Nicholas Royle was born in Sale, Cheshire in 1963. He is the author of two previous novels – *Counterparts* and *Saxophone Dreams* – in addition to more than a hundred short stories which have appeared in a variety of anthologies and magazines. He has edited five anthologies including, most recently, *A Book of Two Halves*, *The Tiger Garden: A Book of Writers' Dreams* and *The* Time Out *Book of New York Short Stories*. His book reviews and other journalism have appeared in *Time Out*, the *Guardian*, the *Observer*, the *Independent*, the *Independent on Sunday*, *Literary Review*, the *New Statesman* and elsewhere. He lives in west London with his wife and young son.

Praise for Nicholas Royle

Counterparts

'Enormously accomplished and ambitious' Jonathan Coe, *Guardian*

'An excellent, odd first novel' Roz Kaveney, *TLS*

'Written with wiry control' Nicholas Lezard, *Guardian*

'Royle's cool, steady prose sets a tone between Pinter and Derek Raymond' Christopher Fowler, *Time Out*

'Complex and thrilling right to the very last page' Maaike Molhuysen, *Strictly*

'The final twist is as deadly as the bitter route it takes to get there. *Counterparts*, Royle's first novel, is a dazzling début' Jo Knowsley, *Maxim*

Saxophone Dreams

'Written with a compulsive energy that makes you want to run to keep up' James Laurenson, *Observer*

'A strong multi-layered novel' Peter Bacon, *Birmingham Post*

'Highly original . . . To read the novel is to pass through a gallery of literary spectacle' Natalia Nowakowska, *Chartist*

'The spirit of solidarity that infuses this novel lingers on as a welcome and much-needed optimism' Liz Heron, *TES*

The Matter
of the
Heart

The Matter of the Heart

Nicholas Royle

An *Abacus* Book

First published in Great Britain by Abacus 1997

A CIP catalogue record for this book is available from the British Library.

ISBN 0 349 10956 7

Typeset by Solidus (Bristol) Limited
Printed and bound in Great Britain by Clays Ltd, St Ives plc

Abacus
A Division of
Little, Brown and Company (UK)
Brettenham House
Lancaster Place
London WC2E 7EN

for Kate

'I had a brief, almost instantaneous glimpse of the real way the world worked and of tunnels criss-crossing under the universe and a sense of infinitely deep abysses folding in upon themselves.'

Robert Irwin, *Exquisite Corpse*

'Heartbeat, increasing heartbeat.'
Ron Mael, 'This Town Ain't Big Enough For Both Of Us'

CONTENTS

SUPERIOR VENA CAVA

The venous trunk, draining blood from the head, neck and upper extremities, which empties into the right atrium: an entry-point into a new cycle of regeneration.

'On the highway between Geraldton and Perth I saw a man break his wife's neck in the door of their Mercedes,' he said. 'It was white. Mercedes 280SE. You know, the one with headlamps like figure 8s. They were heading south. A 280SE.'

He was speaking to me and only to me. He would have elaborated but the woman on his other side grabbed hold of his arm and said she had something to show him which couldn't wait. I don't know what it was.

Throwing a big party at one of the best restaurants in town to celebrate his wedding anniversary, the man was as generous with his stories as he was with his money. They flowed from him all night while the rest of us cracked open prawns and slipped oysters down hungry throats. He would stop for breath, then think better of it and knock back another glass of Chardonnay, stuff one more smoked salmon vol-au-vent into his vast mouth. Never once did the grin leave his face. Not even later, after he'd finished his speech and sat down. He turned to me, that grin still wrapped around his features, took a sip of wine, wiped his hand across his mouth and said what he had to say, about the man and the woman. And the Mercedes.

Although I hadn't really been sold on going along at all that evening, the food was good and this remark gave me

3

something to stick around for even after the tables had been cleared. It was the first really interesting thing he'd said all evening, and I wished I'd heard more. But I didn't get another chance after his neighbour had distracted him. In any case, he was getting drunker all the time, so any further testimony mightn't have been reliable. Not that I even had reason to vouch for his opening line.

It was a question of trust.

RIGHT ATRIUM

The 'Blue Room' of the heart, receiving deoxygenated blood collected from the venae cavae en route to the right ventricle.

One

I'm going to tell you about these people I know. I won't give it to you all at once, there's too much to take in. In fact, I might just leave something out about one of them. I'm not even going to tell you which one. It's more fun for me that way. More fun for you too.

Max – an old acquaintance of mine, I'll tell you later how we met, if there's time – Max is the kind of guy who's always banging on about something or other. Some strange fact, some fascinating statistic, some new obsession. Makes half of them up, I wouldn't be surprised.

This whole business started about six months ago, for me at least. Though, as you'll see, it really began much earlier. Max had this idea that there are insubstantial but clearly defined thoroughfares all over the city. Emotional routes, he called them. As if London's traffic problems aren't bad enough. Max does tend to go on a bit, but I always listen to what he's got to say. He's been right before. Though he's been wrong too.

He told me about an evening he spent with his mate Danny. Which is where he got the idea. They spent a lot of time together, possibly because back then neither man had any better options. There were no girlfriends on the scene and work was, well, just work. They'd go to parties, get pissed in Irish pubs up the Kilburn High Road where hirsute gentlemen played bodhráns, fiddles and pipes, crash another party on the borders of West Hampstead, and end up collapsing into Danny's car around two a.m. It didn't seem to matter how much he'd had to drink, Danny's driving always appeared completely unaffected. As if the car had a mind of its own and was happy just to have Danny sit there in the driving seat, stick his feet on the pedals and rest his hands on the wheel.

Max lived on a fairly dodgy estate behind St Ann's Hospital in N15, and Danny at that time was probably still kipping at Walthamstow, so dropping off Max was on his way home. Most nights Max would spark out and have to be heaved out of the car at the other end – no easy task as Max is a big bloke – but every so often he'd come to sufficiently to watch the strings of terraces being pulled by the car as they flew through the wet-look night. He might not have been much of a driver himself, but Max had taken enough cabs to become familiar with London's road systems: he liked to know when he was being ripped off. And clearly, at two in the morning with sleep an imperative he would expect Danny to take the shortest possible route between A and B.

This particular night they'd finished up at a party in King's Cross. Just south-east of King's Cross, in fact, where it merges into Clerkenwell. They got tipped out with the ash trays and bin bags around three thirty, piled into the BMW and made off up the left side of St Pancras Station, nipping right at the lights into Goods Way, past the huge black and red gasholders at which Danny made some comment Max failed to catch, then left by the Mobil garage – where the former Deputy Public Prosecutor will for ever regret stopping off to buy a KitKat – and into York Way. I don't know why Max should have been alert on this occasion, but he was and he couldn't help wondering why, instead of sticking with York Way and feeding into Camden Road and then heading into Seven Sisters Road, they spun off to the right into what looked like a dead end. Max straightened out the blurred sign: Blundell Street. When it looked as if Danny was about to plough his beloved machine right into the side of a pub, the road twisted through an evil right-hand chicane, which he rode like a steeplechaser. They went left at the end in front of Pentonville Prison, right at the lights, and managed to snick by some mansion block off the Holloway Road, outside of which, Danny pointed out, he'd once French kissed a girl called Kim.

Max was aware of them slowing down through Crouch End, some reference being made to a Clive here, a Jenny there. People Danny knew or had known. By the time they pulled up in the middle of Max's estate he felt he'd been taken on a tour through Danny's address book.

On future occasions he paid more attention and saw that with few variations Danny plotted the same route back home wherever they happened to have been for the evening.

These routes weren't shortcuts or time-savers at all. They avoided the principal roads where possible. Danny made no further references to girls or old friends but Max noticed when his driver's glance happened on a particular first-floor window or strayed over some Muswell Hill attic. He checked his *A–Z* one night after Danny had dropped him and worked out they'd covered at least a couple of miles more than they needed.

When he questioned Danny about it while they were stopped at the lights late one Friday evening, his friend just grunted. Made some private hand signal as they went rat-running through Fitzrovia instead of gliding down Marylebone Road as any sensible person would have done. 'Used to live down there,' he said with a small wave, a surprisingly gentle gesture for such a wiry, highly strung little man. According to Max anyway.

Danny didn't have a name for the routes he took, it was just something he did, but Max is different. Always has to give names to things. Hence emotional routes.

***

Then there's Charlie. Charlie Herzog. A writer and editor, an American. Works out of a booklined log cabin in Deliverance County, North Carolina. Keeps a loaded shotgun by his writing desk. To ward off inbreds and grizzlies. Or so I believed until I checked out his side of the tale. This man mountain, this wild, sun-beaten rock of a man with his crazy beard of scorched desert scrub, lives in a charming, chintzy little apartment in the French Quarter of New Orleans.

Trouble is, he's yellow. The colour of the rye he's been drinking for a quarter-century. The colour of onionskin – he won't write on anything else.

And there's a woman. A doctor. That, in a sense, is where I come in.

Danny, though, he runs this surprisingly lucrative import/export business in Chinese pornography. Not heavy stuff necessarily, just stories, erotic blatherings of pent-up Hong Kong Chinese. Occasionally, you know, you wander past an empty shopfront, some old stationer's or newsagent's in Store Street that's been empty for a couple of months, and there are these piles of softback books tied up with twine, Chinese characters bristling on garish covers, newsprint-quality paper. Lined up uselessly in the window. Well, they're always Danny's. He'll use the space for a month or two then move everything out of town into an abandoned Thai restaurant down the main drag into Sydenham. If you know Danny, or know *of* him as I did, eventually you'll pass by, crawling in a traffic queue, the roads all up between Greenwich and the M2, and you'll spot those familiar Oriental bindings. Max once said it was how he kept up with Danny in the days before mobile phones. Nowadays, Max tried to tell me, when he calls Danny he's always belting round the South Circular. 'I'm in Clapham, you old tart,' he'd shout down the fuzzy line. 'Just on my way to a meeting. I'll call you.'

He never did, but that's not the point.

The point is: Max wasn't telling the truth. You have to watch

out with Max. Danny and telephones never got on. Danny's a
fax man, never uses the phone.

He used to work in a pizza restaurant at Hyde Park Corner,
next to an abandoned hospital – St George's. Before they
relocated to the site at Tooting. I couldn't see Danny as a
waiter but I guess nine years ago everyone was doing something different. Max told me all about it.

Speaking of Max, he's the rule that proves the exception.
He's always been doing the same thing, whether it's ten,
fifteen, even twenty years ago. Drifting, like an unmanned
canoe.

Then he fell in love. Again. He was telling me about it. Met
her outside a pub, which seemed unlikely, but you know what
they always say, he said to me.

I didn't know if I did.

Anyway.

He came to me one day. 'Chris,' he said. 'Here's something
for that book you're never going to write.' For some time I'd
been gathering material for a book. A book about the heart,
although I didn't really know what *kind* of book it would be.
Max, of course, had a pretty good idea.

Max had asked her out to dinner, the woman he met outside
a pub, and she'd pulled the rug out from under his feet by
actually saying yes, so now he had to think of somewhere to
take her. Max isn't exactly dreamboat material, but nor is he
the Date from Hell. A big-boned, bulky character with the
scatty, slightly surprised look about him of a man who has put
his glasses down somewhere and forgotten where. He's always
slightly overdressed, but his clothes are neither smart nor
fashionable – he just always seems to be wearing a few too
many, so he's constantly peeling off another layer. His face is
kindly-looking, intelligent. Overall you sense that if he were to
do something radical like lose a stone and get a couple of decent
shirts and a number-one buzz-cut, he'd look pretty neat.

He was still worrying about dinner. First off, he had to decide on the kind of food – Indian, Thai, French – the only thing he had to go on was she'd said she didn't like bad Chinese.

'What help is that?' he'd wailed. 'Who does like bad Chinese?'

I could think of several places he'd taken me over the years, from hell holes on the Holloway Road to sleazy Soho dives, but I kept my mouth shut. (Had I done so literally I might never have known projectile vomiting, but that's another story.)

Then Max worked out that the key variable was not nationality but location. 'If we eat at Lam's, say, or Satay Malaysia, it'll be too close to my place and she'll think I'm trying to lure her back there so I can try it on. You know, like she owes me one because I bought her dinner.'

So he went out and got the *Time Out Eating & Drinking Guide* and picked out a pretty good-sounding Italian in Shepherd's Bush, but when he checked the map he realised it was about half a mile from where she lived.

'Obviously she'd think I was angling for an invite and so would either give me the brush-off or feel obliged to invite me back, in which case I wouldn't *want* to go back. You know what I mean?'

Well, sort of.

Going somewhere in town was no good, he went on, because you're bound to bump into someone you know, either some drunk or an ex-girlfriend. 'Then you've got the whole transport problem. Do you pick somewhere that you can both get to by tube or bus? Or can you assume she's going to drive, or get a cab? It's a minefield. And that bloody guide's no good. Clearly the most important thing is how likely you are to cop off, not whether the meat is barbecued at your table or if they welcome children and take bookings for large parties. Whatyou want to know is, are you gonna score? You know, 'cause some places are designed with that and nothing else in mind. All mirrors, black leather and chrome. Others are so fucking functional you might as well drive up the M1 to Toddington services.'

What Max needed, he explained, was somewhere in between, where his date wouldn't feel threatened but nor would the surroundings preclude intimacy should it arise. 'There should be a copping-off rating with little condom symbols awarded, you know; from five down to one. Five condoms if it's a dead cert. Four if it's just about worth a packet of three. Two, and you needn't worry if you didn't manage to shower. And one – save your money and have another pint.'

I didn't bother to ask what three meant.

They ended up at a fairly expensive Thai place near where she lived. He walked her home and she didn't ask him in – which was fine by him because he'd already decided she was too nice to ruin it by rushing headlong into bed – and he walked another mile to the tube, only to find they'd all finished.

Things progressed – a quick drink and a walk by the canal here, a movie and a curry there – and before you knew it he'd practically moved in. Round there all the time he was, having her cook for him, even putting up a few shelves as if that made it all okay. But there wasn't any problem – it was good for both of them. For a while.

Two

So, anyway, Danny used to work in this pizza place next to what was left of St George's. Me, I know it by the Grenadier pub round the back – I'd had a few beers there in my time, and doubtless a pizza or two in Danny's place. Who knows, the guy might even have served me. You retrace your steps far enough back and you'll find you've crossed paths with just about everyone you know. Anyone who's anything to you. Seriously. Try it.

I think, however, I would have remembered Danny if he'd served me. He's quite striking-looking. Not tall, but lean and powerful, rippling with contained energy. His long grey hair was probably dark then, his goatee likewise – and it was a proper goatee, trained to a point, not some bank clerk's fashion statement. On the restaurant floor he made few mistakes. After all, it wasn't as if the menu was very extensive. As for the arrogant types who couldn't bring themselves to look up to give their order, they'd get whatever he felt like giving them, usually a garlic pizza with capers, anchovies and extra garlic. 'Serve the cunts right,' was Max's view, and I had to agree with him.

I wouldn't have seen Danny in the Grenadier. He didn't frequent pubs. Max reckoned he was a more 'underground' sort of a guy. Whatever that meant. He worked hard in the restaurant and got on fine with his colleagues, even kidded around with the posh guys in black ties who worked downstairs in the jazz room – possibly where Max's underground thing came from. Could be Danny just knew who he should keep in with. But I don't think so. There's no side to him. Come break time he'd wolf down his pizza – same one every day, American Hot with extra olives – and nip upstairs, through the kitchens and out on to the small triangle of roof where everyone went for a fag.

Danny would climb down to a lower level, jump across a narrow gap, then haul himself in through an open fourth floor window of St George's.

I never knew Danny back then, of course, but the way Max tells it, I feel as if I was in that old hospital with him. He'd roam the empty corridors, check out the dusty wards, dally in rubble-strewn labs where forgotten bottles of brightly coloured liquids just demanded to be taken hold of and shaken till they frothed.

On his third or fourth visit he found some kind of fist-sized object on an old lab worktop, couldn't work out what it was, genuinely didn't know if it was an old chamois leather that had hardened and gone mouldy, or an extracted heart that had inexplicably been left lying around – hardly seemed likely, but it was the look of the thing. He took a camera in one afternoon and photographed it in situ. Never moved it – unless it was fractionally with the tip of a pencil.

The hospital had been empty for three or four years but it looked as if they'd moved overnight. White coats lay draped over swivel chairs, racks of test tubes had been scattered over black and white tiled floors as if upset in some technician's haste to leave. There were signs up everywhere saying that anyone caught trespassing would be dealt with as if they were a terrorist.

'Fuck knows why,' Max said to me and I pointed out the old hospital's proximity to the Palace. What possible other reason could there be? Max had no better ideas.

Danny never mentioned a girlfriend and was not known to have made any passes at the waitresses, but then this new girl started. She was the receptionist. To be honest, even that was stretching her intellectual capabilities. She was something with a zed in it – Zara or Zoë or Zas – lived in her own mews flat in Mayfair, thought Marxism-Leninism was a comedy-songwriting duo: about how bright she was. But when she bent down to slip her Pall Mall back in her Moschino hand-bag she gave you an eyeful down the front of her starched white shirt. Well, she gave Danny an eyeful, and he was hooked. Poor bastard. Within days he was running her around from beauty therapist to elocution tutor in his lemon-yellow BMW 2002ti. Her Mini Cooper had been written off in a three-hundred-and-sixty-degree spin off the Hogarth roundabout, she told him. He would only find out later that she didn't drive at all; she was sixteen. Just.

They couldn't go back to her place, she explained, because she shared with her sister, who was revising for exams at nursing college. And she didn't know him well enough yet to go back to his. 'You could be anybody,' she said. 'I don't know who you are.'

He thought he knew who she was though. He thought he did.

He hired a cottage on Dartmoor – just a weekend, a weekend she wasn't working and he was able to swap shifts. Two bedrooms and she made him sleep in the second one. He didn't complain, never pushed it. Not his style. They went out walking, nothing too strenuous, found a flat-topped rocky outcrop on which he imagined, as they lay there side by side with the sun on their faces, occasionally sneaking the ghost of an embrace, that they lay there fucking each other's brains out. It would wait, it would keep. They had a half of bitter in the pub down the road with the fire that never went out – even in the middle of summer.

Maybe she was doing it on purpose, stoking his fire, not only ensuring it didn't go out, but building it up – in the middle of summer.

He never expected her to go for it, but decided to suggest they sneak into the old hospital together one night after work. Something in her make-up which he hadn't anticipated, some sleazy, danger-loving streak beneath her Amagansett blouse, jumped at the idea, and they sat across the road in Hyde Park until the manager had locked up and cabbed home for the night. Danny used the keys he'd borrowed off the Yugoslav busboy to get back into the green-tiled pizza parlour, allegedly once the hospital's post mortem room, and they slipped upstairs. Of course, by this stage they could have screwed across a table-for-four or given the cockroaches beneath the marble dough-rolling slab a good hammering, but Z was fair wetting her knickers over the promise of penetrating the forbidden portals of St George's, of *getting in* – with Danny. He'd told her about the strange object he'd found, the chamois heart (compounded in his mind from the two things it most closely resembled) and watched her pupils dilate as he described it.

They broke in easily enough and as they slunk down plaster-scarred corridors Danny worried that the security guards whose signs festooned the crumbling walls would spook his performance. Z was stopping every other stride to pick up some cobwebby swab or shattered syringe while Danny placed a light hand on her elbow to urge her along, packet of Gossamer burning a hole in the pocket of his black silk bomber jacket. She leant back coquettishly against the concertinaed elevator doors and lifted her short black skirt to reveal, even in the clinging shadows, a dark tuft which belied the natural blonde image she'd sold everyone in the restaurant. Danny's muscles bunched, his knuckles tightening, and he took a step towards her. She grinned and fled, leaving him clutching at air, cursing and twisting to see her pale legs vanishing around the next corner. He was after her, nervous and turned on in about equal measure, and he caught up easily.

'Where're we gonna go?' she whispered.

He took her hand and they climbed a flight of stairs, stepping over lumps of masonry, avoiding jigsaws of broken lampshades, Danny navigating by means of grainy orange light filtered through windows and skylights. They stopped in a room that was not too big to contain their excitement, the ceiling low enough that its shadows were only shallow. Through the thin walls and a series of grimy windows Danny could feel the incessant grind of traffic around Hyde Park Corner and see the moon reflecting dimly off the top of the Wellington Arch.

There was a cot. Just one. Bare and dusty, stained, musty and damp, but they fell upon it as if it were the most glorious king-sized bed in the hotel suite of their choice. Despite his urgency Danny was the tenderest lover, and Z, whom no one could have called a faker, flung her head back and shrieked God's name as the little man pressed her back on to the scraggy mattress. They made love for an hour, ninety minutes, maybe more, sweat drying on their hungry skins as they rested between bouts. Danny pulled her to the edge of the bed and got to his feet; he acted as fulcrum between planes of pleasure he wouldn't have guessed existed; he experienced sensation so pure and extreme it registered only as the brightest of white lights. He cried once, very briefly, upon reaching his second orgasm. Z was too far gone to have seen his tears. She was beyond emotion. She was a still lake.

Three

Max. I don't know. I didn't know what to make of him back then. He even drew me a map of the emotional routes that led to Danny's night in the old hospital. Paths that criss-crossed each other. To and from her place in Mayfair, when he'd picked her up or given her rides home. Spins up to north London to sit on the grassy slope in front of Alexandra Palace and watch the misty twinklings of the city by night. Destinations that when plotted on a graph showed a distinct pattern, with the low-ceilinged room in St George's at its heart. I don't know if Max was using dodgy maths or if things really did work out like that. He tends to live his life according to other people's, drawing his experience from theirs. It was Max who told me about Charlie Herzog, the American editor. Guy came over to the UK for some bizarre kind of convention. Writers and editors getting together to swap notes, sell stories and get pissed up together. Well, I guess that sounds okay.

So. Charlie hit town for the annual binge and his colleagues were shocked because the guy had turned yellow. As if some reader had tipped up on his imagined North Carolina doorstep with a sledgehammer for Charlie to take full in the face the moment he opened the door. It was yellow like old bruising, you hoped it would go away. Yeah, right. It was bruising, all right, but of a different kind. Charlie liked a glass of rye, a big one, for breakfast. His friends were upset and surprised he'd decided still to fly over. 'Only went yellow this morning,' he announced, running out of puff, beard-stroking in an effort to keep things going.

'Where are you staying?' they asked him, having noticed he wasn't booked into the convention hotel.

He told them about Yvonne. The Fetish Queen. The lady in leather, dominatrix and *Headpress* cover star he'd picked up back home. She needed a little pampering if she was to come to England. The convention shithole would no longer do. 'I went upmarket,' he told them. They'd seen the pictures, the ones the magazine had been allowed to print, and they figured whatever Charlie had to do to hold on to her was probably worth it. At his age. And, they grimly acknowledged, in his condition. Charlie checked into a fancy new hotel on Hyde Park Corner. Built on the site of the former hospital no less. Constructed, in fact, within and around its actual shell.

Charlie had fallen in love with Yvonne despite their twenty-two-year age difference, in spite of the fact she outlawed sex. It was the first time he'd been in love since 1967 and he didn't care. He cherished her. If it led to something, fine; if not, it'd still be worth it. Just to wake up in the same room, if not the same bed – she'd insisted he book a twin room. Her part of the bargain was simply to be with him at the convention, to sit with him in the bar and talk to his friends, to listen to him give his readings, and stand around while he signed copies of his books. She could handle that. She thought she knew what to expect.

She was wrong.

She stepped into that hotel room with its fine view of the glimmering Wellington Arch, its soundproofing designed to keep the roar of Hyde Park Corner at bay – she stepped into the main room from the bathroom where she'd been freshening up after their first afternoon at the con – and she felt an overpowering wave of compassion for the big, red-bearded, dishevelled man who she knew loved her more than anyone ever had. Charlie was standing at the far side of the room, one hand reaching for a bottle of rye, the other scratching his vast chest, and her heart lurched. She didn't want anything to happen to this giant. She saw in a trice his vulnerability as he teetered between bottle and bed. If she felt this she could love him. Before she'd rationalised it any further she was crossing the room to stand before him. She took the bottle out of his hand and put one finger to his astonished lips, and slowly slid it between them.

She undressed him first, then herself. Slowly.

If his heart pumped faster and faster as they made love she was not aware of it. Something in the air between them had made her feel she had to give him what she'd been holding back. She had to give him everything. And she did.

Done, she stopped resisting his bulk, her own heartbeat returning to normal. She listened for his.

He made no effort to get off her. He was twenty stone. Dead weight. She had to lift his head to get a look at his florid face.

The phone was beyond her reach. She wasn't a powerful woman. Not particularly. She heaved and pushed, tried sliding out, realising that seconds were precious. Panic rushed up on her, twisted her gut. Maybe it gave her the muscle power to dislodge Charlie's body. Something did.

She made sure – no breath of air, no murmur of a pulse – then grabbed the phone.

Dialled 0.

Of course, the room Yvonne and Charlie had in the fancy hotel was the same room used by Danny and Z all those years before. Not that many years actually. Nine, ten at the most. When I heard about Charlie and Yvonne, I wondered if it might be the same room and that was why Max was telling me. It was.

What Max didn't tell me was what had taken place in the same room more than a hundred years earlier, long before the hospital's abandonment. I wouldn't find out about Dr George Maddox until later.

They took Charlie to Chelsea and Westminster Hospital but thanks to the Conservative Government's policy on health the intensive therapy unit was full up. There wasn't a single bed to be found, they said, although it was later established there *had* been a bed, but there'd been no staff to man it. So once he got out of A&E he couldn't stay. A bed was found for him at ten o'clock that evening at the Central Middlesex. His consultant cardiologist there was Dr Joanna Mackay.

Yvonne might not have been your first choice paramedic, but she was a decent human being and she wasn't stupid. She knew, once she'd relayed the situation to the guy on reception, the key thing was to get Charlie's heart going again if she could. She'd seen *ER*, she'd sat through the odd medi-doc – she leaned on his chest as hard as she could, but nothing happened. He was a big guy. So she pinched his nose shut and blew into his mouth. Did this a few times then thumped his chest again. Still nothing. But she was a stayer. She kept on until the ambulance guys turned up, didn't find out till later she'd actually got his heart going again moments before they walked in. She'd done it within the required four minutes too, without knowing how important that was. Saved his life *and* prevented irreversible brain damage. She'll do for me any time, I told Max. But that was before I met Dr Mackay.

She was on call the night Charlie was admitted, and whereas she dealt with most of her on-call by phone, in Charlie's case she considered it best to go in. It was just as well she did because he suffered another arrest at two minutes past midnight. According to Max, once she'd resuscitated him – well within the four-minute limit – she stuck around all night to keep an eye on him. Just like being a junior doc again.

I wanted to meet Charlie, just as Max had known I would. But first I had to talk to Dr Mackay. Which for me meant a quick blast down the Westway in my reconditioned Triumph Stag. Max has a name for me and this research I'm doing. A Chronicler of the Heart, he calls me.

When you meet a guy's heart specialist to talk about his life-threatening situation and whether or not it's safe to go see him, the last thing you should be thinking about is sex. On a scale of appropriateness – it just isn't. I'm meant to be fairly business-like. After all, as Max says, it's sort of what I do. I sat there thinking maybe it was the Westway. That sexy piece of engineering, its ups and downs, its curves, the way it so boldly slices through west London. There are residential flats there a few feet from the hard shoulder – the people all dream of cars. Hypnagogic hallucinations – Hondas, Hyundais.

Or maybe it was the Stag. It's a pretty funky car. Changing from third to fourth is a sexual act in just about any car, but in the Stag it's quite special. The combination of the two – the Stag and the Westway?

Or maybe it was the way she looked at me as we talked. A little shyly but in total command, she knew her job and carried it off with confidence. Yet her eyes would dart from me to the wall behind me, and back and back again. Nervously, you'd say. A bit like someone's eyes in the tube when they're trying to read the name of a station while the train's still moving.

They were good eyes, just the right amount of crinkles at the corners. You could tell she smiled a lot. They were greeny-blue, kind-looking. She didn't know how well I knew Charlie, didn't know whether to be sympathetic or wary, her concerned expression covered all bases. And I thought, what a sexy woman. I shouldn't have been thinking it, I know. I'm sorry. But she was, and I was, so there it is.

In a story by the American writer Cris Mazza, someone asks a fisherman what a strike feels like. The fisherman says it's like asking what chocolate tastes like, what a pine forest smells like. It's like nothing. It's like what it is. So if you ask me to tell you why I thought she was sexy, I'd have to give the same answer. She's sexy because she is. She was wearing an attractive slate grey jacket (I couldn't tell you whose it was), a white linen blouse, a moonstone necklace, a long black skirt. Anyone else could have worn those clothes and looked just okay.

She looked relaxed about herself, at ease with her body when she got up to get me a coffee. So I shouldn't have been looking, who cares?

Her hair tumbled forward as she leafed through notes on her desk. Had she hennaed it? Dyed it a little, just to keep things interesting? This woman's a consultant cardiologist. She's what – thirty-five, thirty-six? How interesting is she allowed to be? She folds her hair back behind her ear, her left ear, but leaves a lock hanging in front of her ear, and I want to lean across and do it for her. I want to touch her skin, to see if it's real, that still-young bloom. She looks after herself, though she hardly needs to; nature's been looking after her just fine.

Like I said, she was a sexy woman and I hadn't heard a word she'd said to me.

'He'll pull through,' she said. 'He's strong.'

'His heart couldn't take it?' I asked.

'Let's say it wasn't quite prepared.'

'Suppose it wasn't entirely a physical thing?' I suggested, but she was too professional to be drawn. She brushed her reddish-brown hair behind her ear again, and left that same stray lock hanging loose.

Four

In the early hours of the following morning I woke up in distress after a bad dream.

The way the dream started was more strange than upsetting. It was like that Magritte picture of the apple in the room, only the apple's so big, or the room's so small, that it's a tight squeeze to fit it in. It touches the ceiling and three walls. It would touch the fourth wall only that's where you are as the viewer. It could be used as one of those personality tests. Is the glass half full or half empty, that sort of thing. Is the apple too big, or the room too small? If you're like me you think it's a big apple.

The difference was, instead of an apple, my room had a big heart in it. Not a cartoon heart but the real thing – extracted, greasy, dark red and weeping all over the wooden floorboards. In the dream the room was definitely normal size and the heart filled it just like the apple in the painting. There was even a window on the left-hand wall, through which you could see a blue sky with white clouds. I was aware of heat coming off the heart in great thumping waves.

Gradually I became aware of a noise exterior to the room. A steady drone with an occasional whine laid over the top. And the room seemed to be moving, swaying. The clouds were moving past the window as if the room were moving through them. I was no longer observing the heart so much as identifying with it. Instead of a sash window in the left-hand wall, there were now portholes. The room had become an aircraft. From the whining of servo motors controlling the wing flaps I could tell we were on a descent. The clouds were now thin and wispy, trailing past the window like cobwebs, but there was no blue sky or ground visible through them. We were trapped in that horrifying grey limbo between sky and earth, approaching the moment when the pilot would attempt the supreme folly of crossing from one element to another, endangering hundreds of lives. In the form of the pulsating heart I seemed to represent a community of souls bound for disaster.

Maybe there was a gap there. I may have stopped dreaming for half an hour. More likely I just turned over in my sleep and the porthole became a compact disc. I was myself again in the room and I was living under a death sentence; not in any legal sense, but I knew that at the end of a prearranged sequence of actions I was going to die, of natural causes. I was reviewing CD singles for a magazine and I knew that when I reached the last review I would die.

I woke up with tears streaming down my face and only allowed myself to slip back into sleep because I was so tired. If I dreamt again I didn't remember anything.

When I came awake for the second time I knew that I hadn't been crying for myself, but for my father.

Much as this may purport to be Max's story, or Danny's story, or Christ knows whose story, I can hardly not include the death of my father.

He'd been ill for eighteen months and now he was dying. My mother knew he was dying, my sister knew he was dying, half of the time *he* knew he was dying. He'd make jokes about it, or he'd talk to my mother in the middle of the night, as she sat next to his bed holding his hand, stroking the tiny, furry hairs that had started to grow again on his fragile skull – he'd talk to her about committing suicide. He may even, on the darkest nights, have asked her to go with him. She would have been reassuring him – *you don't know, they haven't given up yet* – even though she knew, and he knew that she knew.

Or he'd be brave, smiling for the nurses, trying to sit up for my sister or for me. He knew then, probably, deep down, but he was considerate, decent. At the end of it all a good man. A very good man. Not a man who deserved to be taken, only sixty-four, by the disease he'd feared all his life. This was a man who gave up cigarettes the very morning he heard on the radio that they were definitely linked with cancer. A man who raised many false alarms but in the end was proved right when tumours started appearing all over his lymphatic system like stations on the tube map. They'd zap one to kingdom come, only for another to show up a week later. And all the while, the chemo stripped his head of hair, drained his body of energy.

The only time he didn't know he was dying was when the fever took him in the night. He would sweat and ramble until exhaustion claimed him at dawn, and my mum would slump in her chair, grab an hour's rest before he woke again. He told her he was the captain of a ship. He asked her about work colleagues he hadn't seen in twenty years.

And at the end – when they pumped him so full of morphine he made no sense whatsoever for days at a time.

Even after they moved him to the hospice he would talk about getting out of there in a few weeks and getting cracking on the garden. It almost broke my mother. You can't make someone accept that they're dying.

If any good came out of those painful months it was the revelation that my father's heart was bigger than any of us had ever known. He and my mother formed an unbreakable bond during the last weeks. We all knew this would make it harder for her after he'd gone, but she remained, as she always had been, utterly selfless.

The first time Dr Mackay let me go and see Charlie I followed her into his room – he had a side room off the intensive therapy unit – and she introduced me. She said I was a friend of some friends of his, then looked round at me for a prompt. She wasn't altogether clear on where Max fitted in.

'I'll explain to Charlie,' I said, moving forward, dismissing the subject as lightly as I could. 'Hello Charlie. Thank you for allowing me to see you.'

He barely moved his head. He was all hooked up with drips and stuff, and his long hair and puffy cheeks made it hard to see his eyes properly.

'We'll be fine,' I said to Dr Mackay, and she seemed to accept this.

'Let me know if I can help further,' she said as she left.

'I will, Doctor.'

Charlie and I sat in silence most of the time. I didn't know to what extent he was aware of me. I looked at his notes on the end of the bed. They didn't mean much to me. There was a line coming out of his jugular and wires attached to his chest. I watched the blip on the cardiac monitor. I spoke his name softly a couple of times but there was no response. After about a quarter of an hour I got up to go. As I reached the door I heard his breathing change. I went over to the side of the bed. His eyes opened slowly, hesitantly, like some creature being born. Then he was looking straight at me. Without moving his head he switched his gaze to the bedside table. On it stood a jug of iced water. I poured him a glass and held it to his lips. He inclined his head as much as he could and I tilted the glass. Inevitably a trickle of water escaped at the corner of his mouth but I didn't do too badly. His head returned to the pillow with a grunt from his lips. His eyelids were heavy.

In a low, guttural voice he said, 'You a friend of Max's?'

I nodded, my throat constricted.

Then his eyes closed again and his breathing slowly became deeper. The interview was concluded.

I like the Westway precisely for the reason a lot of people dislike it. The road surface is made up of prefabricated concrete slabs and it makes this noise when your tyres hit the join – *chnk*, *chnk*. There's a stretch of the A45 near the Cambridgeshire-Suffolk border where the same thing happens. I guess most major roads in the country have similar stretches, but it's a lot more fun when you're up in the air.

I was just leaning into the right-hander by Westbourne Green when the phone went. I got a carphone fitted in the Stag when they were all the rage, that is before mobile phones overtook them. And boy, did they overtake them. Obviously, a mobile leaves your average carphone standing still. Because (a) you don't have to leave it in the car when you get out to go somewhere; (b) you keep it in your pocket rather than on the dashboard, so you don't look like an arsehole all the time you're driving your car. Unless it rings, of course. And (c) you don't need a telltale aerial sticking out the back of your car with a pennant attached saying 'Please break in'. That 'c' is especially pertinent if you happen to have a soft-top model, which of course I have. I only say 'of course' because it's a measure of how stupid I am. The car's been broken into seven times. Thieves have taken my leather jacket, a Nikon camera, three stereos and a virtually irreplaceable cassette of Slovenian folk music I bought in Ljubljana. That makes six, I know. The one other time was near Highbury. I didn't have a radio in the car at the time – it had been stolen in Clapham three weeks earlier. I was accompanying Max and a friend of his who had never been to a football match, we were going to see Arsenal play some team, I don't know, some northern team. I left a note in the windscreen saying, 'There is no radio in this car', and when we got back to the car it was to find the soft top slashed and my note turned over. On the back of it they'd written 'Just checking'.

And the game was a drag. Nil-nil draw. It figured, Max said.

So the phone rang and it was Max. Could we meet up? At my place? He had something he wanted to give me. For some reason I preferred to meet him on neutral ground. I said the name of a pub in Islington, the Narrow Boat, I think. It'll do. I met him there that evening. It was September, and there was still some summer left in the air at the end of the day. You can't beat the Narrow Boat on a summer evening. It may not have the dramatic sweep of the Barley Mow, E14, from where you can see for miles down the Thames in either direction; or the upriver cosy feel of the Dove in Hammersmith; but the Narrow Boat has something quite particular, whether you sit up on the terrace of wooden boards and wrought iron or slump on the towpath with your back against the bare brick wall of the pub itself.

I walked up from Great Arthur House. It's only a mile, if that, and the evening was humming, yellow-soft. Not being in the car meant I could have more than a couple of drinks; also, I wouldn't feel compelled to offer Max a ride home, which, as long as he stuck it out in N15, was pretty much a long way round for me. Max was already there when I arrived. The weird thing is, he always is. No matter how early you turn up somewhere, Max will always be there first, looking as if he's been there all day and is perfectly comfortable. Then he'll turn his attention solely to you, no longer even acknowledging the waiters and bar staff you get the impression he's been cultivating for hours on end. And they don't take offence. It's as if he lives there. He seems to belong everywhere. Partly, I think, because he actually belongs nowhere. His place in N15 was a bolt-hole, a fastness, but you couldn't describe it as homely. A ground-floor council flat with wire grilles over the windows on an estate patrolled by crack dealers on mountain bikes. More mobile phones than Tottenham Court Road. Customised, skirted red and black BMWs sticking half out of lock-up garages, Mark Two Cortinas stripped down to their shells, never fewer than six motors up on bricks. Kids flogging tyres down the Seven Sisters Road.

There were two girls playing jazz near the bar. One shifting her feet nervously as she fingered an ironing-board synthesiser, the other blowing into an alto sax as if it were a breathalyser.

'Pretty good, aren't they?' Max jerked his thumb in the girls' direction. 'I've got something better for you though. Get a drink?'

Was he telling or asking? I waved my hand and he remained in his seat.

When I got back from the bar with a bitter for me and a lager for Max, I nodded my head towards the window. 'Let's go outside,' I muttered through clenched teeth – I was carrying two bags of crisps.

'You saw Charlie,' Max said when we were outside. Table on the little terrace.

'I saw him.'

Max said: 'A lot of heart that guy.'

I didn't know what to say.

Max went to the bar for another round and when he came back he produced something from the pocket of his jacket. 'You'll like this, Chris,' he said.

It was an odd thing for Max to give me. He occasionally did give me things out of the blue, but they usually had some relevance to stuff we'd been talking about. I turned the packet over in my hand – it was one of those small padded bags. Inside was a cassette of Laurie Anderson's 'Bright Red'. Her new album, I imagined.

I remembered my dream.

As long as I didn't have to review it for a magazine.

'Check out "Freefall",' Max advised, wiping beer from his upper lip.

'You trying to give me nightmares, Max?'

Five

Hospitals. I'd never liked them. Always feared them. It was nothing pathological, merely associative. My grandmother died in hospital. It was an old, cold, green-tiled aquarium of a place where you swam down interminable corridors thick with the smells of the dead and dying. I saw her high up on an all-white bed, head propped up, chin falling away. She only came home again to lie in a box in the front room for two days. My sister's curiosity got the better of her when she found the post mortem scars on the back of my grandmother's neck.

My grandfather died in hospital before I had a chance to go and see him. My last glimpse came as they carried him out of the house late one night to a blue-light ambulance.

So now I found myself travelling to two hospitals. South to see my father, west to see Charlie. And Dr Mackay. I'd find myself phoning to check that she was on duty before getting in the car. I'd go and see Charlie, then find out if she was free for a chat. Charlie was making slow but steady progress. Much of the time, Yvonne was sitting right there with him, her integrity unquestionable. I'd talk with her for a while, but found that I was anxious to get away and catch Dr Mackay before she went off duty.

'If you assume that at rest the stroke volume of the heart is sixty-six millilitres and the rate is seventy-two beats per minute,' Dr Mackay said to me across her desk, 'the left ventricle has a minute volume of five litres. That's a daily output of seven thousand two hundred litres. A normal, healthy heart has great reserve power which can be increased by physical training. During exercise, there's a greater venous return to the heart and a consequent increase in diastolic filling and stretching of the muscle fibres. The natural response to this is a more vigorous contraction – according to Starling's law – and blood pressure is raised.' She tapped her pen on a lined notebook open on her desk. I nodded for her to continue. 'The rate of contraction also increases during exertion and these two factors can raise the minute volume to seven times that of the resting state. This kind of physiological performance can only be maintained if the myocardium is healthy, if the valves function efficiently and if the conducting system of the heart coordinates contraction of the chambers.'

She stopped and looked up at me, her eyebrows forming question marks. Clearly she thought this was all over my head.

I merely asked her to continue.

She turned slightly to one side and spun the tracking ball of her PowerBook, double-clicked to open a file.

'Put simply,' she went on, her face reflecting numerous colours from the little screen, 'the blood supply to the myocardium was impaired through diseased coronary arteries.'

'Charlie likes a drink, he smokes a pack a day—'

'Smoked,' she rightly interjected.

'He smoked. He's overweight. He's – what is he – a writer,

he writes crime novels. That's a fairly sedentary occupation. Sounds classic, doesn't it?'

'Ischaemic heart disease,' she remarked, closing the file with a single click. 'The scourge of the western world. The biggest killer, accounting for over a third of all deaths in this country.'

I wondered if I should worry: my own heart was starting to beat faster. Was she such an expert in her field she'd be able to tell?

I apologised for taking up her time. She said it was quite all right. As long as she still had the odd five minutes here and there she was happy to talk. She meant about the case, about Charlie.

'The way things are going, soon I won't have time to do anything other than sit on committees, go to meetings, prepare tenders for GP fundholders and present arguments against whatever latest ridiculous scheme the management and the chief executives have come up with. If this hospital doesn't watch it, it won't be here in five years' time. And somehow, amidst all that, I have to find time to care for patients.'

'I really am grateful you could spare me the time, Doctor.'

'I'm sorry,' she said and smiled. Both rows of fine strong teeth came into view. There was a slight overbite, compensated for by a full bottom lip and thinner top lip, a combination which I found uncommonly attractive.

'What's your prognosis?' I asked. 'For Charlie.'

She sucked in some air. 'That depends,' she said. 'I wouldn't have expected him to arrest again so soon after the initial arrest. Nor would I have expected him to rally so well considering his general state of health. He clearly drinks far too much.'

'Drank?' I offered.

'Who knows?' she said, smiling a tiny smile. 'I can't watch him all the time.'

Driving down to Tooting, the destination of St George's Hospital after abandoning Hyde Park Corner, I inevitably got caught up in slow-moving traffic. It often felt as if I was already following my father's cortège through the grim thoroughfares of Clapham and Balham. My parents had been living in Earlsfield for some years, so my father more or less had to be taken in at the new site of St George's. A coincidence, it seemed to me, although Max had another word for it.

When someone close to you is very ill you're torn. You don't know what's best. You want to see them, obviously, as often as you can. But on the other hand you don't want to alarm them. So you act as if it's not that serious. Even if they know how serious it is and you know too, you both act as if it's something that's going to blow over.

There was nothing wrong with Dad's heart. It was being let down by the rest of his body. He had peripheral T-cell lymphoma, a subgroup of non-Hodgkin's lymphoma. I didn't know what that was when Mum told me. I still don't. All I knew was, it was bad news. It was an aggressive cancer, but caught early enough it was the sort of thing on which the doctors would give you pretty good odds. In my father's case they didn't seem to catch it early enough, despite the fact he had been complaining of a sore nose for eighteen months before a diagnosis was made and radiotherapy was used to get rid of the first tumour, behind his nose. He lost some of his hair, it grew back, but then the tumours grew back also, at other places around his lymphatic system. Under his armpit, above his elbow. Each one was dealt with, by radiation treatment or surgery, then the disease mounted a more businesslike assault. It had just been messing around before. New tumours appeared even while he underwent chemotherapy. He was in and out of hospital, in and out of fever. Mum looked after him at home for as long as she could. She'd be up changing his sheets twice during the night as he sweated constantly and rambled. Forty-eight hours after they took him into St George's again the consultant told my mother she ought to gather the family, there might not be long. She phoned me and she phoned my sister. We got there as soon as we could. He was asleep. It was late in the evening, approaching midnight.

My mother sat leaning over his bed, cradling his soft skull, stroking it. The lights in the ward were switched off but there was a muted Anglepoise over my father's bed. From a distance the scene resembled an old Dutch painting – people huddled around a light seeking more than literal illumination.

Although he never became lucid that night, he did open his eyes and look at Mum several times. Not at any point was he aware that my sister and I were there. His lips were dry, his mouth opening and closing like a fledgling's. Mum dipped tiny sponge squares into water and then placed them between his lips. He used all the strength he had to squeeze the moisture out of them. Then sometimes he couldn't move a muscle and my mother pressed them against his lips for him. The only way I knew he was still alive was I could see him swallowing. The blanket lifted and fell as he breathed, but it was almost unnoticeable. His tiny frame lay on its side, shaking very occasionally when coughs ripped through his body like sudden tides and we would look at each other in panic. Mum's eyes implored us, me and my sister. What could we do, any of us? It was the longest night of my life and I knew that Mum had spent dozens of them both at home and at St George's. She'd excited comment and admiration among the nurses who were used to relatives who came and went, some who turned up once a week only to sit at the end of the bed and deliver a string of complaints.

We sat there with him, convinced all three of us that he would not see out the night.

My sister and I felt our eyelids falling and had to walk around to keep ourselves awake. My mother sat through the whole night virtually without blinking. We could see he was suffering, and we were suffering for him. How is it possible to wish your loved ones dead? And yet I know I thought to myself it would be better if he died sooner rather than later. What was the point in hanging on till seven o'clock? Why not go in the middle of the night? We rationalised our feelings by reminding ourselves how he was suffering, but still we felt soiled by our thoughts.

Around mid-morning he was sitting up in bed, wide-eyed and frail but indubitably, triumphantly alive. I felt tears sting my eyes as I looked at the harsh planes of his ravaged, formerly handsome face and wondered if it had been a Pyrrhic victory.

We didn't know whether it was the chemo, the antibiotics he was on for the ugly red weals that had started to appear on his forearms, or the fever itself – we didn't even know, and I include the doctors in that 'we', whether the fevers were drug- or disease-induced – we didn't know what was causing him to ramble. Part of the time he was lucid, and he'd be smiling, then the smile would become slightly exaggerated and out of no-where would come a remark. Sometimes it appeared nonsensical and that would break the tension. 'That custard's not very clever,' he said with a puzzled look at his untouched dessert. Mum would laugh. My sister and I would look at each other and smile in desperation. Then, at other times, he would make us cry. That afternoon he whispered confidentially: 'I saw the children trying to go upstairs.'

There were no children. There was no upstairs.

Mum turned away from him, her face distorted, tears aglitter in red-rimmed eyes.

Married forty-two years they hadn't been happy all the time but they'd done pretty well. Over the past few months the bond had strengthened and my dad realised before it was too late just how much she loved him, and always had. When the disease threatened to tear away the remaining shreds of his dignity she was there to make sure it didn't happen. She was wife and nurse rolled into one. She, apart from the dwindling thread of his fighting instinct, was what got dad through night after night when by rights death should have had him. My sister and I looked on. It frightened us to think what effect his eventually going would have on her whose raison d'être for the past six months had shrunk to a pure channel of love and dedication.

Their love and interdependence had become a kite-string between them.

***

My flat at Great Arthur House is on the eleventh floor. It's got a balcony. Facing west. A lot of people reckon on south, to face south is best, you get more hours of direct sunlight. But I want to see the sunset. It doesn't matter that I only get the sun from early or mid-afternoon. I get it at the important time. When it's on its way out again.

A former council flat, it's not particularly grand or anything, but, as I say, it's eleven floors up and that gives me a hell of a good view west. The sun sets over there somewhere between the Houses of Parliament and the BT Tower, depending on the season, and I can sit on my balcony and drink up every last drop. Anyone who says London's not a beautiful city wants to come up to my balcony and sit and watch the sun go down. From soft peach to smoked salmon it does more shades of orange and pink than a Dulux colour chart.

It's how I relax. My flat and my belongings behind me – books, music, my collection of old Ordnance Survey maps – the evening in front of me. Planes droning distantly through thick strata of dusty light on their approach to Heathrow. A cold beer as well, that helps. I put my feet up, have a beer and watch the planes. Have you ever noticed how we always look up when we hear a plane? As if we don't know what it is. We know, sure enough. But still we crane our necks. Why?

Because we know deep down that the plane has no right to be up there. Someone somewhere is cheating and they don't always get away with it.

You can produce all the technical drawings and 3D computer simulations you like, rattle off formulae and equations, and make the evidence appear watertight, make it seem to be proof, but you'll never convince me that something so big and so heavy has any business up there in the sky.

Planes fly. Planes crash. It's as simple as that.

Statistics, you say. Look at the statistics. The safest form of transport. According to the statistics. Well, excuse me but the statistics must be strung together by some seedy guy in a polyester suit working for Planes R Us, hidden away in an underground office somewhere near Shepperton. So fewer people are killed in air disasters each year than on the roads. That makes it safe? I don't think so. There are so many ways to dismantle the proposition that flying is safe I don't know where to start. If I began with A I'd exhaust the alphabet.

If you're in a car and you see trouble approaching, sometimes, just sometimes, you can avoid it. You've got your hands on the wheel – turn it.

Say you're only the passenger and you see trouble ahead. Well, you could keep quiet and hope the driver sees it as well – which is what you might as well do if you're on a plane – or you could raise the alarm. Often you don't get any warning because everyone drives up everybody else's exhaust pipe, in which case there's an accident. You could die. But you might not. It's that 'might not', you see. Strikes me you've got a much bigger 'might not' in a car than you have in a plane. Less far to fall.

If they redid the statistics taking into account how many people survive plane crashes against the same for a car wreck, you might not think flying was such a safe option. And all these people who go on about statistics, don't they realise that someone actually has to make up the statistics? They all have a go at winning the National bloody Lottery, these people. Look at the statistics there. You're more likely to develop multiple sclerosis than win the National Lottery Jackpot. Someone's got to win, you say. That someone could be me.

Just like someone's got to be sitting in seat 14B on the next 737 that nose-dives because of rudder problems.

It's not the fact that pilots fall asleep, that the co-pilot might be having a bad day. Nor the fact that for ninety per cent of the flight time you're in the hands of a computer programmer – pilots only manually fly the plane on take-off and landing. Nor is it the report I read about pilots being unable to override these same computers.

It's the sneaking suspicion that in our rush to go faster and faster, and squeeze more hours into all of our lives, we just might have overlooked some vital thing and therefore be reducing our chances at securing an allotted span.

Icarus made the same mistake and we've still to learn from it.

I felt much safer gliding over the Westway, watching in my wing mirror the planes heading on down to Heathrow, watching them because they're beautiful. Terrifying and beautiful. And because watching them keeps them up there. When nobody looks up, that's when they go down.

To reach the Westway from Great Arthur House, I would fling the Stag into corners, and while Danny may not have been big on saving time, I found shortcuts I never would have been able to work out had it not been imperative. I belted down streets that weren't even on the love-letter-thumbed pages of the road atlas. Traffic lights became knots on a rope that was pulling me in to where I wanted to be. If it looked too heavy on the Euston Road I'd get off on to Judd Street and weave my way across Gower Street and Tottenham Court Road, not surfacing until just before Baker Street. I was locked on course, a heat-seeking missile. The deck sections of the Westway bumped under the wheels of the old Stag. 'Freefall' came on two days running at the same place, as I was just nipping through the last set of lights on the Marylebone Road and heading on to the Westway. The track matched the time it took to get from the start of the Westway to White City. I bought the 'Bright Red' CD and recorded 'Freefall' on a tape loop.

It was the things I noticed by their absence as much as Joanna Mackay's qualities which attracted me. She wasn't too thin; there were no yellow patches on her fingers, brown scratch marks on front teeth or nicotine wake as she walked past you; no broken or bitten nails. The complete absence of signs of madness. I mean, you can't be sure until you've known someone a hell of a lot longer, but it was looking good. There wasn't even a wedding ring.

Flying across town, wheels barely touching the tarmac – one

heart to another – I checked the pulse of the city: a white light winking at Canary Wharf. The BT Tower's red flash. The lights' intervals were the same. Beating at the heart of the city.

As long as I dragged one side of the Stag through the gutter as I launched it over the speed humps, and as long as I continued to time my dash past police cameras by the city's heartbeat, I'd be okay. There was a trend just picking up back then for fixing neon lighting under your car and making the road glow mauve, pink, blue, green. Did I need some of that? I don't think so. My emotional route was burning up.

I knew that whatever happened, the Westway would always remain warm to the touch.

Six

'*Psychic News*,' Max snorted, then paused. 'Why do they bother?'

Joanna laughed. I liked watching her laugh. Her lips drew back so that I could see both sets of teeth – so white, so clean.

'I mean, why do they go to the trouble?' Max worked his gag, but we'd understood.

It hadn't been my idea. I'd spent a bit of time planning an invitation to dinner, sure. Although it hadn't involved Max. He just happened to be at the hospital visiting Charlie at the same time as I was and we all ended up back in Joanna Mackay's office. I'd even tried one or two subtle manoeuvres to lose him so I could talk to Joanna on my own. It might have been my imagination but I thought she gave me a couple of looks, as if she'd had the same idea. However, Max lofted the plan of going for a pizza and that's how we ended up in a Pizza Express on Chiswick High Road. Max came with me in the Stag and Joanna followed us in her Renault 19. I kept having to check in the rearview mirror that we hadn't lost her by jinking through the last set of lights or doubling back round a tight right-hander, because Max was so insistent on finding a Pizza Express. If we were going to have a pizza it had to be Pizza Express, he said. When, with the three of us seated around a table, I asked why, he practically exploded.

'Where else would you suggest?' he demanded. 'Have you ever tasted a Pizza Hut pizza?'

I had and it hadn't been anything special.

'Nothing special?' he roared. 'Nothing special? They're bloody diabolical. I've never eaten a worse pizza, not even ones I've made myself and I can hardly open a tin of beans. I've eaten better pieces of carpet. Domino's are no better. And as for Perfect Pizza. Perfect fucking Pizza. If ever someone was asking for trouble . . .'

I looked at Joanna. Her gaze darted between Max and me, her eyes flicking to and fro.

'Danny worked in a pizza restaurant,' I reminded Max.

'Course he did, mate. Of course he did. And do you know which one?'

I thought about Hyde Park Corner, St George's, tried to imagine the restaurant.

'Pizza on the Park,' Max announced proudly. 'Belonged to Pizza Express in those days.' He swallowed a mouthful of Peroni. 'Why d'you think I let him work there?' he said without a trace of irony. 'He'd never have worked there if it hadn't been a Pizza Express.'

I didn't know how seriously to take Max a lot of the time. On this occasion I also felt an obscure need to apologise for him to Joanna. It was early and we were the only people in there, but that didn't stop Max – he was on top form. He was shouting. He was just getting warmed up.

I suppose I didn't really appreciate how well Max and Danny knew each other and had known each other back in the early days. Sometimes I got the impression they knew each other so well, even back then, that they were practically the same person, or at least that their personalities overlapped. Other times they seemed so impossibly distant I wondered if Danny existed at all. It was odd that I, who also was amongst Max's inner circle, had never met him. When Max had given me the picture of the chamois heart, he had also shown me a photograph of Danny apparently taken at the pizza restaurant, upstairs at the back where the waiters and busboys used to go to eat their Venezianas and Fiorentinas at break time. He was just as Max had described him. Short and wiry, earnest-looking but with a flint in his eye – from the photo you couldn't tell if it was white hot or ice cold. Long hair drawn back in a ponytail. Small goatee teased and stroked to a point. Behind him was a Belgravia roofscape and, in the left foreground beyond a twenty-foot gap, the window through which he had broken into the abandoned hospital. It was a sash window in a modest row of sash windows, the lower half pushed up so that it looked like a missing tooth, its neighbours reflecting late afternoon sunlight like a toothpaste ad.

It looked fairly ordinary, that gateway to mysteries, that heart valve.

Had Danny been through it at that point, when the photograph was taken? Why else would it be open? Max had used the phrase 'broken in', as if Danny had had to jemmy the window. I could imagine him telling the photographer, Z perhaps, or the Yugoslavian busboy, to make sure and get the window behind him in the picture.

How much, if anything, did he know about Dr George Maddox at this point, as he posed awkwardly for the camera? If he had already been inside the hospital – and I guess he had from the open window – then he had at least crept down some of the same corridors once patrolled by that mad visionary Maddox – a driven loner, like Danny himself. Would they ever, the two of them, have stepped across the same threshold with exactly the same angle to the head, or impetuously jumped the last step in a small flight of stairs between the third and fourth floors in the east wing? One unconsciously mimicking the other, matching his movements in space, but separated in time by more than a century.

When our pizzas arrived, Max ordered more beer.

'So who's been to see *Amateur*?' he asked. The new Hal Hartley film had been out for two weeks. Joanna and I looked at each other. Neither of us had seen it. 'Christ,' he continued. 'Don't go. Whatever you do, don't go. I thought his last one was bad. I fell asleep in his last one. I'm not kidding – I literally fell asleep. Can't even remember what it was called. Saw it at the Metro on a Sunday afternoon. I've got this friend, all we ever do when we see each other is go to the cinema and we always seem to go to the Metro on a Sunday afternoon. And it's always a Hal Hartley film. You know? It's my own personal hell. Sartre was generalising. Hell is Hal Hartley films shown on a continuous programme.'

Max attacked his pizza, drank some beer, didn't wait to empty his mouth before carrying on. Joanna and I got on with eating and drinking, and watching Max perform – I imagined he only blossomed like this outside of Danny's company.

'This one, he could have made it in an hour, an hour and ten, if only he'd cut out the meaningful pauses. Every shot's held for ten seconds longer than it needs to be. The dialogue is appalling, the plot is ridiculous, the irony about as funny as a funeral. I don't know, I think cinemas that show Hal Hartley films should be shut down by the bloody council.'

'I've not seen any,' Joanna interjected, 'but they can't be as bad as Louis Malle.'

'Hmm,' I added gnomically.

'Good call,' said Max. *Vanya on 42nd Street.*' He shook his head. 'Any film that uses the tag line "FROM THE CREATORS OF 'MY DINNER WITH ANDRÉ' " . . .' He nodded then at the waitress who had asked if everything was all right. 'I mean, that's a seriously sad line to put on a movie poster. *My Dinner With André.* Have you seen it?' Joanna was nodding. I'd seen it as well. 'Two guys having dinner. And you keep thinking any minute there'll be a flashback, a dissolve, a flashforward even. Nothing. Not a bloody thing. They just sit there and have dinner and talk.'

Max was right. If you haven't seen the film, set aside one evening out of your life. Afterwards you have to reappraise all the crappy action films you've ever seen and judged too harshly. *Die Hard 2, Jaws 4, Nightmare on Elm Street 116 –* they're all better than *My Dinner With André*. Auto-trepanning is better than *My Dinner With André*. Or *Atlantic City*, for that matter. Those of Louis Malle's films I haven't seen have been just as warmly recommended by all I know who have seen them. Apart, that is, from serious film critics.

'Critics,' Max scoffed and a tiny fragment of green chilli flew across the table. I tried not to follow its trajectory. 'Take *Time Out* for instance. Do you read *Time Out*? You must read *Time Out*. Everybody in London reads *Time Out* – everybody hates it, absolutely hates it; it enrages them week after week. But everybody reads it.'

Joanna was smiling, sawing unselfconsciously at her Capricciosa.

'I'm right.' Max marched on. 'But it serves its purpose. It serves its purpose brilliantly. I find the film section in particular invaluable. If they loathe something, there's a bloody good chance I might like it. And if they praise it to the skies, I know for sure it's one to avoid.

'*Time Out* love Hal Hartley,' he added. 'Come the millennium they'll do a special issue with a top ten. *Time Out*'s top ten films of the millennium. They love all that shit. And you just know what'll be in it. Godard, Bunuel, Tarkovsky. The bloody *Bicycle Thieves*. Bresson. Fassbinder. Wenders – but only early Wenders, mind, none of his decent films, certainly not *Paris, Texas*. That Portuguese rubbish a few years ago about some old guy painting the tree in his back yard. All of Hal Hartley's films, including whatever gems he produces in the next couple of years, and, guess what, who'll be at number one? You guessed it. Louis fucking Malle, with *My Dinner With André*.'

'No,' Joanna said, with her mouth full. 'There's a consensus. Everyone would put *Citizen Kane* at number one.'

'*Modern Times*,' I said.

'No chance,' said Max, thinking for a moment. 'Could be *The Third Man*, you know.'

And we fell to silent contemplation of our own favourite films. As we dawdled over filter coffee, Joanna listed *Diva*, *Harold and Maude* and *Repo Man* as her favourites. I had to stop myself blurting out something crass in approval. The thing was, I liked her top three. They might not have been mine but they'd have come close.

'What about you, Max?' Joanna asked.

'Jacques Tati's *Playtime*,' Max said without hesitation.

'Mmm,' Joanna murmured, then drank the last of her coffee.

They were both looking at me. The axis of the evening had shifted, but only momentarily, as long as I answered the unasked question.

'Oh, I don't know,' I said. '*Fearless* by Peter Weir. *Alive!*, *The Survivor*.'

'Something of a theme developing, I think,' said Max.

'What?' said Joanna.

'Films about plane crashes,' said Max.

I said, 'Films about plane crash *survivors*,' and watched their reactions. Max stared blankly at me, a half-smile catching his upper lip. I looked at Joanna. She, unconsciously it seemed, had turned her body towards me. Throughout the meal we had both been facing Max – he'd done most of the talking. Now they were both looking at me.

When we left the restaurant I told Max I'd had too much to drink and would not be able to drive home, so I couldn't give him a lift. He hailed a cab and I went to follow him into it, but then stopped in the act of climbing in and said I was going to stick around and see that Joanna got home safely. He made as if to get up but I stepped back, shut the door of the taxi and gave the driver Max's address. They sped away, leaving a thick ragged U of black exhaust. Joanna had waited for me and I let her drive me back to her house, which was only five minutes away. Once inside I discovered that she was a big fan of orange (she called it terracotta) and had some worryingly New Age-type CDs (Deep Forest, Enigma) mixed in with the Lou Reed and all sorts of Latin stuff. We didn't sleep together, though I did stay the night. In the spare room, which felt like the right thing for the moment. Over breakfast she told me she was going away to Australia – Western Australia, she said, as if it made any difference – in a month's time. She was going for four weeks. Too late I remembered that my car was parked on a single yellow line. It was Saturday, a busy shopping day in W4. Joanna got dressed and drove me down there, but the Stag had gone. I collected it from the car pound that afternoon, after she'd allowed me to buy her lunch at a flash new caff. It was an expensive day, but money well spent as far as I was concerned.

TRICUSPID VALVE

The heart valves direct the blood forwards, between chambers or into the circulation, without impeding flow. Thin white cords, the chordae tendineae, or 'heart strings', anchor the three flaps of the tricuspid valve to the ventricular wall.

Dr George Maddox strode proudly through the grimy pits of Whitechapel, knee joints crackling, wide eyes flashing messianic zeal. Appended to his blistered lower face were flaccid whiskers, not so much mutton chops as scrag end of lamb. Few would stand in his way. There was purpose in his march, distinct threat in the way his rheumy eyes swept to and fro across the human scum washed up against the sides of every cobbled alley. Dr Maddox was looking for something.

Dr Maddox was looking for some*one*.

With swishing cape he would stop abruptly by a lit doorway and ask a brief question of the weathered old crone leaning against its frame. Then he would move on, his boots striking the shiny cobbles, his brass cane top glimmering under the gas lights. Ragged bands of children ran at his heels until he turned and flourished the cane. As if it were a game, they would scatter, then re-form once he had completed his turn and follow him until, their surroundings no longer familiar, one by one they fell back.

He crossed Commercial Street, the stark moonlit chiaroscuro of Christchurch rearing up giddily behind him. He glanced back, looked on. Dived into Spitalfields' maze of alleys and passages where he questioned cripples, petitioned prostitutes. Recognising the mark of a gentleman they afforded him a little respect, answering his query with a 'No sir' and a curtsey. Tirelessly he pressed on into the night.

His quarry, after all, should have been easy to find. How many blond-haired, green-eyed giants could there be in the whole of London? Never 'mind the East End. Given that he already had one of them tucked up in bed in an isolation room, the other should have been all the easier to find. Christopher Lovegrove, wealthy landowner with houses in Belgravia, was Maddox's patient; Lovegrove's identical twin brother William, a pox-ridden, penniless outcast, his last hope. And he was every bit Maddox's last hope as Lovegrove's. There was no shred of doubt in Maddox's mind that he would find the unfortunate twin. He had to find him. It was inevitable. It was his destiny. Just as it was William's destiny to sacrifice himself for Christopher, so was it Maddox's lot to make medical history. William had come second to Christopher all through his life, and now his was to be the ultimate sacrifice. Maddox's name would for ever be spoken in awe. They would have no choice but to rename the hospital after him. So had it been named from the beginning, some would say, by some kind of psychic foreshadowing, and Dr George Maddox was not a man to squash such outrageous claims. Not so long as they featured himself.

This was the doctor's third night spent trawling the diseased waters of east London for Lovegrove's brother. Three hours' kip was all he'd had in the early mornings, then back to work. Lovegrove's time was running out. The man had paid handsomely but that wasn't the point. The point was immortality, and the brother would secure that for the doctor.

Maddox doubled back, convinced Whitechapel held further scraps in the paper chase. A woman with the complexion of a rotting rose standing at the corner of Hanbury Street and Commercial Street muttered something about Artillery Passage and Maddox slipped her a crown before dashing back across the road, narrowly missing the dung-shovelling boy, and plunging into Fleur de Lis Street. The dim glimmer of Artillery Passage beckoned. If that were the sheen of destiny, it could do with a spit and polish. But any lead had to be followed up.

Lovegrove – his ankles had swollen up like balloons that morning, leaving Maddox only a day and a half, two at the most. Dropsy. He'd treated the emerging symptoms with digitalis. But the patient's condition had deteriorated. When he lay flat he soon became breathless and couldn't move around without severe difficulty. The heart itself was enlarged, the apex beat displaced laterally to the left, practically in the man's armpit.

Maddox approached a public house, raucous drinkers thronging the saloon bar and spilling out on to the cobbles as he passed. One man came tottering out of the opened doorway, carried on a froth of voices and alcohol fumes, falling into Maddox's arms. The doctor lost his cane, took the man's weight. He was very heavy, far too heavy. Maddox buckled under the strain, could only slow down the rate at which the man slumped to the ground, his head a mop of blond curls. Maddox's breath caught in his throat. Eureka. He'd got him.

Getting him back to St George's was easier than he'd imagined. An urchin ran and got Maddox a cab on the promise of tuppence ha'penny, and the driver climbed down to help load the precious cargo. During the ride across town, William Lovegrove occasionally stirred and muttered unintelligible fragments of speech which Maddox didn't trouble himself to decipher. Two burly porters assisted at the other end. If William hadn't anaesthetised himself with alcohol Maddox had been prepared to use strong-arm methods. But by midnight the Lovegrove twins were lying in separate beds in adjacent rooms at the heart of the hospital's east wing and Maddox sat waiting, a spider at the centre of his web, juices flowing.

By morning, Christopher's ankles were so badly swollen the more likely diagnosis would have been elephantiasis. Maddox knew he should wait no longer. The moment was at hand.

William, bound to his cot in the next room, slept sweetly in the arms of the opium Maddox had thought it wise to administer before turning in.

A last-minute restraining hand of caution: Maddox slept. He would have expected his excitement to have rendered sleep impossible, but knew that fatigue could unsteady his fingers. Nothing must put the operation at risk.

He slipped into sleep with the ease of a trout rejoining the stream. If he had dreams they were no more than the fluid trajectories of any animal's brain in repose. Nothing disturbed his rest. No narrative was more important than the one he was about to set in motion. He woke, fully refreshed, after two hours. Maddox either slept the full night through or he snatched a two-hour refill; five minutes longer and he would have lain in the doldrums tossing and turning for hours. But his body clock was inseparable from his mind. He swept the sheets aside and strode to the bathroom, a driven man, splashing his body with cold water and towelling himself dry with a touch of the ceremonials.

Three men were going to assist Maddox in his quest to change the course of history. Four if you counted Christopher Lovegrove. And five if you considered his brother.

Two auxiliaries, assistant surgeons who in Maddox's eyes played the role of handmaidens. Faithful lieutenants, they had been sworn to secrecy during the months of planning. Not that Maddox had relied unreservedly on their fidelity: he had planted weeds in the soil of their surgical careers within the past year. Tiny errors that had shown up in the wake of unsuccessful operations, shown up only because Maddox had shone a bright but dishonest light on their individual records, falsifying details of treatment, amending figures on long lists, even copying out entire reports to insert one deadly alteration after the event. Both men owed their continued practice to his silence. Both men owed Maddox a lot. And both men were good surgeons. Why else would he have chosen them? They would help him make history, then quietly step back as he took the bow.

The third man, Maddox's disciple and faithful acolyte, the so aptly named Hope. Alexander Hope. Aspiring chief surgeon at St George's and vital lynchpin in the world's first heart transplant operation.

The principle was not unknown. Maddox had seen Mantegna's work. The National Gallery not a mile away held a painting which had enthralled the young doctor, its image penetrating his dreams as deftly as a needle entering a vein. The diseased leg of the white man. The grafted black leg from a negro donor. The artist's audacity in presenting the idea of transplant actualised in flesh to a world yet innocent of such science. He, Maddox, would be hailed as the first truly great human confluence of art and science. Da Vinci's achievements would grow dim in his brightness.

Hope, the junior, would be Lovegrove's heart bypass while the brother's organ was made ready. For two, maybe three minutes, Lovegrove's deoxygenated blood would pass through Hope's right auricle, slip through the tricuspid valve into the right ventricle, whence it would be expelled via the pulmonary semilunar valve and find its way to Hope's lungs. Oxygenation would take place and the blood would flow back into the heart – left auricle, mitral valve, left ventricle, the powerhouse of the operation, and with an almighty pumping action back into Lovegrove's arteries and around his body. All while the donor heart could be fixed up for insertion. In a sense there were two donors, but Hope was only lending his support. William Lovegrove was giving his life for his brother, which in effect had been the deal since birth. Only now was that deal actually being struck. And Maddox its humble broker.

He did occasionally experience delusions of humility.

As if he were playing a role himself in the Lord God's great design.

And so to work.

'Gentlemen,' said Maddox, turning to Salthouse and Copthorne, the two assistant surgeons. They snapped to attention and regarded Maddox, who stood over William Love-grove's prone form. 'This man is dying. His condition is fatal and no drugs we can give him would prolong his life. We are in agreement?'

Copthorne and Salthouse nodded, aware there was no possible argument.

'Indeed so, sir,' added Salthouse.

In the time he'd been in their 'care', William Lovegrove's condition had deteriorated – Maddox had simply not given him the dosage that could, feasibly, have prolonged his life by, say, an afternoon. The man had gone to Whitechapel to die – there was no question of that not being the case. He had sought the anaesthesia of alcohol by which to enter the end stage: for he had known as surely as Maddox intimated the measured approach of destiny that death was at hand.

He was not expected to last out the day. His breathing was very shallow, his skin pale and papery. And Christopher Lovegrove likewise was heading for a point of no return. Maddox's hair practically stood on end with the electricity in the room. Hope lay waiting, anaesthetised. Salthouse and Copthorne watched Maddox's lips. The only sound now came from William Lovegrove's dwindling breathing. Destiny was at hand, history upon them.

'Begin,' whispered Maddox, and his assistants set to.

Maddox wore a long leather apron over his dress coat, metalwork slotted into pockets sewn on to its skirt. Salthouse and Copthorne were unprotected.

'Sir,' exclaimed the former as he hovered over the ailing William.

And Maddox saw that the Lord had obliged. William Lovegrove's life winked out as he watched. The candle flame guttered one final time and expired. Maddox fancied he saw the poor man's soul depart its body in a tiny puff of smoke. Such ideas were nonsense, he knew, but within his own solid chest beat a heart capable of romance. He was, after all, a visionary.

'Gentlemen,' he announced. 'The Lord has provided. *Carpe diem.*'

And like a scatter of surprised doves, their hands flew into a blur. The transplant was underway. Incisions were made along dotted lines and tiny saws worked against breastbones. Rib cages were split asunder, great chests flung open and their glittering contents revealed to the world. Maddox stopped for a moment in awe of the sight: Christopher Lovegrove's heart and Hope's heart both now beating against the open air.

The three patients lay on benches in a half-star formation, their heads pointing inwards forming the three points of an isoceles triangle. William Lovegrove's feet pointed east – back from whence Maddox had brought him – while Christopher Lovegrove and Hope lay almost side by side, their feet pointing west. In the space at the centre between the three men's heads, Maddox marshalled his two assistant surgeons. Copthorne was already severing the blood vessels around William Lovegrove's stilled heart. While he lifted the glistening purple muscle clear of the dead man's body and laid it carefully in an ice-filled bowl, Salthouse was making a start on Christopher Lovegrove's anaesthesia. The man was unconscious anyway, but Maddox didn't want to take the risk that he would wake up mid-operation and panic, only to die from shock. Maddox himself cut a hole in Christopher Lovegrove's superior vena cava – the main blood vessel entering the heart – and clamped the vein below the hole. Then he inserted a length of rubber tubing and quickly clamped the end of the tube. Salthouse was cutting a similar hole in Hope's superior vena cava. This done, Maddox slipped off the end clamp and threaded the tube into Hope's superior vena cava. Salthouse then incised a tiny hole in Hope's aorta – the main artery leaving the heart – and slipped in another tube, its end clamped. Maddox had already snipped at Lovegrove's aorta and inserted the end of the tube which Salthouse handed him, sweat dripping from his brow. He slotted it home.

The strain on Hope's heart, now that it was pumping two

lots of blood, was enormous. Maddox was fully aware of this and so indeed had Hope been. The man had a keen sense of responsibility. But that was not all: there would be a scandal quite unprecedented in scale if the truth about Alexander Hope and Mrs Olive Dunwoody were to emerge, Mrs Dunwoody being the Chief Surgeon's good lady wife. Maddox knew about the pair, Hope having confided in him one drunken evening. Just as Hope knew he could die on the operating table, so could he also die at the hands of the Chief Surgeon or his henchmen. The Chief Surgeon was a most formidable man and one crossed him in any way at all at one's peril.

Maddox stood up straight, his backbone grating and clicking, and he surveyed their position. Salthouse looked calm. Copthorne's eyes glittered from deep within shaded hollows – the younger of the two assistant surgeons had been awake for many hours. Maddox hoped for the thousandth time that he was up to it.

'Gentlemen,' he said, but it came out hoarse, high-pitched in his mingled terror and excitement. 'It is now time.'

Drawing his scalpel from the pocket on the front of his leather apron, already darkened with a little blood, Maddox leaned back over Lovegrove and sliced across the major blood vessels leading to the heart. He pocketed the scalpel – Salthouse and Copthorne were too busy looking after Hope for either to act as nurse – and reached into Lovegrove's chest cavity. Having freed the heart he lifted it clear, as long thinning strings of fluid maintained a ghost of a connection with the suddenly heartless body.

For a split second or less, Maddox watched the proceedings from outside himself. He saw a tall stooped man in a bloody leather apron holding a man's heart in one hand, the future in the other. Then he shot back into his body like a genie into its bottle and slipped the old heart into a waiting pail. Copthorne, ever alert to Maddox's needs, approached with the brother's cooled heart in his cupped hands. For a brief moment Maddox apperceived not Copthorne but a butcher's apprentice stepping gingerly across the pools of blood on the floor, a swollen pig's heart spilling from his grasp.

As both men worked and Salthouse kept a close eye on the struggling Hope, the bare floorboards of this hidden room at the heart of the great hospital opened themselves up to the shallow reservoirs of spilt blood. Infinitesimally slowly the grain in the wood parted and the dark stuff of life seeped in. Sticky patches remained on the boards themselves but some of the blood coagulated within the fabric of the hospital, so that it became part of the very structure of the behemoth.

Maddox took hold of William's stilled heart and slipped it easily into the cavity from which he had taken Christopher's. A snug fit, the pericardium nestled in between his two greyish-pink lungs. Taking a needle and silk from one of the pockets of his apron, Maddox began to reattach the major blood vessels, unhooking the tubes and quickly sewing up the holes in the superior vena cava. The whole operation took no more than twenty minutes. To Maddox, as he stood back and watched Salthouse and Copthorne diligently stitching away at Hope and Lovegrove, it seemed as if a whole era had shifted and they stood now, actors on a stage, silhouetted against a new sociological and historical cyclorama.

Now it was a question of keeping Lovegrove alive long enough to be able to pronounce the operation a success. And Hope, for that matter: he had played his part and one hoped he would suffer no ill effects. Though, viewing it with the cold eye of professionalism, as long as you chose your participants with care, sacrificing two to save one was still an acceptable deal.

'Mr Salthouse?' Maddox inclined his head towards Hope as Salthouse looked up from his work.

'He will be fine,' said Salthouse. 'I think.'

That was good enough for Maddox.

'Gentlemen, you will do two things for me. You will dis-pose of William Lovegrove's body by means of the hospital incinerator. And you will be careful to recall the conditions under which we have been working. Conditions of total secrecy. You will be kept informed, both of you, of any developments. But there must be no further contact between us until you hear to the contrary. Is that clear, gentlemen?'

'Perfectly clear,' said Salthouse.

Copthorne was nodding as he wiped his hands on the sides of his trousers.

'Mr Copthorne, I must hear it from your lips.'

'Clear, Dr Maddox.'

Could he trust them? He had to.

It turned out he was right to trust one but not the other. The mistake he had made was not to distinguish between the two men, not to view them as individuals. To him they had been a team, each man as trustworthy as the other, each one as ambitious as his competitor. That much was true, but alongside his burning ambition Copthorne regrettably accommodated an excessive enthusiasm for the ale served at the Grenadier Inn behind the hospital. Stories reached Maddox's ears of Copthorne stretched out on the wooden floor as if on a rack, his mouth full of sawdust, beer and tales of wonder and astonishment. He gathered quite an audience.

Of course no one believed the stories he told – fantastic tales of bloody resurrection, of men cast as gods – but listeners were sufficiently affected to use them as currency in their own day-to-day conversational transactions. Rumours spread down corridors and into lecture rooms with the swift and sure whisper of forest fire.

Over the next fortnight, Maddox monitored Hope and Lovegrove closely. He kept them on separate wards so that no other member of hospital staff should ever think to link them. When only two days had passed since the operation it was clear to Maddox that Lovegrove, although he had undergone significantly more profound trauma than Hope, was faring the better of the two. When he sat in his room in the east wing late into the night, doodling with a quill pen and periodically looking out of the window at the dim splendour of the Wellington Arch, Maddox admitted to himself that if it had to be a choice between the two patients, he would have to choose Lovegrove. Hope was a good, but foolish man, and few would mourn his passing. Mrs Dunwoody might well be alone in her grief, and that would be private by necessity. As far as Maddox had been able to ascertain, Hope had no surviving family, which was not considered that unusual for a forty-two-year-old bachelor in such times. Nor did Lovegrove have relatives – it was one of the reasons why Maddox had selected him for the transplant – but he did have a lot more riding on him. Give him a year's good health, Maddox mused, and he could go public on the operation. He could risk everything for his place in history.

By the end of the first fortnight, Maddox was growing impatient to announce his secret to the world. But as Hope lay ailing, and more and more outlandish tales were exchanged in the byways of St George's, Maddox realised he had to face up to his mounting problems. He appeared at Hope's bedside shortly after dawn, having slept little himself. Since no one waited for his return at home, Maddox tended increasingly to bed down at the hospital and rise before any of the day staff arrived.

'Mr Hope,' he said just loudly enough to wake the patient.

Pale of face and short of breath, Hope opened his eyes, which seemed as heavy as the hospital's great front doors. He tried to speak, but the words rattled around in his throat like dried peas in a whistle.

'Ssh.' Maddox put his finger to his lips, then took hold of Hope's left wrist to feel for his pulse. It was still irregular. A thought had occurred to Maddox in the night and every symptom he saw in the patient now seemed to support it.

'Still no chest pain?' he asked.

Hope gave a slow shake of the head.

'But I can feel my heart,' he croaked. 'Beating.'

'Yes.' He decided he couldn't spare Hope's feelings any longer. 'Mr Hope. No one else is on the ward, so we may speak freely.' Hope's eyes opened wider. 'Is Mrs Dunwoody a healthy woman, as far as you know?'

Hope looked confused.

'I believe so, Doctor.'

'This is an indelicate matter, Mr Hope. As you are aware, I know of your relationship with her, and you will appreciate why I cannot speak to Mr Dunwoody about this matter.'

Hope nodded, weakly trying to sit up and failing.

'Your symptoms are consistent with those of a Dr Charles Patin, a Frenchman and professor of surgery who upon his death was found to be suffering from an aortic polyp. I read about the case some years ago and it came back to me last night. It is most likely that the polyp indicated a syphilitic aneurysm of the aorta and I do believe that you are suffering from the same complaint. The stress placed upon your heart two weeks ago in surgery did not cause your current condition – of that I am now certain – although it may conceivably have exacerbated it.'

Maddox waited for Hope to catch up. At the far end of the ward, a patient stirred, and two corridors away a bell rang shrilly.

'Lovegrove is in splendid shape, I am pleased to report. It's my belief that we should not delay in repeating the operation we performed that night, but this time with yourself as recipient. What is your answer?'

Maddox had had second thoughts about Hope. If he died, Maddox would never be able to declare his operation a success. In his own terms it would still be an outstanding triumph, but the sacrifice of Hope would be deemed unacceptable by parliament and the authorities. His work would have been in vain. Hope had to be kept alive and the very fact of Lovegrove's continuing rosy pallor pointed the way to the clearest and most obvious solution. There was the further advantage that it would allow a couple of loose ends, which were causing Maddox increasing anxiety, to be tied up.

Hope was struggling to take it all in. He knew he was sick and that something had to be done. And at the back of his mind, of course, he knew that Maddox held the key. Maddox watched as Hope's mind worked to assimilate this new information. What it implied about Mr Dunwoody, chief of surgery, might not yet have hit home. Maddox had had several hours to consider all the ramifications, one of which, it could not be denied, was the possibility that there might soon be a vacancy in a very senior hospital position. A vacancy for which a surgeon who had recently become famous throughout the world for his pioneering heart transplant operation would have to be top choice. In truth, though, the job was but a bauble. The real prize was immortality.

'But a new heart, Doctor? Where would you find one? And whose heart would substitute for mine at the moment of transplantation, in the way that mine stood in for Lovegrove's?'

'Allow me to worry about that, Mr Hope. It shall not be a problem, believe me. Do I have your agreement to go ahead?'

Hope looked down the ward where a rumbling round of chesty coughs and rattling catarrh announced that more patients were beginning the struggle to get through another day.

'Yes, Doctor. My life is in your hands. Once more.'

Maddox touched Hope's shoulder briefly and marched purposefully from his bedside, coat-tails swirling like bat wings as he turned the corner at the end of the ward.

Maddox sat at his desk in his room overlooking Hyde Park Corner until late in the night. He was still plotting furiously when the medicine-bottle sky behind the Wellington Arch began to turn the paler blue of a nurse's dress.

The plan had occurred to him a good while previously but Maddox didn't want to rush into anything. He had to run through the operation from all angles, taking into account the enormous risks. The basic operation he had already performed once, so he knew he could do it. But on his own it would be far more demanding, the risks greater. However, by dawn, he had decided that what had been achieved by three could also be performed solo. It would require all his skill and quick thinking and, above all, dexterous speed. His vast experience guaranteed that.

Copthorne and Salthouse would lend their support, of course, but at a far more essential level than before. It was risky, yes, but not as risky as leaving them free to blab about heart transplants in the Grenadier or on the wards. True, Salthouse had not yet given any indication that he was unable to keep a secret, but it was too great a risk having him running around free, muzzled by nothing stronger than the twin gags of loyalty and ambition. In a moment of weakness, both motives could be undone as easily as the bow on Mrs Dunwoody's latest hat box.

As far as Hope was concerned, there was little time to waste. Maddox himself sought out Copthorne and Salthouse and told them he needed them right away for a repeat performance. Both men acquiesced without much resistance. Neither suspected anything, as far as Maddox could tell. The operation was set for that night. Salthouse and Copthorne were to meet Maddox at midnight on the stairs that linked the third and fourth floors in the east wing. By eleven, Maddox had wheeled Hope back into his own room, where he had previously performed the transplant on Lovegrove. His own heart rate was up; he could hear the blood thumping in his temples.

Maddox was waiting on the stairs at five minutes to midnight. A rain-streaked window revealed the deserted open spaces of Hyde Park Corner and the dark shadow of the park itself over to the left. Although he was operating to a strict timetable by arranging to meet his 'assistants' at midnight and turning up five minutes early in order to secure his advantage, Maddox felt as if time had never been more subjective. In one sense it moved with the slow elasticity of melting candle wax, as the seconds ticked silently away and destiny seemed to retreat down a long, gloomy corridor. In another, he felt it almost as a physical sensation, swirling around his legs like a shining will o' the wisp from the great river that flowed a mile and a half away.

Suddenly, Maddox became aware of footsteps on the stairs. Leaning over the banister rail and looking down he spied Copthorne and Salthouse making their way up. He straightened his spine, tugged at his waistcoat and with a dab of spittle smoothed the wings of his moustache.

'Gentlemen, good evening.'

The pair mumbled a reply.

'It is my belief,' Maddox grandly announced, 'that we should mark this auspicious occasion with a toast. Please, come this way.' So saying, he pushed open a swing door and led the way down a short corridor at the end of which they were able to access the vestibule to Maddox's rooms.

'A fine port,' he declared as he rounded the workbench where he had already prepared three glasses. His own was the one with the slight chip out of the rim. He ran his finger over it just to make sure as Copthorne and Salthouse reached out to grasp theirs.

'Gentlemen. To the heart! A remarkable powerhouse and the receptacle of the soul. You are earning your place in history.' And he raised his glass to clink against theirs. They stood, the three of them, in an isosceles triangle formation, the two assistants keeping their distance from Maddox but staying close to each other for mutual support.

The three men drained their glasses and replaced them on the workbench. Maddox looked from Copthorne to Salthouse and back again. Both men returned his gaze somewhat blankly and he felt a slight wooziness of his own, as if he'd just stood up too abruptly, and panic began to steal over him. But the sensation left him and he reassured himself that he had drunk from the right glass. It could not work so swiftly in any case. Nothing could go wrong. At least not yet.

Copthorne looked uneasily at Salthouse. If they suspected

something it was too late now. The laudanum would already be well on its way to their stomachs, whence it would be absorbed into the bloodstream, and then out they would go like gas lanterns. While they were still standing he could engineer them as close as possible to their ultimate positions so he would have less work to do shifting their heavy bodies. He talked to them about the almost unqualified success of the last operation and how this new transplantation would lay to rest the few quibbling doubts he still had. Their names would go down alongside his own, he assured them.

Copthorne was the first to show signs of affect and they were not lost on Salthouse, who looked quite alarmed as his fellow assistant held his head and simultaneously lost his footing. Salthouse went to grab him and Maddox rushed to help, a mild anxiety twitching at the corner of his mind, the thought, just the slightest fear, that the younger man was somehow immune to the laudanum and he would have to subdue him in some other way . . . When suddenly the young doctor's body folded in on itself like an empty suit dropped to the floor. Relaxed by the drug, he landed safely. Maddox wasted no time, for he genuinely had none to waste, and hauled Copthorne up by his armpits, dragging him quickly across the room to the waiting table. Well-developed muscles and determination enabled him to hoist the dead weight without too much of a problem. Then he scuttled back to manhandle Salthouse and within a minute he was ready to start.

The now familiar triangle pattern was established, with different apices. Hope the patient; Copthorne the donor; Salthouse the bypass. Hope and Salthouse lying almost side by side. Copthorne, inevitably, was about to play his last card, did he but know it. Salthouse would be following him out of the game shortly after. Hope would appear to take the trick, but of course the real winner would be Maddox.

He quickly administered ether to Salthouse and Hope. The laudanum would keep Copthorne under for long enough.

Maddox took his scalpel and drew a red line down the centre of Copthorne's chest. He drew back the skin like velvet curtains and sawed apart the man's sternum. He levered the chest open, like the jaws of some great beast, and in a flash severed the arteries and blood vessels. Within moments Copthorne's heart was on ice and the man had not felt a thing. Fully aware of the imperative to complete the operation swiftly, Maddox worked faster and more efficiently than he had ever done. His coat tails flapped as he flew from one body to the other, joining up Hope's blood vessels to Salthouse's and whipping out the heart which was to go. There was no time for ceremony and the slippery heart muscle was allowed to subside on to the floor of the operating room. It rolled a couple of feet and came to a rest against the wall, its juices seeping into the floorboards. Did it still beat? Just once or twice? Was it possible? Pumping its last into the fabric of the hospital.

The fact that Salthouse's survival was far from a priority meant that Maddox could work quickly enough to save Hope – or so he had calculated. It was a sacrifice, pure and simple, and one which Maddox felt empowered to make on the younger man's behalf. His fingers flew into a blur, his bootheels skittered on the wooden floor. Sweat stood out on his brow; he became dimly aware of its acrid aroma mingling with the metallic scent of blood. With Hope stitched up, Maddox administered a further dose of ether to Salthouse. The man would not be waking up. Maddox could not take the risk. Salthouse had played his part and should have known from the start there would be no winning in this particular game. Maddox felt no guilt. He watched Hope's chest rise and fall over his new heart and knew he was right to have done what he had done. As history's humble servant, really he had had no choice. He surveyed the room. One dead man, one dying and one resplendently, gloriously alive. He himself felt more alive than at any previous stage in his career. His own heart pounded furiously against his ribs. George Maddox – visionary. Pioneer.

***

The first fingers of the day would prise open his eyelids towards seven o'clock. Long, searching, prodding shafts of dusty light, they penetrated the shuttered windows without too much difficulty. Even if he slept huddled up beneath the windows and allowed daylight's vanguard to stream over his head, he soon became aware of the play of day on the far wall. The patterns the light made on the wall, if he dared open his eyes, and the shadows it created simultaneously with such little effort, stoked his anxiety.

The corridors of St George's soon rang less resoundingly and less frequently with George Maddox's bootheels. He retreated within himself and stayed for longer and longer periods in the small room on the third floor of the east wing where he had performed his clandestine operations.

Hope stayed with him, though the patient had little choice in the matter. Salthouse and Copthorne were long gone, their ashes scattered across Park Lane by the joint offices of hospital incinerator and westerly wind. If Maddox were mad, his madness was quite reasonable: the larger the space he occupied, the greater the chance it might include one or more of those who might seek to undermine the success of his operation. There were jealous surgeons just as there were jealous lovers. When colleagues passed him on the wards their looks were loaded with meaning. They were only biding their time before propagating rumour. The truth must only emerge when Maddox was ready, which would be when Hope was ready. And so he spent longer and longer periods holed up in the east wing, emerging when necessary to find food. If asked by anyone he told them he was managing a particularly difficult case which needed his near constant attention. People seemed to accept this, as if they simply wanted to see the back of him.

The atmosphere in the room thickened. Whenever Maddox returned after a short spell he became suddenly, nauseatingly aware of the mingled smells of sickness, death, sweat and blood.

Day passed into night by a conspiracy of shadows. Maddox would light a gas lamp for warmth and inspect his patient, who showed signs of neither progress nor deterioration. And in this way they both waited out the season. With the coming of spring and its rising temperatures Maddox could no longer ignore the sad fact of Hope's condition. He stood over his patient, staring at his splayed chest, and wondered once more if by fastening the man up again he would have given him a greater chance of survival. He had wanted to watch the heart – the *new* heart – chug and pump. A flash of memory – the sodden, crimson muscle bunching and unclenching, bunching and unclenching: blood pumping, the lungs flapping away like bellows, the pinkish tinge to Hope's strained expression revealed by candlelight. Sadly now a memory; the once vigorous heart still and sticky and furred with dust, never to move again.

Maddox's retreat from the world did not go unnoticed and hospital staff started to exchange outlandish tales. Before too long, the darkest of rumours were seeping under closed doors and coiling up stairways like smoke. A couple of eager young doctors were quietly despatched to ascertain the truth.

When they did finally penetrate Maddox's fastness to find him quivering beneath the table on which Hope still lay – despite the slow drip, drip, drip of his deliquescence – there was an impression of noise, of sensation, which was felt by both young intruders. They later spoke of thumping headaches brought on by the heat and the shock. But in the early hours of subsequent mornings when they started out of nightmares panting and sweating, they recalled the quick horror of that sweltering, putrescent chamber. Hope might have been long dead and Maddox completely out of his mind, but there was life yet in that room – that was the impression the young men had formed, each one independently of the other.

Gagged by order of the authorities, the pair soon moved on. Sought positions elsewhere and took a drop in pay if that was what was required, to leave the horrifying compass of Maddox's room, to rid their ears on hot days of the pounding of the blood in the temples. Maddox was dealt with, incarcerated in an institution to the south of the city where he was visited with decreasing regularity by a functionary from St George's until one cold November, when the rain and the biting wind sweeping in across south London proved too much for the old representative and the visits stopped altogether. Maddox's nurses had to listen to him ramble on without respite. The delusion that he had performed the world's first human heart transplant in a secret room at St George's Hospital plagued him – and his nurses – until the very end. Which didn't come for a number of years. And when it did, there was no one around to witness it. His secret, although he would divulge it to anyone willing to listen, in effect remained his own, shared only with the great building itself – St George's.

RIGHT VENTRICLE

Although the right ventricle is the largest cavity in the heart, this is due partly to its having thinner walls than the left ventricle. The Arab physiologist Ibn al-Nafís, who died in Cairo in 1288, noted that blood could only pass from the right ventricle to the left ventricle via the lungs, where it became perfused with essential spirit.

Seven

When I'm flying – and, clearly, if there's a feasible alternative I take it – I have to sit in my allotted seat. Otherwise, the plane will crash. I know this as surely as I know the date of my birth. It is a sequence of events that would be incontrovertible.

In the first place, I choose the seat myself when checking in and I choose it for good reasons. Obviously, not next to an emergency exit: the sense of contained panic in the words themselves is enough to set me off. Then there's the terrifying responsibility of having to be emergency exit monitor. Further to which, the distant but nonetheless conceivable possibility that I will lean across and open the emergency exit door in my sleep. Also, you get a dodgy deal on extra leg-room – there's so much space in front of you, it's like being in the front row at the theatre. I value my privacy over the questionable luxury of being able to stretch out my legs: people come and peer out of your window at the sunrise as if it were the only one on the whole bloody plane.

I once delayed the take-off of a 737 because I was late boarding and I found that someone had taken my seat, carefully chosen next to the aisle in the tail section. Tail sections break off and very often that's where the survivors are – if there are any at all. I like sitting in the tail section, as long as it's a non-smoking flight. When I say I like it, that's relative.

I allowed the stewardess to seat me in the row in front, jammed between two businessmen. It's not my seat, I told her. It doesn't matter, she said. And at first, although I wasn't happy about it, I accepted that. But as soon as the aircraft began taxiing, I came out in a sweat. I had to sit in my own seat. It was the only way to prevent us crashing. You see, it's not just my own life I'm concerned about. We would all die. The entire plane-load. And it would have been preventable. I caught the eye of the stewardess and told her I *had* to move. A simple 'I'm a nervous flyer' was all it took. They're very sensitive to it. They have to be.

The plane was delayed while I switched seats. Passengers cursed me but they should have thanked me for saving their lives. A hundred and twenty-three of them on a 737 bound for Zürich. Half of them were Swiss nationals. Maybe I shouldn't have bothered.

For this reason I don't like to leave boarding until the last minute. On the other hand, you get on too early and you've only got to sit around getting nervous for longer. And you set yourself up for disappointment thinking you've got an empty seat by you only for the most obese man booked on the entire flight to turn up at the aforementioned last minute and take his place, right next to you. He'll look at you and grin one of those shit-eating grins you just have to ignore. You can always use being a nervous flyer as an excuse for this kind of behaviour. If only to justify it to yourself. Anything to distract you from the terror to come.

So I sat down, stowed my hand luggage at my feet, belted up. The plane was a Boeing 747. United Airlines 1043 Heathrow to Washington. I was on my own, three seats to myself (the flight was not full – it was beginning to look as if I might be lucky). Joanna was already in Australia. Her holiday had been booked months before and it was impossible to get on the same flight, even for me to get something around the same time. So I would meet her there. Not only that but I would go via the US. A connecting flight would take me from Washington to New Orleans, where I had an appointment to keep.

I read the laminated card out of the seat pocket in front of me from cover to cover.

Twice.

In the unlikely event that you have to evacuate the aircraft, the emergency exits are here, here and here. Cute pictures of the plane landing on water. It actually does say 'In the event of a landing on water . . .'

In the event of a landing on water.

Correct me if I'm wrong, but a piece of metal weighing five hundred thousand pounds that falls twenty-nine thousand feet out of the sky – that's the height of Mount Everest, five miles high – doesn't *land* on water.

It parts the waves.

It leaves one element (air) and enters another (water) without a moment's pretence at the one you should never have left (earth).

Let's say it's travelling at nine hundred and eighty-six km per hour, an average sort of cruising speed, and the engines pack in, as they are wont to do – they're only mechanical things after all, metal fatigue and all that – the engines fail for whatever reason and the plane falls out of the sky. Well, of course, it wouldn't fall like a stone. It would glide for a bit. It'd be really cool to watch. If you were on the ground. Or in a boat. But something that heavy doesn't glide for very long. There's the whole gravity thing. It would hit the water, part it like, well, I'm sorry, but there just isn't a metaphor. It's the kind of thing you use as a metaphor for something else. He dived into the conversation like a 747 into the Atlantic. There'd be a splash, I guess, but not much of a one.

Morbid fascination draws me to it. I read all the reports. Make a special effort to catch the TV news. Keep mental lists – types of plane, airlines to avoid. But the details which distinguish one air disaster from another are just that – details. I know that one day the significant detail will be my own name's inclusion in the newspapers' sombre roll call. Until that happens, each new crash is like another stratum of rock laid down in a macabre formation, its fossils the dreck and sludge of another hundred lives.

As I write, reports are reaching London of an air disaster in Romania. All fifty-nine people on board the Romanian Tarom Airbus A310 Flight RO371 perished when it exploded three minutes after taking off from Bucharest's Otopeni airport. The dead passengers comprised thirty-two Belgians (the flight was headed for Brussels), nine Romanians, three Americans, two Spaniards and one person each from France, the Netherlands and Thailand. The crew of ten were all Romanian.

Flight RO371 went down and fifty-nine people died. Maybe the snowstorm which the plane hit just after take-off was to blame. Maybe in a crisis the pilots were unable to override the plane's computers, the black magic of fly-by-wire. Don't you ever think there are just too many maybes?

Most of us take a supposedly philosophical line: you've gotta go some time; if your time's up there's nothing you can do about it; he had a good innings; all that nonsense, those placebos. If anyone had said something similar to me about my father they would have known about it. It's the platitude of an innocent, the guff of someone who's not known grief. Someone who does not love life sufficiently to have a healthy fear of death. Show me someone who's not scared of death and I'll show you someone who's not lived. Doesn't know how to. How else can you explain their indifference?

He had a good innings.

Someone actually said that to me, not about my dad, but about a writer I knew. A brilliant writer underrated for most of his career, which only really took off a few months before he died of liver failure. Most of his old novels were suddenly being reprinted. The BBC had commissioned a series of dramas based on his detective stories. He was happy in England again after years in another country. He was happy at home, the world had caught up with him – and then he died. He suffered, friends cared for him, but he suffered and he died. Just when he was about to be everywhere, suddenly he was nowhere. He died. Finished. 'He had a good innings.' What was he, sixty-four, sixty-five? About that. A good innings? I don't think so.

Who was it, the person who said that to me when all I wanted to hear was a sympathetic remark? Does it matter? Someone for whom life is nothing more than a cricket match. Well, perhaps that person should just retire and leave the game to those of us who love being out there. Those of us who are always last off the field. Straining to see the ball in the failing light. Dusk's uncertain goalkeepers. Tennis players who don't get a chance to swing because the ball comes out of nowhere. Out of the gloom. Anglers who can no longer see their float, yet still they squint. Unwilling to admit the inevitability of the diminishing daylight. I play for that team and I'm afraid I don't understand anyone who doesn't. Don't you love life? You'd better: it's all you've got. Or so I firmly believed until Charlie Herzog and I talked. But that comes later.

My father didn't want to come in when he was called. He wasn't ready. He was sixty-four. He still had a few lines out. Bait on hooks. He was still waiting, still casting. He loved life, had long been scared of losing it. He had enthusiasms: his Dixieland LP collection filled several shelves, the hi-fi cabinet was stuffed with old reel-to-reel recordings of 'Jazz Record Requests'; he fell in love with tomorrow's computer technology when today was already slipping past him – still digging up the roots of his family tree even when he knew what the missing numbers by his own name would be. I wonder if in the early hours of one of the darkest nights he ever keyed them in, then deleted them, those remaining digits – 94. Obviating the need to repeat the 19. 1930–94. Only another six years and he could have anchored his genealogy in a new century. A new millennium. But somehow he was supposed to accept that he would not?

And now *I* am supposed to accept that he *could* not? How does one accept the unacceptable? One accepts it over time. You accept it or you go mad. Mad. Max objects to the word. Mad. Perfectly good word in my view, but Max deems it offensive. Perhaps because he knows there're people out there who would apply the epithet to him. Mad Max, yeah right. Max and his ideas, his theories. Emotional routes – well, okay. But as for his idiot contention that time does not exist, expressed and expounded upon one night in a filthy Chinese restaurant in Kentish Town where time certainly didn't exist as far as the waiters were concerned, there I draw the line. Or at least, there I *drew* the line. Now I know the question is more vexed than straightforward.

The last time I saw my father alive was on a Sunday afternoon in early September. The sun was beating down, coming through the window at the side of his bed, and he was sitting up and smiling when he recognised me (Mum was there all the time). I wanted to tell him I loved him – I didn't know if I ever had – and that I admired him in his brave struggle. Where was the self-pity I might have expected? Fallen ill, he took it like a punchbag. Kept swinging back. Didn't lie there crying. If he felt sorry for himself he didn't show it. Maybe that's why it was difficult for me to demonstrate my own sympathy. It was as if we were all pretending. But what's the point in pretending when death is staring you in the face?

At this stage they weren't pumping him full of morphine. That came later. The fevers had given up on him. He was lucid, but weak. But he smiled for me when I walked on to the ward that afternoon. He smiled and listened to my chatter, said a couple of things, largely through my mother. My limbs felt hollow, as if sudden movement would snap them, my head swirling with the things I was too shy to say. In case they forced on him a deeper intimacy with his disease and his death. Could be I was projecting my own terrible fears on to him, but I couldn't bring myself to utter more than a few words of empty encouragement. I wasn't lying to him exactly, but I wasn't speaking the truth. I didn't want to remember him catheterised and helpless, I didn't want to see him die.

When I left I held his hand briefly. I squeezed it too hard and he winced. Then I walked past the end of the bed and he followed me with his eyes, still smiling. Could he have known he would never see his son again? Would his awareness of death have given him a preternatural awareness of life? Was there a pattern which at that point he and only he could see? And if he'd known, would he have said anything, or simply smiled as I left? When I looked back, through the glass partition at the ward entrance, he was staring past the end of his bed, his gaze at ninety degrees to my own, his eyes still open. Mum had said she would see me out. We'd left him alone for a moment. I tried to imagine the loneliness he must have felt whenever Mum left his side. There's no doubt that if it hadn't been for her vigil he would have gone long before. I hugged Mum hard enough for both of them. We both knew. We all knew. But to say it out loud in front of him – to him – would have broken some kind of spell.

I often wish I'd broken that spell.

But maybe I only wish that for myself. I'm in no position to know if that would have made it easier or harder for him.

I walked out of the hospital into a wash of sunlight. It was so bright it made my eyes hurt. My head was shaking and I couldn't see clearly. I had to sit down. There was a bench up ahead, if I could just cover another twenty yards. All that went through my mind was that he shouldn't have to die. Not yet. Not at sixty-four.

It was as if his plane had gone down but they hadn't yet released the number to call. All we could do was wait.

Falling in love with Joanna didn't so much comfort me as completely take my mind off Dad for short periods. I was experiencing highs and lows and one didn't seem to affect the other. I'd be out with her somewhere and an image of my father would enter my mind but for some reason it didn't spoil the experience of being with her. It was too new an experience. She was so very different from other women I'd known in recent years. At thirty-five she was older than me by four years, which was a welcome relief after the sulks and whims of twenty-three-year-olds, girls who had seemed fun and exciting for a while until they began to pout when I didn't want to go to this club or meet that ex-college friend.

I was growing up and maybe it was about time.

She lived two or three miles south-east of the Central Middlesex Hospital, where she worked. Just the other side of the A40, which was why I used the Westway to get over there. We'd met in August, so the days were getting shorter and I had to be quick to catch the sunset. Driving along the Westway into the setting sun to meet a beautiful woman – I'd not done it before – is an experience I can recommend.

We went down to Hammersmith, drank at riverside pubs, held hands across tables in the tapas bar across the street from where she lived. She played me records: Arturo Sandeval, Guy Ropartz, Joni Mitchell. She loved Joni Mitchell, she told me – she was a big fan. I looked through her collection, wondering how big a fan. I was a fan too.

'I can only find "Blue" and "Hejira",' I said, bent down on the floor in the corner where she kept her LPs. 'Maybe you've got more on CD?'

'No, that's it. Great albums.' She smiled.

'Yes . . . but . . .'

I stopped. Why on earth would I want her to be like a man? She was a big fan of Joni Mitchell: she had two of her records. She had two Joni Mitchell records: she was a big fan. I had, what, eleven, twelve – I don't know. But I'm male, I behave like a male. I collect, I tick off, I complete. I slipped 'Hejira' out of its sleeve. No inner sleeve, I noted – another female trait. Didn't mean she loved the music any less. The track record of the record could be read all over it – all over its tracks. Surface marks – the kind you used to have to pencil on to a card at the record library – and scratches and gouges. Thumb prints, grease marks. Didn't mean she wasn't a big fan. Just meant she wasn't a guy. She wasn't uptight. She wasn't mad.

I put the Joni Mitchells back. Flicked on through the dog-eared covers. Found a Sparks LP – 'Kimono My House'.

'Now you're talking,' I said, rocking back on my heels and tipping the familiar Island label out of its sleeve. 'The best.'

She laughed. 'The best?' she said.

'The very best. I suppose it's the only one you've got? Or you might just about have "Propaganda" as well?'

She shook her head.

Sparks are the only artists whose complete works I owned, and still own. I even have the two early LPs they recorded before 'Kimono My House'. I have 'Big Beat' and 'Introducing Sparks', two albums they did after their big three ('Kimono My House', 'Propaganda', 'Indiscreet') and which weren't really up to scratch. I have twelve-inch picture discs of 'Beat The Clock' and 'Tryouts For The Human Race'. 'Number One Song In Heaven' – the best song title ever bar none – on green vinyl. French CDs featuring both the best and the worst of Sparks. And the latest album, a new release, 'Gratuitous Sax And Senseless Violins'.

Joanna wondered out loud if that wasn't lifted from Talking Heads, but I gave her a look that put an end to *that* speculation.

I have *Rollercoaster* on video – Sparks feature in the film playing a funfair gig. 'Black Rain' – a nightclub scene.

So? I'm a man. It makes me happy.

I took off 'Hejira' and put on 'Kimono My House'. It begins, of course, with the one Sparks song everybody, but everybody, knows – 'This Town Ain't Big Enough For Both Of Us'.

I'm not saying I fell in love with her because of her record collection, because it contained some Sparks and a couple of old Joni Mitchell LPs, but it didn't do any harm. And she made me laugh – professing to be a big fan of Joni Mitchell when she only had two LPs. But she probably knew those two LPs inside out – she made me laugh *at* myself and *with* her. She made me laugh a lot, right from the beginning. For once I wasn't stranded in 'Amateur Hour': I seemed to know what to do at what time. I didn't rush in and ruin it. I didn't hang around so long she got sick of waiting either. For once I didn't mind being expected to make the first move because I sensed how right it was. There was no game-playing, no dissembling. There were just the two of us, one night in her house after another excellent dinner, and a kiss.

A kiss that went on for ever.

I had to learn how to kiss all over again. Any woman who kisses, rather than simply allows herself to be kissed, does so in a manner entirely her own. Once I'd kissed her for the first time I became a different person. Largely similar but actually different. I'd kissed her, she'd kissed me, there was no going back on it. We kissed some more.

I'd bought her a copy of 'Gratuitous Sax And Senseless Violins'. Brought it round all wrapped up. She laughed when she opened it. Later we turned the lights off, lit a couple of nightlight candles in thick purple glass holders and put it on. My favourite track, 'Hear No Evil, See No Evil, Speak No Evil'. Russell Mael's voice, extraordinary when he wasn't even trying, like bubbles of helium bursting in vast dark halls, looping over notes a man shouldn't be able to reach. Still doing it, twenty years after 'This Town'. Swooping up through the octaves as if they were mere musical theory. It wasn't just an unusual voice, but a beautiful voice. Like artists located on the edge of any sphere of influences – outside it altogether, even, true originals – the effect was to move you and thrill you. She was there with me on this one. She liked people who were *out there* and somehow *on the edge*. The sort of people – bands, writers, painters, whatever – about whom the mainstream media would rarely say anything more generous than that they were 'curious' and 'interesting', but not as 'accessible' as they might be.

I hoped she wasn't going to turn out to be mad. The signs were good, but they'd been good before. (You don't want to know.)

I stayed the night. The spare room didn't get a look in.

I'm not going to go into details, but I woke up in the morning with new sunlight streaming in through new windows. The world felt a little bit different. Slightly unsteady, but exciting. As if in the night I'd been fired into orbit and I hadn't yet made it once around the earth. Scary but good. Then she woke up and smiled at me.

I wanted to get up, make a coffee and go and sit in the back yard, in the sun, and think about how it all seemed to be working out pretty well. Just have a couple of moments' reflection on the past few days. But Joanna had other plans.

I was at home when I heard. Back at Great Arthur House and Joanna was with me. It was about nine o'clock in the morning. We were asleep in bed, having a lie-in because we'd had a late night. It was a Saturday. The phone rang and it was answered by the machine before I had a chance to wake fully and scramble out of bed. Mum's voice – chilling, factual, strained. Tiny hairline cracks at the edges of it.

'Your father died at ten past eight this morning.'

I picked up the phone and we talked for about ten minutes. Then I walked back across the room to where Joanna was sitting up in bed. She said nothing, just put her arm around me and held me. We stayed that way for some time. The night before we'd been to a Cranes gig in Clapham. Afterwards we drove back north of the river, had a wander on Hampstead Heath, sat by one of the pools, diesel oil by moonlight, and talked about stuff. Romantic stuff. Finally got back to my place, eleven floors up. Enjoyed the view from the balcony for a while, then went to bed.

My mother didn't want to see anybody. We had to respect that, my sister and I. It didn't matter that I thought it was strange. It didn't matter that Joanna thought it was strange. I could understand it. My sister had her boyfriend. I had Joanna. Mum – I imagined her walking out of the hospital that morning. After three or four nights sitting by his side she'd taken the doctors' advice and gone home for a night's sleep. Woke early to their phone call. 'You'd better come in. There's been a change.' Of course, when she got there it was too late. He'd gone.

He'd been asking for her and they told him they'd spoken to her on the phone and she was coming. He knew she was coming and he tried to hang on but he simply couldn't. Maybe the knowledge that she was on her way made it easier for him to be on his.

Joanna was on call and she had to go in to Central Mid to see one or two patients. I didn't want to sit around at home. My natural desire was to be with Mum, but I had to respect her wishes.

Two and a half hours later, Joanna and I were in the Stag, leaning into the Westway's curves. Paddington Green, Westbourne Park, back on the straight over Ladbroke Grove. After Joanna had been to check on Charlie and told me he wasn't doing too badly I went in and sat with him. He was lying there with his eyes closed, on his back. Didn't react when I said hello. There were monitors and drips and a catheter. Some of the stuff my father had had around his bed. And which hadn't done him a fuck of a lot of good.

'My father died,' I said. Perhaps I said it because I knew Charlie wouldn't hear. I don't know. It just seemed ridiculous sitting there and keeping it to myself. 'This morning,' I added. 'Ten past eight.'

It occurred to me that my father and Charlie had this in common if nothing else. They had both died. The only difference being that Charlie had come back – been revivified. They didn't bother with cases like my dad. What was the point? They'd been waiting for him to die for weeks. They'd done their best to avert the course of the cancer, they said. How did you know whether to believe them or not? We hear about cases where there's a five per cent chance with this or that treatment, but if you're over eighty, forget it. If you're sixty-four, well, I guess you can forget it as well.

Charlie had been there and come back. What was it like? We all want to know, after all. If there's something, or just nothing.

'What's there, Charlie?' I spoke quietly, not loudly enough so as he'd hear me. He didn't even appear to be conscious. Really I was just thinking out loud. 'What is there? What is there *there*?'

Charlie grunted.

I looked at him. Looked at the daisies and chrysanths in a glass vase next to his bed, a tag stuck among the stalks, lots of love from Yvonne. I looked at the orange on the nightstand.

And at the single card. Plain white with a naive image of a heart on the front. For all the world like a Valentine. Signed simply, and dead centre in the available space, 'Max'.

With a shiver of realisation I saw that Charlie had opened his eyes and was looking at me.

'Charlie.'

In an uneven, phlegmy voice he said: 'This doctor of mine, this heart specialist . . .'

His voice just seemed to run out.

'What about her, Charlie? Dr Mackay? What about her?'

He was silent, apart from his ragged breathing. His eyes closed, then opened again.

'That hospital,' he managed quietly.

'Hospital? Which hospital?'

I wondered if he was rambling, if I should call for Joanna or for a nurse. He coughed, a terrifying, mortal saw tearing through his chest, then fading to a tickly rasp. His eyes opened again.

'That room,' he said. 'In the hospital. It's some kinda place.'

I was bewildered and about to run for Joanna when he added: 'Don't be too upset. He's okay, you know. It's okay.'

I suddenly felt very cold.

I gripped Charlie's arm.

'He's okay,' he repeated.

'Who?' I asked. 'Who's okay?'

Long pause. During which I hardly dared breathe. And then, almost inaudibly, Charlie whispered: 'Your father, you asshole.'

I started to speak but choked back my words. I realised I was still holding Charlie's arm. I let go. Tiny little crescents of white quickly turned pink again.

'What do you mean?' I said. But he'd gone, really gone this time. Fast asleep. Out of it. His great chest continued to rise and fall, but he'd switched off. I shook him gently, but released my hold when I heard a nurse rustling into the room behind me.

'I think perhaps Mr Herzog needs some rest now,' she said as she cast her gaze over the instruments. She pulled his covers up, finally turning to me with a rather grim expression. I rose. Quashed an instinctive apology and moved into the corridor feeling shell-shocked and numb.

What did he mean by telling me that my father was okay? The man was dead. I may not have seen his body, but my mother had. I hadn't wanted to see his body any more than *she* had wanted anyone going to see *her*. It was best to keep out of the way. His body would be just that. It had been bad enough seeing his lifeless expression when still alive. In death his features would have shed the invisible web that kept them in true. As if someone had severed the string on a bag of oranges. The chin would have started to go, the eyes would have rolled up. I didn't want to remember him that way.

I looked back to see that Charlie's eyes were open again. And around the back of the nurse, who was leaning over him, he'd raised a thumb in my direction. He was almost smiling, the old bastard. I felt something give.

I went and sat outside for a while watching cars go by, people waiting at a bus stop, the walking wounded besieging the entrance to A&E. I was detached from it all, like an actor in the wings, my part played. None of these people knew my father was dead. None of them cared. They just carried on going about their business as if it were the most natural thing. I realised I was crying. I was crying for my mother as much as for my father. I imagined her like a rubber band that had been pulled tighter and tighter, then snapped. How was she going to cope? Especially alone.

Joanna came and found me and we went for a drive. It was tough for her. She hardly knew me and suddenly she had this to contend with. Talk about putting strain on a relationship. She was accustomed to death, though not so close to home. For her it was part of the process. If a patient died it wasn't necessarily seen as a failure. You can't save them all. Some of them are going to go, however hard you try to hang on to them. It was the children that got her.

And it was my dad that got me.

Eight

Much to everyone's pleasure, Charlie had made a full recovery under Joanna's care and had returned home to New Orleans. He was throwing a big party for his fiftieth birthday. I think it was for more than just his fiftieth birthday, but that was what he said.

He and I had spent some more time together after he'd made his strange remark about my father, about him being okay, but, despite my shy promptings, he'd not enlarged on it. There'd been more talk about the hospital, or the former hospital, at St George's – the hotel as it was now – but that was all. We talked about various stuff, got to know each other. I told him about Joanna – his doctor. I didn't know if he knew about Joanna having invited me to join her in Australia when he invited me to his party. I mean, it was a long way to expect someone to come, and he seemed perfectly serious when he issued the invitation. 'A man's only fifty once, Chris,' he'd said, and he knew that I knew we'd got pretty close in the short time we'd known each other. Max had been around a fair amount, spouting his theories. The link through him had helped as well, of course.

The seats either side of me on the 747 at Heathrow remained empty. The cabin was only sparsely populated, which was fine by me, when the stewardess started her routine. I had to put the laminated card back in the seat pocket and pay attention. This was another key thing. If I didn't watch and listen, then I'd actually need the advice she'd been dispensing. There would *be* a sudden decrease in cabin air pressure. There would *be* a landing on water. I watched. I listened. I coped.

When Joanna had first suggested it, I'd assumed she was joking. Me going to Australia as well. I wasn't wild about the idea of us being separated for four weeks just when we were getting to know each other. Just as we were falling in love. With the relationship at that early, critical stage, it was vulnerable.

I had this scenario: she'd stick it out for three weeks in the desert, then succumb to the charms of a blond surfer down at Margaret River called Wayne. I'd be cool, I'd be relaxed – for about a day and a half. Then I'd start wondering why she hadn't written. Couldn't she get to a phone?

I wasn't keen on the idea of separation, but going along as well and spending all that money – flying around the other side of the world, more to the point – never really occurred, until one night we were out having a drink with a doctor friend of hers and someone – Joanna, I think – suggested it. I thought nothing of it until I was standing at the bar getting in the next round when I suddenly thought, *Why the hell not?*

I couldn't wait to get home after that and look in the atlas. See how far it really was.

Then Charlie asked me to go to New Orleans and I had that dilemma to carry around for a few days as well. I looked in the atlas again and thought if I was going to go all the way to Australia, I might as well go via America, since I'd been invited and since I couldn't travel with Joanna. Charlie seemed still to have things he wanted to tell me. 'Come see me in New Orleans,' he'd said. 'It'll be easier to talk there.' It was as if he was preying on my insecurities, and yet clearly there was nothing in it for him.

The plane was taxiing, rumbling across the macadam, for all the world like an oversize double-decker bus. I began my mantra. Kept it up until we reached the end of the queue. Through the window I saw them, a huge line of elegant white birds snaking around to the beginning of the runway. Within seconds we were joined from behind. Slowly, one by one, we moved up the queue as planes were lifted gracefully out of the line and slotted into the invisible groove of the runway's crossbow.

My chest was thumping, my mouth had gone dry. I alternately gripped and let go of the arms of the chair. The seatbelt felt absurdly reassuring. I thought of a picture I'd once seen in *Paris Match* of the Sioux City disaster – guy still strapped in his seat slumped over on to the runway. You think I do this on purpose? I wished fervently I hadn't decided to go. Especially the way I was going. Right around to the other side of the world. The wrong way. I hadn't figured just how many planes it would take. Somehow I'd conjured up an image of two short hops. One to New Orleans and one to Australia. Without looking out of the window I could sense our turning circle. I picked up my mantra, quietly, under my breath. I had to repeat this now until we were in the air.

The engine pitch rose, in a way I still never expect it to. Should you really be able to hear something so mysterious, so magical, as the engine that will propel two hundred and fifty-nine human souls into the air? This increase in engine noise is so banal, so ordinary, I instantly lose faith. Which I never even had in the first place. And I keep repeating my mantra. We move suddenly, surprisingly quickly for something so huge. You want to get up now, right now, and run down to the cockpit and demand that they stop. You fight it. Repeat the words, around and around and around they go in my head, protecting me, protecting my loved ones, protecting everyone on the damn plane whom I couldn't care less about – but if they go, I go. Then I'm knocked back in my seat with the initial acceleration. Around and around go the names muttered under my breath. My heart, under increasing pressure, fights back as if it's trying to get out. The plane tumbles and rattles down the runway, wheels rolling like thunder beneath us, and we pick up speed, but it's not enough, because it's *never* enough. The pilot'll lift the nose too soon. Without getting up enough speed. The wheels will leave the ground, we'll tip, bank and crash-land on a wing full of fuel.

The front end lurches skyward. I'm pressed right back in my seat. Now the joy, the exhilaration, undoubted, undenied, mixed with the fear, the abject terror. The knowledge that it's too late to back out. If something this big falls back now we'll know about it. The rear end clears the ground. Delicious, terrifying pole-vaulter's swoop across the divide from one element to another. And the ascent, the first-gear sprint to the top of the hill. Don't run out of breath. Your legs are tired, your calf muscles straining so hard you think they'll snap, you've got to reach the top – stop before you do and you're straight back down again. Climbing, still climbing, acceler-ating, keep going, faster, faster – and you're there. The first plateau. Still ascending, but it's easier now. Relax a little. The worst is over. Until it comes to landing. Several hours to look forward to *that* particular delight.

It takes about ten minutes. We've got to be above the clouds and in the sunlight. Somehow it's tempting to believe the clouds, once passed through, become a solid, spongy mass beneath you that would take a falling plane and cushion it. In the event of a landing on clouds . . . Tongue-like chutes depending from the sides of the fuselage, tiny figures sliding down them, standing up on the clouds, stretching, walking away, huddling in groups. Everyone walks around for a bit, asks how long it will take to get the plane fixed, or will we have to be airlifted down? Children want to know why they can't stay up there.

I'm pleasantly surprised to learn the flight is only about five hours. Then there's a change, of course – internal flight to New Orleans.

Charlie's fiftieth. A lot of people, including himself, thought he wouldn't make it. Quite a thing to go there and come back. Why did they call them NDEs? Near Death Experiences. Why not PDEs – Post Death Experiences? I was hoping Charlie would tell me more. I was sure there was more to tell.

I was banking on it. This impulsive, mad flight to New Orleans was predicated upon it.

I slept. Not especially comfortably, but I slept and when I woke up I found we had been in the air two and a half hours. Halfway there.

I thought about Charlie taking this trip a week earlier. For a normal, healthy person, flying is a wearying business, the low air pressure in the cabin meaning the oxygen levels are lower than those we're used to – unless you live in the mountain kingdom of Bhutan and work out a hell of a lot. But for anyone with heart or lung problems, whose oxygen levels are lower to begin with, the effects can be more severe. Of course, cabin pressure could be made to be the same as at sea level, but to prevent the obvious consequences the aircraft's skin would have to be so much tougher, making the plane heavier, and that costs money. So we cruise with air pressure equivalent to that outside at around seven thousand feet.

I know Charlie arrived safely because I checked. I called him from London to let him know I was coming. I was hoping the distance between us might in a sense bring us closer together and he would tell me over the phone whatever it was he'd been holding back. But I was hoping in vain. And in any case, I'd already made my mind up to go.

I got up and stretched. Had a bit of a wander. Got myself a drink.

Eventually the embossed, crenellated patterns of the strangely solidified Atlantic gave way to land – and what land! A shining, shimmering silk-merchant's window display of golden browns and brassy yellows. New England in the fall. I hoped we wouldn't. Fall, that is. Laurie Anderson was singing about it in my earphones. I'd been listening to the tape Max had given me for the past hour. There's no way she didn't record those songs – or write some of them at least – at twenty-nine thousand feet. She conjures up the feeling of being that isolated, that small – a tiny dot in the vast sky. And yet, somehow, there's a shred of comfort in her voice. Even in the lyrics. It's a record about what it feels like to be in orbit. If we fell out of the sky now, it would be less a matter of falling to earth than falling to the bottom of the sky.

When I was little, the house we lived in backed on to a large area of common parkland. Thinking back now, it was neither one thing nor the other, neither golf links nor wilderness. My sister and I used to play there; it was called Briar Dene. There was a stream running through it, at the bottom of a gorge. It seemed a gorge to us then. If I were to go back now, no doubt it would be nothing more than a gentle slope. We would cross the stream and make bivouacs in the trees on the other side. We would play elaborate games of chase. My sister once took a swing with a rusty old golf club and hit me, accidentally, just above the eye. She herself dreamt that she was chased across Briar Dene by the dustbins that were kept around the side of the house.

One spring morning I got up early for some reason, which was unusual for me, and wandered downstairs. I could tell from the mess that someone had been up. I also knew who it had to be, given that there was any mess at all. Mum would always clean up straight away. My sister slept even later than I did and was never known to get her own breakfast. Dad always left the same telltale pool of milk in the bottom of his cereal bowl. He wasn't inside the house though. I headed for the back door and stepped outside. It was crisp and bright, not really as warm as you'd want it to be, but the sky was clear.

I found him in the garage, working away at something on his bench, some construction of wood and brown paper. I watched from the doorway as his hands fluttered over thick brown parcel paper that seemed to fold itself, and blond wooden sticks that lashed themselves into a cross without his having to hold them in position. Intense · concentration ploughed his forehead, rendering him deaf and blind to me as he continued to conduct the work in progress. I distinctly had that feeling, that he was allowing something to be made, rather than actually making it. I felt slightly dizzy for a moment, then stepped forward into the garage, scuffing my shoe on the corner of his bench. He looked up just as his hands came into contact with the surface of his construction. He just had to snap the lateral strut outwards like a bow and then it was finished. He smiled as he held it aloft for me to admire.

It was a kite, diamond-shaped, made out of that stiff brown paper he always used for wrapping our Christmas and birthday presents. On it he'd painted a face with black arched eyebrows and a grinning red mouth. 'I just have to . . .' His voice trailed off as he rummaged in an old Quality Street tin where he kept an oily selection of nuts, bolts, screws, washers and rings. I imagined his antenna-like fingers becoming smeared with grease, feeling for just the right piece. He lifted out a split ring. 'This'll do,' he said as he attached it to the ends of the three cotton tapes that trailed from points on the kite's frame.

'Come on, Christopher,' he said, gathering up the brown paper kite and a reel full of string. 'Let's try it out.' I had to run to keep up with him as he marched into the back garden, down the crazy paving between the rockery and the roses and lupins, up the two little steps at the end and vaulting over the white wooden gate. He was already disappearing into the distance by the time I had clambered over the gate. I ran, my feet dragging in the long grass, my breath in my throat. When he wanted to, my father knew how to infect people with his enthusiasm. He strode uphill without even looking around. He stopped at the crest of the field's gentle slope and laid the kite on the grass, kneeling down to attach the string to the split ring. I reached the kite's squashed, grinning face in the grass as Dad pulled the distance of string between it and himself, a further fifty yards away, taut. He mimed that I should pick it up and hoist it. The wind caught that paper diamond the minute I pointed it heavenward. It leapt out of my hand and soared upwards, arching with the unwavering power of a vertical bridge, the wind drum-rolling on the stiff, new paper.

I looked quickly over at my father. His hands holding the reel were tucked into his midriff. His head angled upwards, chin jutting excitedly, glasses flashing in the early sunlight. His arms swung to the left and the noise the kite was making changed. It skimmed across the sky, swooped like a hawk, the paper, drum-tight, snapping and beating against the frame. The grinning face buzzed the earth only yards from where I was standing, then climbed rapidly, widening the angle of the string with the ground.

My father let out more twine and the kite was suddenly so high I toppled over backwards watching it. When I sat up in the grass I realised that Dad had retreated some distance as he paid out more and more string. Backwards he walked, feeling his way with the backs of his legs in the long grass. I lay down again and rolled over, impossibly happy, aware for a split second of just how enormous the world was and how huge and exciting my own place in it could be. I loved the feel of the grass brushing against my cheek. I plucked a long thick blade, folded it in half, cupped it to my mouth and blew. The high-pitched squeal sailed across the field. I sat up and saw my sister running from the house. I did a quick somersault, rolled over again, stood on my hands unsteadily and tumbled panting into the grass. Lying on my back. My sister running towards me. Dad taking further steps backwards away from me. The three of us held together by three invisible ties like some earthbound copy of the heavenbound kite, itself secured to us by three slender threads.

Did I think these things then or superimpose them later? Well, what do you think? But I was aware of something. My sister running shrieking with joy across the long grass to where I lay. My dad playing the kite as he would later show me how to play a crucian carp – giving it its head, letting it run from one side of the sky to the other. And me lying in the grass.

In my memory, my sister never reaches my side and plunges in the long grass next to me, winding me with a flailing arm. She never arrives. She's just always in the act of running towards me. And my father is flying the kite. And I'm lying there. Watching this kite-shaped thing, this brown paper heart, climbing higher and higher into the sky. Trying to get away from my father yet unable to. Between them stretched the string that held it to the earth. Obvious stuff, but it got through to me. Just as later that same day I watched another kite – the kitemark, the British Standard kitemark – flying across the sky as we drove into the country. Slumped in the leathery back seat of the old green Jag, I watched the kitemark etched into the safety glass on the corner of the car window as it made steady progress across the sky. In the kitemark design, of course, was a heart. I watched that but saw the kite from that morning, soaring, ascending. My father turned his head and looked my way. I caught his eye and there was a look about him. The skin at the corner of his eye crinkled. His mouth twisted a little. He knew, I decided. He knew.

I went back to watching the kitemark on the window, feeling strangely comforted.

Something kept the plane up. Not physics, or chance, or the hand of God. But something. Some kind of kite-string.

Nine

The changeover at Washington Dulles Airport was achieved with minimum fuss. Those of us flying on to New Orleans were separated off from the rest of the passengers as we deplaned from the 747 that had brought us safely from Heathrow.

I didn't catch the number of the internal flight. I usually make a mental note, just another superstitious thing, but not a particularly heavy one. The flight was full, the plane another 747. I had an aisle seat on the left side about five rows from the back, next to a youngish couple who looked as if they might be musicians. She was late twenties, auburn hair, make-up, nice eyes; her boyfriend was a little bit older, long dark hair streaked with grey. He had a little grin that came and went as he talked to her; his eyes lit up when she smiled at him.

Stuff like that can make a difference. I felt good about them, so less scared about the flight. But only marginally. As we taxied for take-off I must have been gripping the arm-rest quite hard, or had failed to keep my muttered mantra under my breath, because she turned to me and asked if I was okay. I said I was a little nervous. She wasn't all that keen either. Her boyfriend was fairly relaxed. He explained he'd done so much flying when he was younger he just got used to it.

As soon as we stepped off the plane at New Orleans, even though we were still inside the terminal building, I was struck by the heat and humidity. I took a cab into the city.

It was dark, local time getting on for ten thirty p.m. The cab was a huge, low-slung car which rode the dips in the prefabricated road sections like a dolphin might ride the swell. The female driver was polite but untalkative. We passed by a cemetery, graves crammed into a high walled yard swept virtually underneath the freeway. My sense of direction had deserted me. I thought we were headed completely the wrong way. Bright and jumpy with extreme tiredness, I sat back and relaxed.

The cab dropped off the freeway on to a multi-lane highway for half a mile or so before taking a ninety degree right into a much narrower street. There were weeds growing up out of cracks at the side of the road. The traffic was single-file, one way. Houses, shops and bars with sheltered sidewalks, balconies and verandahs drew up to the side of the roadway. My driver had to brake suddenly to avoid a horse-drawn tourist trap at the next intersection. The car's shock absorbers took the strain without complaint. Driver's elbow up on the window ledge. Cigarette behind her ear.

We reached Rue des Ursulines. 'Which hundred block do you wanna go?' she asked. I responded, 'Six-one-six', and we were there, the car still rocking softly to and fro as she climbed out to free my bag from the trunk. I tipped her and she was gone in a chug-a-chug cloud of sound. I was left in the thick, moist night air of the French Quarter. It felt almost as if it were raining. A sort of Hebridean drizzle or Kenmare mizzle, but warmer. I wanted to get my head down but knew I'd dump my stuff and be right back out here to explore. Just one drink.

You know the early part of a relationship? The good ones, obviously, or the ones you think have a reasonable chance of being the good ones. Neither the Kafkaesque nightmares in embryo, nor the Munchian disasters in waiting. But the real ones, the ones with promise and more than half a chance of becoming something. When even after several weeks there are no gaping holes in the road, no bitter exchange of deep-seated resentments, no signs of madness. That early part of a good relationship when you can't get enough of a person and can't bear to be apart. You fly halfway around the world and hope they'll have left you a message at reception for when you check in.

It's not reasonable to expect this kind of thing, and someone like Max, say, never would expect it, even after several weeks' separation. It's quite all right for him to entertain fantastic whimsical notions about emotional routes and the non-existence of time, but he'd never be so weak-kneed pathetically human that he'd expect a message from his loved one as he checked into his hotel halfway around the world, and even be prepared to be disappointed if there wasn't one. And in this sense, clearly, he's less of a disaster than I.

I, on the other hand, am hopelessly vulnerable to my own niggling inner voices, a dead loss, useless.

There was no message.

The guy was friendly, a white-haired sixty-odd-year-old in a burgundy polo top and one of those permanently pleased expressions, his lips always slightly parted, eyes glittering with some half-remembered joke. He offered to help me upstairs with my stuff. I said it wasn't necesary. Moments later I was closing the door of my room behind me.

I have a routine with hotel rooms. I go around and I open every drawer, switch on every light. I stand in front of my reflection in the bathroom mirror, to see the hotel around me. I test the bed then unpack and stash my stuff in cupboards and drawers. I inhabit the room. I open all the windows and step out on to the balcony, if there is one (there was).

The air out there was thick and damp and hot. My head felt the same after nine hours' flying, but there was a strange brightness also. I couldn't have just lain down and gone to sleep. The hotel was constructed around a central courtyard but my room was on the outside of the building facing out of town. I didn't know if that was west or east because my bearings had been scrambled. I didn't know where the airport lay in relation to the city. In the cab we'd driven alongside a waterline but it hadn't felt like the sea, and even if it had been, the land-sea divisions were too complex down here for me to be able to orientate myself. My sensitivity to elemental distinctions had already been thrown awry by the business of flying.

I sat down on one of the wrought-iron chairs. Had there been a bar in the hotel I would have ordered a beer. That would have been perfect. That and a message from Joanna. I couldn't call her, I didn't know where she was, only that she was somewhere in Western Australia, probably in or around Perth. It would be three days before we met.

A long, low-slung car bounced over the intersection to my right, its red tail-lights glowing like Chinese lanterns in the sticky dark. From a bar two blocks away there rose the faint buzz of activity, fading in and out. A police siren dopplered by on the highway the cab had brought me in on.

Deciding to leave the French windows open, I got my wallet and keys and left the room. I nodded to the guy on the desk. He gave a little wave and I bounced out into the night. I walked two blocks without thinking. A humming, glowing ball hovering just above the ground a couple of blocks down Rue Decatur turned out to be Jimmy Buffet's Bar and Grill. I went in and got a beer, sat watching people go by. Everyone looked relaxed. I drank an ice-cold Miller and thought about calling Charlie. His party was just two days away. I decided to wait. Above all, I needed rest. I got another beer.

Strolling down the centre of Decatur, arm in arm, came the couple from the plane.

I thought I'd sit and watch them for a moment before calling out. Enjoying the damp warmth of the night air on my face, the refreshing kick of the Miller as it slid down my throat. And then, just as I was about to shout a greeting, they wheeled to the right and went directly into another bar across the street. I felt my heart kick, my pulse speed up slightly, and wondered why. Should I have called sooner? Should I have called at all? It seemed odd that I should have seen them, a coincidence. Or a pattern. But if it had been a pattern, shouldn't we have ended up making contact? Maybe New Orleans was smaller than I'd thought and it wasn't such a big deal. I waited until I'd finished my beer, then got up to pay and wandered out into the street. I approached the other bar and I don't know why but I had this weird feeling that I would look in and find it empty. Not because it sounded dead – there was a juke box pulse emanating from the doorway. I had the strange idea that it was a heart and the people from the plane were blood corpuscles who had been sucked into it and pushed out again at the other side. Its walls were myocardial muscle, its main room the right atrium. The pool hall at the back, the right ventricle. Beyond that . . . I could see the guy with the long hair pretty clearly bending over the pool table to line up a shot, his girlfriend standing nearby.

I left them to it and headed back to Ursulines. I must have fallen asleep on my way into the room because I woke up the next morning fully clothed with the sun streaming in through the window and the telephone ringing by the bed.

There was a rumbling sound on the other end of the line, like when you suddenly feel a tube train tunnelling beneath you in a theatre. It was a voice but I didn't recognise it. I lay the receiver down for a moment to rub my face and shake my head, then when I picked it up again, the rumbling was still there.

'Hey,' I heard at last. It was as if the train had come out of the tunnel and I could see it.

'Charlie?' I hazarded.

He grunted, uttered some mixture of laughter and vocalised shrug.

'How are you doing?' I asked him.

'M'doin' okay,' he murmured. 'Why'n'cha c'm'on over here?'

I had some trouble with this for a moment.

'Two blocks down, three across,' he said more clearly. 'Get your ass over here. Let's go get somethin' to eat. I'm hungry, man.'

Outside was as warm and damp as the shower I'd just got out of. I was excited about seeing Charlie and I marched jauntily across intersections, looked in at shop doorways and fancy window displays.

I saw a guy sitting out on his balcony. Big guy with a ginger beard, long hair. 'Stay there,' he shouted. 'Comin' down.'

Once he was down at my level he stood a few feet away from me, slightly awkwardly, looking around and tugging on his beard, muttering about where we could go. I wanted to give him a hug or at least shake his hand.

'C'mon,' he beckoned. 'S'go get a sandwich.'

We had muffalettas – Italian bread stuffed with cold meat, olives, salad, some kind of paste – washed down with draught Budweiser. He asked me if I'd had a good flight and I told him I had. Considering.

Cars glided across the intersection, long, low Cadillacs, their suspension bouncing over the camber, stop lights glowing, exhaust softly growling.

Charlie ate and drank like a man in perfect health. He

knocked back three beers to my one in twenty minutes. I saw his eye twinkle, but he said nothing.

'Tomorrow night,' he said at length, dabbing at the corners of his moustache with his napkin. 'Whole thing starts around ten.'

I watched a couple stop by a shop window. He wanted to move on but her hand was in his jeans back pocket and she wanted to stay looking. Her arm snaked as the gap between them widened, but he allowed himself to be pulled back, slowly, lazily. I missed Joanna for a sharp instant, wondered where she was, what she was doing. Lying by a pool somewhere with a dozen surfies eyeing each other up through their fringes.

'Tomorrow night, guy.' Charlie had stood up. His bulk blocked out the sun. The couple had moved on. I nodded.

He wasn't going to tell me anything. Not yet.

After I left Charlie outside his place, I wandered through the Quarter, turning left then right, left then right. I remembered from seeing a map that the area was bound on one side by the highway and on the other by the river, but I had no idea which lay in which direction. I drifted along, stopping every few minutes to listen to street bands, informal arrangements of folk gathered around a sousaphone or double bass.

I hit Jackson Square and lay down on the grass, still jetlagged. Within moments I was lost to the world. Strange patterns of light fracturing over my closed eyelids. The feeling of the sun on the skin of my arms. Joanna's face came into my mind. Then I was gone. I didn't dream so much as have some loud ambient house gig play intermittently inside my head for the next half-hour. Fortunately I turned over on to my front at some point and shielded the unprotected side of my face with my hand.

I sat up and rubbed my eyes. As I looked around the square, and the sights and sounds of bustling tourist activity impinged on me again, I had a sense of having crashed out in the corner of the room while the party went on around me. I wandered east on Chartres, pretending to be, and consequently feeling a little bit, part of things. At the intersection with Toulouse I

went south, then east again on Royal, down St Louis two
blocks and right into Dauphine. I gridwalked for half an hour,
an hour – you could do it your whole life. Past cute little
jewellery stores, loud booming music bars with women torn
apart by thongs and gyrating on tables, retro diners where
huge grizzled old guys ate hash browns and drank strong
coffee. If you had no purpose you could create one here. Stay
here long enough to meet some people, ignite new desires, you
could lay down a few emotional routes.

I ended up on Bourbon. When I saw the sign for the
Preservation Hall Jazz Band I went straight in without hesitating.
It was time to face up to the fact of why I'd come here. Time to
cope with some stuff I'd swept back behind a neat set of purple
curtains. I got myself a little table near the back, near the open
windows to the street. Sat down. Ordered a bottle of Dixie
Blackened Voodoo Lager. On stage a group of seven or eight
middle-aged guys were piling their way through a trad standard. I
didn't know any of the names but I knew all the tunes. I'd listened
to them many, many times in my childhood.

This was my father's music. He played it all the time.

And this, New Orleans, although he'd never been here, was
his favourite city. He'd never even been to America. But New
Orleans was the one place he'd wanted to go more than anywhere else. He couldn't come so I'd come for him. I'd thought
about buying him and my mother a couple of flights when he
got ill, but to have done so would have acknowledged just how
ill he was. So this was the best I could do.

In a bar in the French Quarter of New Orleans a young man
realised he'd not done the simplest thing, the one thing he
could have done. He'd allowed his father to die without lifting
a finger. Just one man in one bar in the entire tight little grid of
the French Quarter, which hummed and glowed liked some
kind of circuit diagram, growing smaller and more insignifi-
cant as it was left further and further below on the earth.

Ten

The Quarter is a strange place to have a party, since there's a party going on there all the time. Bourbon Street is one long party. And Dauphine. And Royal. Especially on Halloween.

·As I strolled down Royal Street the following night there was madness in the air. Every single bar, every restaurant, each and every jazz club was decorated with skulls and jack o'lanterns, wispy shreds of cobweb and dangling luminous skeletons. I was thinking about Joanna, while around me men and women were abandoning themselves. Young men gathered on balconies to throw cheap beads down to girls who had to earn them by hitching up their skirts or dropping the front of their tops. Choruses of whistles accompanied showers of plastic beads and girls' shrieks.

One woman, swaggering down Bourbon in a close-cut elasticated flower-print dress, stopped short when the cries and jeers of the balconied youths reached her. She swayed in the middle of the street as she cocked her head on one side and watched them from under her curling fringe. There was here, in the way she'd been walking, in the way she swayed on the sidewalk, a kind of unstoppable sexual momentum that pushed against her social superiority over the men. She didn't need to submit to their chanting and wolf-whistles, so clearly was she their better as they panted and salivated, drawing in behind her like a pack of subordinate dogs, and still her power could be expressed in yet more dramatic fashion. She pulled at the front of her dress and leaned forward, allowing them a tantalising glimpse of cleavage. They bayed for more, jangling their beads. I watched her turn away from them and lean forward, long sable tresses cascading about her face as her hands came up to grasp the front of her dress. In one fluid motion she spun around, tilting her body backwards and pulling the front of her dress down. Heavy breasts swung free, large dark nipples pointing momentarily, at the zenith of their arc, right at the crowd of cheering, squealing admirers.

It rained beads.

With perfect poise she scooped two strings out of the air and turned away, twisting her spine once more for privacy, to recapture her shivering bosom.

I watched her walk away, so full of confidence, so happy, so clearly in control. That in itself was almost as much of a turn-on as watching her show off to the gallery. Yeah, almost.

Within seconds she was gone, vanished into the stream of bodies. There were men in leather chaps with tight buttocks protruding, studded black straps delineating their pectorals. Women naked but for all-over body paint – quite unerotic, although Max would have been in his element. I remember once sparring with him in a lively argument about Nicolas Roeg's *Castaway*. Quite apart from it being so disappointing, given the track record of its director, it featured the unedifying spectacle of Oliver Reed and Amanda Donohoe walking about without a stitch on for ninety minutes.

'Exactly what makes it worth watching,' Max had maintained.

'Bullshit,' I had said. 'In *The Music Lovers*, yeah, maybe he was worth a look.'

'I'm not talking about him, you arsehole. I'm talking about Amanda Donohoe. She's absolutely fucking gorgeous.'

'Look: (a) she's not; and (b) even if she were, given that she's got her kit off for eighty-six per cent of the film, it's not that interesting. There's no eroticism. If there's no juxtaposition of concealment and revelation, there's nothing to get excited about. Basic stuff, Max.'

I remember him chewing on whatever we were eating, then countering with the considered 'Great tits though'. Just a little bit too loudly for the place we were in.

I returned to the hotel to freshen up before heading out to Charlie's, although if I was honest with myself I was missing Joanna and I guess I was hoping there might be a message.

There was. The white-haired guy gave me his little grin as he handed it over. I took the message without looking at it and didn't unfold it until I was lying back on my bed with two pillows under my head. It was brief, unfinished. 'Joanna says hi. Looking forward to seeing you in . . .'

The guy had had some trouble with 'Joanna', having attempted three different spellings, so I figured he'd simply lost it altogether by the end of the message. Most likely she'd have said Australia, or Perth. Or 'Looking forward to seeing you in a couple of days'. Although I was set to leave New Orleans the next day, which was Tuesday, I wasn't due to land in Australia until Thursday. Somewhere along the way I was going to lose a day. Wednesday – I was not going to have a Wednesday. This had been bothering me so much I hadn't allowed myself to dwell on it. It was the sort of thing I just was not able to come to terms with. When I was little, I was the kind of kid couldn't understand how we could change the time merely by changing our clocks. Every spring my mother and father would go around the house moving all the clocks forward an hour and in the autumn they'd go around and move them all back. How on earth dared we presume to mess about with something so immutable as time itself? I never got my head around that. I still haven't.

I was going to lose a day. I couldn't get my head around that either.

Most of us lack some small part of the human brain. With some of us it's money – balancing the economy, currency exchange, why we can't just offset poverty by printing more money. With me it's time and what happens when we start messing around with it.

None of which made any difference to the fact that Joanna had rung, she'd said hi, she was looking forward to seeing me.

I went and stood out on the balcony, watched the city lights flicker, listened to cars chugging along Rue Chartres, revellers laughing and drinking on Decatur. I was all set for Charlie's.

I don't know why, but I wasn't all that surprised to find the couple from the plane at Charlie's place on Royal Street. I saw them on the balcony as I approached. The auburn-haired woman was deep in conversation with a heavily made-up goth girl, but the guy with long hair was leaning over the handrail gazing into the street. He smiled when he saw me, he too looking quite unsurprised, which made me feel a little odd.

The entry was at street level but then a flight of stairs took you straight up to the first floor, to Charlie's apartment. It was heaving. Bodies everywhere. A constant buzz, the splash of beer and clashing of glasses, the glug of wine poured from freshly opened bottles, insectile rasping and clicking of lighters. The hiss of air sucked through cigarettes, like creatures burrowing through undergrowth. No immediate sign of Charlie, but people were friendly and as I crossed the room to get to the balcony, I met a middle-aged Merseyside writer with a booming voice, who introduced me to a tanned, healthy-looking American novelist. With them was a screenwriter of indeterminate origin. Charlie seemed to know a lot of writers. Which figured. I was told everybody's names and promptly forgot them. When I finally made it outside I saw Charlie.

The apartment occupied the corner of the block and the balcony was therefore L-shaped. Charlie was leaning back against the wall of the house on the other leg of the balcony. Before I could make my way through the tight knots of people enjoying the muggy warmth of a late New Orleans evening to get to him, my sleeve was tugged by the auburn-haired woman from the plane. Her boyfriend appeared by her side and we exchanged the inevitable remarks about coincidence and fate, but I was eager to see Charlie – after all I had flown three thousand miles to see the man. I excused myself and, on my way over to where Charlie was, reached into a huge tub of melting ice for a beer. Dixie Blackened Voodoo Lager. An opener hung on a string attached to the tub.

I clapped my hand on Charlie's shoulder from behind. He was saying my name as he turned around – how he knew it was me I didn't know – and I was delighted to see he was looking better than at any stage since I'd known him. His big round face was glowing, having shed all traces of the yellow cast it had reportedly worn when he'd arrived in London. Green sparks glinted from within the soft creases around his eyes, like fragments of jade cushioned in velvet. He leaned across to give me a hug.

It felt strangely as if I hadn't met him at all for lunch the previous day.

I'd noticed this about Charlie in London – that he had a tendency to come and go – but had assumed it was a symptom of his illness. This now seemed like the real Charlie. Had I got a beer, he wanted to know. 'Then get another one. There's more beer here than in the whole of Bourbon Street,' he said. He didn't appear to be taking Joanna's advice in terms of alcohol consumption, but it was hardly my place to say any-thing, not on his fiftieth birthday. I noticed that he had taken a step back from me and had his arms stretched out wide as if to take in the whole party, to embrace all his friends who had come, presumably from all over the States, as well as flying in from around the world. A huge, beatific grin split his face in two and coming from somewhere deep in his chest a chuckle recalled my old Stag responding reluctantly to ignition on a February morning. He was teetering, about to topple back-wards against the flimsy rail. Adrenaline fired my system, enabling me to shoot out an arm and steady him.

His balance recovered, Charlie stumbled inside for a refill. I staggered along the balcony a short way and grabbed an empty chair. With my feet up against the rail and an unfinished bottle of Blackened Voodoo in my hand I tried to relax.

By Charlie's apartment, Royal Street strayed west into a predominantly gay area. At a bar on the opposite corner, boys leaned over the balcony to whistle at men in the street. The downstairs bar pulsed with Marc Almond, Freddie Mercury, Gloria Gaynor. Two men were ejected from the door to roll around in the street. They picked themselves up, blew kisses up at Charlie's balcony and re-entered the mêlée.

I finished one beer and started another, barely aware that Charlie had sat down next to me until he started speaking.

'All these people,' he murmured, with a sweep of his hand indicating the range of his guests. 'If you can imagine all these people who've come here, imagine they're not all discrete individuals – which they're not. They are – and yet they're not.' He stopped in order to swallow a mouthful of Jack Daniel's, regarding his empty glass afterwards with a mixture of pride and surprise. 'They've come from all over America, east and west coasts, from Colorado, New Mexico, Maine and Vermont. They've come from London, England . . .' Here he squeezed my shoulder and looked briefly in the direction of the couple from the plane. 'You all of you lead separate lives. You'll go away from here and never see most of these guys again. You may never see *any* of them again. Some of these guys know each other pretty well and will see each other from time to time, but essentially, whether they see each other or not, they all have their own lives, which they imagine are quite distinct. Right?' He looked at me, his green eyes questing from out of the shadows of his big round face. 'Right?'

I nodded.

'Wrong,' he said, his face folding up into a big smile.

'Wrong?' I helped myself to another beer from the tub.

'Wrong.'

'How wrong?'

'It's the reverse.' He unscrewed the bottle of JD by his feet and poured another glass.

'You want me to get you some water for that?' I offered.

He shook his head, grinning. 'They're all connected. All of 'em. Every last one. Did they but know it. Ignorant fucking bunch.' And at this he cracked up, unsteady laughter hacking through his lungs. He bent over, bucking with each fresh cough. Eventually he was quiet again. 'All connected,' he squeezed out before tipping more whisky down his throat.

'That room,' he continued, and I guessed he meant the room in the hotel at Hyde Park Corner, 'that room ain't no ordinary room.'

'I know that,' I said. 'From talking to Max.'

'I saw things in that room . . .' He tailed off, watching two cropped-haired men with heavy moustaches cavorting on the balcony across the street. 'It ain't no ordinary room. But more to the point, there's something about us that ain't that ordinary neither. Or about the world we live in. You know what I'm saying?' His eyes shone. 'This ain't no *ordinary* life.' His hand fell on my knee and squeezed hard. 'We think we know all the answers,' he drawled. 'And we don't know shit. But after I came out that room, I knew a lil bit more 'n before I went in.' He poured another tumbler of JD. 'But I guess that's all bullshit. All I really knew when I came out that room was how lil I knew when I went in.'

Which left me absolutely nowhere nearer to understanding what the hell he was going on about, and before I knew it, he had melted away back into the party. Irritated, I plunged my hand into the beer cooler and came up with a bottle of Bud. I snapped off the cap and guzzled at least half of its contents in one slow slug. I got a rush to my head and an electric tingling in my hands, which was something at least.

After that, things became a little less distinct for me. It seems, looking back, that I stayed there a long time. I may have talked to the couple from the plane. I may have talked to some other friends of Charlie's. But I don't remember what I said to them. Nor them to me. What I do remember is Charlie talking to me again later – I remember his words as clearly as if they were spoken yesterday – his voice booming out on the sweltering balcony, while the party swung on through the early hours, both in the apartment and out in the Quarter.

'You know you got yer subtle body,' he was saying. 'Well, you also got yer subtle heart. And when you're up there, man—' he swept his arms high in the air '—you can see everything. The whole fuckin' lot, you know. It's all connected. Each one connected to the next in a giant fuckin' web. A net. Whatever you wanna call it. It's the World Wide fuckin' Web of the heart, man, if that's what you wanna call it.' He knocked back another JD, poured the next. 'And if you gotta subtle heart, man, you got other stuff too. 'Cause when you think about it, the heart is the cradle of time and space. Think about it. I have. I've a lot of time to think about it. An eternity.'

He sat back and I realised my hands were tightly clasped over my knees, my knuckles white.

'This might have packed in once or twice back there,' he continued, thumping his left breast, 'but my subtle heart didn't. They don't. They just keep on going.' He sat back, placed his enormous hands over his knees and gave me a long look. 'It's *not* the end of everything. That's all. What I wanted to tell you, it's as simple as that.'

He didn't look as if he was going to say anything else, and he didn't need to. I felt a curious but undeniable lift inside my own heart which felt like a mixture of hope and comfort.

Just when the party seemed about to fizzle out, it suddenly picked up again; like a sagging balloon getting a fresh breath of air it became buoyant once more. Charlie had drunk himself to a new, strange state. He'd gone beyond the plateau of lucidity to a steeper slope of consumption so high in the clouds no one, least of all him, had known it was there. Nothing more would I get out of him that night. In any case, I sensed that was it. He'd told me all there was, in as straightforward a manner as he knew how.

As I left the building and stumbled carefully across the street I was aware of a figure resting on the first-floor rail watching me go. Long dark hair, a patient, indulgent attitude. The guy from the plane. Almost as if he had been detailed to watch me go.

Eleven

When I awoke I had no idea of the time.

I also felt anxious.

I lay there in my sweltering hotel room with no real idea even of what day it was. The sun was high in the sky, which wasn't a particular help, and as to which day of the week it was ... I thought hard, tried to burrow backwards to the night before and then realised my problem. I'd been asleep only about two hours, having walked back from Charlie's – and having taken the long way around. There was a good chance I'd been through all the districts the white-haired guy on the front desk had told me were no-go areas. Most people simply advised you not to go east of Canal or beyond North Rampart, but the guy on the desk shaded out a whole area of my map and shook his head gravely. Just about anywhere north of Bourbon got the big no-no from him. I guess he was just over-cautious because I got back okay. I couldn't move my arms or legs more than an inch, but no doubt that was sheer exhaustion rather than anything more sinister.

I still felt anxious. But without any real focus. It was as if there were a little guy in an old bi-plane assiduously crop-dusting the back of my mind with unformed-anxiety powder.

Then I remembered I was flying out that day – and soon. I felt that grim foreboding you get before exams, trips to the dentist, anything that scares you. I reached for the phone and called the front desk to see how I was doing for time. I was doing fine but I'd be doing a lot better if I got up. Turned out they had an airport shuttle service, some kind of minibus that shunted around the hotels in the Quarter and took you all out to the airport in one go. Cheaper than a cab and, well, that was just about its only advantage.

I got up and looked in the mirror. Leaned forward over the washbasin. My hair really was getting longer, I noticed – I was letting it grow.

I had time for a relaxed breakfast down in the cool green shade of the hotel's courtyard. As relaxed as it could be, given I was about to take the longest international flight of my life. Four hours from New Orleans to LAX, then sixteen hours to Melbourne, via Auckland. The coffee and croissants with marmalade didn't taste quite so good as on previous mornings. I packed quickly and efficiently then sat out on the balcony. I still had over an hour before it was time for the shuttle. A small leaden sac of anxiety distended my stomach. I watched a wino in a doorway down in the street and felt a mixture of pity and envy. At least he didn't have to do what I was about to do. It wasn't as if I could just grin and bear it. Not for sixteen hours. Two calendar days. Bye-bye Wednesday. Possibly that was the hardest part.

No it wasn't. Who was I trying to kid? The fear of breaking up over the Pacific was the hardest part. My eye followed a fan of telegraph wires to the point where they were clutched together and attached to a pole, but this made me more anxious. Mere apprehension of the real connections in the physical world, normally something to cling on to, was now a source of distress. Sitting out on the balcony with a good view of the skies above New Orleans was not helping.

I went out, down to the end of the block where a coffee-house occupied the corner with Decatur. I'd been meaning to visit this place since my arrival. I went in and stood in line for a couple of minutes. Got myself a *caffè latte* in a tall glass and took it to a table by the window. There was some piped jazz playing, a trumpeter. It sounded pretty good. I went up and asked who it was. Dizzy

Reece, the guy with a tea towel stuck in his apron said, and the CD was called 'Asia Minor'. I'd have to buy that if I ever got to Australia in one piece. If I ever got back *home* again. Back to London and my flat at Great Arthur House. I'd sit out there on my eleventh-floor balcony listening to Dizzy Reece and thinking *Thank Christ, I made it*. And then, get this, I noticed the headline on the newspapers in the vending box outside the window of the coffee shop. I watched a guy put his quarter in the slot and remove a paper, then stand right there, side on to me, so I could read his paper. Like it was all carefully arranged: someone somewhere was having a bit of fun. The headline said '68 DIE IN PLANE CRASH'. I am not making this up. That is a direct quote. You can check, you go back through the newspapers and you'll see. I don't *need* to make this stuff up. It's happening. The crash occurred just outside Chicago, I think. There was talk of adverse weather conditions.

Max – and I don't know why this should be predictable, but it is – claims to enjoy turbulence. He enjoys flying in bad weather. He reads the papers like you or I, sees the reports on aircraft coming down in fog, rain, snow, ice and high winds, but still he gets a kick out of flying through that stuff. He likes it when the plane gets shoved about in the air – it's a big fairground ride to him. Likes the physicality of it. The risk element.

I didn't go and buy a copy of the paper, but I read as much as I needed to over this other guy's shoulder before he moved on. I don't remember reading if there were any survivors; that's the bit I always have to be clear on. I imagined there weren't. There usually aren't, after all. (There weren't. I checked.)

I could have done without this. I still had some time to kill before the airport shuttle came around, but this piece of news had done for the coffee-shop. I couldn't hang around there any longer knowing the full details of the crash were waiting in a vending box just outside. I wandered down Decatur as far as Jackson Square, watching people, wondering about Charlie. Alternately discarding and reconsidering his theories. As I had always believed, it would be nice to think there *was* something.

Afterwards. Some kind of survival. A belief in it was even more enticing now, because of my father. The stakes were higher.

I heard a familiar noise up above. A high-up, subsonic drone that wavered in and out of frequency. A portent. I would look up. I would have to look up. I knew what it was but I would have to look up.

I leaned back, shielded my eyes and looked up. Two hundred and fifty souls were being drawn across the arc of the sky. I wondered where it had taken off from. Where it was headed. Where the midpoint was. Where the kite-flyer stood with his – or her – reel of string. And suddenly I had a better understanding of Charlie's role in this whole story. Not only did he bring Joanna and me together – and it was his heart, of course, which had done that – but he was also, in a sense, acting as middle man in my journey to reach her.

Perhaps *that* was why I had to go via New Orleans. He was there at the centre, right at the heart of it. He *seemed* so trustworthy. It seemed safe to have him there playing that role. I hoped no one had secretly cast him as the double-crosser.

Twelve

The first leg of the flight was to Los Angeles. A short hop. Only four hours.

Only four hours wedged in between two of the biggest guys flying anywhere in America that night. I stayed right where I was for the whole flight. I listened to Laurie Anderson. You know things are bad when you take comfort in someone singing about your greatest fear.

I'm not going to go into detail about the rest of the journey. You know my position on flying by now.

At LAX they called the flight – UA841 – with about an hour still to go and as we funnelled down towards the departure gate we were all looking around, wondering who we'd be stuck next to. We were taking off around eleven p.m. on Tuesday and landing in Melbourne at eleven ten a.m. on Thursday. As for Wednesday, it just wasn't happening. As I think I have made clear, I couldn't quite get my head around this. You're crossing the International Date Line, my travel agent had said to me by way of a full explanation. As if that was all you needed to know. As if that could explain something so outrageous as the loss of a whole day. What would Joanna be doing during that day which for me would not exist? How *could* it not exist? What about my father? Would that day exist for him? For his body? What would Charlie be getting up to down there on earth while I was cradled up there in the sky?

The implications of this temporal theft were even more worrisome. What if I kept on going past Australia without stopping – supposing it were possible – how many more days would I lose? By how many days would I hasten my own death? And what if I went the other way around the world? Would I gain a day instead and then another and another and so become immortal? Suddenly the idea seemed to hold some promise.

Then I noticed the guy who was to be sitting next to me as we hurtled towards the other side of the earth. He looked agreeable enough, well dressed, thirties, not over-friendly. He reached across me to fiddle with the light switches, exposing me to his armpit. My heart, that vulnerable vessel, sank. This man's armpit, next to which I would be sitting for a whole day, more or less, on end, was as pungent as the Mississippi.

Little things.

The odour of the guy in the next seat; the impassioned, determined way in which passengers stuffed huge bags into overhead lockers despite clear warnings not to do so; the man in the denim shirt who passed my seat trailing a nicotine cloud all the way from the toilet, the stewardess in slightly ruffled pursuit. The rules were clear: smoking anywhere on the aircraft was an offence punishable by a fine of up to two thousand dollars.

Little things bothered me. Amplifying my unease.

They doused the cabin lights. I wondered whether to try to stay up and sleep later. What was the point? I drifted off surprisingly easily. I was asleep when we flew over the International Date Line, which must have made it easy for them to make off with my Wednesday.

There was breakfast. Maybe I slept again, I don't know. We'd been in the air now for so long it was almost normal. The same things turned over in my mind – Joanna, my father, Charlie – when suddenly I thought about my mother. Down there on earth alone for the first time in forty years. My father's illness had been so severe towards the end we'd kidded ourselves that for him to die would be a relief. Clearly a relief for him, and for my mother and sister and me as well. Of course it hadn't really felt like that. Intellectually we'd believed it was a good thing that his suffering was over, but grief is an unstoppable force and we are not immoveable objects.

I looked out of the porthole window and thanks to clear skies saw the Pacific many thousands of feet below. It looked like one of those cheap stereograms on sale at street markets and novelty shops now the world over. Only this time there was no hidden image to find.

Uselessly, hopelessly, my heart went out to my mother.

When we finally reached Melbourne, I was in a daze. Someone was playing time as if it were a concertina and I expected I would have to pay for it at some point. My missing day was still bothering me. I seemed to be in that bright state of artificial wakefulness that follows a sleepless night. You know that sooner or later it's going to catch up on you and so you proceed slowly with a mixture of surprised satisfaction and quiet dread.

I was conscious for a short time on the flight to Perth, as we overflew the bright sharp edge of the Nullarbor. Although at that point I'd never heard of Ken Ambrose, I realise now that if I had stared harder and concentrated, I might well have seen a tiny cloud of dust raised by the former teacher's camper van as it crawled across that vast empty plain.

For most of the 'time' I drifted in and out of a flux hammock of semi-awareness. I had a beer. I may have eaten a meal, but by this stage my head was stuffed with cotton wool. I tried to construct chronological scaffolds that would enable Joanna to leave wherever she was at the right time in order to meet me when we landed in Perth. But they all tumbled like insubstantial things, insectile limbs, whenever 'time' was inserted into the equations. I was rapidly losing faith in the idea of 'time'. Note the use of rapidly. It's unconscious. I didn't know if it was rapid or very gradual. I wondered if I was losing my mind, or just my sense of 'time'. I might have had another beer. If I opened my eyes during the last hour or two I could see that the sky was darkening – had darkened – had become quite dark – was totally dark – as we narrowed the gap between plane and ground, bumped home again and taxied around interminable airport buildings to reach the terminal itself.

I stepped into hanging curtains of warm, clinging moisture. I knew we weren't, but it felt as if we were in the tropics. My stomach was going around and around. Fears which I hadn't dared acknowledge – that Joanna would have had time to realise what a terrible mistake she had almost made, that she would choose some point in the next ten minutes or ten days to tell me that – stamped their feet on the bare boards of my mind's stage. I told them to shoo but seemed to have no control over my nerves. My stomach, as I said, was going around and around and around. I walked down that smooth, tiled corridor, wrapped in the damp heat of the Perth night, as if I were on deck and the seas below were pitching and roiling.

She wouldn't even be there. She would wisely have decided in favour of a no-show. Back in England she would resist my attempts to find her, thinking that sooner or later I would give up, and I would, but only because I sensed she wanted me to. In this way she would leave me, possibly believing it to be the least hurtful way to do it. I rounded the final corner, my little heart thump-thumping away at the bars of its cage, and my eyes fell upon the milling crowds in the arrivals hall. Luggage was already going around and around on the snaking carousel but there was no immediate sign of Joanna. I picked up my bag, which appeared without delay, and threaded a path in and out of the folk hanging around.

Just before going away, Joanna and I had spent an evening at the Dove in Hammersmith. We sat up on the upper terrace and looked out at the river. We talked on and on into the night, forever avoiding the subject we both knew we should be addressing. We had only just made the decision that I should also go to Australia. We'd had a couple of days to get used to the idea, but hadn't seen each other since. We'd not really talked about it.

'So, I'm going to Australia,' I said, looking out at the river and hoping for a reaction.

'Ye-e-es,' she said.

But by the end of the evening, as she sat slumped forward, her chin resting on her splayed hands on the edge of the wall, she said to me: 'This could be the making of us, this holiday. The making or the breaking.' I nodded, only realising after a few minutes' silence, watching the river swirl away under the bridge, that she was almost certainly right.

The making or the breaking of us.

I'd collected my own bag and all the rest of the luggage had been around the carousel a couple of times and she still hadn't shown up. My bag was pretty heavy but I could still sling it over my shoulder and have a wander. I made it to the main doors – still no sign. Then I went back to check around the carousel again because there were still people about.

And that's when I saw the woman who looked a bit like Joanna but clearly wasn't Joanna.

She was wearing dark blue shorts and a white linen top and was unfeasibly tanned. She wasn't Joanna, I was certain of that, but she sure looked like her. I watched her for a couple more moments until something clicked, until two plates shifted back on top of each other somewhere in the subtle and delicate machinery of my life, and I knew that of course it was her. After that clear shift, there followed a weird, drunken thirty seconds or so during which she became again the person I had met and known in London. It was a gradual process, like an image taking on definition in a developing tank. After a minute it was a case of, of course it was her, how could I have hesitated?

If, once I'd seen her but before the shift took place, I'd walked straight out the doors and not looked back, she would have been lost to me for ever. She would have been someone different. Not the girl I met and fell in love with but some new creature she'd become in the ten days or so that we'd been separated. Now though, those vast, thin plates having whispered into position and locked together with a soft, resounding click, she was mine again – and I was hers again – and even if I were to walk out at that point, it would be Joanna I was walking away from. Not some stranger. I could see, or sense, a long line stretching into the distance – a dusty road, light in colour, clouds of dust obscuring the end of it – and I determined that I shouldn't lose her. If we worked at this one, we could find it working for us.

I was still standing watching her thinking all this stuff when she saw me and gave a tiny jump. I saw air under her toes for an instant. Then she was running over towards me and I was dropping my bag on the floor and she was grinning, her thick hair seeming to pull her head to one side, and I was closing my arms around her, astonished at how real she felt. She squeezed me and I felt how she was very warm and slightly damp. Her hair smelt of oranges. I was the happiest man in that airport. Christ, I was probably the happiest man in the southern hemisphere at that point.

'Come on,' she said. 'I've got a car outside.'

I picked up my stuff and we walked out arm in arm. The night was so warm and still, it was as if it was the middle of the day and someone had switched the lights off.

'Are you sure you feel like it?' Joanna asked as I took the keys from her.

'This is exactly what I need,' I said, 'to come back down to earth.'

She was a perfectly good driver but she knew I loved driving and she liked to be driven.

The car seemed to move forward of its own accord into the soft night. Power steering and straight empty roads possibly accounted for this to some extent, but there was a feeling of having been set down in a toy car on a fixed track and all I had to do was keep my finger on the trigger. We rolled over inter-sections where the lights were always green, passed strings of telegraph poles and huge warehouses and retail outlets. Now and then a car would swish by on the opposite carriageway. Joanna gave me directions but they seemed only to confirm what I already knew.

We didn't enter the city of Perth but flowed like the Swan River itself down towards Fremantle, crossing it finally on a wide, flat bridge before pulling around to the right and negotiating a tight manoeuvre to enter the grounds of Sunny's, the hotel Joanna had picked for the two of us. She'd been staying with friends of distant relatives, or relatives of far-flung acquaintances, and could have invited me to do the same but we both understood the way forward was to be alone together. At least for a while.

We were installed within five minutes, sitting out on our balcony overlooking the Swan River. *It doesn't get much better than this*, I thought as I put my feet up on the rail and felt the warm night air caress my weary skin.

But it would. It would.

PULMONARY VALVE

A valve in the root of the pulmonary artery. Cesalpino in 1571 described valves as 'special membranes' which ensure the 'perpetual movement of the blood from the vena cava through the heart and lungs into the aorta'.

Ken Ambrose rolled the camper van on to the stony verge, shifted into neutral and pulled on the handbrake. He picked up the towel from the passenger seat and wiped his face. The aircon worked fine but he liked driving with the windows down. Hence the sweat and the fine coating of orange dust over the dashboard and seat covers.

In the back Yasmin stirred; a hand appeared, fingers raking through her short black hair, tugging at knots, a few blonde highlights that would still remind her of Bali. Ambrose turned his gaze away from the rearview mirror, wished for the hundredth time since leaving Melbourne that he'd scored some dope before setting off, and unscrewed the cap from a Tooheys Red.

'Go back to sleep, darling,' he said, half turning around, before putting his weight against the driver's door and stepping out of the van. He reached back in for his white sun hat, his notebook and camera, took a swig of Tooheys and set off back down the highway. He passed the tyre treads that snaked across the road, disappearing as they hit the run-off verge, and he continued until he reached the wallaby. It had been hit by something big. A road train. And flung to the side of the road. Ambrose knocked his hat back and swiped his forearm across his brow. It was another hot one. The wallaby was humming. Scores of big black blowflies rose lazily from the corpse.

The tyre scorchmarks were nothing to do with the wallaby – they were a lot older. He'd only glanced at them as he passed but they looked to be six months old at least. The wallaby had been hopping around as recently as two or three days ago. Most likely it had hopped into the road at dusk. In these circumstances, tourists would have a go at braking or swerving. Australians, road train drivers all the more, would just keep going, not even take their foot off the gas. Some would floor the pedal because it gave them a bigger kick. Them *and* the animals.

Ambrose pointed his camera at the carcass and clicked off a couple of shots. He took the thermometer out of his jeans pocket and bent down with his back to Yasmin. Then, rising to his feet, he made a note in his spiral-bound book. Instead of going straight back to the van he stopped off to look at the scorchmarks.

He crouched down over the tyre tracks, dabbing at them with his finger, then slipped the little steel ruler out of the top pocket of his T-shirt and took some measurements. Scribbled in his book. He thought about Yasmin back in the van. How much did she *really* know about what he was up to? There was no good reason to conceal it from her. He was just a little embarrassed.

They'd have to find somewhere to stop. He knew she wouldn't want to spend another night in the van. In his experience, women liked to spread out a bit more.

He returned to the van, leaned in at the driver's door and took his hat off. 'What do you know?' he said, wiping his forearm across his brow. The heat was pounding against the roof of the van. Yasmin nodded, taking a hit off a Marlboro she'd lit in his absence.

'Let's go, huh?' she said.

He tossed his hat on to the passenger seat, climbed in.

He was aware of her watching him from the back for a while as he drove. His thinning silver hair drawn back into a ponytail, fastened with a fluorescent pink sweatband. He'd let her drive for a couple of hundred Ks across the Nullarbor Plain; when they were driving into the sun, the wheel got so hot it was just about melting. His right elbow stuck out of the window. He'd had plenty of exposure over the years.

The first time he'd seen her, as he pulled up outside the Mundrabilla Motel after twelve hours' solid driving, he'd assumed she was unobtainable. Out of his league. But it turned out he made a welcome change from the local creep, who had been pestering her non-stop. Ambrose didn't mind particularly if he represented merely a convenient escape route for her. That first night they stayed up drinking beer. He told stories that, when he got halfway through, he realised dated him.

'Up all night we were. Paris. Sixty-seven, sixty-eight, I don't know. Jesus, I can remember it now. We found this little jazz club on the Left Bank, this black guy was playing saxophone, we were smoking joints and drinking red wine. We didn't leave till three in the morning. Then went to this discotheque. We were stoned, man. I mean . . . I ended up walking home.'

He couldn't believe he'd used the word 'discotheque'. She wouldn't have been to a discotheque in her life. She'd have been to clubs, plenty of clubs no doubt, but no discotheques.

Why did she stick around? Was it just for a ride? At odd moments he wondered if it could be some quality in him – his innocence, his naivete. Qualities in short supply in Seattle, where she told him she'd started out. Even shorter supply in the dives she'd passed through to reach this wilderness. Istanbul, Madras, Rangoon, Bangkok, Hong Kong, Bali, Sydney, even Melbourne. The jobs she'd done, the things she'd vowed she'd never do, for money or for love. Waitressing in Istanbul, hostessing in Bangkok, worse, much worse in Melbourne, she told him. All just so that she could travel, get around the world (she'd left the Pacific North-West without a cent).

She dropped her cigarette butt out of the window, then caught his eye in the rearview. He hated her doing that. She gestured with her hand, sat back, lay down across the seat, sat up again, tugged at the sleeve of her T-shirt. Fidget, fidget, fidget. She didn't seem to like the desert all that much. What was she doing here anyway? He couldn't actually imagine her wanting to stick around when they reached Perth, with all those other rides to choose from.

There was a roadsign. Norseman 404 km.

At Norseman you went either left or right, south or north, and it was two hundred Ks in each direction to anything approaching civilisation. Ambrose caught himself wondering which way Yasmin might prefer to go. North would take them to Perth in less time – no doubt what Yasmin would want. Although the sex wasn't that unbearable, was it? On the second night they'd wound up in the sack together, and it had become something of a routine since then, an entirely welcome and pleasurable one for Ambrose. He wondered if she worried that he was beginning to like her, over and above the time they spent in bed together.

Maybe he was too prone to thinking. His ex-wife had certainly thought so.

For himself, he preferred to go south to Albany, Margaret River, the vineyards. He liked a glass of wine. Also, it would take a couple of days longer that way to reach Perth, so he could make the most of Yasmin's company.

Ambrose had taught English in Melbourne, sacked when the state of Victoria offloaded twenty-five per cent of its teachers. He'd already lost the wife to a zoologist from Cairns, sort of guy liked to let spiders run all over his hands. Hardly human, in Ambrose's book, but then maybe his view was coloured. Before going into teaching he'd been around the world with the merchant navy. He couldn't go back to that but didn't want to stay in Melbourne with nothing to do, so he took a commission from the national government to do the round-trip of Australia carrying out a one-man survey of roadkill. What got knocked over, where and when. Which species were most prevalent on which roads. He presumed the point lay, at some future time, in preventing so many unnecessary animal deaths.

The methods were scientific. Photographs. Temperature readings – he stuck his thermometer up the animal's rectum. If it still had one. He estimated the age. Determined the sex. All manner of details went in his little book. There was a clipboard in the van but he'd not been keeping it up to date.

The truth was he was becoming increasingly distracted by tyre treads. The tyre treads burnt on to the highway by drivers going into skids, spins, collisions – with animals, other cars, road trains or, unlikely but it was that kind of country, people.

'They're these drivers' last signatures on the world's page,' he explained to Yasmin.

'Ghosts,' he called them. 'Ghosts.'

Yasmin looked out of the back window. The van trailed a cloud of dust.

'Ghosts in the dust.'

Whenever Ambrose and Yasmin stopped at a roadhouse they now had to stay inside to have their pie and cold drinks despite the clamour from kids' parties and the palpable air of madness surrounding the lone Japanese cyclist who always seemed to be sitting at a table by the door. It was much cooler inside than out.

Having lived in Melbourne most of his life, Ambrose wasn't exactly unaccustomed to the heat. But this was exceptionally hot. So hot the steering wheel could not be gripped with more than a hard, calloused thumb and forefinger. Yasmin fanned herself constantly in the back. But despite the discomfort, Ambrose liked it. He enjoyed the illusion of carefree abandon. The irrelevance of passing time. It made him feel better about mortality, even though he was confronting it daily. It made him feel randy and it seemed not to have the opposite effect on Yasmin.

The only problem was the Projectionist.

It was not easy to discern the Projectionist's motives. Was he jealous? Or sadistic? Or, like traffic wardens, orthodontists and state executioners, was he merely doing his job?

Ambrose pulled the van off the road into the dusty forecourt of the Casson Motel. The uneven motion woke Yasmin. Ambrose glanced in the rearview. Her T-shirt was skewed about her neck from an awkward sleeping position, such that he could see the upper slope of her breast. He stopped the van and while she was looking out of the window at the motel he enjoyed the view in his mirror. She yawned, ruffled her hair and looked up, suddenly aware of his scrutiny. But she waited a moment before rearranging her top.

Ambrose smiled in the mirror, desire uncoiling in his shorts. He wouldn't be able to get out of the van for a couple of minutes. Not and retain his dignity. He allowed himself a moment's recollection of the night before. Yasmin's small nipples hard as cherry stones. The sweat that coated their limbs as they intertwined. The rich, dark pleasure of finally entering her, hearing her gasp, feeling her nails digging into his shoulders. You couldn't beat that stuff.

This wasn't going to help prepare him for the walk across to the accommodation office.

Funny how the Projectionist only popped up when you didn't want him to. He'd've been ideal right now. But no show.

Ambrose had previously been able to tame his erections. He had acquired the need when attending Mrs Valentine's massage service in East Kew, as he had done regularly for an eighteen-month stretch, ever since the wife went off with the spider-fancier. And his father totalled his Kingswood in an unexplained accident outside of Broome. Mrs Valentine's eager yet professional manipulation of his deltoids and rhomboids had had an unfortunate result, which was easy to conceal as long as he lay face down, but when the time came to turn over he knew he had to act. Trial and error revealed Bob Hawke's as the only face he could bring quickly to mind that would immediately break the spell. He would have preferred it to have been Joh Bjelke-Petersen or someone of that ilk, not a Labour man. But Bob Hawke it was. And he could hardly be called a Labour man anyway. A Labour man okay, perhaps, but not a socialist.

Bob did the trick. Ambrose swung his Blunnies to the gritty ground and strode across to the office. He emerged two minutes later with a key.

Yasmin collapsed on to the bed while Ambrose dumped the bags and went into the bathroom to run the cold tap. He loosed his ponytail and put his head underneath the tap, rubbing his scalp as the water trickled down his neck and chest. He wouldn't have expected it to be so hot this far south and this early in the year. It was still only late spring. Standing up straight, he ran his hands through his hair, water running down his back. He tugged his T-shirt over his head and dipped his right hand inside his shorts. On the move again.

A quick flick of the shower curtain: all clean, all clear.

He moved back into the main room. Yasmin hadn't stirred. He leaned over and pulled up the bed clothes around her – looking, checking.

'Ambrose,' she complained. 'Do you have to? I mean, every time?'

'You know I do, darling. The time I don't check, there'll be one there. It'll wait till you get in and really stretch out and then bite your leg. You wouldn't believe the ulceration and the scarring. It's not a pleasant sight. Ideally you want to live your entire life without ever coming face to face with a white-tailed spider.'

Reluctantly she stood up, allowing him to pull back the sheets for his peace of mind. Every town, every motel, every bed they slept in had to be checked. Ambrose sensed she almost hoped they'd find one. Just once. Although she was no great lover of spiders herself.

The bed cleared for take-off, she flopped down on it once more, her tanned arms flung back over her head, burnt sienna against ivory sheets. Ambrose pushed his shorts down over his slender hips and stepped out of them as they hit the floor. He approached the bed, pulled down her cut-offs and dropped to his knees, burying his still damp face between her still, damp legs. She giggled and moaned. The tiny hairs at the tops of her legs were crackly with salt. He ran his hands up her body and rolled her T-shirt over her head. His hands catching her breasts, fingers lightly squeezing her nipples.

He caught the briefest of glimpses of the Projectionist setting up. Plugging in his machine. Loading his magazine, checking its orientation.

But Ambrose banished the thought and reached for a condom. Yasmin grinned and writhed on the bed, arching her back, making a noise somewhere between a beached seal and a police siren. And then he was there. Slowly at first, dead slow – she liked that, he knew. Then speeding up gradually to gain a rhythm until he was punching smoothly in and out of her like a sewing machine. Her noises increased in volume until she was producing a throaty ululation. He sensed that unmistakeable stirring common to all men, that loosening, as he liked to think of it, of the bow ropes on the big white submarine. He knew that in seconds he'd be unable to prevent his climax when, predictably had he but thought of the little bastard, the Projectionist stepped in, silently sliding his first image on to the white wall of Ambrose's mind.

The black house spider wasn't one of Australia's biggest, and Ambrose had never actually seen one, despite their common-ness in and around the house, especially in the corners of windows – but it was an ugly fucker. With its thick black legs, spiny-looking hairs and bulbous abdomen. And it did the job. It did the job, all right. His erection dwindled and he slowed accordingly. Yasmin had opened her eyes.

'The Projectionist?' she asked.

Ambrose nodded, wiping sweat from his forehead, blowing air through the gaps in his clenched teeth.

The fucking Projectionist.

Again.

Bastard.

Ambrose rolled off Yasmin and lay on his back, his heart gradually slowing. The image of the black house spider flashed intermittently on to the screen, the Projectionist flicking the power on and off. It was like a series of retinal memories or after-shocks. The image was just as horrible but now that its work had been done it had less power over Ambrose. Gradually it faded.

Yasmin was climbing off the bed. As she disappeared into the bathroom there was an involuntary dip of the left shoulder that signalled her resignation. Ambrose let his head fall back on to the pillow. What was he going to do?

Apart from track down the Projectionist and eliminate him, what could he do?

Perhaps just that then.

LEFT ATRIUM

*Atrium sinistrum, left atrium: the atrium
of the left side of the heart; it receives blood from the pulmonary
veins, and delivers it to the left ventricle.*

Thirteen

The Great Northern Highway, as it leaves Perth, snakes out of town through a thin sprawl of suburbs and light industry and you're pretty much in the country by the time you head left on to the Brand Highway. If that's your route – and it was ours, in order to travel north along the coast. Until you get a lot further north, the road is too far from the coast to see the ocean and sooner or later you get so as you need to see it. You can see too much of the bush and parched scrub and need a break.

It's for this reason that a town such as Lancelin is allowed to continue to exist.

I say town, it's more of a settlement. In fact, less of a settlement, more of a compromise, and not a particularly happy one at that.

It's a disaster.

Lancelin, self-proclaimed wind-surfing capital of the world, is a one-horse town whose lame ass you want to shoot to put out of its misery. It's a small, disappointing town. And the night we visited, it was closed.

It was late when we arrived in our hired Ford Laser among the straggling lanes and tumbledown buildings that constituted Lancelin. We needed a place to stay. Just a mean motel. We knew there were places – Joanna had a book with an authoritative ring to it which said as much. We cruised past a general store that didn't look as if it had ever been open. At the end of that street we took a right, signposted for the beach.

'Maybe the main part of the town is down here,' Joanna suggested. Although neither of us voiced it, we both suspected we'd seen all there was to see of Lancelin. It was a warm night and if it came to it we could probably sleep on the beach or in the car, but it wasn't ideal. Joanna was exhausted after the drive from Fremantle, where we'd spent a few days taking it easy. The most energetic activity we'd undertaken, outside of our hotel room at Sunny's, was take a long walk along Cottesloe Beach one evening. With the sun setting slowly, other folk out for strolls, the odd fisherman standing knee-deep in the soft surf trying his luck beyond the gentle breakers, conditions were perfect and it was hard to think that anything could go wrong. Even if I thought of my father, I found myself becoming stoical. As I was embarking on a new life myself, his loss seemed to hurt me less. Could I really be getting over it already? I doubted it, but the relief was welcome for the time being.

Mornings we enjoyed slow breakfasts of freshly squeezed orange juice and granary toast at the Old Mill. We'd wander around town, pick up secondhand books and head back to Sunny's where Joanna would have a dip and I would crash out, still getting over jetlag. My sleeping patterns were erratic. I was waking up in the early hours of the morning, but only every other night, then feeling completely wiped out at some point the following afternoon. My body didn't have a clue what was going on.

That aside, we had such a restful, luxurious time in Fremantle we never actually made it into Perth. Even when it came to be time to head north we found we could bypass the city. It had looked fairly cool from the main road by the Swan River that first night as we drove from the airport – all gleaming steel, electric blue neon and row upon row of palm trees – but we didn't feel any compelling need to investigate further.

We could have taken pretty much the same view on Lancelin were it not for the fact that we needed a bed for the night and WA isn't the kind of place where you can just drive to the next town if the motel happens to be full (or doesn't exist). The next town could be two hundred kilometres away.

At the beach there was a clapboard hut, locked up and pasted over with windsurfing flyers. 'It mustn't be the season yet,' Joanna suggested. I turned the Laser around and we trundled back in search of a town. After a couple of minutes we spotted a turning we'd missed going the other way. It was little more than a break in the trees. I turned the car into the narrow track and soon the headlamps revealed a rambling one-storey affair about fifty yards down. One or two lights were burning. An old VW camper van was the only other vehicle in sight, painted orange and white with Victoria plates and covered with a fine film of orange dust.

'God, it's like the Bates Motel,' Joanna whispered.

'It's not great, certainly,' I agreed. 'But it's got to be better than sleeping in the car. I'll go and see if we can get a room.'

Joanna nodded. I leant across and we kissed.

'Have you seen *The Vanishing*?' I said.

'The original, with Bernard-Pierre Donnadieu and Johanna ter Steege, or the terrible Hollywood remake with Kiefer Sutherland?'

Was I impressed? I mean, I'd have given her points just for knowing there were two versions, but naming the actors – in the *original*—

She smiled and I climbed out of the car and walked across to the office. It was a warm night. Just walking twenty yards in my Billabong shorts, blue Bravado T-shirt and Blundstone boots, I was sweating. Joanna had bought me the shorts and the Blunnies in a surfies' shop in Fremantle and we'd each got ourselves a Bravado top from a boutique on Market Street.

The swing door banged shut behind me and I leaned on the counter. If there'd been a bell on the desk I'd've rung it. As it was, I only had to wait thirty seconds. When the door the other side of the counter creaked open and a tall thin fellow with a wispy goatee slipped through I caught a glimpse of the room beyond. Well, not so much of the room as of one of the walls, which seemed to be occupied by a large print of an enormous and extremely unpleasant-looking spider. I didn't know what type it was but I did only get a quick look. And the man was looking at me, expecting me to say something. His beard was a creeper that had started at the bottom of his chin and was struggling to colonise the sunken pits of his cheeks with soft spindly fibres like the legs of harvestman spiders. Max was quite clear on beards – and goatees in particular. It wasn't as simple as them being utterly pointless and meaningless and unnecessary – which I didn't have a problem with myself – he took it further than that. Beards were actually a setback to civilisation.

'Singapore,' I remember him bellowing one night when we were having a drink at the Waterside in King's Cross. 'They've got the right idea. Everyone misses out Singapore when they "do" South East Asia, but they shouldn't. It's the only place round there with a decent line on beards. Albania's another, although standards have slipped now. You let in capitalism, soon as you know it you've got arseholes with goatees driving round Tirana in fucking Mercs.'

'What about Danny?' I checked him. We were due to meet Danny at the pub that night, but he'd not turned up.

'What about him?' he asked, sinking the rest of his pint.

'He's got a goatee.'

'Ah yes, but he's always had it. He didn't grow it when it became trendy to grow one. Christ, even I grew one once about six years ago, when no one else on the planet had one. And you could see why. It was fucking hideous. It gave me stomach cramps just to look at myself in the mirror. That's why I'm able to take this line on beards, because I've tried it. And it doesn't work. I mean, look: it's a different type of hair to the hair on your head. There's a line, you can see the join where it goes into your sideboards – we're not meant to wear beards any more than we're meant to walk around without pants on. Buy a fucking razor. Jesus.'

Back in Lancelin, a place which makes King's Cross look like pages out of a travel brochure, I said to the guy with the encroaching Russian vine on his chin, who I doubted had grown his beard because it was fashionable: 'We need a double room, please. Ensuite.'

'Fifty bucks,' he said, handing me a key. 'Down at the end.'

'Thanks.'

He waited till I was gone before opening the door to the back room.

We moved our stuff into number seven and locked the door behind us. Joanna collapsed on to the bed while I went around turning the taps and the lights on and off. Opening the French windows beyond the double bed and leaving them open, though making sure the thin drape was pulled right across. The chirruping of a thousand insects floated into the room on the warmest, softest air. I remembered we had a cool box in the boot of the car and went outside to get a couple of stubbies of Tooheys Red and some meagre supplies.

'Midnight feast,' I said as I lay down on my front beside Joanna. She rolled over and I kissed her, then she grabbed me, playfully but firmly. And we didn't eat for a while.

The next couple of days exist in my memory as a sun-soaked kaleidoscope of images. In a film they would be represented by a montage sequence with unbearably slushy music.

Joanna and I heading into the dunes from the motel; cresting a rise and seeing the sweeping curve of the beach, white sand, empty as far as you could see; kicking through the surf; heading back into the dunes around the far side of the bay; dithering for a while over whether it was safe to make love, then collapsing in fits of giggles at the sound of a tour bus revving madly just beyond the dunes; the oscillating drone of a spotter plane; skinny-dipping and offshore drilling; heading back along the shoreline to whatever new motel we'd found, trailed by a lone dolphin which broke the surface again and again whenever we thought it had tired of us and swum back out to sea.

In the Nambung National Park we saw our first kangaroos, two of them, western greys, standing still in the scrub only a few feet from the car. We stared at them and they stared back, like a couple of bartenders taking it easy. An idyllic stretch of beach at Hangover Bay, miles of glittering quartz sand, the soft, lulling whisper of surf – turquoise expanse.

We stayed at the Cervantes Pinnacles Motel, which was everything its equivalent in Lancelin wasn't, but never made it to the Pinnacles themselves. Maybe if we had, things would have turned out differently. Certainly they would have done. We intended to head out there – Joanna particularly wanted to – but we put it off and put it off and by the last morning neither of us felt like making the trip, a twenty-kilometre slog across an unmade-up dusty road.

'We're due in Geraldton,' Joanna reminded me as we sat in the car at the intersection outside Cervantes on that last morning. Right for the Pinnacles Desert or straight on to the Brand Highway. She was right. We had an appointment in Geraldton with friends of Joanna's and would stay there a few days. 'We can go to the Pinnacles on the way back down.'

We should have visited the Pinnacles right there and then, but we didn't know that.

We headed east along the Cervantes Road, back to the highway. Every couple of kilometres, it seemed to me, we'd pass an empty bottle, stubbies thrown out of car windows, mostly brown glass, Tooheys Red or Tooheys Blue. As we headed further north we noticed more roadkill: wallabies, lizards. No 'roos. The heat was phenomenal. Our only air conditioning was to open the windows all the way and for me to put my foot down. On the back roads this kicked up an enormous cloud of red dust and proved fairly uncomfortable as the much abused Laser's suspension attempted and largely failed to deal with the poor surface.

On the Brand Highway, Joanna dozed off while I maintained a steady hundred and ten kmph. The speed limit was just about ideal for cruising. I kept noticing bottles by the side of the road, lying on the gravel verge, and constructed an image of the guy employed to drive around Australia with a truck full of stubbies. He'd tootle along at seventy-five, left hand on the wheel, right hand holding his stubby, his elbow catching the sun. Every couple of Ks he'd take a swig, then when the bottle was empty he'd stick his right arm out the driver's window and sling the bottle over the roof of his cab to land by the side of the road. The scrubby, sandy gravel would cushion the fall so the glass didn't break. He'd check in his rearview mirror that he'd not missed, then crack open the next one—

Whoooah!

Daydreaming, I didn't see the wallaby until the last moment. The very last moment. It was dead already, but hitting it would have messed up the front of the Ford and could have put us into a spin. I braked abruptly and brought my left hand down hard at the same time.

Not the best idea I'd ever had.

The back end swung around dramatically and would have smacked into the oncoming stream of traffic, had there been any. Joanna sprang awake. We arced balletically through a hundred and eighty degrees and juddered to a halt, missing the dead beast by inches.

I put my hand on Joanna's leg.

'I'm sorry.'

I breathed out, loosened up my shoulders, wiped sweat from my face.

'It's okay.'

The car was tucked neatly on to the run-off verge, albeit facing in the wrong direction, so by unspoken agreement we opened our respective doors and climbed out. Legs a little shaky. Joanna came around to my side of the Laser and we took a few steps away from the road before sitting down, resting our backs against a dead eucalyptus.

Joanna was looking at the wallaby we'd just managed to miss.

'Could have been nasty,' I said.

'Yes,' she said, 'I'm tired, Chris,' and laid her head in my lap.

Within minutes her breathing had slowed and I knew she was asleep. Although I wasn't actually aware of dropping off myself, I realised I had when I woke up.

The thing about snakes – in Australia at least – is that they're silent.

When I came to, my mouth dry and my head throbbing from the sun, I found that I was looking directly at a Western Brown snake.

Having double-checked that I was not dreaming, that I was definitely awake, I stared quite hard at the snake, trying to figure out its programme. Was it on its way towards us or sitting there oblivious? Clearing off altogether? It had assumed the position – figure 8 – on the dusty earth about a foot from Joanna's bare leg.

In the car we had a book, *Venomous Creatures of Australia – A Field Guide*, an indispensable volume if you wanted to build up any level of creepy-crawly paranoia. Australia's full of them. Spiders as big as your hand; spiders that live in trees (which has *got* to be considered cheating); and spiders that get right in bed and wait for you. And there were snakes, pages and pages of them.

This one by Joanna's leg, I thought I recognised from the book.

A Western Brown.

Coiled into two equal circles of double thickness.

I doubt that they actually were, but its eyes seemed to be looking at me, so that my own gaze locked into the snake's.

It was like one of those shots they've perfected in a certain type of film: the dolly brings the object of view into full screen and the focus-puller has a job to keep up, but keep up he must. Only the snake existed. The snake and me. Object and subject. Subject and object. The bush vanished, melted away into its own heat haze.

They say a cobra can mesmerise you with its stare. It was the Western Brown's figure 8 that transfixed me.

The link was Danny.

Danny had always been a car obsessive. He got through motors like someone with flu might work their way through a box of tissues. Even I knew that much about him. German cars specifically. When he'd first met Z he'd been driving that lemon-yellow BMW 2002ti, and he'd followed that up with a VW Karmann Ghia in pale metallic blue. Then he'd progressed to a red Merc, a sports machine, two doors, but he'd always had half an eye out for another particular model. A particular model with vertically stacked headlamps, I remember Max telling me in a seedy boxing pub down the Old Kent Road where Danny had been supposed to meet us for a drink.

Danny, of course, never turned up, so Max attempted to fill in for him, assuming his mantle of car obsessive.

'They're like figure 8s,' he'd said, a dull light flickering in his eye, the muffled sound of punches thrown to accompany our conversation. 'One on top of the other, two either side of the grille, like 8s. You know, like figure-of-eight knots or the shape your mother stirs in her Bechamel sauce.'

'I know what a figure 8 looks like,' I told him, lifting a half-pint glass of some disgusting house bitter to my lips. 'Isn't there another car with similar headlamps he could get instead?'

'There's the Pontiac Parisienne but there the twin headlamps on each side are mounted *latitudinally*. Like infinity symbols. That's no good. He likes the figure 8s. It's got to be the 280SE.'

'He's completely mad, is he?'

I'd only intended it half-seriously, but Max went very still and quiet. At length he turned to me and leant in so he could speak softly: 'Never,' he said, 'never say that about Danny.' I raised my eyebrows, shrugged, looked down at my drink. 'Especially to his face. Okay?'

I didn't like being talked to like this by Max of all people. I toyed with the idea of acquiescing, but I only toyed with it.

'Truth hurts, eh?' I jabbed. 'Maybe that night in the old hospital turned his mind?'

I picked up my glass half expecting Max to sweep it out of

my grasp with an upper cut. But I was able to get its rim to my lips and take a sip. Max had gone very, very quiet and intense, his shoulders hooked over his rib cage like some kind of vulture. If anything this was more disturbing than the thought of him losing it altogether.

From the far side of the high-ceilinged room came the hard impacted slap of leather on flesh and the mingling smells of stale beer, sweat and linament. We'd come here because Danny had developed an interest in physical combat sports, according to Max. He'd bought himself a pair of secondhand gloves and was even considering getting in the ring.

'Who told you about that night?' Max asked in measured, low tones.

'You did, Max. You did.'

He was silent for a moment, his guard up. Then he knocked his head back and swallowed a mouthful of lager. 'Then perhaps,' he said, 'you don't know as much about that night as you think you do.'

I stared at him, but he wouldn't be drawn further on the subject. We gave Danny another ten minutes then headed out. My car was parked around the corner. I was giving Max a lift home. Throughout the half-hour journey he sat shaking his head, clucking his tongue and giving occasional low whistles at girls on the street.

In a different car on a different road with a different passenger – all of them an improvement on transporting Max in my too-cosy Stag through Stamford Hill, dodging impossibly long and badly battered Volvo estates – I reached for the sunblock: my arms and legs were taking a direct hit through the open windows and sunroof of the Laser. I was wearing a black baseball cap of Joanna's, a small, trim design, the only one I'd ever tried on that wasn't so built up at the front it looked like a busby. Of course she'd have got it in South Africa or Israel or some other distant place I had no desire ever to visit, so I'd never be able to get one the same.

'No,' she'd said. 'I got it in Gap.'

But that was just as bad because I'd tried all of Gap's baseball caps and they were all ill-fitting monsters as well.

'You got an old line,' I'd said. 'They've withdrawn these ones because they're too good.'

'You can have that one. I never wear it. You look good in it.'

My hair was long enough now to pull it out through the hole at the back and not look too ridiculous.

'Your hair looks good,' she said. 'You should keep letting it grow.'

The Western Brown snake had eventually untied its own knots and moved on, breaking the spell it had cast over me, but I found the image of the figure 8 stayed with me while I drove.

Fourteen

From Cervantes to Geraldton was about the same distance again as from Perth to Cervantes, yet we did it in a day. Not a great distance – little more than two hundred Ks – but the combination of heat, dust, long straight roads, mirages, whirling willies and road trains can get to you in a relatively short time. It didn't get to me. I felt myself relaxing – my body, my mind, even my emotions. The driving itself, overtaking road trains, watching the mirages play over the dusty surface, skirting roadkill and stopping at roadhouses for hot meat pies, cold beer and ice lollies – this was a million miles from home.

But it was a little too much for Joanna. I think if I'd been the passenger I'd have felt the same.

We reached Geraldton around five p.m. Joanna's friends, Eddie and Nick, lived just south of the town, which was small by my standards but a major centre in WA.

I was a little nervous about meeting them. They'd known Joanna for about twenty years.

'Turn in here,' she said, gesturing wildly. Joanna avoided using left and right because she tended to get them confused, with potentially disastrous results. ('It's a good job you're not a surgeon,' I'd said to her as I three-point-turned out of the first of several cul-de-sacs to which we had paid brief, unexpected visits. 'Surgeons are all bastards,' she'd retorted. 'They're all so full of themselves. They think they're it.')

'What, on to the lawn?' I asked.

There were already three vehicles lined up on the grass. What damage could one more do?

'The four-wheel drive and the silver car are theirs,' Joanna said. 'I don't know about the other one. Babysitter? Nanny? Dunno. Don't worry. It'll be fine.' She squeezed my knee as I pulled on the handbrake.

The door was opened by a little boy who then stood on one leg and regarded us timidly, catching his left foot with his hand.

'Hello Sammy,' Joanna said, reaching down to pick him up, but he stepped backwards into his approaching mother. Eddie was a tall red-haired woman with an easy, friendly smile. A dog appeared, a black labrador, which bounded up to us, singling me out as being unreasonably frightened of dogs. Then there was another little boy, Sammy's older brother by a couple of years, and behind him, shirt flapping open, was Nick. He threw his arms wide and shouted his welcome in a deafening basso profundo which set the dog off barking, so Nick scolded the dog and, unseen, something fell to the floor and shattered and a little girl started crying.

For the briefest of instants, a mere half-blink in eternity, I regretted ever meeting Joanna. A quick montage flashed across my mind-screen: me dropping the bag I was carrying and running to the car, shredding the lawn in my haste to reverse back on to the road, wheel-spinning and laying down some rubber to regain the highway and the long, straight, peaceful, hot road to nowhere.

As I said, the briefest of instants; before manners took over from panic. Introductions were made. I shook Nick's hand as hard as I could. He was laughing about something, grinning all over his wide face, then suddenly he was throwing me a beer. Joanna picked up Sammy, who seemed to have recognised her by now (she'd last seen the family two years previously when they'd made a joint trip across Australia), and ruffling the other boy, David's, hair. We went inside. In the kitchen were Helena, who looked about three and was managing both to hold a fluffy toy possum and to pull her skirt up over her head, and Georgie, who was having a fine time picking bits of orange off the tray of her high chair and flinging them randomly about the kitchen.

The dog started barking again and Nick bellowed at it to keep quiet. Joanna and Eddie were roaring laughing at some old shared joke.

'I'll get the stuff out of the car,' I said, backing out of the house.

I sprang open the boot of the car and hid behind it for a minute. I wondered about jumping in and pulling the lid shut. A big, noisy, chaotic household just wasn't, had never, been on my wanted list. For whatever reason I found it difficult to cope with. They were decent people. Eddie was nice – straightforward and friendly – but Nick was actually so loud I couldn't tell if he was nice or not. Joanna had tried to warn me, saying he was 'larger than life'.

I told myself to get a grip. We were only staying a few days; they were Joanna's friends and if I wanted to stay with Joanna I had better get on and like her friends. I could always play with the kids if it got too much.

I carried the bags into the house. The dog barked at me. Nick came to quieten it down, grinned at me and in answer to my mimed question concerning the bags pointed to a flight of stairs leading to the basement. Down there I found a kids' play area and a guest room with its own little ensuite shower room and toilet. I dumped the stuff and locked myself in the loo for a few minutes until I heard Joanna come looking for me.

'Come on, hurry up,' she shouted through the door. 'It's not long till we go out.'

We were going out for dinner. Eddie and Nick were celebrating their wedding anniversary and it had all been planned so that we could attend.

I joined everyone out on the sundeck. Nick offered me another beer. Getting drunk wasn't a bad option.

'You're going to really enjoy yourselves here,' Nick grinned, looking first at us, then out at the view, which I had to admit was pretty impressive. The bungalow was built on a hill which sloped down to the main road, then across to the beach about a kilometre away. Beyond that, of course, was the ocean. The sunset would be quite something.

'Come on, Nick.' Eddie arrived on the sundeck, Helena clinging to her legs. 'It's time to go. You've got to get ready.'

'Okay.' And he jumped up, shirt tails flapping as he disappeared back into the house. Joanna took hold of my hand under the table.

Within ten minutes everyone was climbing into the Land Cruiser – except the kids, for whom a babysitter had arrived.

There was something about Nick I found daunting. He was so many things I wasn't. Big, rambunctious, outrageously extrovert. I'm not saying I can only get on with my spirit double but it's possible that out there somewhere is the man who is the exact opposite of you. And it's perhaps not a good idea ever to meet up.

I hauled myself up into the passenger seat, so I was alongside Nick, who drove without seatbelt and with one leg slewed across the gearbox housing. Grinning, he kept twisting his head round to share in some remark made by Eddie or Joanna. The result was that the focus somehow turned on me without me really contributing anything, so I just smiled and nodded along to whatever was being said and watched Geraldton float by. It was a small town of lawns, bungalows and roundabouts. As we entered the centre, with its three or four streets of shops, I saw one or two brown faces and commented on this.

'Ten per cent,' Nick said, shouting over the noise of the engine. 'There was a rape last week. Eight-year-old girl. And a revenge attack on the fellow who did it. In prison.' He sucked on his teeth and shook his head as he turned the Cruiser in a graceful arc around another roundabout. 'You know, there's a lot of whistle cocks among the fellows in prison.' Nick and Eddie were lawyers and often handled cases involving Aboriginals.

'Whistle cock?'

'It's a tribal thing.'

'There are tribal Aboriginals here?'

Nick didn't answer for a while. Just grinned and sat with his arms straddling the wheel like a bus driver. I would discover he did this occasionally; held up the conversation for whatever reason. Back then, I thought it was for effect, to make sure everyone was listening. I was wrong. It was just his manner.

'Of course there are tribal people. Lots and lots of them. Had a case a couple of weeks ago. Little boy was wasting away, only he didn't have any disease known to the doctors. Poor kid died and there was nothing wrong with him. Turned out he'd walked in front of a lawman who was pointing the bone at another man. The other man was okay but the boy died.'

I heard Joanna exclaiming something in the back and Eddie confirming what Nick had said.

'Here we are,' Nick said, turning the Cruiser in a wide circle to park on the other side of the road. I climbed down and waited for Joanna then we followed Nick and Eddie over to the restaurant.

It looked as if most of the other guests were already there, sitting around a long table in the centre of the restaurant. Bottles of champagne lolled in ice buckets. Huge platters of oysters and crayfish sat waiting in the middle of the table. Nick was exuberant and ebullient, greeting everyone, leaning across to kiss smart, smiling women and swap jokes with genial middle-aged guys. Eddie meanwhile was introducing Joanna and myself to some of the guests. Names went in one ear and out the other with me. I tried to match them up after the round of introductions was finished and found I couldn't, so calculated that the atmosphere was so lively and noisy I might just be able to have several beers and blend into the background. Take it easy. Someone started eating. Joanna asked me if I liked oysters. I admitted I'd never tried them but had always been curious. I tipped my head back and allowed the oyster to slip down the back of my throat. I gulped instinctively and it was gone, leaving a trace of the sea. A tantalising salty, fishy smear on my palate. I helped myself to some more. Then to a beer.

Nick got up and gave a speech, naturally. He dinged the nearest champagne bottle with his fork, spread his arms to embrace us all, and dived into his largely improvised address with such vim and enthusiasm I couldn't help but warm to him. That aside, the speech itself covered a lot of ground and included many names I knew little of; Joanna was mentioned once or twice only. Other friends of hers, whose names I had heard over the last few weeks, did not figure and I admit I allowed myself to be distracted, wondering where Nick and Eddie fitted in and whether or not I would ever see them again. Would Joanna and I stay together? Did we want to? Was there a chance, that if we did want to, we would? I had another beer and sat a bit lower in my seat.

A round of raucous applause burst into my consciousness. All smiles, Nick warmly thanked everybody for coming – there was a thoughtful special mention for Joanna and me for having come so far – and urged us all to continue to eat and drink until we could do so no more. Given that he was picking up the tab – which he later did unostentatiously – this was exceptionally generous.

Once he'd sat down and various conversations had already picked up around the table, he turned to me and said: 'On the highway between Geraldton and Perth I saw a man break his wife's neck in the door of their Mercedes.'

Having leaned forward conspiratorially in order to be able

to hear his lowered voice, now I leant back to get a good look at him. He was still smiling.

'It was white. Mercedes 280SE,' he continued. 'You know, the one with headlamps like figure 8s. They were heading south. A 280SE.'

It was the way he stressed the car, not the act. I was about to ask why, when the woman on his other side shook his arm and demanded his attention. I guessed he was either being perverse or had drunkenly latched on to the wrong detail. I didn't get a chance to speak to him again until we were in the Cruiser heading back to the house, Nick very unsteadily and terrifyingly in charge of the vehicle, and it no longer seemed the right moment. I could feel Joanna's hands tightly gripping the back of my seat. Eddie was begging him not to drive another yard. But Nick was oblivious, his loon's grin turned a ghastly green by the dashboard display as he weaved either side of the white lines in the middle of the road.

Fifteen

North again. Due north. North-West Coastal Highway.

I had ended up enjoying the time we spent at Nick and Eddie's so much I almost didn't want to leave: there was a trip up the Chapman River to swim in a bottomless pool, endless playing with the children, both there and back in Geraldton, and a fair amount of sitting out on the deck drinking beer and watching the sun go down over the Indian Ocean.

But it was good to be on the road again. Tiny settlements –

Ogilvie, Hutt, Binnu – shimmering in the heat haze ahead, only to dissolve in the rearview mirror. North of Geraldton there was a marked change in the character of the landscape, the nature of the highway. Rough scrub followed by bush. Eucalypts the only living thing above five feet. The road trains now had three wagons; as they passed you coming the other way you heard *vrooom-vroom-vroom* with a rattling undertow. If they were going north too, they represented an even greater challenge than the two-wagon rigs south of Geraldton. Joanna drove for a bit. I touched the soft skin behind her ear and stroked the back of her neck. She told me about the near-miss she had last time she was in Oz. When she was driving across the interior somewhere, with Eddie and Nick, and was overtaking a road train when a kangaroo appeared out of nowhere and hopped in front of their hired four-wheel drive. 'I did some kind of handbrake turn,' she said. 'I didn't really know what I was doing, I just yanked on the brake and the car spun. Luckily we were all okay, a bit of whiplash but there wasn't much you could do about it out there, so I just started it up again and drove on. After about five minutes Nick suggested I turn around and go back the other way.' She turned to look at me. 'I'd spun through a hundred and eighty degrees and so when I'd set off again we were going back the way we'd come.'

'Exactly what happened to us with that dead wallaby,' I pointed out, once we'd stopped briefly and swapped positions and I was driving again.

'The kangaroo was all right. They do that though,' she was saying, her bare feet up on the dash to allow cooling air to blow up her skirt. 'Kangaroos. They come out of nowhere. I'm not kidding, you've got to be really careful. Especially at dusk.' I raised my eyebrow. 'And especially when I'm asleep and can't keep a watch out for you.' She dozed off sometimes on long stretches. Awake or asleep, she made me glad of her company. I couldn't think of anyone I'd rather have in the passenger seat than her. Not Max certainly. Oh, he'd be a change and fun for half an hour – he'd have some controversial view on the road-houses or other drivers or the landscape. But the novelty would wear off. I wondered what it would be like to ride with Danny and imagined he'd sit there quite self-contained and tense, staring out the window on his side the whole time.

Thinking about the hospital. Thinking about the pizza restaurant. Thinking about Z.

Maybe he'd tell me the one about the squaddies.

When a gang of squaddies from Knightsbridge barracks started giving Z a hard time as she walked past their table.

'Oi sweetheart,' one of them called her over. He was stocky, fair-haired, number-one back-and-sides. He wore a yellow polo shirt and Wrangler jeans without a belt. Danny didn't hear him, but noticed when heads started turning throughout the restaurant.

Z had stopped in her tracks – turned and smiled. At first she looked in command of the situation, then Danny detected the slightest twitch in her smile. He knew she wasn't handling it.

'Come sit on my face, love. Bring us a couple of beers as well.'

She tucked a lock of blonde hair behind her ear. She appeared to be trying to work out how to wrest control from the squaddies. The deputy manager said later she had it under control: she was staring them down. Most of these guys were cowards and couldn't hack it if you actually confronted them. Danny knew though – or reckoned he knew – she stopped because she was frightened. She was like a deer – or a 'roo – caught in car headlights. Frozen. Rooted. Unable to go on or go back.

He couldn't watch. He stopped thinking for a moment and snapped into action, marching straight across to their table. At some point he put down the mixed side salad with Thousand Island dressing he'd been taking to table fourteen – didn't drop it, but calmly placed it down on the nearest flat surface. He was on auto-pilot. He walked between the tables, arms swinging lightly as he went, biceps twitching. The deputy manager said he'd never seen anyone picked up by the shirt-front before. It was the sort of thing you saw in films.

The squaddie's knife and fork clattered to the floor. His beer glass was knocked over and Peroni splashed on to his friends' trousers – they all scooted back away from the table amid protests. The squaddie was twice Danny's weight, but his feet cleared the floor when Danny lifted him by the scruff of his polo top. No one could hear what Danny said to the man but they could see that it was punctuated by vicious little prods to the chest. He'd picked him up with his left hand, so it was with his right that he was jack-hammering the man's left breast.

I could guess what he said to the man. It was no accident that he prodded him where he did. Over the heart. Danny was already a man obsessed. He'd been in St George's maybe a couple of times by this stage, but had yet to take Z with him.

Would he have told me that himself? Or was Max his sole confidant? In a bizarre way he probably needed Max as much as Max needed him, as an outlet for his stories.

He didn't need Max like he needed Z. And I didn't need either of them like I needed Joanna.

There hadn't yet been a single moment when I'd wished simply, as I had occasionally in the past with old girlfriends, that no one was with me. I hadn't felt the need to be alone. The open road was mine and it was ours – they felt like the same thing. In any case, I would never have been there without her. As she dozed and as I drove I would place my left hand on her knee and hear her faintly murmur.

Next stop was Kalbarri. Another road through another national park with another vestigial town at the end of it. I turned in a gentle curve through the gravel off the North-West Coastal Highway on to Route 66 and headed north-west to the ocean once more. With the window down, hot, dusty air caught my hair. I slotted Joni Mitchell's 'Turbulent Indigo' into the tape deck. Joanna muttered something but didn't open her eyes. A large lizard flicked its tail at the car and vanished. The land was flat and covered with uneven bush and vivid wildflowers. I noticed a brown bottle lying on the run-off verge.

I decided to phone Max from Kalbarri. To talk about what Nick had said at the anniversary dinner in Geraldton. Just to check it out and eliminate the possibility.

A phrase stuck in my head from the Joni Mitchell. Usually with Joni Mitchell it was just the voice. A voice that could pierce a shroud and wake a dead man, so alternately mournful and joyful, so far ahead of the competition you wondered why other girl singers ever approached the mike. Because of a combination of engine noise, the drumming of the sun inside the skull and the tyres on the road it was difficult to hear much of the middle section of the tape. But near the end, on 'The Sire of Sorrow', the sound engineer or somebody hiked the volume so that even with background noise you could clearly hear her singing about the *janitors of shadowland*. Out there, miles from anywhere, in that sun-baked paradise, that line, that single phrase, cast a shadow. It chilled me. Who were these guys, these *janitors*? And where was *shadowland*?

I had a hunch about what Nick had said at the restaurant in Geraldton. I hoped I was wrong.

We started passing signs to tourist spots. Ross Graham Lookout. Hawks Head. Later: Z-bend, Nature's Window and the Loop. Joanna woke up and this time stayed awake. She always seemed to be able to sense when we were approaching our destination. She looked at me sheepishly, although there was no need. It didn't bother me that she fell asleep. With her job I reckoned you grabbed – and earned – all the Zs you could get. As it were.

'Kalbarri,' she said, reaching into the back of the car for the *Lonely Planet*. She'd picked up some tourist stuff in Geraldton as well, leaflets and a little map to the Kalbarri National Park.

We drove around Kalbarri; it was bigger than Lancelin but still pretty small. Two parades at either end of the town comprised maybe ten shops in all, among them a baker, a fishing tackle store and a small general grocer's with instore post office. The heart of the town seemed to be at neither shopping area but between them, somewhere among the guest houses, motels and self-catering apartments that presumably accounted for most of the town's business. These establishments lurked within stands of extravagant vegetation – eucalypts, lots of palms and blackboys – which waved to and fro in the warm breeze, like something vacillating in a tropical fish tank, as we drove around the tidy streets in search of the right place.

Reef Villas looked right to both of us: self-catering two-bedroom villas with private pool and barbecue. Fifty bucks a night. Between us. About fifteen quid each. I stopped the car and walked across to the office. As I entered, a big man in his early fifties with jet-black thinning hair drawn back over a tanned skull stepped into the narrow space behind his counter by means of a sliding door. He smiled at me.

'Well, hello there. How's it going?' he said, the smile perfectly natural.

'Fine, thank you. We're looking for a place for a night or two.'

'Well, you've definitely come to the right place. We've got villas standing empty, just gotta be used. Why don't I give you a quick tour?' He lifted a section of his counter, at the far end, and slipped through. 'Have you come far today?'

'Just from Geraldton.'

'Lovely place, isn't it?' He pushed open the door and I stepped back outside. Joanna had got out of the car.

'Hello there,' he said. 'Now listen, my name's Ray and my wife Margaret and I run the place together. What are your names?'

I told him.

'Okay then, Chris and Joanna – let's go and have a look around.' He pushed open a side gate and led the way. I looked at Joanna and she grinned.

'Right, okay guys, do you like swimming? You must like swimming. Anyway, whether you like swimming or not, here's the swimming pool.'

It was a small but beautiful pool surrounded by clean white tiles and a few loungers. The water gleamed electric blue. Despite not being much of a swimmer, I knew I would enjoy this particular pool. The manager was off again. His white polo shirt was soft and spotless, his cut-offs clean and not too raggedy. On his feet he wore faded black pumps. He was a big man but very gentle, in the way he spoke, the way he moved.

'This is our barbecue area.' Two huge hot plates, spare gas bottles, decent-sized spatula, pile of old newspapers. 'We ask our guests to clean up after they've used the barbie. Here's the light switch.' He pointed to the wall marking the end of the barbie area, which was also surrounded by thick gum trees.

He showed us into one of the villas.

Villas is stretching it slightly, but at two storeys, the master bedroom with a wooden balcony overlooking a clump of sub-tropical trees and a Bali hut at the front, all for fifteen quid each, we were not complaining. Far from it. I could tell Joanna had fallen in love with the place, as indeed I had. Part of that was to do with the manager. This guy had come out here from Melbourne or Sydney with his wife and they'd worked their fingers to the bone to get Reef Villas looking how it did. Then they continued to work around the clock to maintain it that way. The lawn at the back between the barbie and the pool could have been used for a bowls tournament. I'd seen Joanna running a finger along a shelf inside the villa, looking for dust and not finding any. So why did it seem to me as if he had just materialised here one day, appointed guardian of this magic hideaway? It appeared that way because he gave that impression. He was a genius, a master of his art.

'Well, we can't stay here, obviously,' Joanna whispered to me when he was far enough ahead to be out of earshot.

'Clearly,' I said. 'It's far too nice. We need to find somewhere more disappointing. Somewhere a bit grim and dangerous.'

When we reached the end of the block, he was standing there holding the key between his forefinger and thumb, an innocent grin splitting his genial features. I held out my hand for the key.

'We'll stay two nights,' I said. 'If that's all right.'

'All right? Of course it's all right. We hope you'll have a wonderful time in Kalbarri.' Joanna and I stood there beaming at him. 'If you just pop back into the office,' he continued, looking in my direction, 'you can sign the book and I'll give you your phone messages.'

Sixteen

'**None of which explains** how he knew you were *here*. At Reef Villas.'

'I don't know,' I shrugged. 'Maybe he's left messages at every motel and self-catering place in town. All over the state, who knows? Western Australia peppered with phone messages from Max in a single day.'

Joanna wasn't only puzzled by the revelation that Max had phoned and left a couple of messages, she seemed quite cross about it. But then so was I. Jesus, you fly right around the other side of the world and you can't even get away. He's a friend and everything, but there's a time and there's a place. And what on earth could he want anyway? My first instinct was to phone him up straightaway and find out, in case it was something urgent. But knowing Max it could just be a whim. He thought, I know, I'll phone. Doesn't matter that he's in Oz. The world's not that big a place.

Evidently not.

'I can't phone him right now anyway,' I said, looking at Joanna's watch.

'Why not?'

'It's the middle of the night in London. I'd wake him up.'

'Oh what a tragedy,' she said. 'Do you think he worried about that when he phoned you?'

The two messages had both been left the day before. The first one said: 'Max called. Can you call him back'. Dated and timed. The second message was to the point: 'Max again'.

'Maybe he wants a lift somewhere,' Joanna suggested.

'Yeah, it's the dreary fag end of some druggy party in Upper Norwood and he's thinking how on earth do I get back to Harringay. Well, how do I usually get back to Harringay? I know. Quick phone call.'

We were sitting out on the balcony of our villa looking down over the sub-tropical grove and the Bali hut. I sort of wanted to call Max to see what the problem was – after all, I had been going to call *him* – but at the same time I didn't want to feel I was his lapdog. And I didn't want Joanna to think I was his lapdog either. He was just the sort of person who'd ring up either for no good reason at all, or because he'd thought of some absolutely compelling reason why he had to get hold of me immediately. Which, two days later, he'd have forgotten about. And in any case, it *was* the middle of the night in Maxland. Come to that, it was always the middle of the night in Maxland.

'Let's explore,' I said. 'Have a look around Kalbarri.'

We took the car and cruised the town's wide streets again, found a restaurant that had kangaroo satay and crocodile steak on the menu. We'd go back later for dinner. Where the Kalbarri River hit the sea – after the harbour and the sandbar at its mouth where pelicans and anglers shared the last strip of land before the ocean – huge, deep-red sandstone cliffs reared out of the surf. When the sun started to go down, we headed back. I had a shower, then joined Joanna on the balcony. She smiled. I smiled too when I saw how the green of the trees in front of the balcony had turned darker and more lustrous with the light of approaching dusk. The sky beyond the trees was deep magenta and all around, it seemed, insects and frogs and toads were tuning up for a nocturnal symphony.

We ate dinner at the restaurant we'd found earlier; again we sat on a balcony. It was already dusk by the time our kangaroo satay arrived. We watched the sky turn through a colour chart from burnt chocolate orange to African violet as we ate. A bottle of Vasse Felix Chardonnay and we walked back to Reef Villas arm in arm, the surf swishing to and fro like curtains on smooth runners. I still hadn't phoned Max but I put that to the back of my mind. Very easily. I lay naked on the bed, the covers thrown on to the floor, the shutters and door to the balcony wide open and the mozzie screen in place, while Joanna finished in the bathroom. The sky was quite dark now, the moon bright and clear and tiny stars winking in and out, but in the trees by the balcony a single peach-coloured light attracted a host of fluttering insects batting against its shade. Bigger, more mysterious creatures croaked and chirruped, seemingly in a semi-circle around the front of the villa. Like an audience sitting around a proscenium arch and applauding.

At dinner Joanna had asked me how I was feeling about my father. I told her the truth. That there were black spells that would come upon me with no warning, when I was driving and she was dozing or at other times when I found myself alone: I was waking up in the early hours every other night, still jetlagged, and some of those times it would get me. It was like a black curtain coming down and there was no way I could fight my way through it. It was simply a question of waiting behind it, trying to think it away, but it never went. I'd fall asleep and in the morning if it was still there I wasn't aware of it. She asked me if I felt guilty for being happy with her, and I told her I didn't, which was the truth. She'd never met him, didn't know him, and in truth hardly knew me, so there wasn't that much real support she knew how to give me. Most of the time I was happy with her and some of the time, when I was on my own, I felt the weight of that black curtain come down again.

Lying on the bed at Reef Villas while she clattered about in the bathroom, I felt no sadness. His death had released him from pain and we all had to go on. My mother, my sister and I, we had to go on with life. I couldn't feel guilty about that. If I felt guilty about anything it was that I had deserted my mother. She wanted to be on her own, to work through her grief in her own way, and I had to respect that. But maybe flying twelve thousand miles to the other side of the world was respecting that just a little too much. I resolved to call her before I called Max.

Joanna came in and stood in a patch of moonlight. She was wearing a T-shirt which she slowly lifted over her head and dropped on to the floor. The soft light washed over her body like gentle surf over an untouched beach. She turned to face me and smiled. I laughed as I reached up to touch her and she started faintly, softly, to giggle.

Seventeen

The phone was in the laundry room, which was outside by the pool. The manager was supervising his automated pool-cleaning device – a long tube thick as a conger eel which roved across the length and width of the pool picking up debris.

'G'day,' he called to me as I pushed open the door of the laundry room.

'How's it going?' I replied.

''S'going all right, mate.'

It was eight o'clock in Kalbarri which meant it was three o'clock in England.

'Mum, hi. It's me.'

'Oh Christopher, you shouldn't. What did I tell you? You mustn't. It's too expensive.'

She sounded okay – bright and alert. I was relieved. There had been sharp, acute grief for her to get through at the beginning and that had gone on for a long time, but it had been expected to. What worried me was that she would slip naturally into a depression and find it impossible to climb out. I could only imagine what it did to you to lose the person you've lived with for forty years.

'It's very cheap. Don't worry about it. The phones here are practically free. Wherever you go, people come out of their homes and offer you their phones.'

'Oh, you clown.'

'Look, how are you doing, really?' I watched the manager through the window. He was wearing another white towelling polo shirt, a pair of tan shorts and the same deck shoes. He worked thoroughly but with a lack of urgency that spoke of a man relaxed and happy with his lot. I wondered if he and his wife were happy together. If I would ever be as settled and as happy about it as he appeared to be. With Joanna.

'I'm all right, love,' my mother said. 'Really, I'm okay. How's Joanna?'

'She's fine. It's all fine.' I watched as he used a long-handled broom to sweep the tiled poolside area. 'How are you, you know . . .' I didn't know how to say it.

'I'm *all right*.' Maybe she was. She sounded it, but she was good at that. There'd been times with my dad when she'd had to make it seem as if everything was all right. Most of the time, of course, it was, but whenever there was a problem, whenever he gave her a hard time, she'd shield us from it. Because she wanted to spare me and my sister any suffering and because she was devoted to him.

'Mum, I'll call you again soon,' I said.

'Don't be silly, love. Just get on and have a good time.'

I rang Max's number. The manager was clearing up his conger eel thing and storing it in the little shed at the far end of the pool. Max's phone rang and rang. I pictured the green Trimphone purring away on his knackered old writing bureau. I was with him in Camden Lock market when he bought the phone, a genuine mid-seventies period piece – just like Max. There was a ticket on it that said £25 and Max offered the guy a tenner. 'Twenty-five, mate,' said the stall-holder not unreasonably. 'How do I know it's gonna work?' Max pressed him. 'It works, mate, it works.' The guy had been right – though he did come down to twenty under pressure – and it still worked now, ringing out in Max's cluttered flat. I pictured the undulating dunes of discarded newsprint, the jumble stalls of dirty clothes that needed tidying away, and wondered where he was.

Suddenly: 'Pronto?'

It was Max. A paranoia thing – always wanting to make sure he was one step ahead of whoever might be calling him. Just in case it was a set-up of some kind. Or someone he didn't want to talk to: he could keep it going for up to ten minutes. The Italian deli owner. He'd gab on, about the Neapolitan sausage not having been delivered that morning, throw in a couple of Channel 4-derived Serie A results and *La Gazzetta dello Sport* headlines. It was good enough for some some suckers, but not for me. I'd heard it all before. I let him run with it for a few moments longer before it dawned on me that I was paying, and the dollars and cents were being ticked off before my eyes.

'Max, hey Max.'

His babbling fell silent.

'Max, can you hear me?'

'*La prestazione dell'Inter è stata deludente.*'

'Max, for fuck's sake.'

'Oh it's you.' He sounded disappointed.

'Yeah, who d'you think it was? The President of the Board of Trade?'

He muttered something I didn't catch, then, speaking up: 'Do you know, sixty-one per cent chose Pepsi! Sixty-one per cent.'

'Max.'

'Sixty-one per cent. Like that's something to shout about. It's a fraction above a half and given that fifty per cent is what you'd expect *anyway* it's hardly an exciting statistic, is it?'

'Max, what the hell . . .'

'Their latest advertising campaign,' he said, dismissively. 'Posters all over town. Sixty-one per cent! Big fucking deal!'

'Max. You had me ring you from the other side of the world to tell me that?'

There was a pause and all I could hear was rustling followed by a rattle.

'Max, what are you doing?'

'Hang on,' he said and put the receiver down on his bureau with a clunk that rang in my ear. He was gone twenty seconds. I had to slip more money into the slot. 'Sorry,' he said breathlessly. 'Had to get some milk. Just about to get a bite to eat when you rang.' He started chomping on something. 'Bowl of Shreddies,' he said. 'Go on,' he said, his mouth full.

'What do you mean "go on"? You rang me. What did you want?'

Chomp, chomp. Followed by an inarticulate throaty sound as if he were trying either to form a word or to decide what to say.

Then: 'It's Danny,' he said. 'He's in Australia. You should watch out for him. You never know.' And then he broke down into a fit of sniggering, Shreddies catching in his throat and causing him to choke. The phone was dropped and a loud, hacking cough ensued. I had to feed more change into the slot. Eventually Max picked up the phone again at his end. 'Just, you know,' he continued, 'watch your back, that's all.'

'What's he doing out here, Max?'

'What?'

'I mean why did he come here? Is he following me?'

Through a mouthful of half-masticated breakfast cereal: 'Why on earth would he be following you? Why should I know what he's doing out there? I don't know what he's doing. He got religion, I don't know. He's an eschatologist – seems like a good place for it. Doesn't it to you?'

'If I knew what eschatology was, maybe I could answer you. Stop talking in riddles, Max.'

'Who doesn't talk in riddles, old boy, who doesn't?'

I paused, exasperated. The manager had packed his pool cleaning equipment away and was walking back towards his office, the hairs on his legs catching the sunlight and making his legs glow around the edges.

'The study of last things, young man. The end of the world. Western Australia seems as good a place as any.'

'I thought he was your closest friend, Max.'

'He is, he is. He's just a little unpredictable, that's all. You know that. I've told you enough about him.'

Ray disappeared around the corner. I thought of Joanna probably still lying in bed or standing in the shower or leaning over the balcony rail.

'What about his wife? What about Z? Did she come with him?'

'I don't know. I should imagine so. You don't go that far on your own, do you?' Sharp little squeaks summoned up a picture of Max sucking bits of food from between his teeth. 'Although, Danny is the sort of person who just might. I've known him however many years, but I still don't *really* know him. Anyway, he was born out there.'

'Was he? I didn't know that.'

'Why should you?'

And then we got cut off. I'd run out of change. Although I'm normally superstitious about getting cut off – I have to call the person straight back in order to sign off properly – with Max on this occasion I couldn't be fucked. He'd started to irritate the hell out of me.

For a while I stood and watched the corner around which the manager had disappeared. I was thinking about Danny and about the man Joanna's friend Nick had seen, the man who had broken his wife's head in the door of his white Mercedes 280SE. I was thinking about figure 8s. And about Max's reaction that time when I'd asked him if Danny was mad. When I'd wondered out loud if the night in the abandoned hospital had affected his mind.

One of the many things I didn't know about Danny was how exactly dangerous he might or might not be.

Watch your back, that's all.

So Danny was born somewhere out here. Why was that so surprising?

He's just a little unpredictable, that's all. You know that. I've told you enough about him.

Had he though? Had he told me enough?

Although history will show that Danny left London in the summer of 1992, there were still reports coming in of his various activities in and around the capital as late as the following winter. Reports which came mostly, it has to be admitted, from Max, who wouldn't be your first-choice witness. But in Danny's case, unfortunately, he's just about all we've got. Z was no use when she was around and is slightly less use now.

Danny's last incarnation before he quit London gave no hint he might be disappearing to Australia. He was alternating his old lemon-yellow BMW 2002ti with the metallic blue Karmann Ghia, parking them up outside a variety of addresses in central and south London. From mansion flats in Ridgmount Gardens, WC1 to a converted Victorian terrace in Rye Hill Park, Peckham. Max said he was moving Z around so that she wasn't at any one location long enough for another man to draw a bead on her. It wasn't that he was obsessively jealous, just that after what had happened that night in St George's, he was taking no chances. 'He's a mad cunt,' Max used to say. *He* was allowed to say it, if I wasn't. Although I don't think he ever meant it in the technical sense – 'mad' that is. Whether he did or he didn't, a clinical psychologist would have had a field day with Danny.

In those last weeks or months he was working as an importer. If you asked him what he imported he'd have said just about anything, but in truth it was mainly alcohol. Eastern European spirits: genuine Slivovic from Prague and Bratislava before it became fashionable, and therefore before he could charge anything like cost for it; homemade brandies and poitín from what was Yugoslavia; and he was the only man in the West importing ponç from Durres, Albania. He was the only man in the West importing anything from Albania in the early nineties, if you discounted whichever enthusiast kept the shelves of the Albanian Shop on Betterton Street stocked with Hoxha busts, double-headed eagle flags and cassettes of folk music. If the markets for Danny's Bulgarian wines (the ones the supermarkets didn't buy on their own trips) and Transylvanian plum brandy were small, the potential for making money out of ponç, a thick, syrupy orange-flavoured liqueur the colour of early rosehips, should have been virtually non-existent. But there were several offies around Soho, ones you'd never think about patronising in a million years, which snapped up his ponç when he told them it was forty per cent proof and he only wanted a couple of quid a bottle. They cost him less than a quarter of that, and in dollars, which at the time was good news for Danny and others like him. If indeed there was anyone like him.

What happened was he shifted so many bottles through those dusty-windowed liquor marts you reached via Meard Street and Percy Passage he made a small fortune in a few months – enough to vanish off the face of the earth with Z and not have to do anything to earn cash for the next few months. He wanted to give Z and himself a new chance in the wide open spaces of WA. He left behind a temporary craze among the meths drinkers and vagrants of lower Fitzrovia, Soho and Chinatown for the sweet charms of Albania's only drinkable drink, because the off-licences, finding they couldn't offload them at a tenner a bottle to the trendy set, downpriced them to three quid fifty just to clear the shelf space.

Danny was laughing. Or his mouth was opening and closing in that eerie, silent way that passed for laughter on his planet.

He did a dodgy deal with a Finsbury Park pornographer called Howell – he was one of those guys ran a business printing off tarts' cards for public phone boxes with increasingly better-quality photos of Swedish models who bore about as much resemblance to the girls whose numbers appeared on the cards as the serving suggestions on the sleeves of microwave meals.

Danny had graduated from his genuine Hong Kong newsprint erotica to scams: he got together a couple of dozen digest-size Danish skin mags and slapped covers on them ripped off *Les Lettres Albanaises*, an Albanian literary review published in Tirana but printed in French – two hundred and forty pages, offset litho, saddle-stitched. Howell, fair frothing at the gash, offered cash for the warehouse-load Danny promised him, and Danny was the kind of man could get even a guy like Howell to cough up before he'd properly inspected the goods. There was indeed a warehouse – it was out by the Lea Bridge Road – and it was full of magazines that looked like *Les Lettres Albanaises*. Bundled in polythene and heavyduty plastic tape, they looked sufficiently like the real thing to fool Howell. The only trouble was they *were* the real thing. Ninety-four thousand copies of *Les Lettres Albanaises*, 1981–86, which Danny had seen dumped in a disused factory outside Durres. He'd made enquiries, filled out a few pointless shipping forms that would be torn up once his back was turned, and counted out a few hundred dollars to a bunch of guys who'd do the actual shifting, or who would pay other guys a handful of leks to do it for them. As long as it got done, Danny wasn't bothered either way. He was in for the kill and he made one with Howell.

Of course, after that, after his quick exit from the warehouse, it was imperative he disappear. This he pretty much did. Even Max didn't know where he'd gone. Australia was the last place anyone thought of looking. Howell could hardly go to the cops and he didn't have the manpower to watch the airports. Or the imagination.

This was spring 1993, but if you'd checked the records you'd have found Danny left the UK several months previously. Which was certainly true: he'd been to Albania, for a start, but had not yet entered Australia, although the stamp in his passport said he had. Max would later explain this by referring to his theory that time did not exist.

'We've had it drummed into us from day one,' he would say as he leaned against the bar in some grim Clerkenwell boozer, surrounded by Farringdon bookdealers sipping at pints of Tennants. 'But it's a dimension that can be taken out of the equation. Say you and I both throw our Grolsch bottles against the wall of the pub. I put more energy into mine, so mine hits the wall first. But it also makes more of a racket. More energy in, more energy out. That's what's important, not which bottle hits the wall first. It's all about energy.'

I would have been shaking my head, continuing to drink, looking around for distraction.

'Look,' he said, sliding his bottle along the bar and indicating for me to place mine next to it. He took hold of both bottles and tried to make one pass through the other. 'It won't go. They can't occupy the same space. It's exclusive simultaneity. It's nothing to do with time. Not really. Exclusive simultaneity.' He knocked back another mouthful. 'I know what you're thinking. Simultaneity includes the concept of time in the very word. That's only because it's been made so much a part of our language we can't escape from it. It's a question of going back to basics. A level playing field.'

I looked at him, wondered how serious he was being.

Whether he actually believed in his theory or not, he'd spent hours developing it.

'To make you get it,' he said, 'I'd have to sit in my room for a whole weekend just to get back to the beginning of it myself.

To get the real sense of it. If *I* can't feel, what chance is there of convincing you?'

Confused and irritated by Max, and a little anxious, I walked out of the laundry room into the blinding sun. I closed my eyes and lifted my face up, let it wash over me. No matter how hot it became, I loved it. Just as my dad would have done. Soon as the sun came out, you wouldn't find him indoors. He'd always be doing something – reading the home news in the *Guardian*, completing a new box kite made out of an old nylon sheet, annotating his exercise book catalogue of reel-to-reel tape recordings – but if the sun was shining he'd make sure he could do it outside.

He'd never had the chance to come out here, just as he'd never been to New Orleans. He once said he'd like to have the Eureka Brass Band of New Orleans play at his funeral. Of course, when it came to it we never arranged anything of the kind. We were all numb, caught up in a seemingly unstoppable train of events. Non-believers all of us, my father included, we went along with the basic religious service, in case by not doing so we would have given offence or failed to give whatever comfort could be given to the other mourners. My mother's wishes should have been paramount – she wasn't falling for any religious crap, she'd lost my father, her companion of forty years, and she knew that nothing would bring him back nor speed her to him – but, as always, she thought of others first.

Everything I experienced now I was experiencing for him as well, because he couldn't. I moved by the pool and sat on the edge of one of the white plastic loungers.

Joanna found me with my head in my hands half an hour later. When I looked up at her, she was all blurred and streaky against the glare of the sun.

'Chris, you shouldn't sit out here without some cream on,' she said before she got a good look at me. When she did she sat down next to me and wrapped her arms around me. Sometimes the grief was so raw it seemed as if there would never be any consolation.

We had to hope, she'd said to me one night as we lay anxiously awake in the dark, that although the process of getting to know each other and becoming more intimate was inevitably speeded up by my loss, no disaster would befall us later as a result. Once the words were out we both lay still, reflecting on their implications. I had to admit, from my own experience of rushing into these things merely because of impetuosity, it was possible to go so fast at the beginning you missed stuff.

'I hope we're going to be all right,' she whispered to me in the night, her voice mixed just above the insectile susurration of the sub-tropics.

'We'll be fine,' I said, holding her closer, and wanting to believe it.

Eighteen

Shark Bay was as far north as we were going to go. It was as far north as the insurance on the Laser would allow us to go. In fact, it was probably what we'd come all this way to see. Though it was hard to imagine – as wildflower scrub drew steadily past the car on both sides and the road unrolled before us – that any place could be the equal of Kalbarri, that any time could match the hours we'd spent there together. It was our zenith.

We'd spent our last day in Kalbarri visiting the river gorges. In the morning we'd hired a small dinghy with an outboard motor and pootled around in the harbour for a while before turning our backs on the ocean and heading upstream. Not very far upstream, it has to be said, but far enough to find a secluded cove where we could pull the boat up on to the shore and have a swim. Over the past few days Joanna and I had been reading passages to each other from *Venomous Creatures of Australia – A Field Guide*. It was for the sea creatures that Joanna reserved her profoundest concern.

The jimble, the dusky flathead, the butterfly cod. The Portuguese man o'war, cone shells and stonefish. Step on a stonefish and you'll know about it, promised our much-thumbed guide. It spoke of extraordinary pain lasting for several hours and of permanent tissue damage. Yet we paddled barefoot, believing ourselves far enough upstream to be in safe territory. One night Joanna had dreamt of sea snakes – a writhing, seething mass of them miles out in the ocean, thousands of blackcurrant eyes and paddle-shaped tails. Swimming off the beach she'd drifted out to sea and remained unalarmed by the image of the receding coastline until she found herself drifting inexorably towards the matted caravan of serpents. The swell rolled and pitched her forwards abruptly into the great green maelstrom.

She woke up, sweat standing out on her forehead, mozzie screen banging against the wall. I held her until she went back to sleep.

We swam in the little cove, our feet slipping on the muddy bottom as we came ashore to dry off. Soon we were chugging back towards the harbour where the boat hire guy was giving two Aboriginal girls a hard time. They wanted to take a boat out and he didn't trust them.

We took the car out of town towards the gorges.

At the Loop we parked up and walked down the winding path to Nature's Window, a natural hole in a sandstone bluff that offers a view up the Murchison River gorge. We each took a photo of the other sitting by the window. Joanna was wearing black Lycra shorts and a pink T-shirt with a little pocket I had bought for her in New Orleans. On her feet, dusty black pumps. Ray-Bans, a big smile.

At the Z Bend we sat on a huge rock overhang and gazed down at the river, hundreds of feet below. The water was shallow and unbelievably clear. The rocks that formed the bed of the river were sharply defined. We climbed on to a bulbous outcrop that afforded another view back up one stretch of the river and sat dangling our legs. 'Think what this place must have been like,' she said after a few moments.

'What do you mean?'

'Four hundred and twenty million years ago.' She leaned forward, her head tilted upwards as if to sniff the scorchmarks of time as it scraped through our lives like some inexorable earthmover. Some cosmic JCB that would never stop, only appear to slow down and speed up. Right now, for me at least, it was fixed at dead slow and I wanted it to stay that way. 'They found the world's oldest footprints here,' she said.

'Who did?'

'I don't know. The men from the museum. Fossil men. Palaeontologists.'

'Which museum?'

'Which museum? I don't know which museum. It doesn't matter which museum.' She turned round to hit me on the arm and I pretended to fall off the edge of the rock. She grabbed for me and we messed about like a couple of kids. 'In fact, Chris,' she continued, 'I think you might be one of them.'

'What? One of the men from the museum?'

'No. One of the eurypterids.'

'The eurypterwhats?'

'Eurypterids. Don't tell me you haven't heard of eurypterids.'

'They must have passed me by.'

'They're like scorpions only they grew up to two metres in length and as they floundered across the sand they left footprints. Or paddle marks. They used paddles to get about.'

'So they were like sort of prehistoric canoeists?'

'Yes, that's right. I bet you like those animal pictures in the back of the Sunday supplements.'

'I don't see the link, but yes: my Sunday is never complete until I've read the animal picture caption in the back of *You Magazine*.'

'The link is anthropomorphism. You're one of those poor pathetic human beings who can only conceive of animals if they're in some way related to us. Turn a kitten into a little man, put a crap caption underneath it and you delight half the country.'

'You and Max should get on. He likes people who hold strong views.'

'I hate *You Magazine*,' Joanna said. 'I hate it more than the *Sun*, even more than the *Mail*. I hate it because week after week it accompanies one of the most objectionable collections of prejudice and intolerance and acts as a soft cushion for it. It's lazy, it's smug, it's mediocre.'

'That's why I love you,' I put my arm around her and leant my head against her left breast. 'Your heart's in the right place.'

She was silent for a moment and all I could hear was the faraway rustling of the Murchison River.

'No, it's not,' she said.

'Oh yes it is.'

'No it's not, Chris.'

Then: 'It is.'

'I'm telling you, it's not.'

And the funny thing was, I couldn't hear it. My ear was pressed right up against where it should have been and I couldn't hear it or feel it. A warm breeze brushed the hairs on my legs but I felt a momentary chill.

She said: 'Do you believe me now?'

Dextracardia. Having the heart located on the right side of the body instead of the left. There are no symptoms and rarely any problems associated with the condition. It was just something a bit different. I'll admit I was shocked. It's just something you take for granted – and there was the irrational feeling that she should have told me previously. But why? Why should she? It didn't matter.

Another long drive up to Shark Bay, from one dusty horizon to another. Through tiny settlements marked only by a roadhouse and a skimpy bar. 'Where do their customers live?' Joanna asked, watching the skimpy bar disappear in the rearview – she was driving for a short stretch. I imagined a bar room full of greasy-browed locals who once had run distant farms and cattle stations but having made a single trip to the bar found themselves caught in its sticky web of cheap beer, social intercourse and skimpy barmaids. Back at their farms, wives waited on front porches scanning the horizon for dust clouds that never materialised.

'See the bottles?' Joanna said.

The run-off verge was host to the usual brown bottle parasites, dotted a couple of kilometres apart. I shook my head, reached for more sunblock.

We switched and Joanna rested her eyes. I woke her just in time to see three emus trotting across the road before they disappeared between gum trees, their tail feathers bouncing. Still we hadn't seen any more 'roos. Joanna kept saying we would. We did see a mad Japanese cyclist just after leaving the North-West Coastal Highway and heading west on the road to Shark Bay. At first he was just a bead bobbling about in the dazzling sun directly ahead of us, like an optical trick that you hoped would go away. But he got bigger and bigger and suddenly we sailed past him. Dressed in white – singlet, shorts, even a white helmet – with huge panniers on the back of the bike. Pain scribbled across his involuted features.

It was on that last stretch that for the first time we bickered. We didn't yet have anywhere to stay in Denham and evening would be on us by the time we arrived. We'd passed several phones on the way, at roadhouses, but for some reason I'd delayed calling. We had a few numbers of places to stay in the *Lonely Planet* and it would have been an easy matter, but, I don't know why, I'd kept putting it off. Probably because Joanna kept telling me to do it and I can be a stubborn bastard at times. I felt anxious.

So now we were heading towards Denham, still more than an hour away, dusk was coming on and we had nowhere to stay. Sure, people have known worse situations than this, but for a little while it seemed to Joanna as if she had not. We snapped at each other and looked out of opposite windows, sulking and wondering if the whole thing had been a sham. Or at least I was, because I have no sense of proportion. When something's right it's perfect, when it shifts off-centre it's a major disaster. I slotted the Joni Mitchell tape into the stereo and 'The Sire of Sorrow' seemed suitably gloomy accompaniment to our journey. I looked across at Joanna a couple of times but she remained stony-faced. We passed an airstrip, then the road cut through a large saucer-shaped depression where the vegetation was markedly different to that surrounding it. The ground was bare except for evenly spaced clumps of some tightly packed non-flowering ground plant. It looked like a former lake, but of a curiously uniform shape – more or less a perfect circle.

'Weird,' I muttered, glancing at Joanna, hoping to break the ice. She shifted in her seat but said nothing. 'Looks like this was under water at some point,' I persisted.

She grunted and I pulled the Laser to the side, eased on the handbrake.

'Just going to have a look,' I said.

She showed no sign of wanting to join me, so I swung open my door and stepped out. The bare earth was compacted sand which scuffed and billowed in tiny clouds as I walked on it in my Blunnies. I bent down to examine one of the plants. The leaves were heading towards rubbery, almost like a succulent. I picked a stem to show to Joanna and straightened my back. A bird flew high overhead. From somewhere came a low murmur, possibly the ocean. I thought we'd better press on.

Returning to the car, I showed the plant to Joanna. When she reached out a hand to take it, I touched her fingers with mine and gently held her hand. She didn't withdraw it.

'Hey,' I said, and apologised.

'I'm sorry too. Let's not fall out. Especially over something so trivial.'

We arrived in a wind-swept Denham exhausted and hungry. There was in fact no shortage of places to stay, even though we arrived after dusk. It was still off season. A lively wind had got up, jumping in off the ocean and lashing the narrow strip that incorporated a gas station, general store, tourist office and a few self-catering places. Inky waves danced on the shore across the road. The air was still very warm.

We took a self-contained unit at Tradewinds Chalets, booking for three nights in advance, and went straight out to eat at the Old Pearler. Constructed out of shell blocks, it was Denham's only sit-down restaurant. Joanna had eaten there before on her last trip. 'One day,' I said, 'we'll find somewhere you haven't been before.' We sat in a tight little wooden booth and were waited on by a tall, dark-haired waitress who chatted to us about the dolphins at Monkey Mia. We said we would probably go to see them the following day. Joanna had been reading up and there were plenty of other places she wanted to go as well. Eagle Bluff, Shell Beach, Little Lagoon. It was a question of fitting them all in. 'They come right in to the shore,' Joanna was saying when the waitress had gone to get our order. 'Every day of the year just about. All these dolphins. It might have got really touristy now though.'

We ate well – seafood, obviously – and ambled across the little road to the beach. The tide was in and a buffeting wind wrought strange phantasmagorical shapes out of the shallow waves. At the end of a short wooden jetty a single naked bulb cast a cosy moist cone of yellowish light. Dove-grey clouds were drawn across the navy sky as swiftly as props in an amateur diorama. We sat down on the wooden boards at the end of the jetty, our feet dangling

inches from the tossed tops of the waves. 'I love you.' Her hair on
my cheek. Her soft breath. 'I love you too.'

   In the sparse, beige bedroom of the modern villa, while
winds whistled and bent palm trees double beneath their
warm hands, we lay together and made love. Afterwards
Joanna fell asleep straightaway, exhausted by the day's
travelling, but I was restless, lying with my head propped up
on two pillows staring through the open doorway into the
main room of the villa. The movement of the palms outside
caused strange shadows to be drawn this way and that across
the walls. I got up and walked into the main room. Closed the
door to the bedroom so as not to wake Joanna, and switched
on the television. A politician with a Liverpool accent was
talking on one newsy channel. I was puzzled by his accent and
the fact that clearly, from the content, he was an Australian
MP. A bad American TV movie barely enlivened the next
channel. Cricket on another. The wind howled, seemed to be
getting stronger. I settled for an old black and white film.
Vincent Price playing a suspicious widower. I allowed myself
to be drawn into the film's cloying world. The spell was
hardly broken by the commercials. I slumped further down in
the chair, my grasp on the waking world becoming
intertwined with threads of understanding regarding what
was going on in the film. I imagined the palm trees bending
outside the windows turning into the plant that Vincent Price
kept in his wife's bedroom, the plant that sapped her strength
and sucked the life out of her. I went to bed and sank into
sleep like a jet dipping into the cloud layer as it begins its
descent. Dimly aware, as I went, of the winds still moaning
outside the villa, the palms stretched like elastic bands.

   I woke in the middle of the night, my mind made of rubber.
It was hot, the trees rushing under hair-dryer winds. The
windows were open. Had we opened them? I couldn't remember. We should have closed them. Put up with the motor racket
of the aircon.

For a while I lay still, edging my way out of sleep. I became aware that I had reached a threshold. Took one more step, made one further move, and I *knew* there was someone else in the room with me. Someone apart from Joanna. I knew it was their noise that had woken me. I knew they were there. Somewhere. I could either go back to sleep or make another move. I had to choose. I was a figure in a game. A counter. A cypher. I couldn't hear Joanna breathing. I should have been able to: she was lying right next to me.

I kept taking another step and then another out of sleep until at last I became aware of being awake. I realised the rubber was just the taste in my mouth. I reached for my glasses – looked at the time. The red figures on the clock snapped into focus: one twenty-five. I got out of bed. The room was in darkness. The curtains were only thin but there was no moon. Joanna stirred slightly. I kissed her to reassure her because I knew that was all she needed and then she would remain asleep.

I prowled the villa in the dark, passed through the main room. Went into the bathroom. The little window high in the wall above the toilet was open. The wind failed to drown out the cicadas. Less than an hour south of the Tropic of Capricorn. I'd never been here before, I'd never be here again. Sharks and dugong out in the bay.

I sat on the toilet. There was a mirror on the wall opposite. I raised my head but could not see my reflection.

It was hot. Very hot.

Then I saw my reflection, crawling in through the little window above my head, its face tied in tight little red knots with effort. Adrenaline flushed my system. Muscles went into spasm. I thought involuntarily of being cradled at twenty-nine thousand feet, swung from one continent to another, a helpless but persistent heart inside the ribcage of the 747's fuselage.

I rubbed the back of my neck. Splashed cold water. Tried to force myself awake.

I heard a noise in the main room. Crept back in from the

bathroom. I imagined an intruder, fantasised scrabbling for a knife in the unfamiliar kitchen. I looked back into the bathroom. The wind sang. It was three fifteen.

When I awoke again in the morning, with a head like a dustbowl, I could hear Joanna in the kitchen. I heard a tap opened, water splashing into the kettle. 'Good morning, darling.' I kissed her and shuffled into the bathroom, cleaned my teeth. Looked at the relative positions of the mirror and the little window.

'We need milk,' she said. 'I'll go and get some.'

'I'll go,' I said, pulling on my Billabong shorts and slipping my feet into my Blunnies. I kissed her again, picked up last night's pink T-shirt from the back of a chair and checked in my pocket for cash.

'I'll come with you,' she said.

'Back before you know it.' I looked at her as I opened the sliding glass door. If she really wanted to come then she could come, but I guessed she was just being nice. And I felt I could handle walking down the seafront a couple of hundred yards to the store. Let the wind blow the dust out of my head. 'See you in a minute.'

She blew me a kiss and I stepped outside. I noticed a couple of cars parked in front of the other villas, one or two vague hulks silhouetted in the glare of the main street. But my eyes were on the ocean. Calmer than last night and the tide further out. A couple of small boats patrolled offshore. There weren't many people around. I picked up some milk and a loaf of fairly dry-looking bread at the general store and headed back. I couldn't have been gone more than ten minutes. If that. And when I got back she was gone.

Unable to see her at first, I called her name. The sliding door had been open, although I had closed it behind me when I left. She could well have opened it to get some air. Maybe she'd gone for a little walk as well. I quickly scanned the kitchen, the bathroom and bedroom. No sign of her. The

Laser was still out front – I could see it through the bedroom window. It crossed my mind that she could be playing a joke, lying in wait to surprise me. Casually I headed for the bathroom again. There was a back door to a tiny triangle of scrub behind the villa between the kitchen and bathroom. I jerked the handle but it was locked. The key was in the lock. I opened the door and swept my gaze across the empty garden.

My heart was thumping but I didn't want to acknowledge the fear. It was too early. There were still numerous rational explanations. I walked back to the main door, having to stop myself running headlong into panic. I was sweating now. Just ten minutes in the sun without Joanna's baseball cap to protect my forehead and there was a noticeable tightening of the skin. I'd have to get some sunblock on it. After I'd found Joanna.

She'd gone for a walk. She must have gone for a walk. I trotted down to the side road and looked in both directions. Then down to the main road along the seafront. No sign of her. The wind disguised the ferocity of the sun. A woman stepped out of a Holden Kingswood thirty yards down the road and without locking it walked across to the little tourist information office. In the other direction a man and a girl stood talking to each other outside a low building, the girl occasionally pointing out into the bay. I screwed up my eyes against the sun just to make absolutely certain it wasn't her.

As I walked back to the villa, the fear seeped into every hidden corner of me like sea water rushing into the keel of a ship. My mouth had gone dry, my hands were starting to tremble. Still it was entirely possible Joanna had nipped out for a walk or even was playing a joke. But underneath these pathetic reassurances I knew she'd gone. I knew the goodness had leached out of my life. Someone had whipped out the plug and all I could do was watch my happiness spiral away. I searched the villa and found nothing. I ascertained that her clothes were gone. The clothes she'd been wearing the day before. Blue shorts, dark green T-shirt from Fremantle and worn black deck shoes. I couldn't see her Ray-Bans anywhere. I sat down at the table and composed a little list. Her bag was on the bed, but all along she'd had her passport in the back pocket of her shorts.

There was a horrible feeling growing in my stomach. That I knew exactly what had happened. But I didn't want to think about it.

She hadn't walked out on me. Yes, life can turn around and slap you in the face. It's done it to me before. But this wasn't one of those occasions. It couldn't be an accident that everything had been destroyed.

Suddenly I was aware of my body rising from the table. I'd had a sudden thought, a tiny point of light on which terrible misery and blessed relief pivoted – I strode across to the fridge. She'd gone for a walk and left me a note in the fridge, because that's where I'd go immediately upon returning from buying the milk. And because it was a bit of fun. A message in the fridge. It was a laugh. We liked to laugh. Share little jokes.

The fridge gleamed at me. Empty save for two stubbies of Tooheys Red.

No message. No note scrawled in ballpoint – 'Darling, just gone for a walk. Back in five minutes'.

Nothing.

I went to the front of the villa and stepped outside. Put my hand against the bonnet of the Laser. It was warm but only from the sun. The car had not been disturbed.

There were scuff marks in the gravel. Not necessarily tyre marks, but marks of some kind. *Could* have been made by a set of tyres. Could have been. There were no signs of a struggle. Not even inside the villa.

I ran across to the office, bounded up the narrow flight of steps and pushed my weight against the door, jarring my shoulder because the door was locked. I banged on it, heavily enough almost to break the glass. Even when I could sense movement inside I knocked again. The woman I'd seen when we'd checked in appeared, unlocking the door. She looked alarmed. I was breathless.

'Did you see someone? A few minutes ago. Did you see anyone?'

She looked baffled.

'A car. A man on foot. Anything. My girlfriend's disappeared.'

'Could she have gone for a walk?'

'No!' I shouted and the woman took a step back. 'I'm sorry. Look I'm worried. I don't know where she is. She's disappeared and she hasn't gone for a walk. I was only gone ten minutes, getting some milk. Are you sure you didn't see a car or hear one? Someone must have seen or heard something.' I was getting desperate.

'There *was* a car around at some point.' She was shaking her head and frowning as she concentrated. 'It was kind of in the background? I mean, it could have been one of the guests going out for the day. I don't know.'

I gripped my jaw with my hand, aware that it was trembling.

'Think, please. What did you see? What colour was it?'

The woman screwed up her face. 'White, I think. Yeah. There was a white car.'

'Did you see her at all, my girlfriend?'

She thought for a moment. 'I'm afraid I didn't.'

'I'm not imagining her, you know. I . . .' I didn't know what to say or what to do and I sensed that time was vital. It was slipping away as I panicked. 'I want to call the police.'

'The nearest police station is in Kalbarri,' she said. 'I can get you the number.' But as she turned to go inside I swivelled around on the step and ran back to the villa. I had to do something. I couldn't sit around waiting for some country cop to come bumbling over to see me. I grabbed a couple of things out of the villa and jumped into the car. Maybe I wasn't thinking straight, but I had to do something. I scribbled

Joanna a quick note and ran back inside with it. As I reversed out of the lot, wheelspinning in the gravel, I realised I was erasing the scuff marks I'd seen earlier but that was too bad. As the Laser swung around and bounced on its front suspension I caught sight of the woman who had returned to the top of the steps, her face a flash double-exposure of concern and suspicion. I gunned the old Ford up the hill out of town to the east and Monkey Mia.

MITRAL VALVE

Under normal circumstances, the mitral valve – bicuspid, like a bishop's mitre – prevents backflow into the left atrium.

Michael McNally draped the grubby white coat on the back of the chair, just as he'd found it. No doubt belonged to a doctor or lab technician at some point in the not too distant. McNally didn't know how long ago they'd closed down the hospital. It wasn't his business to know. His business was to guard the place against intruders.

His oppo, Paz, found St George's creepy. Didn't like going on patrol. McNally's favourite part of the job. For a start it got him away from Paz for half an hour. The kid asked so many questions. And he was a northerner; McNally distrusted northerners. Scallies looking to steal his job off him, or long-haired Mancs on drugs. He didn't know where Paz was from. Bewsey, he'd said. Wherever that was. Marcus Paramor, they christened him. No wonder he called himself Paz.

A sudden skittering caused McNally to swing around on his chair, shining his Mag-Lite down a festering, plaster-strewn corridor.

Nothing.

A rat, probably, or a pigeon.

Nothing would get in past McNally, save the vermin. He took his job seriously. You had to if you wanted to hold on to it.

But it went deeper than that with McNally. It was personal. He felt more like a bodyguard.

He depressed the off-switch on the Mag-Lite – it affected his night vision if he used it all the time – and got up from the old workbench where he'd settled for a few minutes' rest. He looked at the row of chairs, some tucked under the bench, others pulled out, facing away. Whenever McNally sat down like this for a moment while on patrol, he always made sure to put his chair back exactly in the right place. If he picked anything up, it was put down precisely where it had been. He was careful like that. He'd been brought up to be. Neat and tidy does it. If he came across exposed electrical wires, he gaffer-taped them up, even though the current was meant to be off.

Michael McNally headed for the stairwell at the far end of the lab. He wanted to have another look at the wards upstairs before heading back to his and Paz's station near the hospital's front entrance. Over the last week or so, McNally had formed the impression that he and his oppo were not always the only individuals in the abandoned building. He'd found the odd window open, but couldn't rule out Paz or the Sunday relief guys being responsible. The signs that aroused his suspicion were subtler: a swivel-chair that looked as if it had been swivelled; a rearrangement in the pattern of broken glass underfoot in certain corridors; clear circles on a dust-covered work surface; slide boxes, Petri dishes covered with fresh dabs.

If someone was coming in – squatters, vandals, looters – they'd not get away with it. Not as long as Michael McNally was on the job. He didn't actually need Paz. It had occurred to him to say as much to his guvnor. Get rid of Paz and jack up my wages by fifty per cent – you'll still save half of what you're paying him. It wasn't that he didn't have the bottle, more that he was worried he'd find himself slung out on his ear.

There was his mother to think of as well. She'd not been happy when he was on the dole. Preferred her rent coming in regular. And Michael out of the way instead of under her feet all the time, picking things up and putting them down again.

'Put that down and get out of my way, Michael McNally, you great big lump,' she'd order him about when he followed her from room to room. Not that there were that many rooms to choose from in their Catford conversion. The same place they'd been in ever since his mother and father moved down from Bedford, before Michael was born. Collapsing piles of overdue large-print library books. Pictures of Jesus on every wall. When Michael learned in school that the heart was situated on the left side of the chest, he asked his mother why the pictures showed Jesus with a bloody wound on his right side. Which earned him a sharp clip to the left side of the head.

McNally stopped. It was always difficult to tell where noises came from in the hospital. Many of them were just the building's natural acoustics. A test-tube rolling off a lab-top and shattering in the west wing could set off a chain of reverberations which reached you, in the upper sections over-looking Knightsbridge, as a rubber-soled sneaker squelching through rotten underfelt.

He jumped when his radio crackled into life.

'All right, Michael?'

'What's up?' he said.

'Nowt,' said Paz. 'Just checking everything's all right.'

'Everything *is* all right. Over.'

And out. McNally switched the radio off so that Paz wouldn't be able to call him back. Proceeded down the gloomy passageway that led to the back stairs to the east wing.

McNally had an idea someone might be coming in from the pizza place next door. A few nights earlier he'd disturbed two rats fighting over a scrap of old crust. Another time he'd spotted a red napkin screwed up in a ball. He'd been in there himself for a takeaway one night at the start of his shift, his mother not having bothered to cook anything for his dinner. He'd not been in since. Not his scene. Posh blonde girl had stopped him as he wandered in. Expensive-looking white shirt open to her waist, more or less. He knew what his mother would have called her – a whore. He said the word to himself under his breath, to protect himself, while she took his order. She made him sit down at a table to wait. He admired his uniform in the mirrored wall. Navy jacket and trousers, white shirt, black clip-on tie. Epaulettes, silver buckle and buttons. Name of the security firm on the badge on his cap.

She brought him his pizza in a box. Couple of red napkins on top. Bent double when she gave it to him. Shirt gaping. Whore. He got flustered. Gave her too much money, had to wait for his change. As he scuttled out, vowed never to go back.

Between the restaurant and the hospital there was a bus stop. A group of girls stood waiting. He took a detour so he wouldn't have to walk past them. Were all girls whores, or just the ones in London? He'd hardly been outside the capital. One trip to the railway museum in York with his mother and father when he was fourteen. He'd been to school in Catford, grown up there, looked for work there – building sites, shelf-stacking, security work. The hospital job was the best he'd had. Be ideal if it wasn't for that wanker Paz sitting there with his *Sunday Sport* that he managed to make last all week. By Friday it was all creased and furry. Full of filthy pictures. McNally imagined it was the sort of paper his father would read, wherever *he* was nowadays.

McNally stopped as he reached the top step. Strained his eyes to see in the poor light. Concentrated on the sound he thought he'd heard. Tried to hear it again in his head. A sound he'd heard before too many times.

Like a warped door in damp weather with a dodgy hinge.

Only a woman could make a sound like that.

He first heard it when he was thirteen. Came in the flat one day to hear that sound. Couldn't work out what it was. Thought his mother must be in pain. Silently opened the door to the TV room. His father kneeling behind his mother on the couch, shunting into her. She was on hands and knees, her unpinned hair obscuring her face, and that sound came from her. The sound, the bizarreness of the situation, the confusion as to whether she needed his help or not – these things transfixed Michael so that he was standing there for some time before his father became aware of his presence and roared at him: 'Get over here yer little bastard. If you want to watch, you can watch all right. Watch all you fuckin' like.' He'd marched across the room and grabbed Michael by the arm, dragged him across to the couch where his mother had curled up in a ball, crying, begging to be left alone. His father hit him, then he hit Michael's mother.

Maybe it wouldn't have been so bad in the long run, if his father had left at that point. But he stayed, and every time he wanted to have sex he made Michael watch. He called Michael's mother a whore and he hit her. She never fought back, just started crying.

When he was out – and they could be sure he wasn't suddenly going to come back in – Michael sat with his mother and tried to comfort her. He told her he'd kill him to protect her. He wouldn't let him touch her again. But she just put her arm around him and shushed him. 'It'll be all right, Michael. It'll all be all right one day. You'll see.'

Two years later, he'd gone. No explanation, no note. There one day, gone the next.

The moment they'd been waiting for proved impossible to enjoy. Wherever they sat in the tiny flat, Michael's father seemed to hover within a few feet of them. His mother no longer cuddled him, but Michael forgave her. She wouldn't allow girlfriends in the flat. She wouldn't even allow talk of them. Consequently there weren't any, but Michael didn't need any: he worshipped her. All other women were whores.

The sound came again. Drifting down the long corridor to where Michael McNally stood, his head cocked to one side, at the top of the east wing back stairs.

That warped door sound.

McNally checked his back pocket. Non-regulation cuffs where he wanted them, just in case. He hefted his Mag-Lite and started to make his way quietly down the corridor towards where the sound was coming from.

LEFT VENTRICLE

*The powerhouse of the heart, pumping oxygenated blood
out through the aorta into the arterial circulation. Its ability to
adapt to stress is also its weakness: prolonged stress leads to
maladaption and a rapid decline to heart failure or death.*

Nineteen

From Denham to Monkey Mia is a distance of twenty-six
Ks. The road is not of a bad standard, Monkey Mia, I now
gather, being the major tourist attraction in WA. The idea is
you hang around on the beach at the visitor centre, having paid
three bucks or whatever to get in, until at some point during
the day the dolphins get their act together and swim inshore.
Then you get to wade knee-deep and allow them to come up to
you.

Sometimes you can sit on the beach all day while around you
young girls point ramrod-straight chocolate-brown arms each
time a dorsal fin breaks the surface sixty yards out. The dolphins
don't feel like coming in today and you're not allowed to swim out
within the area marked off by buoys. Apparently the dolphins
respect the markers too and don't swim either side of the red lines,
so that although you might swim out a hundred yards, two
hundred yards down the beach, all you're likely to encounter is a
nest of hammerhead sharks. Oh yes. The bay is teeming with
hammerheads. In addition to sea turtles and dugong. Joanna had
been excited about the possibility of seeing dugong.

I could think about nothing else as I forced the Laser,
screaming in protest at being constantly pushed beyond
the limit, over the twenty-six Ks to Monkey Mia.

Dugong, dugong, dugong.

Joanna had wanted to see some dugong. And it wasn't fair

that she should come all this way and not see any. She hadn't seen them on her last trip. I was determined she would see them this time. If any dugong were currently tooling around in Shark Bay I wanted to know about it and I wanted Joanna back with me so she could see them.

The way the mind works when you're driving.

Making a real effort to stay calm, I skidded in the car park at Monkey Mia, raising a cloud of sand which drifted in through my open window and settled on the dashboard. I noticed the guy at the ticket booth looking at me and I ignored him, gazing instead at the cars parked along the row.

No clues. Not yet.

I had an idea, but it was only an idea. I didn't want to admit to myself the possibility that it might be real.

I left the car and ran to the visitor centre and beach. The place was crawling with young girls from Sydney, Melbourne, Düsseldorf. There was one lone Japanese cyclist. I screwed up my eyes against the blinding sunlight, wondering if it could be him, the same one. I ran into the information centre, tricked into a double-take when a girl stepped up to the counter behind me. Something about her hair, the set of her shoulders – but when I improved the angle I saw she was an over-developed teenager. Back out to the beach where a crowd had formed by the water. I trotted down the soft, sandy beach, sweat beginning to escape from my hairline. A guy in a lilac Monkey Mia T-shirt was standing in the water, two dolphins at his feet and a crowd of smiling people gathered around him. One or two reached out a tentative arm and the guy in the T-shirt offered advice that was friendly but firm. I scanned the faces among the crowd which was maybe thirty strong. Satisfied that Joanna's was not among them, I left the water's edge and headed back up the beach, my mind trying to cope with the first disappointment. It had been worth a try, given that I had no idea where on earth she might be.

But was that strictly true?

As I was leaving the car park I stopped by the ticket booth to speak to the guy. No, as far as he could recall, he hadn't seen an old white Mercedes that morning.

And why should he have done?

Watch your back, that's all.

He would have noticed the headlights, he said, when I described them to him. 'Just like figure 8s,' I said. He shook his head.

After twenty minutes' hard drive I was back in Denham. I checked the villa, which was empty, and went in to pay the woman for another two nights. I felt that might help. To bring her back. At least if she came back now, she'd have somewhere to stay. As I rolled the Laser slowly out of town I fought back hot tears: panic wouldn't help. Not in this situation. I had to keep my head clear. I imagined my mind as a radio receiver waiting for the right signal. I had to keep out the white noise of distraction. I had to think clearly and rationally.

If there was one shred of comfort it was the fact that Danny's car had been facing south, according to Nick, sitting in a kind of layby pointing south to Perth. If indeed Danny had killed Z right there in that layby – and I didn't by any means know that for certain – he'd hardly have turned around and headed back the way they'd been. People who'd seen them together asking awkward questions. 'Where's your wife today, mate?' Having done it, *if* he'd done it, he would surely have carried on going south out of trouble. Not north. Not Shark Bay.

A few hundred yards out of town to the south I performed my first ever handbrake turn, raising a cloud of dust you could have seen for miles, and motored back into Denham, taking the sharp right out of the town – the road to Monkey Mia once more. I'd noticed a sign on my way to and from Monkey Mia, pointing to Little Lagoon. Just five minutes out of town and each time I'd passed it before I'd made a mental note that it might be worth a look.

When I saw the sign for the third time I yanked the wheel

sharply to the left and the tyres skittered over the rough, potholed surface. I came down over the brow and Little Lagoon opened up before me like a picture postcard. Almost a perfect circle, maybe a couple of hundred yards across, with a narrow creek running to the ocean at the western end, and occasional dead trees stuck up in the bush away from the shore on the landward side. Tyre tracks led down towards the lagoon and swung around in both directions once they reached the beach. There were no cars present. I allowed the Laser to roll down the remainder of the gentle slope then turned right, unconsciously avoiding the sets of tracks already laid down. When the car came to a natural halt I pulled on the handbrake and switched off the engine. As it ticked and cooled I listened out for any ambient noise.

There wasn't a single sound.

No birds animated the stark outlines of the two or three dead gum trees. No fish broke the mirrored surface of the lagoon. If any spiders scuttled across the scrubby earth they did so noiselessly. I got out of the car and walked down to the water's edge. It was very shallow. I kicked off my pumps and walked in a few yards. Underfoot the sand here became slimy and slippery. I trod carefully. Recalling how in the past whenever I needed to think something over, the only way to accomplish it was to go for a walk, either in the local park or out on the Dark Peak, whatever, I started walking slowly around the edge of the lagoon, a few yards in, where the water was only inches deep. I had to find Joanna but didn't have a clue where she was. I had an *idea* that someone might have taken her and who that someone might be, but at this stage it was just an idea and I didn't want to give it too much credence for fear of turning it into a possibility. I splashed on through the shallows, imagining Joanna laid out on the long, leather back seat of an old Merc, her hair blowing in the wind that came in via the driver's window. Or trussed up in the boot, terrified and breathless with panic.

I picked up my speed and splashed on around the lagoon. As

I neared the eastern side I found I was trotting through fine scum and a film of bubbles. A faint breeze had stirred and was blowing this stuff across the lagoon from the ocean.

She could be sitting in the front seat, relatively relaxed, having bought some line about Christ knows what. Dodging clumps of seaweed, here a dead Taylor, bold and silver-flanked, there a once-proud black-backed iron bar of a gull. My breath coming in rapid, short, shallow pants. She could be lying in the gravel and dust by the side of the road cast from a passing car like a brown stubbie, one leg bent at an impossible angle, her clothes torn, her neck twisted mercilessly to expose her satin-soft skin to the sun.

I forced the image from my mind, breathing in four stages: two pants in, two pants out. Legs pumping automatically. Rhythmically. Breaking my stride only to wade across the deeper channel where the lagoon was fed by the tide. Back to full stretch by the dead gum trees, but getting nowhere. A tatter of crows collapsing upwards like ashes from a fire. Beating sun on the tops of my shoulders, sweat running down my chest. Joanna driving, while he sits in the passenger seat, a tiny gun pressed into her perfect neck.

Why though? Why would he want to? What possible motive could he have?

I sprawled in the sand by the edge of the lagoon after a complete circuit, praying that she was still as alive as I felt at that moment.

The run didn't help. My thoughts had discovered no better order. My fear had not been mitigated by exercise. My mind still flew from one desperate scenario to another. Above all, I hoped she'd merely deserted. Needed time to think. Maybe even made the decision really to go. Then at least I'd be able to comfort myself with the thought that no one had died – the bottom line. Always the bottom line, no matter what. If you're not alive you're nothing.

I'd always believed it, and yet Charlie had got me thinking. It was the one truth I didn't want to be true.

I started the Laser and slewed away from the lagoon, heading for drier sand, the track back to the road. I noticed the same tyre tracks but thought little of them. They were just there. They'd most likely still be there tomorrow. Few people seemed to visit Little Lagoon – I wondered why. In the time it had taken me to negotiate its perimeter – half an hour or thereabouts – I hadn't seen a soul.

I made the road and turned right, back to Denham. I almost didn't check back at the villa, thinking I couldn't waste the few minutes it would take. But at the last minute I pulled over and ran inside. Made sure. Grabbed my remaining things and was gone again.

Straight out of town to the south-east. Not that there was much choice. There was only one way off the peninsula. Only one road.

My foot lifted an inch as the thought struck me that there were other ways of getting about. She could be on a boat. I remembered from our drive north a small airstrip just near the odd depression where I'd got out and felt the strange spongy vegetation.

My foot went back down again. If she'd been taken by sea or by air there was nothing I could do. I had to do the least that I could. And that was to check back the way we'd come, looking for something, anything. Looking for a clue.

I noticed the sign for Eagle Bluff and swerved wildly into the dirt track, the wheels bouncing over increasingly rugged terrain. A four-wheel drive would have been useful. I didn't wish to consider the possibility that my quarry was driving such a vehicle. If that were the case we didn't stand a chance. I simply had to hope and explore every avenue.

There were two other cars in the parking area at Eagle Bluff. A four-wheel drive Jeep and an older VW camper van that looked oddly familiar. Since there was no one in sight, I sneaked a look inside the Jeep. A road map, a couple of country cassettes, a box of tissues and a big pot of vitamin E cream. A discarded T-shirt and a pair of trainers. Nothing of Joanna's.

The camper van was parked right next to it. I had widened the angle to the lookout point and could now see a man standing with a pair of binoculars looking out to sea. He was little more than a silhouette so I peered into the van. Empty Marlboro packets, cellophane wrappers, a wide-brimmed hat (man's), a towel and a coolbox. On the front passenger seat was a clipboard, looseleaf pages lined with columns of figures. I caught sight of a tracing of a tyre tread.

Interesting.

On the floor a scattering of Tooheys Red bottle tops, a white bra. I studied the bra, which lay partly concealed by a diagram of scorchmarks on the road that had fallen from the clipboard. It didn't look like one of Joanna's but could I be sure?

I straightened my back and stretched. The sun was fierce: I'd left my hat in the car. I hoped this wouldn't take long. If the coast was clear I wanted to get back on the road as quickly as possible. I walked up towards the bluff itself. The silhouetted figure resolved itself as a man of about sixty, hooped T-shirt, big belly and baggy shorts, examining the view through a pair of powerful-looking binoculars.

'G'day,' he said as I came alongside him.

'Hi there.'

The view was spectacular, a vast panorama of clear, shallow bay. The water appeared no more than a few inches deep, yet that had to be an illusion. A few hundred yards away were two small islands – rocky, wild places, overflown by a single, large bird. Beyond those were further islands and promontories. I knew Dirk Hartog Island was out there to the right. And Useless Loop.

Useless Loop. That struck a chord.

'See that?' the man said, pointing with one hand to a black cruciform speck in the shallows.

I squinted, shielded my eyes. He passed me the binoculars.

'Thanks,' I said, refocusing and scanning the shallows, running past the tiny black shape and returning to it. 'Yes. I see it.' It was swimming. The scale was hard to judge. Turtle? Shark? Or just a big ray?

'Dugong,' said the man.

'Really?'

'Dugong.'

I found myself dragging the glasses around to view the rest of the bay. I saw a large bird fly between the two rocky islets in the foreground. Black and white. An osprey. Although I was aware of the man at my side making almost inaudible clucks of impatience, I kept on turning, running the twin 'scopes up the steep cliff to our right until I reached the top – and there, perched at the highest point, were a man and a woman. I lowered the binoculars and screwed up my eyes against the sun to get the bigger picture. A man and a woman – she was leaning against him – he was wearing some sort of bush hat and gazing out to sea.

I handed the binoculars back to the Queenslander (the plates on the Jeep which I figured was his) and he grunted. I started walking in the direction of the pair, up a steep, sandy slope. It wasn't long before I could see that the woman was shorter than Joanna. The man was in his late forties, early fifties, kind features.

I reached the top slightly out of breath.

'How's it going?' the man asked.

I said: 'Hi.'

'It's quite a climb.'

'Yeah.'

'And quite a view.'

The woman slid around from the man's lee side and greeted me languidly. She looked as if she'd only just got up. Dyed blonde spiky hair all awry, baggy T-shirt, no bra.

'This is Yasmin,' the man said. 'My name's Ambrose. What do you know?'

'Chris.' I reached out a hand to take his. 'It certainly is a view.'

'Yeah.'

The only sound in the hot stillness was my laboured breathing and the faintest murmur from the ocean.

'Useless Loop,' I said.

'Useless Loop.' And he chuckled.

'Is it worth a trip?' I asked.

'Can only do it in a four-wheel drive. Not much there. Pretty much how it sounds.'

'I'm looking for someone.'

'Isn't everyone?' I heard him sucking at his teeth. I wondered if I should have played my hand so rashly. 'Won't find anyone there. It's a wild place.'

'Last place they'd expect me to look?'

'Two of them now, eh?'

'May I?' I pointed at the field glasses slung around his neck.

'Be my guest.'

Yasmin sparked up a cigarette, wandered around in a useless loop of her own, kicking up sand, bored.

I couldn't see any more than I'd seen with the older guy's binoculars.

'Maybe you've seen his car,' I said, not lowering the glasses. 'It's quite an unusual one. A Mercedes 280SE.'

'Very nice,' he said slowly. 'But how do you know it's a 280SE?'

'Someone told me. Apparently it has unique headlights. Like figure 8s.'

'Almost unique, mate. Almost unique. Had 'em as well on the 300SEL. Slightly different model. Heavier. And the 220SE come to that, and the 250SE, but you won't find so many of those around these days.'

'You're an expert.'

'Kind of. Self-taught. Bugger all else to do.'

Behind him, Yasmin had started to hum to show how bored she was.

'Yeah, the 220, 250 and 280SE and the 300SEL were just

about the only models to carry the Americana headlights. And the 280SE is by far the most common, which isn't to say there are that many around. Have you seen this guy's car?'

'No.' I handed the glasses back to Ambrose. 'To be honest I don't even know if it's him. But it's all I've got to go on.'

'Not sure I follow you, mate.'

'He's a friend of a friend. I think he lives out here these days. I don't know.' I looked out at the enormous flat mirror of the bay. Once more the osprey flew between the two islands in the foreground. 'I'm here on holiday with my girlfriend. She's gone missing. I think she may have gone off with him.'

'You mean he's taken her?'

'He could have done.'

Sweat rolled down my back. I wondered if it was wise to trust this man. And this woman for that matter. Yasmin had perked up slightly at the mention of a possible kidnapping. She was looking at me, shielding her eyes with one brown hand. Her features were a strange, unidentifiable and attractive mixture of races. She was a lot younger than Ambrose. I wondered distractedly how they might have got together and why they stuck with each other.

But the more I explained, the deeper I felt the fix I was in to be. And not just me obviously: I was anxious for Joanna. Especially if she had actually been taken by Danny; if what Joanna's friend Nick had said to me about the white Merc were true; and if the man in question was indeed Max's old ally.

'I might just be able to help you,' Ambrose said.

'Yeah?'

'If you're sure he drives this car, this Mercedes . . . I'm engaged on a project, a piece of research.' Ambrose's tone had become wistful, contemplative. He was staring out across the bay. Yasmin had become bored again and was picking up stones and lobbing them over the edge.

Two minutes later we were down by Ambrose's VW van with the sliding door open. Ambrose was digging out huge piles of papers while Yasmin curled up on the back seat sucking her thumb. Dozens of pages of diagrams – sketches of roads with arrows off indicating the directions of crashing cars – and graphs and statistical charts and photographs of scorchmarks cascaded on to the floor.

'Careful,' I said, making to pick them up for him. 'They'll get all out of order.'

'They're all in here, mate,' he said, tapping the side of his head. 'All in here. And believe it or not—' he reached further into the vehicle '—I know exactly what I'm looking for and where it should be.' As he burrowed further in and papers flew I stepped back and stretched and took stock. The thought crossed my mind that I was wasting valuable time with this madman when I should be on the road, actually doing something about finding Joanna. The other car, I noticed, the older guy from Queensland, had gone.

Ambrose was leaning back out of the van brandishing a sheaf of papers.

'Here you go, mate,' he was saying. 'I knew they were there somewhere.'

'What is it?'

'Look.'

He passed me sheet after sheet, each covered in diagrams, directional arrows, ghost sketches of a car, one or two actual life-size tracings, like brass-rubbings, of tyre scorchmarks on the road.

'So what's all this?' I asked.

'This is a Mercedes 280SE somewhere between Geraldton and Perth going into a handbrake turn and coming to rest by the side of the road.'

'How do you know it's a 280SE?'

He took a deep breath. 'It'll be a W108 chassis, okay? With the kerb weight of a 108 topping 1.2 tons, it's possible to narrow tyre scorch patterns down to a class of cars in a particular weight class.' Ambrose looked at me. He must have seen that I was still unconvinced. 'Look, mate, there's one quality inherent in Mercedes cars, okay? When the rear tyres are elevated from the ground, they bend inwards . . . if you can imagine the bottom edge of the tyres moving towards the differential and the upper edge moving out, away from the wheel arch. It's down to the central spring-type load compensator. Under heavy stress, the tyres bend inwards even when still in contact with the road surface. A lot of the hydraulic compensators on the long-wheel-base 108s have been converted to spring-type anyway. Only cost you two hundred bucks – get a good secondhand one from a wrecking yard.' He paused. 'It's a 280SE. It's your bloke.'

Something about it bothered me, nagged at me. The car was facing south, which was right. Parked up by the side of the road, in a kind of layby, facing south. I studied Ambrose's diagrams. They weren't drawn for me, they were drawn for him, and it took a while to get inside his head. He left gaps which he and only he knew how to fill in.

'Wait a minute,' I whispered.

Inside the van Yasmin moaned in her sleep.

'It's facing south, okay, but what's going on here?' I pointed to a tangle of arrows, a skein of scorchmarks.

'It's facing south when it comes to a rest,' he explained patiently. 'But it *was* pointing north. Look, they were heading north: she says something and *he* yanks on the handbrake. Suddenly they're heading south, you know? Happens all the time.'

'They spun around?'

'Yeah.'

I stepped back out of the van's shadow, straightened my spine, wiped my dripping forehead.

I felt as if my safety net had been spirited away. Danny had been driving north, not south as Nick had thought, when he did for Z – again assuming it was him – so he would most likely have carried on going north. It seemed increasingly likely, as the sun arced infinitesimally slowly across the huge, unclouded sky, that his and Joanna's paths had indeed intersected in

Denham. A tiny, tiny cross on the world's biggest graph.

'I've got to find him,' I said, feeling utterly helpless. 'Maybe you've seen him. He's short but strong-looking, he's a climber. Long grey hair, goatee, baseball cap . . .' Ambrose was shaking his head. 'I don't even know which way to go. North or south . . .'

Ambrose pushed back his sun hat and scratched his forehead. 'Well, there's only one way to go, mate.'

'Which way's that?'

'South, of course.' Ambrose stood with his hands on his hips squinting at me. My puzzlement must have registered because he continued: 'For a start, there's nothing to the north for several hours. Nobody goes north of Carnarvon in this heat, not if they can help it. But more to the point, after a trip like this he's bound to want to go home and that's where he lives. He lives down there.'

I took a sudden step towards Ambrose.

'Where? How do you know?'

'Well, I reckon he does. His car was certainly down there a few days ago. Monday, Tuesday, I dunno. I could look it up though. Fresh tracks, mate.'

'Where? How do you know it was his?'

'Two 280SEs with erratic drivers on the same road in the same week? I don't think so. Try Margaret River, try Pemberton.'

'The same road! That's several hundred miles away.'

'Long roads, mate.'

As I was beginning to think he really meant what he was saying, his manner was getting to irritate me. Perhaps he could see this.

'Look, if you give me a minute I'll find them.' He waited a second or two for a sign from me, which he must have thought I'd given, before turning back to the pile of papers on the floor of the van. Looking at the VW again, I remembered where I might have seen it before: at the motel in Lancelin. I supposed it wasn't that unlikely. It was a big place, but there weren't that many people rattling around in it.

As he shifted another bunch of papers I noticed something on the floor of the van.

'You have a rifle.'

'Yeah. If I find any that are still alive.'

I didn't say anything and eventually he looked at me.

'Roadkill,' he added.

I turned away.

The sun burned. Out in the bay, dugong somersaulted silently in the shallow crystal water. In a fucked up old Mercedes, a hundred miles from nowhere, Joanna strained at her wrist bonds. And I did nothing. I waited for an armed obsessive in a sun hat to stop shuffling papers around on the floor of his knackered old van.

I had to hand it to myself. I was fucking up big time.

Twenty

It's been said before but I'll say it again. Places look different when you're on your way back. They not only *look* different, they *are* different. Driving south, I was following a route laid down by myself and Joanna a few days earlier, an emotional route for sure, but I was now passing through a subtly altered landscape.

A landscape in which Joanna was, but was no more. Every so often I would check the rearview mirror. Not for possible pursuers but to remind myself of the route north. I felt that the road surface shimmered not with the heat of my passing, but with the ghost track of our journey in the opposite direction.

The drive south was unreal, a bad trip, a long nightmare of unbearable, choking heat and stinging dust devils – whirling willies. Dancing red columns in the air ahead so insubstantial you thought you'd imagined them. They melted away into nothing then re-formed, twisting ever closer and stronger. Your elbow felt it, sticking out of the car window, the spinning sand attacking with the sudden ferocity of a thousand tiny needles.

Ambrose had shown me two more sets of scorchmarks placing the 280SE firstly on the road between Margaret River and Busselton and secondly on Stewarts Lane, a twenty-kilometre dirt track through the karri forest linking two sections of the road from Pemberton to Margaret River. To my untutored eye there was little difference between these marks and the hundreds of others spilling out of his looseleaf folders, but his confidence was utterly convincing. Also, I had to believe there was a way to find Joanna. I pushed the Laser down the coastal highway, occasional gum trees flying past, the ocean a bright blur on my right; I sensed that from the air I would be but crawling through this vast landscape. Sometimes hot tears sprang up behind my eyes, waiting there like sprinters on blocks, and I had to force them back. I couldn't waste a second.

I stopped only when I had to, to take on board fuel. A tank full of petrol. A hot meat pie and a cool bottle of Snapple, then back on the road. I tried to think about Charlie in order not to dwell on Joanna, but whenever I did I ended up thinking about my father. Long car journeys to the Lakes or Northumberland. Scotland. My mother sitting in front of me smelling of Chanel No 5 – my father used to get it for her off the ships. He'd brought his old Phillips cassette player into the car and wired it up to the battery. It sat behind the gear box between the front two seats, a narrow selection of tapes playing over and over. It would seem primitive now, but then it was a small piece of magic. The tapes were bright green and printed with the BASF logo. Annie Ross, Louis Jordan, 'Round the Horne' and the Goons. 'He's Innocent of Watergate' by Peter Sellers.

Back to now: Joni Mitchell – 'Turbulent Indigo'. 'The Sire of Sorrow'. On the other side, 'Beginning to Melt' from Medium Series Volume 1: Richard Barbieri, Steve Jansen, Mick Karn. Blue skies, orange dust, white heat. Ford Laser. One hundred and ten kph. Kangaroos next ninety-six km. Cervantes Pinnacles Motel twenty-six km.

I watched the highway peel away from the earth and twist around towards the ocean, and thought of the Westway by Paddington Green. Nodes of recognition, knots on string. Euston Road, Marylebone Road. If you land on the Euston Road at the right time and proceed at the right speed you can get all the way to the beginning of the Westway on green. You keep to a steady thirty-five mph. I know. I've done it. Going to see Joanna. I'm keeping to a steady hundred and twenty kph now, counting off knots on a different rope. Again a rope, I hope, which will pull me in to her – but a different one, a different route. Same emotions, different route.

An occasional flick of some dark tail at the edge of the road, corner of my eye. Not an abandoned stubbie; a lizard or a snake. Brown, gone. No more than a hallucination. Sweat rolling down my back. Still taking care to slap on some cream. Behave as if normal. Don't let go. Carry on. Panic no help. Geraldton, Lancelin, Yanchep National Park. Stopped somewhere – had to – couldn't just go on and go on. Stopped, got a room. Sun went down. Slept. Wild, vivid dreams. Escaping from somewhere. Another searingly hot day. Itching neck. Easing back into the Laser like into a saddle. Heading south. Perth, Fremantle, a blur. Cars around me south of Perth driven by automata. Elbows sticking out of windows, farmers, tourists. People who haven't got a clue about me or my problems. People with problems of their own. Industry. Billboards. The ocean no longer so beauti-ful, even a few clouds. Fluffy, white. A marina, yachts. Traffic lights. Little towns, suburbs. *Neighbours* country. I put my foot down, passed Kingswoods, Toyotas, Fords, Nissans. A stumpy little Mazda we didn't yet have in the UK and Christ you could see why. Ugly little fucker. Why anyone would buy one, beyond me. Heading due south. Clouds dispersed. Late afternoon. Pull into cute little town, teashop with wooden terrace by road, park Laser, amble across. Aching back. Had enough. Cup of tea. Slice of cake. Think about Joanna. As if I have to try. Can't get her out of my head. Every time I see a white car I start. If it's a Mercedes I taste adrenaline. Real fear. Tension knots my muscles. Sit back, relax. Have another cup of tea. Two minutes I'll be back on the road. Only hours away now. Two at the most.

Twenty-one

By the time I reached Margaret River I had found a new equilibrium. My subconscious must have finally realised that I couldn't carry on at the same frenetic rate. The only thing that mattered was getting Joanna back, and in as many ways as I could think of, the frenzied tension of the last couple of days was not going to achieve that. I don't know if it was the survival instinct, my brain's own startling efficiency or simply the roads. The long open roads and the driving. There's no experience quite like it. You can't think in the same way as when walking or lying still, you can't plot stuff out – I'd tried blocking scenes like a director, placing Danny, Joanna and myself on the proscenium arch that is the bottom corner of Western Australia, and working out ways to close the triangle then break it wide open again. But it couldn't be done, not at the wheel of a car.

I couldn't even fall back on the Method: if Danny *had* kidnapped Joanna, his motive, assuming he had one at all, was a complete mystery.

Driving, your mind is freed up in a particular way and lateral thinking takes over, whether you plan it or not – ideas drift by like vehicles going in the opposite direction, and the most you can hope to do is get a good look at them, maybe establish momentary eye contact with the driver.

I booked into a motel just north of the town. On the edge of the forest. That was its name. The Edge of the Forest. I stayed in a pleasant, wood-panelled chalet-style room with colour TV and a telephone which I used only to pre-order breakfast. I went out and ate dinner in a small restaurant in the town. It was one of those tiny settlements that have one main road running through it and little else. A few shops and places to eat and drink, houses and motels, a garage. Everywhere I went I kept my eyes peeled for a white Mercedes. I even made a few casual enquiries, at the filling station and with the waitress who gave me my check. No one recalled seeing such a car. After dinner I drove out of town towards the ocean to check out the surrounding area. The scenery was green and the air pleasantly cool in comparison to Fremantle and beyond. Impassive-looking 'roos eyed me from the paddocks as I rolled by in the Laser. When I reached the edge of the land I pulled on the handbrake in a little car park on top of a bluff and watched a surfer way down below glide in on a curling carpet of waves, finally collapse after a number of near misses close in to shore, and slowly swim back out again, a hundred yards or more. I watched him for several minutes, dully impressed by his dedication to an apparently pointless but obviously addictive pastime. In a way I envied him.

When I checked out of the motel in the morning I hung around in the lobby flicking through the rack of leaflets for local tourist attractions. I kept one for Jewel Cave, slipping it into the back pocket of my shorts. The manageress was still annotating her booking forms at the desk behind me. When I'd arrived the day before she'd taken a note of the Laser's licence plate. I asked her if a man and a woman had stayed here recently. White Mercedes, old model. 'I don't remember. I'm sorry,' she said. 'We have a lot of visitors this time of year.'

'I'm sure.'

I got back on the road, driving slowly through the town, headed south. It was like being either in a different country, or a different season. Compared to the north, this was more like spring in Scotland. A warm spring, but refreshing after the arid conditions beyond Fremantle. There was a tiny gas station on the south side of town. I rolled the Laser round by the pump and tugged on the handbrake. I filled the tank and trotted inside to pay. There was a drinks cooler behind the guy who took my credit card. Behind him to the right, my right not his. His left. I could see the exterior of the gas station and the road reflected in it. A white car had gone past. Just a blur now, but a white blur. I spun around and just made out its rear end as it motored south.

I looked back at the guy. He was still waiting for clearance to come through. I got agitated. It mightn't have been them. Probably wasn't even a Merc. But it might have been. There'd been more than a hint of an old Merc's subtly squared-off back end.

'Did you see the car that just went past?' I asked the man. 'Did you see it?'

'What's that, mate?'

'Nothing. Could you hurry, please? I'm in a hurry.'

'Just gotta go through, mate.'

I thought it was going to take for ever. As soon as he handed me the card and the receipt I snatched at them and ran outside. I had the engine turning and first gear selected before I'd even closed the driver's door. I didn't check to make sure the road was clear before swinging into the left-hand lane and throttling down hard. Two hundred yards ahead another white car turned into the main road from the left. I swung out to the right to overtake but there was something coming from the opposite direction. I hung on desperately thinking he'd shift over or slam on the brakes, but he just kept on coming. I kept on going and he kept on coming, but I gave in, pulling sharply back into the left lane. His horn distorted as we passed each other and finally I was able to swerve back out and pass the white Mazda. I had, however, lost some valuable time.

Soon I was deep inside the karri forest, dwarfed by huge trees some forty metres tall on both sides of the road. I kept my foot on the floor but there was no sign ahead of the white car. When the signs for the caves started appearing I debated. I didn't have long. I reckoned I'd do a sweep of the car park from the road without having to stop, but when Jewel Cave approached fast on the right I saw it had its own turning. The car park was some fifty yards away through the trees. I couldn't be sure and I didn't want to overrun. I laid down a scorchmark for Ambrose to pore over at some future point as I swung around at the last minute and headed down to the Jewel Cave car park. Instantly I saw that my instinct had been correct.

In the car park, close to the exit, was an old white Mercedes with Americana headlamps.

There was little room either side to squeeze the Laser and in any case, there was a parking attendant beckoning me towards the far corner of the clearing in the forest. Reluctantly I jerked the wheel around and rolled over to the spot he was indicating.

I left the car unlocked and ran across to the ticket window, noticing that a group of brightly coloured tourists was already being swallowed in the mouth of the entrance to the cave. The figure in the ticket window, bobbing about behind the glass, indicated I would have to hurry. It was an hour and a half until the next guided tour, he was telling me as I shoved the money across the counter. I ran across and was the last one in through the big iron door which was then snapped shut behind me. Panting for breath, I counted heads. I was with about fifteen people in an airlock. At least one party had already made it through to the next vestibule. The guide was explaining to the crowd why it was important to maintain the airlock system. Her words drifted over my head as I covertly scanned the other faces.

Unless he'd had extensive plastic surgery in the intervening years (since the photograph I'd seen), Danny was not here. Nor, clearly, was Joanna.

'. . . up to twenty-five thousand years old, which is actually very young. Old limestone can be up to four hundred million years old . . . So now we go down and be careful of the steps, they can be a little bit slippy.'

Beyond the airlock was a fifteen-second elevator ride followed by a series of steps. At the foot of the steps we hit a wooden platform where the first group was waiting. About the same number but with their backs to us, they stood at a guard rail gazing out across the first chamber of the cavern. There were several figures, indistinguishable from each other in the semi-gloom, who could just about fit the bill from the back. Our newly arrived group shuffled forward to peer over the shoulders of those already present. I was shunted towards the right-hand edge of the mass and couldn't get a good look at any of the Danny candidates. The guide was explaining something to do with the limestone formations but I wasn't taking it in. I was craning my neck to get a look over the taller people close to me. For once it was a definite advantage not being taller myself. Danny, too, was a small man. But I imagined him as wiry and packed with strength, muscles twitching in his arms as I came at him. The guide was stepping out along a wooden walkway which became a bridge over part of the chamber before reaching another set of steps where we descended further. In between the shuffling of moccasinned feet you could hear the age-old drip-drip-drip of the water that made the limestone. Strategic spotlighting illuminated sections of the cavern where the limestone stretched and gaped like some

twisted, inflamed human anatomy under the surgeon's endo-
scope. Delicate membranous skin pulled taut by invisible ropes
of time across the earth's windpipe. If this were a body it was
one that had lain undiscovered for some months. Garish
photographs scattered throughout the glossy pages of the
Colour Atlas of Forensic Pathology. The corpse was bound and
gagged in the back of an old saloon car. Harpstrings of saliva
furred with salty deposits petrified by the intense heat. A
Mercedes 280SE. White. Americana headlamps.

Surely this place more than any other would disabuse Max
of his ridiculous notion that time did not exist. I wished he
were here now. I could show him the rows of stalagmites and
stalactites, closing on each other as slowly and inexorably as
the enormous jaws of a T Rex.

At the bottom of the next jerry-built staircase people had
gathered again but in the semi-darkness and with the density
of the group I didn't have a hope of spotting Danny. Plus I had
to keep out of his sight. It was possible he would recognise me,
the same way I would surely know him if I were to get a clear
look at him: years back, Max might well have shown him a
photograph of me. I hadn't changed that much. Darker
shadows under the eyes maybe, and longer hair, but still pretty
much the same guy. It could be in his interest to create a
commotion and claim I was harassing him, get the guide on his
side, have me arrested. The guide meanwhile was saying something about one of the forms on our right. In a rustling
movement, everyone turned to gaze at the longest, thinnest
stalactite you could imagine. Longest in the world, she was
saying. 'The carbonated water trickles down the length of the
stalactite and forms a drip at the end. Over thousands of years
this is how it continues to grow.'

As I watched, I could see a drop forming right at the tip. It
swelled and swelled. I imagined getting right up close to it, so
close I could see the bloated, convex reflection of everyone in
the group, with a clear image of Danny standing there, arms

loosely hanging by his side, in the middle of the front row, a half-amused, half-bored look on his face. Knowing full well I was there a few feet behind him, biding my time. But he was biding his too. Muscles bunching, tendons cording in his neck, a tic working furiously at the corner of his eye.

We were off again. Down more wooden steps. Still I couldn't get a good look at the people at the head of the group. I was becoming increasingly convinced he was one of them, but remained aware that it was with little reasonable basis. It was possible I was completely wasting my time. Led on a merry dance either by Danny or my own fancies.

'This is known as the Shawl,' the guide was saying. 'And you can see why when I do this.' So saying, she flicked a switch by her elbow – she'd stopped next to a discreet on/off switch tacked on to the limestone wall. A bulb came on behind the feature, its light diffusing through the milky rock to contrive the appearance of a shawl. There were one or two gasps – it was okay, but really . . . Then she pulled another switch which plunged the whole cave into darkness except for the light behind the Shawl.

There was a low 'ooh' from the group and several cameras were raised.

'I'd advise against trying to take a picture of the Shawl,' the guide continued. 'There's not enough light and you'll just be wasting your film. If you have an automatic flash it will counteract the effect of the light behind the Shawl and again it'll be a waste of good film.'

Several flashes went off nevertheless as people disregarded her advice. You could see the mingled impatience and amusement on her face as she turned to one side and flicked the light on again.

My head was hurting faintly, something like a moderate hangover, as we negotiated another fairly steep flight of steps. With the tension and the lack of fresh air I figured these were ideal conditions for fainting. I took deep breaths and my head-ache got a little worse, but at least I knew what was going on.

The guide pointed out more features – Organ Pipes, Jewel Casket, and a hundred-and-fifty-year-old possum which had stumbled into the cave and never found a way out again. Poor little bugger had been petrified, curled up in a once-furry ball at the bottom of a shaft. There was a man near the front of the group, a short man with a ponytail. Down here I couldn't tell its colour and I couldn't seem to get alongside at any point to get even a three-quarter profile. But it could be Danny. At the same time as being utterly convinced it was him, I was certain it was not. 'Can anyone guess what it might be called?' the guide was repeating. 'Take a look around. What can you see?' Thirty heads bobbed about, looking for a telltale shape in the rock formations. I saw a distinctive humped silhouette about eighteen inches high but held my tongue. 'Camel Cave,' said a voice near the front which I could have sworn was Danny's, only everyone's voice inevitably sounded different down here, and it occurred to me I'd never heard his voice at all.

And then the lights went out. This time it was all of them, with a bit of guide preamble about how she wanted us to appreciate just how dark it could get down here. She threw the switch to plunge the entire cave into pitch darkness. But just before she did it, I saw him. He leant forward from the rest of the group, pressed over the railing to see the guide as he said, for the second time: 'Camel Cave.'

It was him – the wiry frame, like something hydraulic, an exoskeleton almost, within which his muscles spasmed and twitched; the ponytail; the stalactites of silver goatee. My stomach twisted, my heart kicked against my ribs. Danny.

Then the lights went out.

From this point everything seemed to happen too quickly, as if being in the cave had allowed us to fall into a loop in time and suddenly the loop was caught up, spooled back on to itself. Stalactites and stalagmites rushed to meet each other and form spindly columns. There was the sound of footsteps, almost a scuffle, something of a panic breaking out in the group. The lights should have gone straight back on but for some reason the cave remained dark.

In the total darkness, the sudden flurry of panicky sounds was disorientating. Voices were raised, the guide's among them, and when the lights did eventually come back on I saw that the group had become strung out along the stairs leading back to the higher chambers. I had to turn and trot to catch up with the others, the leaders now so far ahead I had little chance of reaching them before we all arrived at the exit. My head was buzzing, an arc of pain lodged just under the skull, sharp and debilitating. The air had been circulating sluggishly for thousands of years, helping to preserve the limestone formations and now give headaches to tourists. I felt a wave of something very much like travel sickness.

People were running. The guide was shouting. 'There's no need to panic. Please stop running. It's dangerous. These steps are not designed for running.' Still people ran. You can't argue with fear. Even if that fear is irrational. There was no need to flee from the cave. No roof had collapsed. No canary had sung. But one set of feet had set off a stampede and I thought I knew whose. I ran faster than most in order to catch him up, but I'd been further back at the start. Even shoving people ahead of me out of the way I was unable to reach the front of the group. When I got to the elevator shaft, the cage, according to the little orange light, was up at the top. Naturally. I hopped about from one foot to the other waiting for it to come down. My agitation didn't go unnoticed. 'There's a dunny when you get up to the surface,' advised the guide. I nodded. When the lift arrived I was the first one in. I couldn't remember whether we'd entered the same way or from the other side, so I stuck myself against the wall in the middle and waited. The panic had dispersed now and people were wondering what all the fuss had been about. There was laughter and a buzz of chatter. The cage doors were drawn across and we rumbled skywards. There were too many of us to fit in the airlock in one go, but I did at least manage to get into the first group, my head feeling as if it were about to explode.

I gulped at the fresh forest air once we reached the surface; it had never tasted so sweet. The white Merc, of course, had gone. I ran across to where it had been. Deep exit tracks in the mulchy earth. Ambrose would have wet himself. I ran to the Ford and within a few seconds was dithering at the junction with the main road. Left or right? Instinct said right, and so did an insubstantial ghost of leaf mould and karri bark in the shape of twin tracks, which could have belonged to any car but which I fancied were Danny's signature. I guessed he was playing with me now and enjoying it. I opened up the throttle and the back end shivered as I entered the straight, gravel and dust clouding even this cooler, damper air, in my wake. He can't have had much of a headstart and of course it was possible he hadn't know for sure I was down there with him. I tried to remember if Joanna carried a picture of me among her things, and couldn't. It was possible he had no idea what I looked like, or what car I drove.

Unless it was the one tearing through the peaceful karri forest at a hundred and ten kmph?

Underestimating Danny was not a good idea.

Max had once told me about Danny's brush with the law in Shepherd's Bush – not a good place to piss about with the police. Chased around the outside of Queen's Park Rangers football ground by a squad car for speeding down Bloemfontein Road (launching his knackered old BMW over the speed bumps as if it were a tactical weapon), Danny had taken the old fucker up to a hundred on the straight down Ellerslie Road and then clipped one of the front garden walls opposite the end of Ellerslie turning right into Abdale. Screamed down to the bottom of Abdale, left then right into Tunis, then nipped into the police station car park. Waited for the squad car to go steaming past the entrance to the car park and head left on to Uxbridge Road before rolling back out of the car park to escape on to the Uxbridge Road going right. He soon lost himself in the squashed grid of streets beneath Uxbridge, parking up outside the Andover Arms, about a mile distant, and enjoying a Newcastle Brown before picking up his original trail.

When I saw a road signposted Cape Leuwin, I took it, spitting gravel on the bend. Five minutes down there and it was like being in Devon. A narrow, winding single-track road bumping over hillocks, the ocean on my left. And, I soon realised, straight ahead. I was heading right for the point where the Indian and Southern Oceans met. I looked out at the sea and imagined huge shifting masses of hot and cold water merging, sliding above and underneath one another like whales. I could almost see a line in the water where it appeared more restless and agitated than on either side. There had to be a line somewhere. It might shift from day to day, but there had to be a front where the chill water from the Antarctic met the warmer channels from the Indian Ocean.

I parked in the shadow of a towering white lighthouse. There were two other cars. Neither was a white Mercedes.

I climbed half out of the Ford, scanning the skyline. Cape Leuwin was connected to the main road by not one little road, but two. Those two roads and the main drag formed an equilateral triangle dropped into low scrub and bush. The karri forest didn't reach the ocean. So from the point, you could see any traffic on either of the feed roads. And I could see, on the little road I had *not* taken, on the other one heading back to the main road, a white saloon car. An old model. From this distance it was difficult to be sure. It was moving pretty fast, and I could almost see Danny's arm hanging out the window as he lazily gave me the finger. His hand spinning out slow, piss-taking circles at the wrist.

Almost.

Twenty-two

Yeah, almost.

I got back on the triangle and made the main road without too much delay, but of course he was long gone. And did I know in which direction? Did I fuck. So I guessed and I drove like a maniac in the hope I'd guessed right. What else can you do?

And before I'd covered five Ks, I got my reward.

I saw the headlights first. Two round lamps, stacked. A figure 8. Americana headlamps.

I stamped on the brakes, layed down some rubber. The Merc was still eighty metres distant, its nearside front wing sticking out from whatever roadside layby Danny had parked it in. I noticed my leg was trembling slightly on the brake pedal. I released it and crept forward a few metres. All the angle allowed me was a little more radiator grille, not that I needed it.

On the one hand, caution advised getting out and approaching on foot, making less noise that way, but on the other hand I figured if he was sitting waiting in the car then I should not leave my own. He could come screaming out of his corner and knock me flat. So I eased the Ford forward slowly. And inch by inch, my disappointment was fully realised.

The Merc, indeed a 280SE, and a white one, was parked outside a garage, a sort of tumbledown shack workshop thing you could imagine being opened up by a guy in baggy shorts one day a year to work on a couple of cars.

Right next to the Merc was another. And next to that was another. Yeah, there were three of them lined up in a row. Three 280SEs. Not all white, I grant you, but three of what I was looking for, that rarest of Mercs. Well, maybe not quite the rarest, but not so common you were likely to come across three of the fuckers parked up outside a garage in South Western Australia. When you thought you'd been following a guy in one for the past three days.

I got out of the Ford and walked across to the line of Mercedes. I touched the first one. I placed my hand on the bonnet. It was cold. So were the other two. All three of them were dusty and could have been sitting there for days, even weeks.

I felt dizzy. Had to walk back and sit in the Ford for a minute or two, my head in my hands, trying to work out what to do. When nothing came to mind, I pulled the map out of the pocket in the driver's door and studied it, hoping for some clue to be revealed.

Twenty-three

Profoundly deaf, thin as a telegraph pole and never once seen to blink – I don't know why I didn't work it out sooner – Danny would have cut an unlikely figure among the brawny ockers crowding into the skimpy bars of Eneabba and Dongara. But observed against what turns out to have been his natural landscape, the dusty wastes of Western Australia's wide open spaces, he's less of an anomaly.

That's why he never used the phone. Why he didn't know what to serve to customers who didn't give him the chance to

lipread their order. Presumably why he didn't turn up to the
meetings Max arranged for the three of us – too much like hard
work. Having to concentrate all the time.

It's the detail that got left out. Worth waiting for? In terms
of its implications?

Deaf, thin and wiry, unblinking. Australian-born, elusive,
potentially dangerous.

Ring any bells?

The heart of a snake, like all its internal organs, is elong-
ated. Inefficient, its three chambers allow oxygenated blood
and deoxygenated blood to mix. It lacks a way of creating and
maintaining body heat. The popular term is 'cold-blooded'.

It has a heart, but no centre. Only by coiling into a figure 8
can a snake centre itself. The omphalos of the ouroborous.

You could tell he was deaf if you listened. Slightly stilted
accent. A lot of people he came into contact with just thought
it was regional – born in Oz, raised in Oldham.

He took Joanna by posing as my friend.

He said: 'Guess who I just saw, down by the seafront. He
said to come and fetch you. I'm Danny.'

Or: he pulled up in his Mercedes 280SE, leaned out of the
window and said: 'Hey Joanna, I'm Danny, friend of Chris's –
isn't it amazing, there I am driving round Denham and there *he*
is coming out of the fucking grocer's. Jump in. He's waiting for
us outside the shop.'

Or this. He sat on the cooling bonnet of the Merc, folded
his arms across his climber's chest and laughed out loud.
'Christ, you go to the ends of the earth to get away from everyone and there's one of your oldest mates going down to the
shops for a pint of milk. Come on, Joanna, jump in and we'll go
and pick him up. Give him a surprise.'

It didn't matter that if he hadn't actually spoken to me he
wouldn't have known where to find Joanna. She only had to
believe him for a second or two. He used one of those lines, or he
used one of a hundred other variations, but somehow and without

a struggle he got her to fold her elegant legs into the passenger seat of that Mercedes and then he reversed out on to the main road. As he tore out of Denham she'd have panicked, wrestled with him as he drove; but he'd have fought her off, resisting stopping the car and subduing her until they were some way out of town. Then he'd have pulled up, hit her once sharply across the face, gone around to the boot for a rope or a belt. Tied her up, maybe knocked her out with something brought along for the purpose. Spread out on the back seat she'd look like any other long-distance passenger passed out in the heat. Danny could just get on with putting as many miles between them and me in as short a time as possible. His Merc could move all right.

While I fucked about at Monkey Mia and Little Lagoon he was motoring south. Joanna could moan and plead all she liked from the back seat and he couldn't hear a thing. As long as he kept his unblinking eyes averted from the rearview mirror he could just get on with the business of driving. Road trains, roadhouses, road-crazy Japanese cyclists – they were all less than distractions to him. To one so single-minded. He towed a permanent dust cloud behind the Merc like a parachute-brake, only it didn't slow him down. Maybe he stopped once or twice, in towns too small to deserve the name, to refuel on gas and cool drinks. To keep her alive. Would she still struggle or would she give in, conserve her energy?

The terrible thing was, I didn't know. I simply didn't know her well enough. I knew him even less well. I had to dredge up memories of the man provided by Max, hardly a reliable character witness. I wondered if Danny, like Max, believed that time did not exist, and decided that it was almost certainly Danny who'd lofted the idea in the first place, Max who'd picked up on it. At times it seemed as if Max had invented Danny as an idealised version of himself. Or as some sort of totem.

The problem was St George's. It all went back to St George's, and what certain people knew about St George's and what had happened there.

One person had already paid the ultimate price. Z had tried Danny's patience with rather too much application and stamina. Of course, she didn't appreciate that that was what she was doing. If Z had a fault it was that she was hopelessly dim. And that's a generous assessment, believe me. Poor woman. Poor kid.

She knew too much and at the same time she didn't know enough – about how to handle someone like Danny. He was like a piece of software she didn't have the power to run.

Not without crashing.

At least she had an original copy. All I had was Max's pirated version and his memory cache was fucked. If only it was that simple: a little icon of a guy with long grey hair tied back, arms hanging loose but ready by his sides. All I had to do was double-click and give it a few seconds to load.

Under the Options menu I'd find, I don't know, Reformatting or Redefine Parameters.

But it wasn't. As simple as that.

Whereas I *had* thought it was a matter of time, of catching up with Danny in time, now I realised there were other strata and other equations preventing me from reaching him. There were the three Mercedes 280SEs parked outside the lock-up garage. Suddenly I was no longer looking for the only Mercedes 280SE in WA. I was looking for one of many.

Even if I found one in time, which I thought I had just done, it was not necessarily the right one. I shouldn't have to wrestle with such ideas, I thought to myself as I wondered which way to go next.

I had to work out which way Danny would have gone. I had to get inside his head. I needed to understand his perspective on the world. Otherwise what chance did I have? I drove until I found a phone, which was at a gas station not big enough to be a roadhouse. I called Max.

'I don't care *what* time it is,' I said. 'Tell me about Danny. And Australia. He's got Joanna. I've got to find him.'

Turned out when Danny went to Australia he had a very specific destination in mind.

Around about the time the whole liquor importation business was reaching its zenith and Danny was moving temporarily back into porn – for the deal with Howell, the warehouse full of *Les Lettres Albanaises* – Max and Danny got together one evening. It was Danny's valediction, had Max but known it. Danny picked him up in the red Merc from the bombsite in N15 where Max was still living and said they were going somewhere special and Max should make an effort, dress up a bit. So Max pulled on his suit – if it was running to threadbare and had an ink stain by the breast pocket, who cared? It was still a suit. He could just about remember to tie a tie; he chose a regimental number he'd picked up from Help the Aged for a quid.

Danny looked the business. He had on the same silk blouson he'd worn the day he'd taken Z into St George's through the back window. His black Calvin Klein jeans hit his Chinese copper's steel-toecapped boots with just the right amount of crumple. Under the silk jacket was a perfectly laundered salmon-coloured top of softest cotton.

When Max saw what Danny was wearing and wondered why he couldn't have worn jeans and a T-shirt as well, he quickly realised that whereas Danny could look smart in that kind of gear, Max would just look a state.

'They wouldn't let you in, mate. With the suit you'll be fine.' Danny pulled at his goatee. 'Nice tie,' he added, turning away.

Max fingered the unknown symbols of his wash-as-silk number and walked around to the passenger side of the red sports car. Danny was the only man of his small circle of acquaintances who made him feel inferior, and yet it didn't trouble him. It was just one of those things.

They motored west, slewed across Green Lanes and climbed one rung of the Harringay Ladder, then went left into Wightman Road. In the traffic queue at its bottom end, waiting to get around the mini-roundabout, Danny revved hard. He swore at drivers who dithered, unsure whether they had the right of way or not. 'How can they be so fucking stupid?' he snarled, his knuckles white on the wheel.

He shouted: 'It's your fucking right of way, you daft cunt.'

He leant on the horn, got a look from the man in front – young Kurdish lad in a Sierra Cosworth, exhaust pumping out the back like a bus.

'Go on, you little fuck, I dare you.'

Max watched his friend seethe, not especially concerned that he'd start a fight. No one ever did seem to pick on Danny. They seemed to know it wouldn't be wise.

They got around the mini-roundabout eventually and Danny throttled hard down Tollington Park Road into Finsbury Park. He had a shortcut he took from there to King's Cross. Max had directed me that way once when I'd been driving him to a party in Bloomsbury. It involved negotiating a number of tight chicanes and nipping through gaps between bollards, for which Danny tended not to slow down. Pentonville Prison shivered in the rear-view mirror. Danny squeezed the red Merc between the huge red and black gasholders at King's Cross and dropped on to the Euston Road. Got the timing right, fixed his cruising speed (thirty-five mph) and they floated down to Marylebone without a single stop light to impede their progress – at Baker Street he hit an amber and so lifted his speed to forty-five to get through the next two sets on green. Snubbing the Westway, he snuck down Old Marylebone Road and swung around into Edgware Road to Marble Arch.

He parked behind Knightsbridge near the Grenadier in a reserved bay.

'You can't park here,' Max would have protested.

'Watch me.'

And they marched around to the front of the Lanesborough Hotel, née St George's Hospital, at Danny's speed, Max having to trot to keep up.

'Come on, Max.'

And they went straight in under the daunting entrance arch – all new, of course, since Danny's day. A part of him would rather have been scrambling in through a jemmied window around the back.

And another part of him would rather have been anywhere else in the world. The power the place possessed over him was awesome. He could still come here, but he wouldn't consider bringing Z. Max knew better than to ask. Z would be sitting by the window in the flat at Rye Hill Park, the light angling down behind her through settling dust on to the Afghan rug and the oakwood chest, the turquoise bowls and the single framed photograph of St George's as it was. Everything was Danny's. If Z had any tastes at all she either never revealed them through choice or had never been encouraged to. She'd be holding the cordless phone in one hand, turning the pages of her address book with the other. Names becoming instinct on the page, felt-tip pen fading with age. She calls one or two, hears a voice of the opposite sex to the one she expected, and hangs up, silently, gently pressing the button, as if that softens the blow. But the impact is always on her. If one or two husbands or wives have to utter the words 'Hello? Hello? Who is this?' into an answering silence, that's not something that will bother them. But each new number that she tries and gains a response to of this type is another hollow knock on the door of her life. Yes, she had a life once, back when she loved Danny rather than just needed him. When his bursting with energy was constantly exciting. When his enthusiasm for some new car or climbing-wall would fire her own passions.

She could never really understand quite how she fell in love with him, unless she only ever really fell under his spell. He was everything she was not; they had nothing in common. And yet from the very first time she met him she flirted with him like she had with no other man. She flirted with him because she felt she had to have him. He made her feel that. He made her because he could, and because he, in his turn, had to. They were made for each other.

She walked into the restaurant swinging her bag, her white shirt open a button or three too far; she inclined infinitesimally as she was introduced to someone. Not out of deference so much as to give them a glimpse. She went that little bit further for Danny: she bent almost double to get her cigarettes out of her bag and, within the darkness of her top, her young breasts plunged. Danny didn't know where to look as Steve, the duty manager, introduced them.

'This is Z,' he would have said blandly. Zas or Zoë, whatever. 'Z, Danny – he's one of our most taciturn waiters. I'm sure you'll enjoy working together.'

Z put a cigarette between her fuchsia lips and lit it with a steady Zippo but she was trembling inside. Danny's eyes penetrated her, saw through the show, the King's Road gear, the ski-tan, the money wasted on elocution lessons. He didn't care how she sounded: he couldn't hear a thing. His head was buzzing, blood fizzing in his temples. She looked both powerful and helpless and he couldn't deny that he felt a strong compulsion to look after her, protect her from whoever the next guy might be to come along. Although in a sense she would twist him around her little finger, in another she would be that man's plaything and ultimate victim. Danny saw this in a trice and spent the next half-hour in a daze. He felt as if he knew what he had to do.

It was clear to both of them that they would end up together, but Z – 'being a woman,' Max said – made Danny work for it. She behaved like an exiled princess, haughty and aloof with Danny, while scattering favours around for other men. She allowed herself to be spotted in a clinch with Christian, the French pizzaiolo, and went off in a cab one night with Steve, the deputy manager. As soon as they got around the corner from the restaurant, however, she invented a reason to stop the cab and get out. Then hailed a black cab to take her home. These were all just needles to stick in Danny's hide.

He in turn became even more truculent than he had been

before, glancing in her direction while he scribbled down customers' orders, watching her condescend to little old ladies in furs as he filled tumblers with ice and Coke at Ahmed's coffee station. Ahmed would make some remark about Z – from 'I wouldn't mind some of *that*', through 'Now, you don't get many of *them* to the pound', to 'Dippy tart' – and Danny, if he'd been watching his lips, would flash him a glare that would soon shut him up.

Breaktimes Danny was always to be found upstairs and out the back, perched on the highest point of the little ledge from which you could scan the empty windows of the abandoned hospital. He'd already been inside and was itching to get back. It was difficult to say why, but his sudden feelings for Z clearly had something to do with it. He sat there, calmly destroying an American Hot with extra olives, his sharp gaze penetrating one dusty window after another, his heart thumping as he pictured Z downstairs – her white shirt gaping, breasts looming, customers sweating out their impossible desire. Nights when he wasn't working he'd drive down and pick her up after her shift and they'd spin off into west London's sodium-lit maze – street after street of wedding-cake semis and inner-city flyovers stranded by the retreat of some futurist dream. Every one-way cut-through was an unprowled corridor, each precisely curved sliproad a spiral stairway to an unvisited ward.

I eased the Laser into the town of Pemberton around six, six-thirty in the evening. The light was marmaladey. Like midday sun through a particular south-facing section of the glass roof on the Meadowhall shopping centre in Sheffield. Of all places. There was a greenish tinge to it. Pemberton is surrounded just about on all sides by karri forest.

Karri and jarrah.

Huge trees, eucalypts, with trunks wide enough, in some cases, to walk through. (I drove past one such tree that had a hole bored through it. You could stand up in it. If Joanna had been with me still, I'd have urged her to stand in it while I took a photograph. She'd have done the same with me and for some reason her picture, despite being taken on a cheaper camera, point-and-shoot job, would have come out better. Over time, with both pictures filed away in an album, I'd have come to believe that somehow *I* took the one of me, the better one, the one we both remembered when we thought of the tree.)

Had Joanna been with me as I rolled the Laser slowly up the main street, we would have laughed at the incongruity of the name above the chemist's – John Major. We'd have given the likewise improbably named Shamrock restaurant the once-over and hoped maybe we'd find something better. We'd have been staring less intently at the parked cars than I found myself doing, craning my neck to get a look at headlamps and radiator grilles, my gaze trailing across rows of rear lights. In fact there weren't that many cars. It was a small town. Signs pointed through its deserted streets to the Gloucester Tree. I thought about finding a motel. Getting my head down. What the hell else could I do? I had to sleep.

I found a place. The Gloucester Motel. Just up the road, promised a sign outside, was the Gloucester Tree itself. I parked and walked across to a phone booth. It took a while to make the connection, but eventually I got through to the police station in Kalbarri. I'd called in on my way back down, given a statement. No, they had nothing to report. A couple of guys in white Mercs had been pulled over, none had fitted the description I'd given of Danny, not even remotely. Certainly none had had a woman tied up in the back, or the boot. 'You wanna give us the number where you are, we'll call you if there's any news.'

'I'm at the Gloucester Motel, Pemberton. But only for one night.'

'We'll give you a call, mate.'

'Yeah.'

And he hung up, went back to his card game, necked his stubbie, ran his hand through his cropped blond hair, tiny droplets of perspiration flung clear.

I checked into the motel, wondered if I should have a look at the Gloucester Tree just because I was there – act like a tourist, as if everything was normal. I felt empty, numb. So utterly helpless I thought I might as well do that as nothing. But I decided to eat. Turned out the Shamrock was pretty much all there was, so I ate there. Had crab or prawns or something similar. And a bottle of Chardonnay. Jesus, why the hell not? I stumbled back to the motel so tired it was all I could do to unlock the door before collapsing on the bed fully dressed and passing out.

In the morning, a fine mist had settled over the forest; I felt terrible. I stuck my head out the french windows hoping that the cool, moist air would refresh me. It didn't. I wondered if I was hungry, if some food might do the trick. At the bottom of my bag I found an old pack of Weetbix which Joanna and I had started at one of our self-catering places then packed and forgotten about. I munched on a dry briquette of Weetbix until I felt like heaving and tossed it in the bin. Whenever I stopped thinking about feeling unwell or about tracing Danny or finding Joanna, I felt oppressed, but I couldn't identify my oppressor. It *was* finding Danny, and yet it *was not*. There was something else as well.

I got dressed and checked out of the motel. With the bag stashed in the boot of the car I felt drawn to the few streets of the town. I thought I should at least have a brief look around. Danny had been here, I was sure. I sensed him. I could almost smell him, his scent mingling with the cool, damp trees, the lumber and sawdust. The desk at the motel had received no messages for me from bored policemen in the north. I wandered over to a long, low wooden cabin set amid the kind of garden that would have been unthinkable in Shark Bay. There was even a little pond out front. Inside, carved out of karri and jarrah, was every conceivable receptacle and knick-knack. There were tea towels printed with the image of the Gloucester Tree, pamphlets on the history of the Gloucester Tree, and postcards . . . of the Gloucester Tree. I heard the two women who ran the place talking, almost sotto voce, about *the tree*.

I ran my fingers across jarrah jewellery boxes and tiny karri caskets, thinking that Danny might have done the same. One of the things I'd been told about him by Max and had no reason at all to doubt was that he liked to know a place, really *know* it. When he took on the flat in Peckham which overlooked Nunhead Cemetery it was important he went and investigated the great Victorian bone-garden. He couldn't wake up every morning he slept there and look out over its massed graves without having been down there and trailed his fingertips across mossy headstones and tomb-lichen. He had to have read the inscriptions – not every single one, because if he was mad, he wasn't mad like that, he wasn't some obsessive completist – but he had to have felt a tear well up as he imagined the brutally foreshortened life of an eight-year-old girl from Deptford much missed by her loving, bewildered parents; he needed to have empathised with the young husband who buried his twenty-year-old bride only weeks after they had married in St-George-in-the-East.

He also needed – and this was the key – to be high up. The flat at Rye Hill Park was not only on a hill, it was also in the second floor and attic, so that the view down over the cemetery and over London was the best he could possibly get from there. At Ridgmount Gardens – tall mansion blocks towering over Bloomsbury – he rented a one-bed flat on the very top floor. 'Otherwise there's no point,' he told Max, whose ground-floor cage in N15 troubled Danny so much he couldn't even step over the threshold when he went to pick him up.

The Gloucester Tree was only a few minutes' drive outside of the town. I could have walked, but I'd packed up the car, checked one final time at the motel where there still had not been a message, and so decided to drive. I parked in a designated clearing (no sign of a white Mercedes – I checked, naturally) and walked across to the base of the tree. Sixty metres high, its top and much of its upper reaches were robed in mist. The trunk was so thick you'd make little impression on its girth by wrapping your arms around it. In any case, you were prevented from doing so by a series of three-foot-long spikes driven into the trunk at ninety degrees. These were the rungs of a sparse spiral ladder which visitors to the tree were invited to climb. I made my neck ache staring up at the misty perspectives of the disappearing ladder and shrouded tree-top. I knew who would have climbed the bugger if he'd been here, and I felt certain he *had* been here. So recently that I could almost see him, flitting between the boles of neighbouring karri trees. I could almost hear the tinkle of Mercedes keys in his pocket. The bob and sway of his long silver ponytail. An elfin creature, a wood sprite.

Before I knew what I was doing, I had my right hand and left foot on the first two iron spikes and had begun to climb the tree. At first it was easy, because I hardly knew what I was doing. It then became difficult as my body realised what I was asking of it. And then got much freer again – the spikes were regularly spaced and a rhythm could be found. My Blunnies slipped once or twice on the dewy metal but my heart didn't falter, nor my stomach lurch. I was holding on. There was no danger. As I climbed I would sometimes cast a glance upwards and the helix of spikes seemed subtly altered. Was there really only one route up the tree?

It began to seem as if there were two sets of spikes, two spiral stairs. Whichever spike I next grasped, it seemed I chose it over its ghost, its twin. And yet I wasn't consciously choosing. The impression was that of a twin-grooved record – hadn't there been one once, a Monty Python LP or some bizarre Eastern European experimental choral thing. You could play it one way or another from the beginning of the first side. I felt as if my own route up the tree was matched by another identical one which had started half a notch earlier. I looked down through the tangle of spikes and the flimsy wire netting which bagged the climbing area for safety and I couldn't believe I'd placed my slippery Blundstone on *that* three-foot metal rod, I refused to accept I'd slid my rapidly warming fingers around *this* chill, damp spike.

I was by now above the normal tree layer. I could see the canopy begin to curve away but the mist obscured anything more than fifty feet distant. In fact, as I climbed higher, it seemed to thicken around the very tree I was scaling. I stopped again and peered into the luminous grey clouds around me. I could see nothing beyond the tantalising promise of sunlight somewhere beyond the mist. The sound of my breathing gave me a shock – I had not recognised it, believing it to be somebody else's. My arms and legs began moving again, spider-like, towards the platform I could see apparently descending towards me. I covered the last twenty or thirty metres in this way, my arms and legs part of a fluid motion that seemed to require no energy from me to keep it going. And then I was poking my head through into the space at the top.

A wooden platform big enough to walk around. Squared off, with four distinct sides for the four points of the compass. A high rail to prevent you falling off, and criss-crossed stanchions to dissuade you from trying. I climbed the remaining steps and hauled myself on to the platform, panting to recover my breath.

I looked around. The view changed. Not because it was different depending on the direction you looked in, which it appeared not to be, but because the mist was constantly evolving. On the north side it would billow up towards the top of the tree before dispersing; to the west it suddenly fell away, exposing the canopy below, then regrouped and mushroomed. I added to it with my own exhalations, as no doubt Danny had done before me. Because he'd been up here.

He'd been here and he'd stood just as I was, looking out over the vast shifting carpets of mist and treetops. But because he was the front of this great pantomime horse we'd formed, he knew where he would go next and I didn't.

He'd been at the back himself, of course, when Z was in front, leading him wherever she wanted to go. And then he'd had enough of that, he'd just snapped one day, and now he was enjoying being in front.

Or was he?

The key thing was, although I sensed I was following pretty much in his footsteps, seeing the same things he had seen only a day or two previously, maybe less, in fact I had no evidence for any of this. I couldn't be completely certain of anything. For all I really knew he could be in Sydney or in a plane over India flying back to the UK. All I had to go on were my instincts.

Feeling slightly disappointed, I started to descend and almost immediately there came the sensation that I was following one of two possible routes down the tree, as if there had been another trapdoor on the opposite side of the platform leading to a separate set of spiral spokes. And once I'd got the feeling, I couldn't shake it. Not only that, but I started checking over my shoulder, half-aware of a shape in the mist, a shape that was not my shadow but in a sense was exactly that. I slowed down, took stock, looked all around. Of course, there was nobody, but as soon as I started moving again it was as if my half-seen companion had picked up his step as well. One moment he was in front of me, the next behind. The mist-slick metal spokes flew away from my feet, sending me flailing, crashing into an imagined shadow. Would he break my fall or shrug my helpless body off and watch it catch spike after spike on its ungainly, rag-doll progress towards the bottom of the tree? I stopped, shivering in the sudden cold engendered by fear. There was no pursuer, no foreshadowing spectre – none that wasn't the product of my imagination.

Which gave me further pause for thought and niggling doubt.

Slowly, shaking slightly, I inched down the massive tree.

It was possible, wasn't it? It was possible I had imagined the whole pursuit. It was possible I had created Danny. Or that Max had created him. Or I Max. (No. Sadly, Max's existence was beyond question. But Danny's . . .?)

***

The orange car was my marker. If it became any bigger than a toy in my windscreen I eased off the gas. If I lost it in the heat haze altogether I'd put my foot down. It was easier to use the car in front than the speedo. All I wanted was to maintain a steady pace and my brain couldn't handle that on its own.

I was numb. Cold despite the heat. It was all I could do to drive.

I would head back up north, following our emotional route – which hurt. Pick up our stuff from the villa in Denham. Call the police one last time and split. Go to Perth, perhaps, base myself there and kick up a stink until something was done. If you could call that a plan, then I had one. I didn't know what else to do.

Once I got past Perth, of course, I hit the same groove Joanna and I had travelled, the point of our new togetherness and joint purpose diamond sharp. The rumble of the wheels on the macadam, the spitting spray of grit when I swerved on to the runoff verge, the whirling willies that stung my bare elbow – these things were the same. The level blue of the ocean, the rolling expanses of dusty farmland, the *vroom-vroom* of road trains rattling by – these too were the same. All that was different was the orange car in front. And the empty seat alongside.

Twenty-four

The orange car remained a steady three hundred metres in front. The monotony had become almost fluid, as if I were aquaplaning just above or below consciousness. The road was straight, the scenery unchanging. If there was a clump of wildflowers, there was an identical clump a hundred and fifty metres further on and so on. All that kept me awake was the arbitrary determination to maintain the same distance between me and the orange car – and the signs pointing oceanwards off the Brand Highway, which taunted me. Yanchep, Seabird, Lancelin. Christ, Lancelin.

It was even hotter now than before. The sun was relentless. Clouds? No chance.

I was parched. Thinking I had a bottle of water in the Esky I pulled over on to the verge and finally let the orange car go, leaving a faint cloud of dust as its signature. Of course, the Esky was empty. I slammed the boot lid down and wandered off into the bush, my breathing fast and shallow. Tried to distract myself, looking for kangaroos, emus – anything to take my mind off things. Scrubby little bits of dried up vegetation tugged at the hairs on my legs as I walked. I wondered vaguely if there might be snakes.

No, I thought, the snake was long gone.

Once, when Danny had gone climbing in Yorkshire, Max went to watch him. It was hardly a spectator sport, but Max had listened to Danny going on about it so much he decided to go and see for himself what it was like. He drove up without telling Danny. No one had even known Max could drive. Or that he had a car. Seems he borrowed one. An old Saab. And drove up the A1 all the way to Leeds, stopping only once for petrol and a can of Diet Coke outside Newark.

Chocolate brown it was. The Saab.

Max could see the crags from miles away as he meandered across the Yorkshire farmland in the old Saab. He could see, even as a non-climber, that they possessed a beacon-like quality. As he got closer he could see what appeared to be tiny red spiders crawling over them. In the narrow road at the foot of the crags, cars were parked in a long line. Mondeos and Granadas, Citroëns and an old MG. He rolled into position at the end of the line and slowly wound up his window, checking out the view of the crags through his windscreen.

A climber in a turquoise singlet, dark blue shorts and a scarlet helmet moved up the rock face so quickly it at first appeared he was being winched up. But the rope attaching him to the top was slack and his progress was by rapid zig-zag, like a snake. His head over-large for his wiry, supple frame. Even at a distance of a hundred yards, Max could see energy rippling through the little man. He didn't need to see his face to know it was Danny. No sooner was one hand-hold engaged than the last foot-hold was evacuated. He seemed almost to flow up the vertical rock face like some kind of children's toy. Or an unnatural river – and for a moment Max was reminded of his dream of the night before.

He'd been heading upstream in a landscape that was part Peak District and part unspecified. Every so often he would scramble ashore to see if he could see the person (unknown) he was trying to catch up with. The river narrowed to a stream. Somehow, although he had no craft, when he was in the stream he was able to move up it. He saw a small pink butterfly on the bottom, but didn't touch it. Was it worth going on?

'Well, *there's* a journey up the birth canal,' Danny said later, when Max had described the dream.

Max couldn't get the image out of his head of Danny zig-zagging up the sheer gritstone face, energy coursing through his body like the rippling skeleton of a snake.

That was how he described it to me.

As I walked back to my car a large spiny bundle scuttled across my path. I stood and watched it go, its progress busy, single-minded, almost comical. I knew what it was. I'd been wondering when I'd see one.

Echidna.

An anteater. One of the last surviving monotremes. That and the platypus. Egg-laying toothless animals with a single opening for the passage of sperm, eggs, waste. I could still hear its quills rustle like a bag of knitting needles as it put more empty space between itself and me. Apart from being an egg-layer, it had another thing in common with the reptiles from which it had emerged a hundred and eighty million years ago: it didn't dream. It doesn't enjoy the luxury of REM sleep. And as a result, in order to store all the information it gathers in a lifetime – where the ants live in greatest numbers, for example, and how to get there after a heavy night on Termite Tequila in the skimpy bars of Echidna City – the echidna needs a wacking great big cerebral cortex. The rest of us mammals were lucky enough to evolve into REM sleepers; whatever other functions dreaming performs, it sifts through all the crap of our lives while we sleep. Some of it gets stored, some gets binned. If we didn't dream we'd need a cerebral cortex so big, in order to hold all this unprocessed data, we'd have to carry it around in a wheelbarrow. And that's no joke.

With one exception. When Danny took off his climbing helmet, he had a head no bigger than the rest of us. Being reptilian, Danny didn't dream either. But neither did he need to hang on to a lot of useless information. He obsessed over one thing and one thing only.

St George's.

With Max still fretting about Danny having parked the car around the back in a reserved bay, the two men entered the Lanesborough Hotel.

'We're just going for a drink?' There was an edge to Max's voice. He *hoped* they were just going for a drink. Though what he worried they might do otherwise was not at all clear.

Danny turned and winked.

Now that frightened him. The only other time he'd seen Danny wink like that they'd just arrived at a party in north Clapham and Danny was locking up the metallic blue Karmann Ghia. It was a balmy evening, late spring in the early nineties, local elections week, and this suave-looking guy in a suit was doing house-to-house with a load of light blue printed matter draped over his arm. Max saw Danny pause momentarily before straightening up from the driver's door. Saw the way he'd clocked the suave-looking guy and thought *Oh shit*.

It was at this point that Danny caught Max's eye and winked.

Then the front door was flung open at the house where the party was being held and the hostess, who'd obviously made inroads into the wine, looked and saw what she thought was three guys arriving together at her party. The suave-looking guy slipped past Danny and nipped up the front path, offering the hostess a campaign leaflet, which she took without knowing what it was. 'Come in, come in,' she said. The suave-looking guy said something suave like 'Oh I'd love to, nothing would give me greater pleasure, however . . .' before oiling back down the garden path towards the gate where Danny now stood. As well as being spectacularly selfish and mean-spirited and grasping (and, sometimes, suave), most Tories are also of course fantastically fucking stupid. Instead of taking one look at Danny, assessing the pulse in his left temple and the deliberately loose way he allowed his arms to hang by his sides, and taking off down the road at some speed, the suave-looking guy only saw the unspoken question in Danny's eye. As invitations went, this was embossed on quality cartridge, personalised in sepia copperplate.

Ask me if I want one. Go on. Ask me if I want a leaflet.

'Would you like one?'

'Would I like one? Yeah I'd like one,' Danny said quietly as he accepted the flimsy piece of A4 with his left hand and set fire to it with his right using the lighter (one of Z's) he'd palmed out of the pocket of his Amazon silk jacket under cover of the leaflet being passed across. Max had been expecting it, but then (a) Max knew Danny, and (b) unlike the suave-looking guy, Max wasn't a *complete* twat.

The suave-looking guy was too shocked to react quickly enough to prevent Danny setting light to the leaflets he was still holding – a couple of loose ones caught instantly and within seconds the flames were dancing dangerously close to his floppy fringe. If his greased thatch caught it, they'd all go up.

The burning leaflets fell into the gutter and smouldered there. The no-longer-quite-so-suave-looking guy's steel-capped footsteps faded out towards the far end of the street. At the corner he turned back to see Max doubled up with wheezy laughter.

'Cunts,' muttered Danny, and walked up the path to the house, kissing the hostess on both cheeks as he'd been taught to do by Z. All credit to her – Christine, her name was – for appearing unfazed. She said later she didn't know he was a Tory canvasser – hadn't looked at the leaflet. Had she done so, she reckoned, she'd have kicked him into next week.

They might live in done-up Victorian terraces in north Clapham, with back gardens and loft conversions, these people – but they know the difference between the good guys and the bad guys. Not that there is all that much these days.

Was it me or Max felt like that? Both of us, I suppose. But Danny would always be the only one with enough balls to do something. Deep-seated sense of justice? Or a quick temper?

Bit of both probably.

So, entering the Lanesborough, Max was nervous as hell because Danny had just tipped him the wink.

'Good evening, sir,' said the doorman, and they were in.

'This way,' Danny said over his shoulder to Max. 'The Library Bar.'

Max followed meekly, not knowing what to expect. He watched Danny from behind for signs of tension but the little man seemed quite relaxed. From his experience, that was the time to worry. They passed through a narrow entrance lobby where a fire was burning. It was probably false, but didn't look it. In the main lobby ahead of them the biggest flower arrangement Max had ever seen sat on a dark-wood table. The scent from several huge peach lilies filled the entire space. Danny wheeled left and left again into the Library Bar. Mahogany counter, sprays of flowers, books by the yard. Another blazing gas-fed fire.

Instead of going up to the bar, Danny sauntered across the room and sat down in an armchair on the far side. Max took the seat opposite and they sat patiently until a waiter appeared with a plate of canapés and a bowl of dried banana flakes and desiccated beetroot.

'Gentlemen?'

'What beers have you got?' Danny asked, leaning forward slightly.

'Sir, we have Beck's, Carlsberg and Löwenbrau.'

'Is that all?'

'I'm sorry, sir. What would you have liked?'

'A Chimay or a Duvel. You want to get some Belgian beers in.'

'Yes, sir. You come back again and Salvatore will see to it.'

For some reason, Max didn't doubt it. Salvatore scuttled away. He was polite and solicitous without fawning over them.

'I love this,' Danny said. 'I fucking love it. They don't know. They don't know anything.'

'What don't they know?'

Danny just shook his head and grinned.

Salvatore returned with a silver tray bearing two bottles of Löwenbrau, two crystal glasses and two linen napkins which he laid on the marble-topped table between Danny and Max. The half-filled glasses were placed on the napkins and the bottles containing the remainder of the beer slotted into two silver bottle-holders.

'Think of him as a nurse,' Danny said once the man had retreated, then, eschewing his glass, took hold of the Löwenbrau around its neck in the crook of his forefinger. Down the Old Kent Road, Max had seen young fighters barely out of their teens lift their beers the same way. Kids who would normally have raised straight pint glasses now bought bottled beers and necked them in honour of Danny. Perhaps without ever realising it.

Danny didn't drink much. He never had. Either he couldn't

take it or he chose not to. So Max was alarmed to see the bottle remain tipped up at ninety degrees to the plush apricot carpet. Danny was going for it. Once he'd drained the bottle he lifted the cut glass and swallowed its contents in one.

Danny leaned forward and touched Max's elbow. Two tables away a former Premier League footballer, now playing for some first or second division side, sat enjoying a drink with two women.

'It's that kind of place,' whispered Danny.

Salvatore reappeared with a bowl of black olives and a fresh plate of canapés.

'I imagine we'll have to pay for this,' Max muttered.

'Not as much as you might think. And in any case, it's worth it. You're paying for years of history.'

'Yes; yours.'

'Quite.'

They drank for an hour and a half, at the end of which Max was slurring his words while Danny's inebriation was more controlled and contained, but there could be no doubt that he was drunk. They rolled out of the Library Bar and into the foyer, where Danny paused by the enormous spray of lilies. 'So are you in, or what?' he murmured.

'What are you talking about?'

'Are you coming or going? In or out? Black or white?'

'No middle ground then?'

Danny paused a moment longer, his short-twitch muscles tugging against gravity – almost imperceptible tremors running down his arms. The overpowering scent of lilies hijacked Max's senses so that somehow they were all he could see and hear as well as smell. When that cleared, Danny had gone. Max thought he could just see his left foot through the tangle of stems and leaves as he turned the corner out of the lobby on the far side. But he wasn't sure. He hung around the flowers a little longer until the reception staff started giving him odd looks at which point he made for the exit.

***

Possessed by alcohol-fuelled determination and a single, seared memory, Danny prowled the softly carpeted corridors of the Lanesborough. Each room was a room that could have been there before. Every corridor at some point intersected with a channel of space that had existed in the past. He wandered through the same coordinates, inevitably, as he criss-crossed the huge building in his desperate search.

He stood for minutes gazing at an angle of roof and ceiling that he convinced himself was unchanged from his last visit, despite the fact he knew the building had been gutted and built afresh from within. When a passing couple in DJ and ball-gown murmured good evening he ignored them. He wasn't even aware of them. They muttered something inaudible to each other and turned the corner.

Danny moved on too, his blood pounding in his ears. The corridor walls bowed in and out with a sub-aural slough and rhythmic thump and soon they peeled away completely to reveal the blistered paint and flaking plaster of the abandoned hospital. The soft whisper of the Axminster underfoot turned into the crackle of broken glass, the squelchy mulch of mildewed underfelt. Mahogany doors swung inwards to reveal shattered labs, trashed wards, ransacked offices.

The peculiar *whump* of fire doors pulling to is replaced by the cool *plch*, *plch*, *plch* of brown water dripping from crumbling ceiling to sodden parquet. Could he but hear it. Danny prowled on, touching his fingers gently against the walls – *I know this place*. Soon he was navigating not by touch or smell but by some fusion of memory and instinct, as aware of the coordinates of his passage through the great building as a bird flying south for the winter. His breathing was shallow, his heart rate matching that of the muscle-walls which expanded and contracted, expanded and contracted, expanded and contracted . . .

He reached the heart of the east wing, the very centre, the

omphalos. Knocking on some poor bastard's door in the middle of the night.

'Go away,' they called. 'We'll call security. I'm calling security.'

Still Danny knocked on the door – he couldn't understand why it was locked. He didn't pound on the dark wood or get angry or reckless, he just knocked repeatedly, unable to open a door in his mind that he really needed to open if he was to get beyond this.

Security came and took him away. Since he offered no resistance they didn't call the cops, but bundled him into a cab. 'My car's here,' he tried telling them, but they could see he was in no fit state. They didn't want it on their consciences. It was good of them not to press charges. He could have been anybody.

They said to him: 'You could have been anybody.'

He watched them through the back window of the cab as it growled away into the milky, barely translucent air of a Hyde Park Corner dawn.

The echidna trotted off into the bush – a hundred and eighty million years and it hadn't moved an inch. Still couldn't dream, poor sod. I suppose it didn't know what it was missing.

I pulled the car door shut and started the engine, trundled back on to the road. I drove slowly, coasting along with my arm hanging out of the window. The heat haze veneered the furthest visible point of the road in a watery glaze. I saw no other vehicles but within five or six minutes a shimmering bulk materialised on the horizon. A roadhouse. Thirty seconds and I was there. I pulled off the highway and freewheeled under a wide awning into a space next to another car.

The orange car.

The orange car that had been my marker.

I put Joanna's baseball cap on and stepped out of the Laser. Looked at the rear of the orange car. I just had time to clock the fact it was a Mercedes when a figure came strolling across from the roadhouse. He was wearing surfie shorts, well-worn lace-up boots with green woollen socks sticking out the top, a pink singlet and a baseball cap with the letters NWA stencilled across the front.

There was something familiar about him.

Familiar not because I'd ever seen him before, but because he'd been described to me a hundred times. And because I'd seen Max's photograph taken at the back of the restaurant.

I hadn't realised it was *that* kind of Mercedes.

Danny looked both tense and relaxed at the same time. The preparedness was in the taut muscle of his arms, and in his amused, disconcerting gaze. He stopped by the orange Mercedes and took his cap off. Swiped it across the Merc's flank, raising a cloud of orange dust. As soon as this cleared, I found I was looking at a patch of white spraypaint.

A white car, then, in other words.

A white Mercedes. Cabriolet. Hood up to keep the sun and the dust off.

I walked around to the front of the car and had a good look at its twin-mounted figure 8 headlamps.

Americana headlamps.

'Only thirty-six of them ever built,' Danny said.

I looked across the car at him. I had of course never heard his voice before. It was a little strained, imperfectly formed, testament to years of struggle. A driven man all his life, he'd done a good job on it.

'Thirty-six. And this is one of them. Left-hand drive they made loads. Twelve hundred at least. Common as muck. Madonna's got one – she's got a left-hand drive. But the right-hand drives – made for export – thirty-six of them. Jump in.'

I looked back down at the Americana headlamps. Figure 8s. Ouroborous. Couple of snakes eating their own tails.

Jump in.

I rounded on him. 'Where is she? Where the fuck is she, Danny?' I could feel my head beginning to hurt.

He looked at me and shook his head as he went to open the driver's door.

'Tell me!' I demanded.

'Hundred and sixty brake horsepower. Four-wheel disc brakes.'

He was already climbing in on his side. It felt like a pivotal moment. It also felt as if I had no choice. No option but to sit in next to Danny. I opened the door and eased myself in, as if into the electric chair.

The leather seat was so generously padded with horsehair it cushioned my weary frame a split-second before I was expecting it. Now I became aware of how high above the road I was, relative to the Laser. Suddenly the Ford felt like being towed down the road slung in a bucket. Danny spun the wheel and the Merc purred out from under the shelter of the carport. We accelerated on to the highway.

The dials on the dash in front of Danny were aligned to complement the headlamps – two main dials, an 8 on its side, infinity.

There was no sign of Joanna in the car.

Nothing.

Neither a shoe left lying on the floor in the back, nor her sunnies slipping into the crack between cushion and arm rest, one lens cracked in the struggle I assumed had taken place.

I look at Danny, on whom my bristling anger has no visible effect.

He's got his elbow on the frame of the door. I notice the skin on his left arm is peeling – from the sun, I imagine.

'Where is she?' I ask.

He doesn't answer but does move his head slightly. Did he look at the rearview mirror? It's angled towards the passenger seat. My seat. It would do him no good for looking at the road behind. What can its purpose be?

'Where is she?'

'Who?' he asks innocently.

I shout her name: 'Joanna.'

Without taking his eyes off the long straight dusty orange

road ahead he says: 'She knew too much.'

Knew too much. *Knew* too much. Past tense.

I stared at Danny. I didn't know what to say. Suddenly I remembered the dream I'd had the night before – shreds of it floated back into my mind. People were being killed. Tipped off high places. Seaside piers. The victims knew when it was going to happen and could do nothing about it. The more I remembered, the more came back to me. A group of men came to take you away, four or five men, nondescript.

I was on a pier, a busy seaside pier, making my way through the crowds to the scene of a murder. I notice two or three identical skirts – long woollen jobs, wraparound, beige – and sense that that signifies a wardrobe department. The murders are being staged for television. Somehow this doesn't reassure me. Real murders are still being committed.

The dream switched to a flat or bedsit somewhere. Joanna and I lived there together and we were preparing to have dinner. It was some kind of special occasion, but it didn't feel all that special to me. There was a sense of anxiety hovering about the place. A little table had been laid for us to eat at, but there was a third setting and the table was far too small for two to eat from, never mind three. Pushed right up against the wall, it would barely have been big enough for one. Cutlery gleamed with a dull burnish; cut glasses twinkled in the light from a single bulb. I knew somehow that this third person, the one joining us, would be Max.

I wondered how well he knew Joanna. Not that there could be anything going on. At least not like that. But I woke up feeling anxious, more anxious than on previous mornings. There are some people you simply don't like dreaming about. You see them when it suits you and not the other way around, so when they start wandering into your dreams, it's unwelcome.

A shadow bulked on the run-off verge up ahead. Fifty metres or so. As we shortened the gap I grew hideously certain

I knew what it would be. I stared unblinking at the dark mound as the Merc crawled closer. My eyes strained. We passed it. I swivelled in my seat. Saw brown fur flapping in our wake, dust settling over the poor beast's carcass.

'Wallaby,' Danny said.

I turned to look at him. He was still staring straight ahead, no sweat on his brow, sunlight furring the hair on his arm. I checked the wing mirror again on my side, watched the wallaby's corpse recede and begin to shimmer.

A road train materialised in the distance, slowly grew, then rumbled past us. Dust blowing in through the open window on Danny's side. Settling on the instruments. Catching in the hairs on his arms. I felt queasy. I didn't know what to do. With his left hand Danny took hold of his ponytail and drew it forward over his left shoulder, scratched the grizzled skin under his chin, blinked – glanced at me in the mirror, kept on driving. I felt immobilised by my own inaction. I couldn't even fidget. The slightest movement would be scrutinised, apparently casually, but I'd lost my sense of proportion. I was thinking about death. Specifically Joanna's. And then mine. And Danny's.

And, when I considered the door I was leaning against, Z's. Zoë's. Zas's. Whatever her name was. Hers. The start of all this.

Except it wasn't the start of it at all, as I was beginning to realise. It came somewhere in the middle.

The start of it all was before all of that, before he slammed the car door on Z's neck, but she was there. She'd always been there.

It would be another twenty-four or forty-eight hours – I don't know how long we spent in the Pinnacles Desert – before he finished telling me the rest of the stuff that I didn't already know. Or most of it anyway.

Twenty-five

From a distance they might be soldiers, standing guard on the hills overlooking the sea. Soldiers or gravestones. Some short, some tall, so that your sense of scale gets mixed up. In the middle of the day they cast little shadow – they're just there. Waiting.

They're like a giant pin cushion, or a complex set of male connectors waiting for their female counterparts to plug into them from the heavens. Waiting anyway. Waiting, for something.

As Danny piloted the Mercedes around stray rocks which, like buoys, marked out the occasional limits of the track, the vast legions of pinnacles shifted in and out of view behind rolling dunes.

I was sweating. An intermittent pain throbbed behind my left temple.

Danny drove with two hands on the wheel to prevent any sudden dip or lurch wresting control of the car from him. Constantly I imagined different scenarios. I would wrestle with him for the wheel then kick him out his side of the car, move over to the controls and . . . what? I had no idea where to go, what to do.

I would argue with him rationally until he told me where she was.

I would hold a knife to his throat until he took me to her.

He banked around another bend and pulled up on to a firm

sandstone ridge, engaging the handbrake and immediately swinging open his door and stepping out. His boots scrunching on the sandy ground. I looked around the interior of the Mercedes, my eyes travelling over the same surfaces Joanna would have scrutinised. Both of us searching for what we knew not. Her presence in the car was less than a ghost's. Purely imagined. Less substantial than Z's.

Danny was fifty yards away or more. He had the keys with him. I didn't have a clue how to hotwire a car and he knew that. He'd know it just by looking at me. And in any case, he knew I had to follow him.

The sand became finer the further away I walked from the car. I could see Danny up ahead – he wasn't in a hurry, and yet there seemed to be a sense of purpose about him. Sweat started to run from under the baseball cap. It itched as it mingled with the dust on my forehead. I wiped the right side of my brow against the sleeve of my T-shirt. Then did the same with the left. My Blunnies raised little clouds of dust which I could feel settling in the hairs on my legs. Danny disappeared behind a bulbous limestone pillar about twelve feet high, reappeared briefly and was then concealed by its neighbour.

Two hundred and forty-five kilometres north of Perth, the Pinnacles Desert is composed of sand, limestone and air, and not much else. No one's sure how long it's been here in this state, how long it took to form. Some say centuries, some a hundred years or even less. Standing there and looking at it for the first time you have a sense of its age. A light breeze blows the sand around the limestone pillars like grains of time over the years. The invertebrate shells of molluscs and forams would have provided the raw material for the lime sand that constitutes the pinnacles themselves.

'The sand was washed ashore by the waves,' Danny had told me as we were approaching the Pinnacles in the car, 'and whipped up into dunes by the wind. Over thousands of years, the sand hardened into Tamala limestone. The dunes were stabilised by vegetation – cool, wet winters; hot, dry summers. After the rain, acidic water percolated between sand grains, dissolving them, and in the summer the dunes dried out, dissolved calcium carbonate precipitating as a cement which stabilised them from beneath. The vegetation increased the acidity of the groundwater and the process was speeded up.'

Danny was a mine of information – just not the right sort.

Now he'd gone and I suddenly became aware of the sun beating down, burning through the light cotton of Joanna's baseball cap. With my ever-lengthening hair pulled through the gap at the back, I worried that my neck was partly exposed. I leaned back and let the sun shine straight into my face for a second, then blinked back its ferocity and had to rub my eyes with the heels of my hands. Sweat mixed with sand and got into my eyes. I swore, staggered a few steps and fell to my knees. I leaned against a pinnacle – only two or three feet high, topped with a hard calcrete cap.

I saw movement, hoped it would be Joanna, realised it was Danny. He was leaning against a pinnacle. He'd taken his cap off. He was only a hundred yards away. I walked.

The ocean glinted in the distance.

'They look best in the early morning,' Danny said. 'Or at dusk. For the shadows.'

I looked around at the pinnacles.

'It was all underground at one point. Under the sand. You know – the limestone. The limestone dissolved where it was weaker, leaving the more resistant columns. The wind blew the sand away. Blew it inland. There are different theories . . . No one really knows. Nor do they know how long they've been exposed. Six thousand years or less than a century.'

He started playing with his ponytail, running it through his hands like a small animal, laying it over his left shoulder.

'There's no evidence the Aborigines ever knew about this place. It doesn't figure in their legends.'

He said nothing for a while. I could hardly even hear him breathe.

'It's been here always,' he whispered, looking up at the sky.

I asked again: 'Where is she?'

He looked at me, his eyes glittering. His forehead was lined like parchment – corrugated, dry.

'You don't understand, do you?' he said. 'You don't fucking understand.' And then: 'People like you will never understand.'

I didn't want to understand. I just wanted my girl back. Or to know that she'd left of her own accord and was safe. That she hadn't had her head bashed in against the door frame of the Merc. That she wasn't tucked up in the branches of a karri tree six hundred Ks south, eyes pecked out by kookaburras. That she wasn't lying foetally curled and desiccated at the centre of a ring of pinnacles, her spine tenting the blistered skin of her lovely back.

I walked a few yards away from where Danny was still leaning against the pinnacle and squatted down next to another of the shorter limestone pillars. My legs folded beneath me and I ended up slumped on the sand, my head falling into my own hands. I seemed unable to prevent my body from going into a minor collapse. I drew my knees up and rested my forehead on them. My arms gripping each other tightly around my shins.

Some time later Danny came and stood by me. I was conscious of his boots scuffing up sand at the base of the pillar.

For some reason he couldn't just tell me what I wanted to know.

'It's that place,' he said. 'That fucking place.'

Yeah, right. Are we talking about an abandoned hospital by any chance?

They thought it was the perfect place. Or Danny thought it was the perfect place and Z acquiesced, because that was what she did. She acquiesced. She could acquiesce for England.

Danny couldn't hear the broken glass tinkling underfoot but

he could feel it. He couldn't hear the soft ripping sound of the sticky carpet parting company with the sole of his shoe, but he could smell the mildew. He couldn't hear Z's running footsteps in the corridors which he imagined would echo hollowly, but he glimpsed a white shoe as it slipped around a corner. It was enough for him. The eyesight of a hawk. He sensed the light peals of Z's laughter tinkling over the vast ranks of abandoned test-tubes like sea-breezes through a mobile.

Danny had borrowed keys to the restaurant off the busboy, a Yugoslav trying to pass himself off as a Greek. Long-haired kid called Zoran, or 'Nikis' to anyone who looked as if they might shop him for a loyalty bonus. Danny had sought him out even before he clocked the keys dangling from his belt. Anyone going undercover had to be worth getting to know. Someone with something to hide had to have something to tell.

It was late in the summer. The sun had already started to sink into the trees of Hyde Park by mid-evening. Danny had worked hard all night, as always. He did all right for tips, not by being chatty or obsequious, merely by being quick. That is, after all, what's most important to the punter. Food and drink and quick about it. They probably also appreciated the way he looked right at them while they ordered, without knowing that he was lipreading. Once or twice he missed extra cheese or olives or pepperonata because they added it as an afterthought without looking up.

When Danny opened the front door and locked it again behind him and Z, the restaurant had been transformed into a forest of upturned chairs and sudden clearings in the mirrored walls. Cockroaches ran for cover as Z's white Gaultier sandals flashed click-click-click across the shiny floor towards the back stairs. Danny waited and let her go first. The stairs were steep. She swung her arse in his face, Kensington Market ra-ra skirt leaving little to his imagination. He couldn't help himself. Control drained from him, like rain through sand, and he grabbed her waist from behind, shoved his head up her skirt, nuzzled against the soft, warm mound of her knickers. She squealed, twisted, jabbed with a heel and caught him in the chest. Wriggled free. He imagined her laughing as he stumbled and she gained the top stair.

When he clambered into the kitchen she was waiting for him, leaning back against one of the great wire cages where the plates were stacked to dry. She was smoking a Pall Mall with one hand, her left, and rubbing herself with her right. Skirt riding up high enough so he could see her fingers gently drawing circles inside the brilliant white of her clean cotton knickers. She understood about contrast if nothing else. There was no break in the tan on her legs. Sun-bed job.

Danny ached for her.

She moved her head from side to side. She also understood the workings of the sexual imperative, like a mechanic knows his engines, down to the nuts, washers and bolts. Every action was calculated and perfectly measured. Each time she inserted a lock of hair into the corner of her mouth it was with complete foreknowledge of where it would lead. She lost the dead Pall Mall, watched Danny waiting at the top of the stairs, watched him come for her across the kitchen. When he got halfway she moved away from the cages and stopped him with a hand placed flat against his chest. The same hand she then allowed to slide down over his stomach, catch on his belt and deftly manipulate the zipper on his Levi's. She went down on her knees as she rummaged around inside his boxers, took out his straining penis. Slipped her lips over its tip, flick-flick-flick with her tongue. Swallowed the length of him, head back. Fingers cupping his balls, tickling, stroking.

Silently, his own head tipped back. The ceiling – he'd never really looked at it before – was a delicate tracery of imagined crane flies and spiderlegs. Curling leaves of dried-up gloss. Infestations of microbes and mould, cobwebs and plaster.

Shadows bloomed like squid's ink in murky water. Danny's head swam.

He looked down. She moved rhythmically, back and forth, back and forth. He thought to himself he'd never seen a sweeter, more exquisitely poignant sight than Z's crown as she bobbed and sucked. His heart swelled for her.

Through the open door at the back he could also see the abandoned hospital, its white stucco glimmering in the heart of the London night.

His climax was brief, momentarily shattering. He couldn't keep silent. He felt something that was half-grunt, half-groan resonate in his mouth. Then his head fell forward and the only sounds would have been Z's quiet rustling as she cleaned up. The hum of the city. Distant sirens.

The beating of his heart, and hers.

As she got to her feet he held her shoulders and regarded her. Light from the open door washed her half-moon forehead, crater eyes; she couldn't hold his stare for long. It was too intense, too demanding. They both knew the stakes were higher even than *they* were, on this night of nights. He took her lightly by the elbow, propelled her towards the open door to the triangle of roofspace where waiters would gather to snatch quick fag breaks and gulp down pizzas and Peroni. Where Keith, the American waiter with digs in Belsize Park who was obsessed with crisp fivers and tenners, joshed everyone who happened by. Everyone except the cashier who slipped her crispiest notes to the bottom of the till drawer and exchanged them for Keith's grimy litter handed over at the end of his shift. Mutual respect.

They stepped out on to the roofspace. The warm, purple air. The satellites winking miles above the earth. Waiters' fag ends soft dead bugs underfoot. A pizza crust not yet snaffled by vermin. A single empty Peroni bottle, the remains of a cigarette within, standing on the edge of the little brick wall where Keith always sat.

Beyond, the long dark eyes of the hospital. The crazy Escherscape of angled surfaces. Pigeons scooting to and fro like vultures patrolling some vast, derelict city. Aircraft lights winking overhead, red and green.

Danny lifted Z around the waist and lowered her on to the next level, then followed her. A skip and a jump across the gap. Climbing a few feet. Pausing by the open window. He helped her through first. She tiptoed into the dimness of the room and was soon eaten up by shadows.

Vaulting over the sill, he landed on an old bent metal sign. Z had already exited via the door a few feet away hanging off its hinges.

There was a sudden, vigorous disturbance in the air and a black shape coming straight at him out of nowhere. It flew over his head and out of the window. A pigeon.

Hands on his knees, he fought for his breath. He could feel his heart pounding. Z was not close. He could no longer sense her as he normally would if she was within what should have been earshot. Checking his pockets, he proceeded to the door and looked both ways before turning right into the narrow corridor.

Broken glass. Mildewed carpets. Crumbling walls. Armies of shattered test-tubes and scattered slides. A sink furred over with some green substance. He walked on, eyes shining in the darkness. She couldn't be far away. Packet of three rattling in his pocket. He went left, turned right, ran a little, dropped low to check beneath a row of work benches, grinning, breathless. It was a game.

It crossed his mind now and then to be alert to the possibility of security. They were meant to have the place under surveillance. He reckoned it was a bluff. Who would bother?

A flash of white. Z? He cleared an upturned desk, caught his balance at the last minute as he landed in a patch of slippery lino-mould, trotted to the corner. She was leaning back against a set of concertinaed elevator doors, something white in her hand raised over her head. She launched it in his direction. It passed close enough to him for recognition to send blood flooding to his groin. Her knickers.

'Careful,' he said, anxious the elevator doors might give. 'Be careful, love. Don't want to lose you just when I've found you.'

She laughed.

'What are you talking about, you silly prat?' she asked him, possibly unaware there was enough light for him to lipread by. Sometimes he felt she might as well have been a foreigner. She could have been Russian. For all she understood him. But it didn't matter.

They fucked once by the elevator, the exoskeleton and fabric of the concertina doors creaking and wheezing as they moved against it. Z riding higher and higher up, until her feet were off the floor and the muscles in Danny's arms bunched fit to snap, his veins throbbing cords.

By the time they found the room at the heart of the east wing where Dr George Maddox had played God and later Charlie would almost give up the ghost, they were glad of the meagre luxury offered by the stained mattress and cot.

When he flung her down across it and began to make love to her, the coordinates of the position she took up were those of the unfortunate Lovegrove brother, heart donor before his time.

The same points which would be plotted years later when Charlie got seriously into it with Yvonne, the *Headpress* cover star.

In the skies overhead, planes coming in to land at Heathrow described the same trajectories through space. Time after time. Like kites on string. A cat's cradle of yearning. A web of want. A need net.

Danny's second orgasm produced tears, unseen by Z. She was gone. Somewhere else. Beyond emotion. Beyond sensation. She was a still lake.

Into which, then, a stone was thrown.

***

At some point in the noonday blinding brightness – so bright it had begun to get dark – Danny had left me. I got to my feet, stretched, wiped sweat out of my eyes, scanned the horizon in all directions.

Vanished.

Before I knew what I was doing, I was running. Running faster than I may ever have run before. Even where the sand should have slowed me down I forced my legs to go faster and faster still. They punched up and down, up and down into the ground.

Pinnacles flew by me on either side – short, tall, bulbously comic, spindly thin. I caught one with my arm – just an edge – and saw a puff of grit loosed into the air like gunsmoke.

She was here somewhere, was what kept me going.

Or at least he was still here and he knew where she was.

I came to an abrupt halt. The only sound the settling of dust behind me and the beating of my heart. Desperate panting for breath. Sweat rolling down my back.

Running again. Sweeping my gaze across the desert from side to side as I went. No one in this place had ever run faster. I criss-crossed the vast graveyard in search of I knew not which name on what stone. Propelled by the knowledge that the answer lay here, encrypted in the tessellation of energy lines between these thousands of columns. I saw myself from above scurrying from limestone pillar to calcrete post in search of a sign. Somewhere in this heat-cracked crater, this benighted amphitheatre, Danny leant against a pinnacle waiting for me to find him or biding his time until I gave up, in which case, I knew, he'd leave. He'd get in his Mercedes and go. Leave me to the merciless sun, the snakes and spiders. The dreams of sand and drainage.

Again I was running. Pinnacles blurring like bicycle spokes. I ran around. I ran across. I climbed to the top of a rocky out-crop and surveyed the desert beneath me. I bounded down

among the stones, Blunnies rubbing the skin raw on the backs
of my heels, hither and thither until suddenly with a horse-
whip *thwack*, a needle-sharp thud into a limestone pillar two
feet behind me, a puff of grit, a whistle of air – and then,
trailing by soft, elasticised seconds the single, booming report
of a bullet having been fired.

The stone was thrown and its ripples would never cease.

Yanked backwards in one swift movement with a sturdy
rubber torch under his chin, Danny would have had a second,
two at the most, in which to react. But the surprise was too
great. Had he resisted, the guard would have overpowered him
and was always only five seconds away from total superiority
anyway. Taller and bigger-framed, the man loosened his arm-
lock only to snap on the cuffs, one around Danny's left wrist,
the other on to a pipe of a wall-mounted radiator. Five
seconds, six at the most. With the element of surprise. And the
fact Danny had just been fucked out of his skull.

He hadn't been able to hear the man coming, obviously, and
Z was too far gone. Roused by the scuffle, she jerked into a
sitting position and tried to scramble off the cot, screaming
Danny's name. But the security guard was right there. Gaffer-
taping her mouth shut. She lashed out, kicking, flailing her
arms, made contact here and there but the blows glanced off
him. She struck a buckle or a button and did more harm to
herself. A sharp instant little bruise springing up.

'You're both in a lot of bother,' he said, as he lashed Z's
hands behind her to the frame of the cot, using a torn strip of
old bed-linen.

'Leave her alone,' Danny ordered.

The guard whacked him on the side of the head with the
torch.

'You're trespassing,' he said.

Of indeterminate age, somewhere between twenty-five and
forty, the security guard had badly cropped, or simply long-

unwashed, strawberry blond hair. It fringed his white collar unevenly at the back. The beginnings of a beard had brought the pinkish dusting of a rash to his lower face. His eyes were a washed-out, cornflower blue, rheumy and watery. There was something slow, almost bovine, about his movements, as if the initial attack had been a fluke.

'Is that what's given you the horn or was it watching us?' Danny had seen the way the guard's trousers were tented at the front. 'Either way, it's a penetration thing. Don't you think you ought to let us go and we'll forget about the assault? Draw a line under it and forget it ever happened.'

The guard turned away from his consideration of Z and took three steps in Danny's direction. Danny looked up at him, held his gaze, although he didn't feel he was making contact.

It must have been steel-toecapped. The guard's boot.

Danny buried his head, held his jaw gingerly, numbly groping at his teeth with a finger. All there. A little blood flowing. He looked up again just in time to cop another one right in the jaw. If he hadn't seen it coming it could have taken his head off, but he was able to take the edge off it. Still smarted though.

The guard had dropped the torch and taken a two-way radio from his belt and was speaking into it but all he got back when he switched channels was static. He held it away from his ear and looked at it as if that might make it work. Danny rubbed his jaw. The guard swore and hurled his radio at the crumbling wall. It struck something soft and semi-decayed and skittered off into the darkness. Something scuttled across the floor in front of Danny – too big for a cockroach, too small for a rat – momentarily distracting him. In that instant the guard approached Z. Danny saw him leaning over her, placing his big, plate-like palms over her breasts – an almost gentle, entirely misleading gesture. Danny screamed and shouted, yelled imprecations and threats. Tugging at his cuffs, yanking at the radiator until he was wearing two bracelets on his left wrist, one of them silver, the other, beneath it, red. He scrabbled around on the deck, hunting for something he could heft and use as a weapon. Nothing. His hand caught a piece of loose skirting but he couldn't lever it off from the position he was in. He smacked the wall instead, dug his nails into soft plaster. Chucked a handful at the guard, hit him uselessly on the backs of his legs. Made him turn around at least. He lumbered across to Danny, towered over him. The roll of gaffer tape in one hand.

'Fucking touch her again and you're dead,' Danny warned him.

The guard said nothing, just unpeeled the end of the tape and crouched down. Danny caught him on the side of his face with his free hand, a hard enough blow to topple him. But he was straight back up again, his eyes shining.

Fuck, thought Danny as he realised the guard was enjoying this.

He got him again – the guard *was* stupid – in the solar plexus, and he keeled over once more, but the trouble was Danny was only setting himself up for a harder fall eventually. There was no choice. Z was still tied to the cot, bent backwards over it, the way she had been beneath Danny only minutes before.

The guard picked himself up off the floor and Danny saw him reach for something, a coil of old flex. As he came towards Danny he kicked him again. Danny raised his right arm to shield his face and the guard caught it, yanked it backwards, nearly dislocating the shoulder, and lashed it crudely to the rad. He taped his mouth, then stood up, seemed to consider giving Danny another whack with the steel toecap but backed off instead.

Z was tugging at her own bonds, then trying to get to her feet but the cot was too heavy. The guard unbuckled his trousers, pushed down his pants (cheap, broad blue stripe on off-white). Danny was screaming through his gag. Z was doing the same.

Even if there was another security guard in the building, it wasn't loud enough to carry down one flight of stairs. And this could have been their routine anyway, although to Danny it looked like an opportunistic thing. Saw Z on a plate and couldn't say no. The cunt. He *was* going to die. It didn't matter that Danny was cuffed to a radiator, gagged and pretty much relegated as far as the guard was concerned, there had to be a way out.

But it was already happening. Like some tacky seaside novelty corkscrew, he was punching rhythmically but raggedly in and out, in and out. Danny could see Z trying to kick out, but the guard's legs were positioned over hers like a clamp. There was nothing she could do. What chance was there, Danny wondered frantically, that the Yugoslav busboy Zoran might be rattling around the corridors of the old hospital as well tonight? Then he remembered that he had the busboy's set of keys to the restaurant. There was no other way into the hospital – unless you came in with the security guards.

It was down to him and him alone.

I hit the ground so hard I almost bounced off it. Would have done if it hadn't been sand.

I didn't have Danny down as a marksman. It was too clean somehow, too remote. I saw him getting his hands dirty, like with Z. Breaking somebody's neck with his bare hands instead of firing a bullet through it from two hundred yards.

I lifted my head up off the ground and checked out my immediate surroundings. Luckily I was smack behind a limestone pillar. Although it wasn't *that* lucky – you could have thrown yourself to the ground just about anywhere in the Pinnacles and you'd have been unfortunate not to be sheltered. I crabbed the lower half of my body around so it was hidden from what I guessed to have been the direction of the gunfire. Which wasn't easy – sound ricocheting off a hundred or more pinnacles within a fifty-yard radius. I lifted a hand and another bullet struck the pinnacle nearest my left. I got into a crouch behind the broad-based pillar that was currently saving my life and peeped around its far edge.

A hundred yards away stood a man with a gun, a rifle. He looked ready to fire again, as soon as I gave him enough of a target. Even at that distance I could see it wasn't Danny. In fact, I wouldn't have been able to make a positive ID at all if it hadn't been for the orange and white VW camper van parked behind him.

Ken Ambrose.

Trying to kill me with the rifle he used for putting half-dead kangaroos out of their misery. At least I had to assume he was trying to kill me, rather than just wing me. I drew back behind the pillar and sat up against it. My breathing was fast and shallow, my heart racing. I scanned the desert for any sign of Danny – there was none. Had Ambrose not seen me clearly enough to recognise me? Did he think I was Danny? Or was he just running amuck with a gun. Christ, just my luck.

Another shot pinged off a nearby pinnacle, reverberations scattering like a pinball in a machine.

Yeah, I could sit and wait for him to come and get me. Sit it out until he used up all his ammo. Wait for Danny to show up and make it interesting. Or I could actually do something. I'm usually happier doing something. So I got to my feet behind the pillar – it was one of the taller ones, over six foot – and ran like a bastard to the nearest big pinnacle, which was only a dozen yards away.

And a dozen yards closer to Ambrose.

A shot rang out. The card I had chosen to play was the one that said he didn't know it was me he was shooting at, and as soon as he did, he would stop. Before running to the next pillar I picked a stone up off the desert floor and chucked it twenty yards in the other direction where it struck one of the shorter pinnacles – sure enough, it distracted him sufficiently to allow me to get closer. I called his name. There was no wind. I didn't know if he had heard me.

'Ambrose. It's me. Hold your fire.'

It wasn't a wide pillar and I was standing right up close to it to minimise the chance of him getting sight of my body behind it. The stone blurred before my eyes until I refocused. Tiny grains of sand swarmed all over the surface like ants. My breathing was too fast, uncomfortable, risky – I could hyperventilate if I wasn't careful. The peak of my hat kept hitting the stone column's calcrete cap so I bent it upwards to allow me to stand as close to the stone as possible.

'Ambrose,' I shouted, not having to worry about Danny hearing me. 'Ambrose. It's me – Chris.' And I stepped out from behind the pillar.

Ambrose had moved. He was standing ten yards away with a silly expression on his face, but it was too late because he'd already squeezed the trigger.

Danny was able to loosen the flex holding his right hand to the radiator by waggling his hand vigorously. In his haste, the guard hadn't tied it as well as he might have done. But still his hand wouldn't slip through the loop. Danny could imagine Z's screams and he began to think this was more terrible than actually being able to hear them. The guard had stopped a couple of times to slap her on the side of the head or bury his own face between her legs, which only made Danny redouble his efforts.

He felt his skin give. For the first time in his life he thanked God for giving him fucking snakeskin. Photosensitive dermatitis, the doc called it, showing how much *he* knew. The skin around the base of his thumb shredded, slipped its moorings and allowed the flex that infinitesimally reduced width it needed. It slipped over the thumb and then it was a simple matter to draw his hand completely out of the plastic-coated wire.

Without pausing to congratulate himself on this small progress he wrapped his free arm around the radiator and gave it a tug. Nothing. Using the left arm as well, still cuffed to the actual rad, he heaved and attempted to lever the thing off the wall. The fabric of the wall was soft. It had to work. There was no other way. If he was lucky, the radiator would be screwed in no deeper than the plaster. He tensed his muscles for one more tug – and it came free. One pipe still attached the device to the wall, but it was old and thin.

Danny pulled the entire thing free with such force he himself was jerked away from the wall into a crouch, from which he unfolded his body, radiator notwithstanding, into an upright position, and then ran, screaming as he went in the hope that the man would turn around and move away from Z – he didn't want to pile into him while he was still inside her.

Z saw the whole thing. Although she'd wanted to close her eyes during the assault to block the event out of her mind, to pretend it wasn't happening, she couldn't. For one thing, it hurt too much, and for another, she was searching, all the time he was moving in and out of her, for a way to stop him. She tried kicking, she tried bucking her body up at the waist, but he was too strong and in an unassailable position. She cursed and screamed behind her gag, but nothing put him off. His own eyes remained open also – they were lost-looking, pale blue in the dim light that filtered through the grimy windows behind the cot. Even when his gaze met hers he showed no emotion. Still she screamed. And still she squirmed on the thin mattress, jarring her hip bone on the side of the cot. Tied down, she'd been unable to see Danny until he'd already wrenched the radiator free of the wall and had come running up behind the guard, his screams joining hers and ringing through the crumbling corridors of the old hospital.

The guard turned at Danny's final approach, his limp penis slithering fish-like, wrung-out and discoloured, from her reluctant grip. Had he not taken half a step to one side in a vain attempt to avoid Danny's onslaught, both men would have landed on top of her and she doubted she would have survived the fall. But the guard took that vital half-step – vital for Z, less so for him – and the radiator, which preceded Danny like the prow of a ship, caught him in the throat. Z saw his Adam's apple collapse before both men flashed past her in a blur and fell to the floor. She tried to follow the struggle but, even with her head turned in that direction, she couldn't see. It didn't last long. Danny's first strike had done enough damage, though that didn't prevent him from bringing the radiator crashing down on his head three more times.

Z heard – and, she admitted later, was glad to hear – the damp crack of the security guard's skull.

Then a brief silence – before the thump of her own heartbeat and Danny's ragged breathing fell in time with each other.

Danny located the guard's keys and released himself from the cuffs; the radiator rolled off the guard's body and clanged on the floor. He knelt to untie her hands, then carefully removed the strip of gaffer tape from her mouth and sat holding her, rocking her, stroking her hair, murmuring intended comforts. She was crying. They were both shaking. He increased the pressure of his embrace, his chin jutting over her left shoulder, so that their two hearts pressed as close to each other as they possibly could – beating, it seemed, as one.

Beyond the cot, just out of sight, lay the body, leaking blood – *more* blood – into the already bloodied boards of Dr George Maddox's former transplant chamber.

The bullet creased my arm. Just above the elbow on my left arm. On the inside edge, so about three inches from my heart. Either he managed to shift just off-target, or he was aiming to wing me – or he was a bad shot. Or I managed to move that vital couple of inches. Whichever. I was still around. Bleeding, in extraordinary pain, but still around.

Ambrose helped me over to his van. In the midst of fulsome apologies – 'I thought you were him, the guy you described. The long hair, the cap . . .' – he patched me up using a cleanish strip of cloth torn from one of his shirts, and together we scanned the skyline.

'It's quite possible he's simply gone,' said Ambrose.

'His car . . .' I began.

'Not like that.'

I looked at him.

Ambrose suggested that the Pinnacles Desert was no ordinary place. 'People come and go here,' he said. He called it the Repository of Lost Souls. *Christ, not another one*, I thought. I told him I could do with simply finding Danny and forcing him to take me to Joanna.

'Let's walk,' he said, and we left his van. 'Certain spots are more potent than others.'

Could be he simply meant you got a better view from higher up.

'Something like that,' he nodded.

You could always tell when there'd been a row in our house – when my parents had disagreed over something and taken that disagreement beyond a point it was ever meant to be taken.

When they rowed it was as if they had taken hold of a bird – a big bird, a gull or something – thinking they could manage it. They'd fought over it, wresting it from each other, until the bird got aggressive and took control of its own destiny, beating its wings and throwing its weight about in a bid for freedom. They could never control the bird after that. Logic, rationality and civility lay in tatters on the floor and the bird flew haphazardly around the entire house beating its head against windows trying to get out. It would sometimes take days or even weeks to find an open window. Even if my sister and I had gone around opening windows for it.

You'd walk around the house on tiptoes until the bird was free, frightened of causing it to stir. You'd close doors slowly and quietly and with gentle determination. You'd talk to each other in whispers for fear of upsetting it further.

We used to sit upstairs if Dad was downstairs. Stay inside if he was in the garden. It was him we were scared of, not Mum. But we were nervous of spending too much time around Mum in case we appeared to be avoiding him. It was a difficult balance and a lot of time was wasted playing these ridiculous games. Many hours of childhood. Time which then you didn't realise was severely rationed. We thought we would live for ever. I can still remember what it felt like thinking I was going to live for ever. When a lifetime was so impossibly long, it stretched ahead of me into the fields beside the house and beyond them into the country paths we would explore several times over the course of a summer holiday. Even a six-week school break was an eternity. When you multiplied that by however many you needed to make a life, it was such a fantastic idea, you couldn't get a handle on it. Yes, we were going to live for ever. If we wasted a few hours creeping around the house being domestic diplomats, we had no idea that time was precious. Oh to have it now. To get that time back and give it to my father. He'd have known even then that his time was valuable. How could he bear to waste so much of it – *any* of it, even?

Times when arguments would coincide with trips out. Deathly silence in the car. The overpowering smells of leather upholstery, Chanel No 5 and dubbin on the hiking boots. No one daring to say a word. My father storming off, leaving the rest of us to catch up. Me knowing I was expected to walk with him, while my sister kept my mum company. The strain on her beautiful face, the pain she rarely allowed us to glimpse. Rows like any other couple, problems like any other marriage. How could she allow those moments to slip by? She couldn't stop them. He was in charge. He was the time-keeper, the time-waster. He wasted their time together, some of it, our time with them. Only by a few hours, twenty-four hours, say, over the course of the years.

A lost day out of so many days. Did that really matter so much?

Twenty-four hours of dead time. It lay there, sloughed off down beside the track of my past like little careful piles of dead snakeskin. Brittle and fragile, like the ghost of a once-coiled spring.

At the end, time meant nothing to him. He'd stand motionless in the corridor just outside the ward on his way back from the loo, staring at the wall, until one of the nurses came and helped him back to his bed. Didn't have a clue some of the time. Didn't know what was going on. The sky changed colour outside his window and the flowers on his bedside cabinet dropped their petals, but time meant nothing to him any more. It no longer existed.

'I saw the children trying to go upstairs.'

No, you didn't.

His soft hair growing back on his fragile skull. My mother cradling his head as she dabbed at his parched lips with those tiny pink pieces of sponge. Hair continues to grow on a dead man for thirty-six hours.

Why can't I get these final images of him out of my mind? Will they be the pictures of him that I carry to my own grave? Will my life *ever* return to normal? *Is* this normal? I guess it is.

They tell you to visit the Pinnacles Desert early morning or late evening. The light's better. Longer shadows.

When I came to, I couldn't quite believe the level of discomfort I was in. My cheek had fused with the limestone pillar I was slumped against. It was a gradual process levering myself away from it and working out that I hadn't been tied up, merely fallen asleep leaning against one of the pinnacles. Ambrose was nearby, sat cross-legged, head bowed, apparently still slumbering. No immediate sign of Danny.

But the column I had slept against, when I finally peeled my face away from it, revealed itself as one of those many in the Pinnacles Desert to bear a resemblance to a human face.

It all came back to me – Ambrose and I had covered a lot of ground the night before. He told me the place was full of secrets and surprises. He told me he was looking to it to return his father to him, if only briefly (and illusorily, presumably – but how did he know anyway? About *my* father? *Did* he at all? I guess not). We wandered through the Pinnacles Desert, drinking Tooheys Red from the Esky in Ambrose's van, and talked about fathers, mine and his. He told me about the accident outside Broome in north Western Australia, his father's Kingswood the only car involved. They found it upside down in the dust some twenty metres from the road. Signed off with a meaningless doodle, enough scorched rubber to resole fifty pairs of Blundstones. No flash flood, no dead animals. Now I saw the need for Ambrose's pages and pages of diagrams, understood how he was able to hold the entire collection in his head.

Danny was never far from our minds but we didn't see him. I remember thinking he was probably watching us all along. Training his sights on us throughout the night. Then I woke up slumped next to one of the pinnacles, my face indented by the surface of the hard calcrete cap – which, as far as I was concerned, when struck by the rising sun, was the perfect image of my father's face. The sunken cheek, the broad, intelligent forehead. Eyes shallow shadows. It was him all right.

During the last part of the night, in that half-dreaming, half-thinking state that may precede dawn, I'd conceived an image of the Pinnacles, which had then repeated itself in my mind over and over again, becoming more intricate and complex each time. An aerial view of the stone pillars showed me that they were joined by something. At first I was simply imagining lines drawn between them. Drawn once and then twice and then over and over again. A cat's cradle of insubstantial pathways traced around and between the stone columns.

In a fantastic conjunction of technology and nature, I imagined the tracery to be computer-generated, like rapidly repeating and increasingly complex patterns on a screen-saver program. As each new pattern was drawn and then wiped away, etched and erased, a vital new layer was left. Imperceptibly but unquestionably there. Lines of energy you could almost see. As if thermal imaging of a football field were to produce a picture not only of the players, but of their running and passing, their warm channels of displaced air.

All of this created a net, a web – all it wanted now was something to catch. It waited there in my dream, sticky as a spider's web. Waiting. Almost thrumming with energy. Alive.

I thought about Charlie. And I thought about my father. Maybe Charlie had something, I don't know. Maybe I wanted to believe in Charlie's crazy spirit world. Maybe I wanted to look up and see a plane in the sky. Maybe I did. I looked up and maybe there was a plane there. Is the Pinnacles under a flight path? Those jets that take off from Perth and head for Singapore, they have to fly somewhere. Just because the Pinnacles is in the middle of nowhere doesn't mean there's no one there holding the kite strings. So I looked up and there was a plane. A tiny speck in the vast blue. A cargo of souls. And I prayed for it to stay up. I thought of the people on board. Hearts beating in fuselages of muscle and bone. Launched on their own trajectories across existence. Hoping for a safe landing. They would all crash some time. And maybe some of them knew that, but only some of them *really* knew that. Only some of them *felt* it, knew it in their hearts. Those who'd already lost someone. Was it possible that the pain of losing my father had been supplanted by the realisation of my own mortality? Was that the power of this place? To throw a switch in my heart?

Ambrose was scanning the horizon. As the sun climbed in the sky the shadows shortened. There were fewer places for Danny to hide.

'I'll find that bloody Projectionist,' Ambrose said. 'Bane of my bloody life.'

I didn't ask. Not then.

'I'll get the bastard, once and for all.'

Yeah, right.

AORTA

*The main trunk from which the
systemic arterial system proceeds.
Exit from the heart.*

Twenty-six

Figure in a landscape. Woman, by the look of her.

I've come a long way for this, I'm thinking. It'd better be worth it.

Why is she standing so still? Why is she standing there at all, exposed to the elements like that? My Blunnies crash through the heather, occasionally slipping – they weren't designed for this kind of terrain. I windmill my arms to regain balance. The figure on the horizon grows no bigger, as if I'm falling foul of contour lines and never actually getting any closer – a not unfamiliar feeling.

I'm reminded of Australia.

Constantly.

I can hear my heart beating, my breath coming shallow and fast. I'm hot despite the temperature and the bitter winds.

Dartmoor.

The middle of winter.

The woman is always just off to the right. I stop and survey the lie of the land. If I continue in a straight line I'll end up having to climb out of the gully currently to my left. If I break my line and head right, I might bring myself at least on to the same altitude as the figure.

Why does it look, as I do now start to get closer, as if she has no arms?

And why do I assume that she is standing on the grid reference I'm aiming for?

The grid reference I was given.

When I stop and check the red directional arrow on the compass, it still points towards her, as it has been doing since she became visible. I experience a sinking feeling, by now very familiar. I can no longer remember the taste of Joanna's kiss, the scent of her skin. Some small part of me tries to prepare itself never to know these sensations again.

If Danny is mad then he is unpredictable – that is the only thing one can be sure of. Just because he snapped Z's neck in the door of his Mercedes is no reason to *assume* he's done the same to Joanna.

I offer myself bets on the outcome and turn them all down in case inversely or directly they influence the outcome. I recognise the first tendrils of magical thinking and realise I must guard against losing my mind. I have to believe she's still alive. I *do* believe she's still alive. I've spoken to her since she got back. But not since *I* got back. Anything could have happened during my return flight.

And so I walk on through the heather, down a narrow gully where sheep scatter, up the other side and at the top I stop for breath. I push my hood back. The wind tugs at my long hair. Cool, fresh – bitterly cold, in fact. Not exactly Western Australia.

A dark cauliflower soup of rainclouds boils in the western sky. There's no sign of a break in the icy winds which flatten the heather. Straight ahead, though separated from me by more ravines and knolls, the armless woman, still locked in position. To my left I can now see several Dartmoor ponies, manes and tails whipping this way and that in the wind, necks bent as they bury their heads in the heather in search of food.

Behind me also to the left, an enormous flat-topped outcrop of rocks, a mile or so from where I'm standing. The compass points to the figure ahead of me. With a deepening leaden sense of foreboding I press on.

I've come all the way from the other side of the world for this. But my heart grows sick at the thought that what I'm looking at might be quite literally what I've been searching for.

Ken Ambrose's opinion, once I'd told him everything I knew in the VW van on our way down to Perth, was that Danny was highly disturbed. A psychopath, he said. I was still praying otherwise. And who was Ambrose to go calling people psychopaths anyway, considering the obsessive nature of his fixation on the Projectionist?

The woman is no more than two hundred yards away now.

There are no other figures in the landscape. Just me. And her.

Danny left me a grid reference. SE 681817. Scratched into the sand in the Pinnacles Desert. I knew what it was as soon as I saw it. Either he knew I'd find his message before the wind erased it, or he didn't care, but my guess was he was watching me and Ambrose all along and was playing us like a sea angler with a couple of big pollock on a feather rig. Once we'd picked up the grid reference, he was away. The Mercedes, there one minute, was gone the next. I believed I'd learnt enough about Danny over the last few weeks – and through what Max had told me about him – to guess this was a genuine message, not a smokescreen, that if I followed it up I'd find Joanna. Unless, of course, we were by now operating on completely different planes and he'd murdered Joanna long before and no longer knew the difference between right and wrong, life and death, whatever. But an Ordnance Survey map reference – that was pretty specific. I simply had to put everything I'd got left on that and hope for the best. It was partly instinctive now. I could have stayed and scoured WA once more but I didn't have a clue where to look and here he was giving me one, a clue – a big one, *the* big one, or so it seemed.

Ambrose took me to Perth airport, glad to help me out further but chuntering from time to time that he'd still not got his Projectionist. I suggested he come to England, leave him behind. He said it wasn't that big a deal. I think it was though.

I asked him how he came to be there, at the Pinnacles Desert, at the right time. He told me how he'd tracked Danny up from the south – a couple of medium-sized 'roos he'd hit, heaped by the run-off verge, blood still cooling; occasional scorchmarks on the road where he'd missed other animals but as good as signed his name on the macadam. As he'd got closer, the burnt rubber patterns on the road surface got warmer.

'Until I found myself crouched over a really good tyre track just east of the Pinnacles that was practically smoking it was so fresh. I'd lost Yasmin by this stage, of course. Jumped ship after we'd come back up through Perth. Probably working some skimpy bar on the Brand Highway, serving beers to the government guy who drives around dropping stubbies by the side of the road.'

At Perth before flying out I checked with the police once more and with the place we'd stayed in Denham. Neither had any news. Moments before I was about to pass through the departure gate, I had another idea.

Eddie and Nick. Joanna's friends in Geraldton. The only people she actually knew on the entire continent. Had she been able to call anyone, she might well have called them.

I found another public phone.

'Oh Chris, thank God you've called,' Eddie said.

Joanna was in England. She was unharmed. There was even a number. That was all she'd been able to tell them.

I called the number straightaway. It rang and rang and rang. The minutes were ticking by. I should have been on board. I didn't want to miss the flight, especially now I'd had an indication Joanna was back in the UK.

A voice answered eventually. I didn't know whose. I just asked for Joanna and after what seemed like an age she came to the phone. The world seemed to stand still for a moment. Then start up again with a dizzying jolt. What we both had to say we said in a rush and at the same time as each other. A lot of it went over my head. I couldn't take it all in. The bones of it were that Joanna was somewhere on Dartmoor, staying in a pub. Max was there too. Danny was not: he was still in Australia. I was to meet Joanna – and Max! – on Dartmoor. At the map reference. There was more but it could wait.

It would have to wait. I had a plane to catch.

'I'm all right,' she kept saying.

I told Joanna I'd see her on Dartmoor. Gave her my ETA and ran to the gate.

I flew back with Singapore Airlines, their staff rendering the whole ordeal as painless and comfortable as possible. The male and female attendants alike were beautiful, unruffled, calm. Solicitous without being patronising, sympathetic to my anxiously repeated questions without becoming alarmist, they cosseted me. I was a type to them, no doubt, but one they knew how to handle. I read their names off their badges, thinking this would protect me, in addition to my habitual *sotto voce* mantra. Vienna Mok, Jasmine Goh, Woon Num Hin. They floated up and down the aisles in their perfect skins, their minutely judged yet apparently natural smiles, their air of absolute professionalism. Not even a landing on water would faze them.

We de-planed in Singapore and had to hang around the airport for an hour or so. I tried calling the Dartmoor number again but there was no answer. I climbed back on board the 747 and went through take-off hell once more. Vienna Mok was still on board; Jasmine Goh reappeared after we had overflown India. I don't know what happened to Woon Num Hin. I guess he hit the sack in Singapore.

The rest of the flight passed in a woozy waking dream. I'd scored something off Ambrose before leaving WA; whether it was a regular sleeping pill or a downer of some kind I didn't really know, or care, but it knocked the stuffing out of me for the final eight hours or so. I hallucinated regular dream-like visitations by Vienna Mok and Jasmine Goh – they soothed me and reassured me in my anxiety. I was sufficiently conscious at one point to think that *Speed*, a film which ends with a jumbo jet bursting into flames, was possibly not the most appropriate in-flight movie.

I drifted off, pictured myself cradled in the plane-as-kite, Joanna holding the string down on earth. Danny cutting the string. Ambrose catching the ends and tying them back together. But not before my father had escaped – somehow, from somewhere, I don't know where. And there was Charlie, whispering his guttural comforts. My mother standing on the end of a pier where she'd often gone with my father, the wind pushing her hair back from her face, tears springing from her eyes, a well she must be thinking will never dry up.

Naturally it was raining in London. I say naturally not because it always rains in London, but because it always rains, if it possibly can, when my plane is coming in to land. That's just the way it works. As we overflew the City I had to content myself with picturing the silvery snaking of the Thames through London's glittering mica. We swooped over the reservoirs at Shepperton and bumped rather than touched down amid a thin grey drizzly sky whose skirts trailed along the runway.

I rang the Dartmoor number again from the airport, but, although I let it ring for five minutes, no one picked up. I took a cab into town and called in at the flat just long enough to get suitable gear and check there were no important messages, and to observe, when I finally reached the supposedly secure underground car park, that someone had broken into the Stag and stolen the car phone.

Soon I was heading south-west out of London, a 1968 Ordnance Survey map of Dartmoor (it couldn't have changed that much) in the pocket of my Geltek coat, a cross marked in red ink on Danny's coordinates. I felt curiously light-headed and quite confused as to the real time of day or night.

As the sky started to darken, I didn't know if that meant we were getting into morning or evening. I automatically slowed down behind a dawdling white Mercedes on the M4 and had to kick myself to get going again; it wasn't even an old model.

I stopped at some services when it was dark, found a parking bay and lay down on the back seat of the Stag. I was asleep before my head hit my rolled up rubber coat. Confused dreams. Something, or someone, going around and around, in some way, trying to get somewhere and finding itself, or himself, merely going around in circles. I woke up shaking with the cold. Ice had formed on the insides of the windows. I got out of the car, my bones aching, and ran around the car park until I started to feel that my dreams had been some kind of psychic dress rehearsal for the day to follow rather than something closer to the other way around.

Within half an hour I was urging the Stag down the M5, digging my heels in. I was prepared to accept that it might be morning, but I wasn't convinced. I felt like an actor trapped in a series of scenes, the changes in the backdrop artificially accelerated. I don't know what time it was when I reached the edge of Dartmoor; I never wear a watch and the clock in the Stag is one of those that are right only twice a day.

I pulled into one of those gritty car parks that appear scooped out of the moor and have room for half a dozen motor bikes and a Nissan Micra. I gathered the stuff I needed and eased myself out of the Stag.

I wrap my arms around her in a tight hug. I feel momentarily as if my search is over even if it isn't. I hold on more tightly, press my cheek against her cold grey shoulder. When I pull away there's a meniscus of chill moisture that stretches between us. I catch a glimpse of it, laced with tiny dark particles of grit, just before it divides into a single string of concentrated saliva and eventually snaps. My eyes struggle to make sense of the surface six inches in front of them. Pitted; grey, brown and silver; alive with lichen and minuscule organisms, red spiders, tiny insects, but otherwise stone dead. Heavy, damp, cold. Warmed little by my breath. A lump of stone.

Carved and then weathered, a mass of granite.

Once perhaps a cross, a Christian or possibly pagan symbol; now, after centuries or mere decades of bitter winds, freezing rain and vigorous frost action, the unmistakeable figure of a mutilated woman. Her arms mere stumps a few inches long. Above these, once the proud angular head of a stone cross, now the softer profile of a woman's skull released from within it, one sculpture having been worked on by the elements to produce a second. This is the one that had always been the ultimate work, the aim of the original stonemason, had he but known it. Doubtless she would change again and in time completely disappear, but for now she is in her prime. This is her apogee.

I take a step back and try to think about her in relation to Danny. And Joanna. A nagging thought plays an irritating pizzicato on my brainstem. Joanna. Where is she? What did he do to her? Is she all right? What might have happened to her since our brief conversation? Is this stone woman some kind of model? Danny's idealised woman? Impenetrable. Double amputee.

My breath freezes on the air as I look around. A line of dark green conifers two, three hundred yards away, beyond the figure. The road, I now see, curling back and cresting a gentle hillock off to the south-west. A solitary building. Back the way I came, a handful of Dartmoor ponies and in the distance the rocky flat-top.

I slump down with my back resting against the stone woman, something teasing my mind towards despair. Has Danny, after all, dragged me halfway around the world merely for his own entertainment?

The new figure appears while I'm looking in its direction

and has actually emerged before I'm aware of it. I'm watching the line of conifers, wondering why one of them seems to be swaying in the wind more than the others. Why it's getting slowly bigger, extruding from the perimeter of the wood. Then I squint through the drizzle. Is it someone running? Joanna? I don't want even to start to believe it. And yet don't I feel numb now, as if Danny has taken a soldering iron and cauterised my emotional nerve endings? What if it were Joanna? How should I feel? Relieved, happy, victorious? These are just words.

She didn't run – that was an illusion. She walked towards me slowly. I don't know at what stage she realised it was me, or I her. Although she walked and I remained where I was until the last moment, I had the impression of watching the scene played out differently. My camera angle switched to one from above, in which she ran across the moor to meet me, and I stood rock still as she threw herself into my arms. Some subtle body of hers, perhaps, which ran ahead of her to confirm it was me and not a trick. My own wispy outline dissolved as I broke free of my moorings and ran to meet her. The moment of contact was replayed over and over again, shot from all possible angles – the different edits all played at the same time, as if the world were a multiplex, each screen running a different cut. Together, the final cut, the combination of all the director's wishes and intentions, now broken down impossibly into his – or her – various dreams of the scene. Is it like this all the time, I wondered, as I felt – actually felt – the moist warmth of Joanna's neck against my shaking fingers, as I buried my face in her hair and held her as tight as a drowning man clings to a life-raft, squeezing her upper body with the desperate strength of a boy latching on to a fixed point, an overhead locker, a seat, whatever illusion of safety, in a plane whose nose has been ripped off – a broken cigar flashing through the sky at five hundred miles an hour, knowing he has ten, eleven seconds at the most before the fuselage is scoured by implacable winds and the plane's contents ditched in the coldest of oceans.

We hug each other so hard we fuse. I'm scared to let go in case I look at her face and see someone else's. Our legs buckle and we fall and roll, hitting the heather, tears mingling on faces that still haven't quite settled into the features each remembers of the other from before.

We draw back, look into each other's eyes, see relief, happiness, but also something dark, something elemental and hurting that we both sense could take years to heal. We'll always know it's there, waiting. Some alternative reel, shot but never used. Distributed maybe to one single movie house in the interior of a sun-blasted desert in the middle of nowhere and played there over and over again. A different ending. An entire different film. The lighting more subdued, the angles all screwy, the actors nervy and haunted, their faces pinched, eyes fogged plates. Imagine your life shot by a consortium of doomy auteurs – Lynch, Antonioni, Bergman, Von Trier, Hooper, Cronenberg – but without the laughs. No constant stream of gags. No light relief. No tongue in cheek. An endlessly repeating darker version of the real thing; a shadow, a subconscious cinema – playing twenty-four hours a day in one outback movie theatre. A shackful of empty seats, a deserted dusty ticket-window, a tiny crooked booth, the projectionist from hell.

Maybe Ambrose wasn't so mad after all.

'Was he violent?'

'Not much. A bit. He pulled up outside the place in Denham while you were getting milk and suggested I get in the car. He could see I was standing my ground, so he got out and grabbed hold of my arm. He was so quick . . . I don't know, I didn't have time to react.'

'Quick as a snake,' I said.

'There was a scuffle but he was too strong. He made me get in the car on his side and slide across so he could keep hold of me, twisting my arm. I shouted for help but no one heard.

Seconds later we were heading south out of Denham. I'm surprised you didn't see the car.'

'Must have been while I was actually inside the shop. Damn it, I'm sorry I left you. You wanted to come with me. I should've let you come with me.'

'Forget it. It doesn't matter. It doesn't matter now.'

'Of course it matters.'

I looked into her eyes, squeezed her hands, tried to unpick the memories knitting her brow.

'Why though?' I asked. 'What was it about? What was he doing? What's going on?'

We don't have long together before Max turns up.

'Let's go,' I'd said.

'No we can't,' she'd told me. 'We have to wait. We have to do this.'

'Why?'

Max comes shambling through the heather. I can hear his old-fashioned waterproof trousers brushing through the wet clumps, his heavy boots springing on the spongy earth. He's carrying a shovel.

I step in front of Joanna. I can hear her breathing shallowly behind me. But as Max approaches she steps out from behind me.

'Don't,' she said to me. 'It's not Max's fault. It's not Max.'

I look at both of them.

I say: 'Would somebody please tell me what the fuck is going on?'

Four people standing in the middle of the moor, you'd have thought, from a distance or from above. Standing close, presumably waiting for something. Joanna, Max, me. And the stone woman.

'We're here because of Danny,' Max says.

'I'm a bit sick of running around after him,' I say.

I wonder what new experiment in psychogeography we're

involved in. What fresh psychogeomantic fantasies we're acting out for him. We're just pawns. Intelligent pawns, but pawns nevertheless in some elaborate game of temporal translocation.

Max chucks his shovel on to the springy heather at the foot of the stone amputee.

Like a weathered, stunted X, she marks the spot.

'The locals call it Bennett's Cross,' Max says, slapping the granite cross with his right hand. 'It's a Norman name – Bennett. Means blessed.'

He turns to look directly at me.

'I suppose I'd better get digging,' he says.

Hacking through the tough heather proves tricky, but then the peaty earth subsides fairly easily beneath the shovel. I notice that the drizzle has stopped, though presumably not for long. The light is sparse, compressed, making Joanna's magenta hiking socks shockingly vivid against the dark earth. Still Max digs. Joanna watches the hole as it grows deeper. Max's skin begins to glow under a thin varnish of sweat.

Eventually the blade of his shovel strikes something hard and I feel myself tensing along with Joanna. Max pulls back from the edge and straightens his crackling spine. Joanna has started to chew the inside of her mouth. I can almost hear Danny giving his orders: *Get the box out, Max. Get the fucking box out*. Max bends over the hole once more and uses the shovel to prise the box free of the earth, then tosses the shovel aside and drops his long arms into the hole to grasp the box. He grunts with the effort and curses when it catches on a root, but then up it comes. Heavy – clearly – from the look on Max's face. It could be lead. Max drags it up against the side of the hole he's dug and finally gets the box to the top, where he leaves it balancing on the lip. He uses his foot to move it away from the very edge, then gets down and examines the box, presumably looking for a way in.

I am wondering whether Danny buried it himself or, as now,

got Max to do his dirty work for him. Not that I have the faintest idea, at this stage, what is in the box. I just wonder if, on the other side of the world, Danny is having a laugh at our expense.

The three of us are bent over the box, warm air streaming from our nostrils and mouths and freezing on the air in ballooning clouds like a convocation of dragons. Max is still looking for a seam or a catch. He brushes more peat off the case and his fingers find the device. We all hear the release – a muffled click – although no lid springs open. Max takes hold of one side of the box in his left hand and eases it up. There are tiny squeals and scrapes and gritty scrunches and finally the lid is free, lying on the exposed peat next to the box.

Our collective breath hovers over the box for a moment, obscuring its contents, then dissolves into the cold, damp air, and we all get a good view.

Inside the lead box is something about the size of a large fist. As if to blend in with the surrounding landscape, its colouring is dull – peaty brown, pale speckling, lead grey, the slippery black of hinted-at corruption, and shifting between these a hint of crimson, a red wash added to a predominantly dark palette.

There are folds and crevices in the material. Lacking any distinct flux or whorl, the thing seems created by chaos. Looking at it cold, there's no way you'd guess what it was. Perhaps. Unless you knew, or had a pretty good idea.

It resembles the chamois heart. The unidentifiable object Danny found in the old hospital all those years ago, which was neither an old window-cleaner's chamois leather scrunched up into a ball, nor an extracted heart inexplicably left lying around. There's no denying its close resemblance to the thing in the photo Max once showed me. Max knows this and I know this. I suspect Joanna knows it too. The thing he spotted from across an abandoned laboratory and slowly circled like a cat with a dead shrew. Prodding it lightly with a pencil, photo-

graphing it from every angle, without ever actually touching it
or moving it from its resting place.

That's not to say I knew what I was expecting it to be.

Just not that.

Twenty-seven

With Max carrying the lead box and contents, we trooped
down the road to the pub where Joanna and Max had been
staying while waiting for me to fly back from Perth. It turned
out to be the solitary building I'd noticed earlier on my
approach to Danny's coordinates.

'They have a fire going in here,' Max said. 'It's not been
allowed to go out since 1845. They say it's to ward off the devil.'

'Really.'

I pushed open the door to allow Max, carrying the box, to go
in first. I looked at Joanna; she gave me a tiny smile and nodded,
as if I'd asked her a question. I suppose it must have felt as if
every time I looked at her I was asking her if she was all right.

We followed Max into the dark interior.

'The rooms are a bit poky,' Max said, looking up at the
ceiling. 'I suggest we stay down here.'

I bought a round of drinks, because I couldn't see Max
volunteering.

Eventually, we got settled, the three of us and the lead box,
around a little table.

Max began. While he talked, the patch of sky I could see

outside the window behind his head grew both darker and more luminous. Night fell quickly here. Middle of winter and no light pollution. Max and Joanna shared the narrative.

I quickly gathered that Joanna's involvement in the whole business was limited to her knowledge of what had happened that time in St George's, which, for Danny, had been reason enough to snatch her.

Once Danny had broken free of the wall in the abandoned hospital and brained the security guard with the radiator, he and Z suddenly found that they had a body to deal with. Going to the police was never really an option at the time, although looking back, it was not easy to see why not. The attack was in defence of Z, and for the three extra blows to the head with the radiator you'd be looking at mitigation due to extreme provocation. So incensed was Danny that he couldn't prevent himself. But at the time, they just saw the body. Plus the fact they were trespassing. An investigation, Danny believed, could have buried them along with the guard.

Once Z had become reasonably calm, Danny went off to look for a gurney. The little man loaded the body on to it himself, despite the guard's weight almost doubling his own: he didn't want Z ever to have to touch the man again. Danny, of course, knew the location of the hospital incinerator from previous visits, and it wasn't too far from where they were now. It might not have been used for some time but an incinerator was an incinerator and all he'd need would be some fuel and there was no shortage of that – bits of old furniture, unstable door jambs, white coats; the place was full of flammable materials.

Danny reckoned there was probably a second guard, since their attacker had tried to use his radio before throwing it away in frustration, so he collected materials without making too much noise. The incinerator was towards the back of the hospital, away from the likeliest places for a guards' station. And if there *was* a second guard, Danny figured, he wouldn't go out on patrol at the same time as his colleague.

It gave Danny no pleasure to cremate the guard's body; an element of grim satisfaction only, perhaps, which lasted until the grisliness of the operation became too distressing. Danny had told Z to keep away, not to watch, but she was determined to witness the burning. Possibly she thought it would help her in the long term to get over the ordeal he'd put her through. Or maybe it was the simpler, more immediate desire for the fullest possible revenge. Once he'd got a fire going with some old curtains torn down from the windows in one of the empty wards, Danny bundled the guard's body through the portal of the incinerator. He slammed the door shut and locked it despite protests from Z. She wanted to watch – or thought she wanted to watch – while every last hair on his head sizzled, his flesh bubbling and melting. But Danny put his hands on her shoulders and moved her back. They watched together from a distance as grease spattered against the glass of the incinerator door. Eventually Z turned away and sicked up that evening's pizza in a corner.

Danny didn't know whether the fire simply lost its strength or whether it was just the kind of bad luck they were bound to encounter, but when he opened the door with an iron rod fifteen minutes later, something of the security guard remained intact.

'His heart,' I said, looking at Max. 'Right? The heart doesn't burn easily. Like Joan of Arc. Her heart survived cremation and had to be thrown in the Seine.'

'The ancient Greeks,' Joanna said, 'couldn't conceive of anything spiritual without giving it a place in the body. One of Pythagoras's pupils – Alcmeon of Crotona, who was a doctor – maintained that the soul was situated in the brain. Hippocrates tended to agree: the intelligence was located in the head.' Joanna looked at me.

'Go on,' I said.

'Plato said the immortal soul was to be found in the head,

while the mortal soul, by which he meant intelligence and feelings, was situated in the heart. Aristotle's view was that there was only one soul, in the heart, the centre of man, as he called it. The brain was cold, Aristotle said, and could not therefore give life. The heart was an inner fire.'

I was reminded of the last time Joanna, Max and I had sat around a table and talked. In Pizza Express. It seemed like years ago.

'The Egyptians believed that a man's heart was weighed after death,' she continued, 'against a single ostrich feather. If the heart was heavier, the man was judged to have been good and he was led towards Osiris. If, on the other hand, the scales went down on the feather's side, his soul was cast down into the Nether Regions.'

I wondered what Charlie would say if he were here now. His line was no less fantastical than the Egyptians', and yet I found it more easily credible, or at least metaphorical.

'That hospital,' Max cut in, 'it was very much at the centre of things. The centre of London. The omphalos. Forget Mudchute, the Isle of Dogs – John Dee and those guys. I drew maps and diagrams and showed them to Danny. Based on stuff he'd told me, about Z and where they went, places where things happened. He said it was over his head, most of it, but he knew what I meant all right. St George's was the psychogeographical heart of their relationship. Their affair was predicated upon it.'

'I studied there,' Joanna said and both Max and I turned to look at her. 'It was still partly functional as a teaching hospital when I started. I used to sit in on certain clinics – clap clinics, psychiatry. Friends of mine did medical and surgical firms there. But within a year or two all the med students were down at Tooting. And everyone else. The place closed down. Shut up shop.'

'I didn't know you'd studied at St George's. In Tooting, I mean,' I said, thinking of my own visits there.

Joanna looked at me and nodded, gave a sympathetic half-smile.

'It never seemed appropriate to mention it,' she said.

'And get this,' Max said. 'Now you work at Central Mid, right?'

Joanna nodded, although I could tell this was really for my benefit.

'If you take a pin and a piece of cotton thread,' Max continued, leaning forward on the settee and looking at me, 'and a map, obviously, and measure the distance from St George's at Hyde Park Corner – the Lanesborough as it is now – to the Central Middlesex, and then do the same for the distance from the Lanesborough to St George's in Tooting, you'll find they're exactly the same.'

I raised my eyebrows.

'Exactly the same,' he repeated. 'Down to one decimal place – five point three miles. No shit.'

'So?'

He sat back. 'So,' he shrugged. 'Seems pretty weird to me. Doesn't it to you? I'm telling you, it's a special place.'

'You'll be telling me next it's haunted.'

'How did you guess? I had an aunt who was a sister there in the war. She saw a lady in grey. But then who hasn't seen a lady in grey? This place is haunted in some other way. Some *more interesting* way.'

Max told us about Maddox. Or told *me* about Maddox. I guess he'd already told Joanna.

About the Lovegrove twins. The eager assistants, Copthorne and Salthouse. And Hope. Long lost Hope. About the transplants before their time. The extracted heart rolling around on the floor of that room. That same room. The blood seeping into the bare boards.

'It's all to do with cardiac myocytes,' he said.

I knew what cardiac myocytes were. Cells in the muscle of the heart that would keep on beating even after a heart had been extracted. They have an intrinsic ability to pulsate. The heart just wouldn't be the heart without them.

'My throat's dry,' Max said, 'with all this talking. Same again?'

Max stood up to go to the bar and I took Joanna's hand.

'You knew about all this?' I asked.

'Enough,' she nodded. 'Enough to make me a player in the game, the game in Danny's head. Charlie knew. He said something to me one day. Max had told Charlie and Charlie told me. I wished he hadn't done, obviously, but he did and then it was too late. I knew.'

'That mad bastard,' I said, shaking my head and looking at the box on the floor. 'I'll kill him for what he did to you.'

'It's over now,' Joanna said, squeezing my hand.

Max had returned.

'Danny decided he couldn't leave the heart where it was,' Max said. 'At the scene of the crime. It had to be taken somewhere. Somewhere that was important to him. So he'd always know where it was.'

'He came here with Z,' I recalled, from a much earlier conversation with Max.

'Dartmoor became another London to Danny,' Max announced. 'He plotted his key points here as he had in London. The two of them. The flat-topped rocks you'll have seen, where he lay with Z and fantasised that one day he'd make love to her. This pub. A cottage where they stayed. All points on their map of the heart, you know? And right at the centre, there was the cross, Bennett's Cross, like a ready-made gravestone. Just seemed the right thing to do somehow.'

Max paused to take a mouthful of bitter.

'And then later,' Max continued, 'it no longer seemed the right thing to have done.'

'Is that why he killed Z? Was she going to talk? And if so, why did he let Joanna go?'

'*If* he killed Z – and no one except Danny, and Z perhaps,

knows that for certain – he did so precisely because she wouldn't stop talking.'

'What do you mean?' I didn't need riddles at this stage. I was tired. I wanted to be alone with Joanna.

'It wasn't working out with Z, okay? It was great at first, obviously – you know all about that. But for one reason or another it didn't last, or it didn't seem to be lasting, and Danny thought a change of scene might do the trick. He took her out to WA—'

'I thought he went to WA to buy that Mercedes.'

'He went to WA because it's where he's from. He was born there, like I told you. They both went out there and he found the Merc. They did a lot of driving, so he fixed the rearview mirror so he could see her in *another* mirror – he had two mirrors going, if you can picture it – so he could lip-read what she was saying while he was driving. He got so sick of her not remembering, not waiting for him to look before she started speaking. So he rigged up this two-mirror system. That way they could chat while he drove. Only they didn't chat. Z just went on and on and on about that night, about the security guard. Someone would find the heart, dig it up on Dartmoor, somehow work out who was responsible and come and get them. It was inane and there was no escape from it. He had to keep the mirrors in place because there's nothing worse than not knowing what people are saying, but when all they've got to say seems dreamt up just to torment you . . .' Max swallowed the rest of his pint and set the glass down on the table. 'One day, he just lost it. He stopped the car, got her out and hit her. Two or three times. With the car door.'

Max look at both of us in turn.

'I'm not defending him,' he said.

'Why do I feel,' I said, 'as if he's always just around the next corner?'

'He didn't harm Joanna,' Max went on, 'I would guess because he never meant to hurt Z, but I could be wrong. The deal was: Joanna comes back in one piece, Danny stays in Australia, and we sort this business out for him. In any case, I think he thought Joanna had a right to know. Having been a student at St George's, saving Charlie's life – she was a part of it, like she said.'

'Max, "this business . . ." What business?'

'It's all going to be put right.'

I didn't like the sound of this.

'Nothing to worry about,' said Max.

I couldn't sleep.

We were staying the night at the pub. It had been too late, when we'd finished talking, to attempt the drive back to London. Especially with me being jetlagged. Now, however, I couldn't sleep.

I kept seeing my father, not as he was at the end, but as he had been. I wanted to phone my mother but it was too late. An owl screeched outside, somewhere behind the pub. I imagined I could hear insects and spiders whispering across the thin, threadbare carpet. There was a wind that was more or less constant, but which produced various different notes as it whistled through the rafters, as if Gheorghe Zamfir and Ennio Morricone had got together to score the rest of my life.

I became aware from the sound of her breathing that Joanna was also awake. I rolled over and looked at her. Eyes open, lying on her back, she seemed miles away. I reached out a finger tentatively, touched her cheek. She didn't flinch or shrug it off. I carefully stroked her face. Propped myself up on one elbow.

'Did he . . .' I began.

The shake of her head was almost imperceptible.

'No,' she whispered. 'The perfect gentleman.'

'Good.'

'The perfect gentleman, but screwed up. Screwed up by that night in St George's. I think he's a very dangerous man.'

My relief was slightly tempered by the other fear, the one I hadn't wanted to acknowledge. There are theories about captives and their captors; bonds that can grow between them. Joanna's heart being in the wrong place – in more ways than one.

'Try to get some sleep,' I said, kissing her lightly on the lips.

She nodded, returning my gaze for a moment.

'When this is all over, we'll go and see my mother,' I said. 'I want you to meet her.'

'How is she?' Joanna asked.

'She says she's doing all right but I don't know how she can be. Though that was weeks ago. Or seems like it.'

'I want to meet her. I'm sorry I never met your father.'

'He'd have liked you.'

She smiled weakly. 'I have to go to sleep.'

I listened to her breathe for a while before drifting off to sleep myself.

Twenty-eight

Max booked the room.

You know which room.

We drove back to London in separate cars: Joanna came with me in the Stag, of course, and Max was in an old chocolate brown Saab, presumably the same one he'd borrowed that time to go and watch Danny rock-climbing in Yorkshire. We could have driven off and left Max to it, but something prevented me from even suggesting it as a joke. I

think by this stage even I needed that sense of closure. Joanna
certainly did.

We found a couple of meters in Grosvenor Crescent. I drew
alongside Max's Saab in order to reverse into the space behind.
Max looked up and I saw him exchange a glance with Joanna,
sitting on my left. Max was the first to look away. I slung the
Stag into reverse and parked it in one fluid movement.

Made *me* feel better anyway.

We trooped around to the front of the hotel like something
out of a miserablist version of a Tarantino movie – no swagger
or half-assed quips, bulky pockets or shoulder holsters. Max,
ever the carthorse, was carrying a sturdy Carlton holdall in one
hand and a canvas tool-bag in the other. Danny, had he been
there, would have had his hair in a ponytail, stroking it as he
walked, pulling it over his shoulder. Joanna looked mildly
stressed: chewing the inside of her mouth, blinking more than
normal.

The guy on the door gave us a seriously funny look but
there wasn't much he could say or do: the room was booked.

The clerk pointed the way to the lifts but Max made for the
stairs. We followed him. Past an enormous vase of lilies. We
climbed a couple of flights and went left, down a long
corridor and left again. A short flight of stairs at the end,
through a set of double doors, right and down another,
shorter corridor. Max stopped outside a door, fished in his
pocket for the key. Slotted it into place, turned – and we were
in.

Max locked the door behind us and crossed the room without pausing to take it in. This was not about vicarious
nostalgia. I pushed a curtain to one side and thought about
Charlie enjoying, briefly, the same view of Wellington Arch.
There was a muffled rumble from the traffic crawling around
Hyde Park Corner, the double-glazing doing a reasonably
thorough job. Max was standing in the middle of the room
looking right and left, all around him in fact, as if trying to

square it with whatever Danny had told him.

'Here,' he said, pointing to a patch of peach carpet. 'Right here.'

He dragged a wing-back chair out of the way, wrenched up a corner of the carpet and rolled it back. Joanna had sat down on the edge of the bed, still chewing the inside of her mouth.

'So this is where Charlie . . .'

I looked at Max. He nodded.

Max went at the chipboard floor with a small saw, following the perimeter of a circle he'd drawn with a marker pen.

I withdrew the lead box from the Carlton holdall.

Would we have one last look?

Using a screwdriver from Max's bag, I levered off the lid and put it down on the carpet. We all looked – even Joanna.

If this was the security guard's heart, which had failed to burn along with the rest of him, how could it also resemble the lump of chamois leather Danny had found in the hospital some days or weeks before the assault? I slipped the photograph which Max had given me out of my jacket pocket and compared it against the real thing. They looked pretty much identical.

'Maybe you're right, after all,' I said.

'What about?' he asked me.

'Your theory about time,' I said.

'Indeed.'

'What theory about time?' Joanna wanted to know.

'That it doesn't exist,' I said.

I looked at the heart in the box again. Was this dried-up thing what a human heart would look like after nine years buried under Dartmoor? Maybe. Maybe not. That was the story, however.

'As far as you're concerned,' I said to Joanna, 'that's a human heart.'

She had a final look.

'Almost certainly.'

Max snapped the lid into place and lowered the box into the hole.

'This is meant to be where he fell,' he said as he reached under the floor, placing the box carefully so that it would rest the right way up.

Max then pierced a couple of holes in the circle of chipboard and attached a thin, perforated metal bracket which ran right across its diameter, extending on either side. He slotted it into place and secured the bracket to the floor with two more screws, then got up and pressed his boot-heel against it. There was just the tiniest amount of give.

Once the carpet was back in place the room was as good as new.

'All done,' said Max.

'I feel as if Charlie should be here,' I said. 'Any idea how he's doing?'

'Charlie's fine,' Max said. 'Never better, in fact. I spoke to him a couple of days ago, before Dartmoor.'

We were silent for a moment. I was thinking about Danny, still in Western Australia. Maybe he'd have the sense to stay there. Or go somewhere else. Just as long as he didn't come back.

'The real problem was Danny hadn't finished with it himself,' Max said, reading my mind. 'So he projected that on to other people. Now, I don't think he cares who talks – though he probably doesn't believe anyone will – because he *has* now finished with it. He had to kill the guy, he killed him and now finally he's had him laid to rest. End of story.'

We left the hotel, Joanna and I walking some way behind Max.

I didn't know how to finish my own business with Max. He should have told me more when he had the opportunity. But being Danny's friend and confidant couldn't have been easy. I caught Joanna's arm and indicated to her that we should let him get further ahead.

By the time we reached the cars, Max was already inside the Saab and starting the engine. I looked at the Saab's bland, inexpressive headlamps, remembering the figure 8s of the Mercedes, infinity signs on their side, snakes eating their own tails. Danny didn't really need symbols if he was the real thing. It made sense, his being born in WA – a lot of venomous snakes were native to that part of the world. I watched as Max pulled away from the kerb, heading off towards Hyde Park Corner, dwarfed by the huge white edifice of St George's on the left.

For Danny – and possibly Max as well – I guessed it would never really be the Lanesborough, but would always remain St George's Hospital.

I pictured him heading up the Brand Highway. Driving with one hand, his elbow sticking out the open window. Occasionally chuckling silently to himself. Wondering where he'd find a new Max; a new me, even.

I pictured him in his dust-covered 280SE, Joanna in the passenger seat, her body angled away from his. He told her he wasn't going to hurt her and he didn't; he just seemed to need to *take* her, to *control* her. She could almost have been anyone.

'Home?' I said, holding Joanna in both arms, determined not to let her go again.

She shook her head.

'Your place?'

'No, I don't really want to go anywhere. Why don't we just drive around for a bit?'

So we did. We headed west and went rat-running through Westbourne Grove, nipped up on to the Westway and – I'm not kidding – drove into the sunset. But then we spun around the roundabout at White City and came back east, the blood-orange disc of the sun enormous in the Stag's rearview mirror. I felt happy that we were together again and reasonably confident that we would eventually put all of this behind us, unlike Danny and Z. There would be some tension to come out and no doubt some rough patches still to get through, but I felt enormously encouraged by the fact that as I downshifted from fourth to third and braked lightly to bring the speed under sixty at the bottom of the Marylebone flyover I glanced across at Joanna and believed I saw, just forming at the corner of her right eye, a single tear. Then she saw me looking and smiled and I wasn't sure any more. I smiled back and gently started to brake for the first set of lights on Marylebone Road. A mile ahead, the red light at the top of the BT Tower would be winking on and off in synch with the white pulse at Canary Wharf and the apex of the three red points on the NatWest Tower – London's own version of Charlie's fanciful but tempting vision of the subtle heart. The lights on Marylebone Road flicked to amber and then to green and we were able to carry on straight through. I knew this meant that if I kept my speed constant and we were lucky with the traffic – as I thought we just might be – there was a chance we'd get all the way through without having to stop.

Author's Note

Material from chapters one, two and three first appeared as a short story in *The Third Alternative* edited by Andy Cox. A section from chapter eighteen first appeared in a different form in *Violent Spectres* edited by Adam Bradley.

I am grateful to the following people for their help and advice:

Kate, Mum, Jo & Simon, Julie & Terry, Denis & Margery; Zoran Petrovic & everyone at Pizza on the Park, 1984/85; Ken McNamara of the Museum of Western Australia; Christopher Fowler & Jim Sturgeon for the 280SE; Don Rotolo, Gary Tan, Adam Bystrzycki and George Theofanous, members of alt.auto.mercedes; Russell Celyn Jones, Christopher Burns, Liz Jensen, M. John Harrison, Jonathan Coe, Mic Cheetham, Richard Beswick, Michael Marshall Smith, Conrad Williams, John Oakey – for their invaluable input; Jim & Angela, Edward & Nichola – for their hospitality; Dr Nigel Brand, Dr Peter Fleming – for help with the heart and the history (any liberties taken are mine, not theirs); Grenville Williams; Tony Binns for the theory of exclusive simultaneity; all the Chisellers & Chisellettes, for being who you are; Steve Jones, Ellen Datlow – for continued support; Laurence Staig for gigs at the Bath Literature Festival; Ray & Margaret at Reef Villas, Kalbarri;

Iain Sinclair, Barry Burman, Mike Goldmark – for inspiration and generosity; Sergio Leone for *The Good, the Bad and the Ugly*; Richard Barbieri, Steve Jansen & Mick Karn for 'Beginning to Melt', Richard Barbieri & Suzanne Barbieri for 'The Wilderness', Ron & Russell Mael for 'Hear No Evil, See No Evil, Speak No Evil'.

In memoriam Russell Royle (1930–94), Karl Edward Wagner (1945–94), Robin Cook (1931–94), Derek Marlowe (1938–96).